the brink of darkness

"Funny, warm-hearted . . . and a beautiful tribute to friendship and family." —Laini Taylor, *New York Times* bestselling author of *Strange the Dreamer* and *Muse of Nightmares*

"A wild, gripping fantasy." —Danielle Paige, *New York Times* bestselling author of *Stealing Snow* and the Dorothy Must Die series

"A must-read for fantasy fans everywhere." —Susan Dennard, *New York Times* bestselling author of the Witchlands series

"Thrilling." —Kami Garcia, #1 *New York Times* bestselling coauthor of the Beautiful Creatures series and author of *Broken Beautiful Hearts*

the edge of everything

A *People* Magazine Pick of the Week
An *Entertainment Weekly* "Must"
A PopSugar Best YA Romance Book

"Gripping. Utterly original. Beautifully written." —Peter Jackson, Oscar-winning director of the Lord of the Rings and the Hobbit trilogies

"Sharp, dark, thoughtful, and romantic." —Cassandra Clare, #1 *New York Times* bestselling author of the Mortal Instruments series

"You won't be able to get enough." —BuzzFeed

"A sharp fantasy thriller." —*People*

"Heart-searing." —*USA Today*

★ "A gorgeous, unearthly ride." —Shelf Awareness, starred review

"[Delivers] with imagination and verve." —*Time*

"Cinematic . . . otherworldly. . . . A delight." —*The New York Times Book Review*

"Reads like a blend of J.R.R. Tolkien's 'The Lord of the Rings' and modern-day horror, such as *Stranger Things*. . . . Highly recommended." —*SLJ*

the brink of darkness

JEFF GILES

BLOOMSBURY

NEW YORK LONDON OXFORD NEW DELHI SYDNEY

BLOOMSBURY YA
Bloomsbury Publishing Inc., part of Bloomsbury Publishing Plc
1385 Broadway, New York, NY 10018

BLOOMSBURY and the Diana logo are trademarks of Bloomsbury Publishing Plc

First published in the United States of America in July 2018
by Bloomsbury YA
Paperback edition published in July 2019

Bloomsbury books may be purchased for business or promotional use. For information on
bulk purchases please contact Macmillan Corporate and Premium Sales Department at
specialmarkets@macmillan.com

ISBN 978-1-61963-757-3 (paperback)

The Library of Congress has cataloged the hardcover edition as follows:
Names: Giles, Jeff, author.
Title: The brink of darkness / by Jeff Giles.
Description: New York : Bloomsbury, 2018. | Sequel to: The edge of everything.
Summary: X is determined to break the lords' hold on him once and for all, but being stripped
of his power pushes him toward a darkness he's never experienced and a past he's never
known. The secrets that surface could be the key to reuniting X and Zoe . . . or they
could mean the destruction of everything they have been fighting for.
Identifiers: LCCN 2017056215
ISBN 978-1-61963-755-9 (hardcover) • ISBN 978-1-61963-756-6 (e-book)
Subjects: | CYAC: Bounty hunters—Fiction. | Adventure and adventurers—Fiction. |
Future life—Fiction. | Love—Fiction. | Brothers and sisters—Fiction. | Montana—Fiction.
Classification: LCC PZ7.1.G553 Bri 2018 | DDC [Fic]—dc23
LC record available at https://lccn.loc.gov/2017056215

Book design by Colleen Andrews and Jeanette Levy
Typeset by Westchester Publishing Services
Printed and bound in the U.S.A. by Berryville Graphics Inc., Berryville, Virginia
2 4 6 8 10 9 7 5 3 1

All papers used by Bloomsbury Publishing Plc are natural, recyclable products
made from wood grown in well-managed forests. The manufacturing processes
conform to the environmental regulations of the country of origin.

To find out more about our authors and books visit www.bloomsbury.com and sign up for our newsletters.

For Lily and Theo

Kiss
the mouth
which tells you, *here,*
here is the world.

—Galway Kinnell

prologue

HE SAW HER AT last—she was up on the grassy dune above the harbor, a pale shape cut out of the darkness.

How long had it been since X had seen her? He had no way of knowing. He'd been in his cell in the Lowlands, deep in the earth, where there was no clock, no sun, no future, only the dead and damned.

She hadn't noticed him yet. She was searching for him, her eyes everywhere. He stood on the dock below her. It creaked and floated up and down, like the water beneath it was breathing.

"Here!" he called.

She turned toward him. She beamed.

"I know that face," she said.

X spread his fingers, and a soft corridor of light appeared—a trail for her to follow to the water. She started down the hill too quickly. She stumbled, fell on her knees, pushed herself up without bothering to brush off the sand.

"Hi, I'm Zoe and I'm a runway model," she said.

He smiled. He hadn't in a long time.

"I love your voice," he said, "even if your meaning eludes me on occasion."

"My meaning eludes everybody on occasion," she said.

He tried not to rush at her when she reached the dock. He was afraid he'd alarm her. She ran at *him* anyway. She kissed his cheeks, his chin, his forehead. He did the same to her, and they laughed at how frantic they were: they couldn't find each other's lips.

"How much time have we got?" she said.

"A few hours, at most," he said. "Then I must return to the Lowlands with the soul they sent me to capture."

Zoe slid her hands under his shirt. Something like silver spread through his chest.

"We need a boat," she said. "I'm having a sudden urge to lie in a boat with you."

"I would lie in a boat with you until the sun dried up all the sea," he said. "When I was young—"

She breathed into his neck.

"Less talking and more boat-getting," she said.

X scanned the harbor. There was a cluster of fishing boats. Otherwise the water lay empty. He peered at the end of the dock, where it seemed to narrow to a point in the dark, and saw an orange rowboat tied to an iron cleat.

Zoe stepped into it first, spreading her arms for balance as it rolled beneath her. A seat—a wide wooden plank—bisected the boat.

"We can't lie down in here," she said. "There's not enough room."

X shattered the plank with his fist, then tossed the scraps onto the dock.

"That'll work," said Zoe.

X laid his coat on the floorboards, and went to untie the boat. The knot was complicated, so he just yanked the cleat off the dock. Again, the sound of splintering wood ricocheted through the harbor.

"Man, they are *never* gonna give you a job here," said Zoe. She frowned. "I've got to stop with the jokes. I just can't believe you're here—and by the time I *do* believe it, you'll be gone."

Whoever owned the boat had taken the oars. X crouched next to Zoe, and pushed the craft away from the dock with a superhuman shove. They flew backward so fast that the boat nearly left the water. Waves rose on either side, and spilled in around their feet.

X had a plan he longed to tell Zoe about, but he was impatient to feel her hands again.

"I beseech you," he said, "do not darken the moments we can be together by dwelling on the moments we cannot."

Zoe pulled him down by the front of his shirt.

"I like it when you beseech me," she said. "Beseech me some more."

part one

Life Without

one

SOMETIMES ZOE FELT AS if she were being hollowed out bit by bit. She had lost so many people in the last six months, and every one of them had carried part of her away. Eventually, she'd be like one of those chocolate Easter bunnies that the stores were suddenly selling again—you could poke her with your finger and her heart would cave in.

It was a Saturday morning in Montana. Early March. Zoe was driving her decrepit old Taurus to a memorial service for Bert and Betty Wallace. The farmlands were drab, gray brown, just starting to recover from winter. Zoe was thinking about the Wallaces, but also about her father and X. She'd had to say good-bye to them all in one way or another. She prayed that her father would never come back—and that somehow X would. She hadn't seen either of them since a terrible day in the snowy woods.

Her friends Val and Dallas were in the car, too. Val looked beautiful, though she hated church clothes: half her head was shaved, the other half a futuristic silvery blue. Dallas was dressed like a jock at an awards dinner (navy blazer with gold buttons, khaki pants, tie decorated with baseballs), and there was a round Band-Aid on the cleft of his chin, where he'd cut himself shaving. Zoe used to go out with Dallas. Kind of, sort of, a little. She thought he looked adorable. Val, she knew, had no patience for him. Val was convinced that Dallas still had a thing for Zoe—he insisted he was going to ask out a girl named Mingyu, but kept putting it off—plus, Zoe had told Val that Dallas used to flex his pecs when they made out.

Zoe had agreed to give Bert and Betty's eulogy even though she dreaded public speaking. The Wallaces had been like grandparents to Zoe and her little brother, Jonah. She'd written out every word of her speech on orange index cards, which sat in a stack on the dashboard. She needed the cards because once she stepped up to the lectern, she expected to go into a terrified fugue state where anything, including ancient Egyptian, might come out of her mouth.

She turned onto Twin Bridges Road. The stack of index cards collapsed, and slid across the dashboard in a smooth orange stripe. Val gathered them up.

"You okay?" she said.

"No," said Zoe. "I'm kind of underwater."

"Do you want me to make fun of Dallas?" said Val. "Would that help? I'm willing to do that for you."

"No, but thank you," said Zoe. "You're sweet."

"Wait, whoa, how is that sweet?" said Dallas.

He leaned forward between the seats. Val pushed his fuzzy, buzz-cut head away, saying, "Back in your cage."

Zoe drove across Flathead Valley. In the distance, the mountains still shone with snow.

"Do you want me to talk about nature?" said Val. It was a joke: Val liked being indoors. "Look at all the nature!"

"You're not helping, dawg," said Dallas. "I'm going to rap for you, Zoe. Val, give me a beat."

"On what planet do you think I would give you a beat?" said Val. She looked at Zoe. "Don't you dare give him a beat."

Dallas rapped anyway: "My lyrics *devastate* / Check this *flow* I create . . ."

"Really?" said Val. "This is happening?"

Zoe smiled, but just couldn't swim up to the surface—it was like her legs were tangled in seaweed. She glanced at the cards in Val's hand. She had rewritten the first sentence of the Wallaces' eulogy 11 times, crumpling so many index cards in the process that the wastebasket by her desk looked like it was full of orange flowers.

Betty had taught Zoe how to use an ax—and Jonah how to knit. Bert, even when he'd gotten senile, used to cut pictures of cute animals out of the newspaper and mail them to the Bissells. Jonah taped them all over his walls. And then, two months ago, a man named Stan Manggold had burst into the Wallaces' home looking for money, and beaten them to death with a fireplace poker.

One of the things that Zoe found hardest was that she couldn't tell Val and Dallas the whole story—the before and the after. How could she? It sounded implausible even to her. So just when she needed to talk most—to vent and grieve—her life had become about managing secrets.

Should she tell them that the nightmare had started with her father? That he had been such a failure as a businessman that he'd sunk to committing crimes with a childhood friend—and that the childhood friend was a sociopath named Stan Manggold? Should she tell them that her father had suggested they rob the Wallaces? That he got scared and had second thoughts? That, when Stan blackmailed him, he was such a coward that he faked his own death in a cave, abandoned his family and ran?

Zoe tried not to let the memories in. But as she pulled up to a stop sign, the Taurus bounced hard in a rut and in that instant, in that tiny moment of fear, her defenses went down and everything came rushing back, like birds to a bare tree.

Stan had gone through with the robbery alone, and murdered Bert and Betty while he was at it. Weeks later, during a blizzard, he returned to their house, convinced they had money stashed somewhere. Zoe and Jonah were there, waiting out the storm. It made Zoe sick just to remember Stan's face: the pockmarked skin, the pink slash of a mouth, the creepy white eyebrow that wriggled like a caterpillar.

Zoe checked for traffic before turning left. There was a fluorescent green SUV coming. It slowed to let her pull out. Dallas was still freestyling—his rap seemed to be exclusively about how good his rap was—but he paused long enough to say, "Look out for the deer."

There were two of them up ahead in the wet field, a doe and her fawn. They were just nosing around in the dead grass. They weren't going anywhere.

"I see them," said Zoe.

Dallas started rapping again.

"My rhymes are *unstoppable* / Like a photo that's *uncroppable*."

Val, miserable, banged her forehead against the dashboard.

Zoe remembered seeing X for the first time. He had come to take Stan's soul to the Lowlands. X was just a blur, a streak of light shooting across the frozen lake near the Wallaces' house. Zoe begged X to let Stan go. She told him that it was wrong to kill somebody—that it wasn't his job. She hadn't known then that it actually was.

Zoe checked the rearview mirror. The SUV was too close. It was a new model, its front end designed to look like a sports car. Even if it hadn't been a pukey green, it would have looked ridiculous. Its license plate was RELOADN.

Great, thought Zoe, *a hunter.*

She slowed, and waved the driver around, but the guy just flicked his high beams so she'd hurry up.

"Seriously?" she said.

She glanced at the deer. They had started toward the road, but she'd be gone by the time they made it there.

How do you tell your friends that you've fallen for a bounty hunter from the underworld? How do you tell them that you jeopardized your life for him, and that you would do it again right now, right this very second? Val and Dallas wouldn't even know what the Lowlands were. She'd have to call the place hell. How do you say a sentence like that out loud? Would it help if she told them that X was an innocent, that he was *born* in the Lowlands? That he was a prisoner himself—and for no reason? The lords sent X to collect evil souls from the world from time to time, but that just reminded him of the life he could never have. The minute he returned with a soul, the lords threw him back into his cell, like it was a mouth they were feeding.

X had forged a family in the Lowlands. One of the lords who ruled the place, Regent, protected him as much as he could. And there was a badass British woman named Ripper who'd trained X to be a bounty hunter. She had worn the same golden ball gown since 1832, when she was damned to the Lowlands for beating a clumsy servant to death with a teakettle. Zoe had met Ripper and loved her, despite the thing with the teakettle. Ripper was on the run from the Lowlands now. She was up in the real world somewhere, searching for her children's graves, which she had never seen.

So, yes, there were people who cared about X even in that hole in the earth. But the unfairness of him spending his life in a cell when he'd never done *anything* wrong, when he'd never even lived—it hollowed Zoe out.

She couldn't tell Val and Dallas any of this. How could she? They were right there, but they were a thousand miles away.

Zoe gripped the steering wheel harder, and sank into her thoughts. She was only dimly aware of Dallas rapping, of Val riffling the orange index cards impatiently, of the SUV surging behind her, of the farmlands flowing past.

"*Deer,*" Dallas said again.

Zoe nodded, and sped up. The driver in the SUV closed the gap between them, then flicked his high beams again.

People: the worst.

Zoe remembered X carrying her and Jonah home through the woods after she convinced him to let Stan go. She remembered how dazed and feverish he got because he hadn't done what the lords told him to do. X spent days recovering at the Bissells' house, sleeping in Jonah's bed, which was shaped like a ladybug, and bathing in the freezing river. But then Stan murdered someone else. X, battered by guilt, left Zoe to hunt him down again and bring him to the Lowlands. Zoe remembered the way X kissed her good-bye—he'd lifted her off the slushy driveway because she only had socks on.

Once X was back in the underworld, he had demanded his freedom. The lords made him a cruel offer: he could be free forever if he returned to the world and brought them one more soul.

But the soul was Zoe's father.

X had searched for him, and found him in the woods in Canada. He brought Zoe there so she could confront her father about what he'd done to her family.

In the end, X couldn't bring himself to take the man's life. The lords of the Lowlands were enraged. They lashed out at Zoe's family to remind X that he'd failed again and that he was theirs forever. An unhinged lord named Dervish led the attack, destroying the Bissells' house and nearly killing Jonah. So X dove back into the earth. He had sacrificed himself because he refused to do anything that hurt Zoe. But his leaving—what could have hurt her more?

Hundreds of times a day, Zoe would think of him and, just for an instant, it was like he stood in front of her: gorgeous, pale, afraid of nothing, wanting only her. A half second later she'd remember that he was gone. The heat and the hope would vanish and it was like she'd been punched in the gut. But this was the thing: That instant before the pain leveled her? The moment before the remembering? It was worth it.

"DEER!" said Dallas. "Zoe, what the hell?"

The doe and the fawn had jumped the ditch that ran along the side of the road. They were racing to cross in front of the car.

A spike of dread hit Zoe's blood.

She stepped on the gas, but the pathetic, piece-of-shit car had zero pickup. Val clenched for a crash.

The SUV was practically on top of them.

RELOADN—what did *he* care if Zoe hit the deer? He'd have the doe strapped to his roof within minutes. He didn't see deer, he saw venison.

You weren't supposed to swerve to avoid a deer. It was better to run into them than to cause an accident. Zoe knew it. Everybody in Montana did. The guy who'd taught Driver's Ed—sad-faced and chubby and always wearing the same chocolate-brown sweater, which was unraveling at the wrist—started every class by saying, "I want to go to your weddings, not your funerals."

Zoe had maybe a second and a half to decide what to do.

She had seen what deer looked like when they died. She'd heard the deceptively soft *thump* they made when the bumper hit them. She'd seen how they went rigid in a split second, how they flew through the air, stiff as stuffed animals.

She knew she should hit the doe and the fawn, but—maybe it was because she'd been thinking about X—all she saw when she looked at them was innocent creatures.

The fawn struggled to keep up with its mother. Its rickety legs were a blur, its frail back speckled white, as if with snowflakes. She could see its big, wet eyes.

Dammit.

Zoe stomped on the brake.

The car stopped so suddenly it seemed to jump. They shot forward in their seats.

The deer darted safely across the road.

Val screamed involuntarily when the SUV struck them from behind.

ZOE TRIED TO PULL off the road, but the vehicles' bumpers had twisted together. The driver jabbed his horn three times—long, longer, longest—then burst out of the SUV.

He stalked up to Zoe's window, and banged on it hard.

"Roll this down!" he said. "Right this goddamn second!"

He looked about 50—doughy and pale, with blue eyes set too close together. He wore a baseball cap with a sexist silhouette of a woman and the words "Booty Hunter."

Zoe made sure Val and Dallas weren't hurt, then looked at the clock on the dash. They had ten minutes to get to the church.

She fished for her insurance card in the glove compartment. When she found it, she breathed out, and rolled down the window.

"My name is Zoe Bissell," she said. "I'm sorry about your car."

"It's not a *car*," he said. "It's a friggin' *truck*."

He was seething. His pupils were so dilated that Zoe suspected he was high on something.

"I'm sorry about your truck," she said carefully.

"I don't give a shit about your *I'm sorry*," he said.

From the passenger seat, Val spoke under her breath.

"I don't like this guy—and his hat is pissing me off," she said. "I'm getting out."

"Stay," said Dallas.

"Did you just tell me to *stay*?" said Val.

"You're gonna make it worse," said Dallas. "I'll handle this."

"No, I will handle it," said Zoe. "*Both* of you stay."

She went to open her door, but the man stood too close. He was trapping her in. He seemed to be deciding if he was going to let her out. Finally, he backed up.

Not much damage had been done to Zoe's Taurus—it was hard to make the Struggle Buggy look any worse—but the SUV's sporty front end was decimated. The headlights were smashed, the grille was sagging. The hood had popped open and been folded in half.

"You see what you damn did?" the man said. "That is a brand-new, thirty-eight-thousand-dollar vehicle right there, fresh off the motherfrickin' lot—and that color green costs extra!"

"I didn't want to kill the deer," said Zoe.

"Oh, the deer!" said the man. "The precious friggin' deer! Who gives a rat's ass if they live or die. There's about a billion of them, you dumb bitch!"

At the word "bitch," Zoe's friends got out of the car.

Dallas, whose first instinct was always to calm people down, offered the man his hand.

"What's your name?" he said.

The man looked at him like he was nuts.

"My name is *go to hell*, you little prick," he said.

"Okay, stop," said Zoe. "You're going to have to *turn down your crazy*. It's just a car."

"IT'S A FRIGGIN' *TRUCK*!"

He screamed it so loud that a bolt of pain seemed to go through his head. He doubled over, and covered his face with his hands. When he straightened up again, Zoe blanched: the guy had burst a blood vessel in his left eye. A red cloud crept across the white of the eye toward the iris.

"Come on, what's your name?" said Dallas. "I'm Dallas."

"It's Ronny, for god's sake," said the man.

"Hey, Ronny," said Dallas. "This doesn't need to be a thing."

"It's already a damn thing!" said Ronny. "It *became* a damn thing when she made me crash the thirty-eight-thousand-dollar vehicle my mother *just* gave me for my birthday!"

He was getting more angry, not less. Zoe didn't like how close he was. He had morning breath.

"Could you take a step back, please?" she said.

He ignored her.

"She asked you to step back," said Val.

Ronny looked Val up and down. He made a show, as men often did, of being appalled by her half-shaved head and the sci-fi color of her hair.

"What are you, her girlfriend?" he said.

"No," said Val, "I'm into fat, middle-aged guys."

"Val!" said Zoe.

Ronny snorted.

"You couldn't even handle what I got," he told Val.

"I'm calling the police," said Val.

"Yeah?" said Ronny. "They're gonna be too late."

He charged to the back of his SUV, and returned with a rifle.

"Whoa, Ronny," said Dallas. *"Whoa."*

Ronny hit Dallas in the stomach with the butt of the gun.

"STOP! CALLING ME! RONNY!"

Dallas fell to all fours, gasping. The tie with the baseballs dangled down toward the road. Zoe went to him.

"I'm okay," said Dallas, when he could speak again. "I'm okay."

Ronny beat Zoe's hood with the rifle.

"How do *you* like it?" he screamed. Zoe couldn't tell if he was talking to her or the car. "This feel good? Does it?"

Dallas tried to stand—he wanted to stop Ronny.

"No," Zoe said. "Let him do it. I don't care."

She looked around for help, but they were in the middle of nowhere: fields, trees, sky. No cars for miles.

Then something caught her eye across the farmland: a bluish glow in the woods.

The rifle went off. Ronny was shooting out her headlights. The *crack*s echoed across the valley.

"How's *that* feel?" he said. "How about *this*?"

Val filmed Ronny on her phone as he bashed the car: evidence.

Zoe turned back to the trees. The light was morphing. It had been diffuse, like a mist on the ground, but now it gathered itself into a ball.

She went to the side of the road. A blurry figure hurtled toward them.

It had to be X.

How had he gotten out of the Lowlands? How had he known to come? Zoe squinted into the distance. He was still out of focus, still a smudge.

"There's stuff I didn't tell you guys about X," she told Val and Dallas.

"This is a good topic for *later*," said Val.

"Yeah, why are you bringing this up now?" said Dallas.

He leaned against the SUV. His shirt was untucked, and he was gripping his stomach.

"Because things are gonna get weird," said Zoe.

Everyone followed her gaze across the field.

The figure was nearly on them. Ronny lowered his rifle, dumbfounded.

"You are *so* screwed," Zoe told him.

The figure slowed as it approached the road.

Zoe felt her heart shrink and nearly vanish when she saw that it wasn't X.

two

RIPPER GAVE ZOE A slight nod, then advanced on Ronny. She looked furious. Her ragged ball gown rustled as she walked.

Ronny shrank backward.

"Who are you?" he said.

Ripper didn't answer. She just kept coming.

Ronny lifted the rifle, fumbled with the bolt, and finally managed to pull it back. He pointed the gun at Ripper's face.

Ripper didn't even break stride.

"I dislike weapons," she said. "Things were about to go badly for you—and now they will go very much worse."

She made a *come here* gesture with her fingers. The rifle flew from Ronny's hands and into her own.

Zoe could hear Dallas and Val whispering variations on *WTF*. She turned to see their expressions. Val had stopped filming. She and Dallas were frozen in surprise, like figures in a museum diorama: *Americans, early 21st century, freaking out.*

"Hey, that's my gun!" said Ronny. "I'm a hunter!"

Ripper regarded him coldly.

"A hunter? Are you indeed?" she said. "So am I."

She reared back and kicked him across the mouth. Ronny collapsed to the ground, blood spilling down his chin.

Ripper pushed the rifle into the pavement muzzle-first. The asphalt tightened around it, seized it like it was the Sword in the Stone.

Ripper went to stand over Ronny.

"Listen to me, you idiotic mushroom," she said. "I was two thousand miles from here and weeping over my son Alfie's grave when a trilling in my brain informed me that Zoe was in peril. In all your world, she is the only one I care for—and I care for her deeply."

"Zoe, you *know* this person?" said Dallas.

Ripper made a lifting motion with her hand. Ronny's body rose off the ground. Then Ripper pushed her palm forward through the air, and he sailed headlong into the ditch.

Zoe went to Ripper and hugged her.

"I thought you were X," she said. "When I saw the light—I thought it was X."

"I'm sorry, dear girl," said Ripper. "But I hate to waste an entrance."

"We could have handled this guy," said Zoe.

"No doubt," said Ripper. "I had a second purpose in coming here—I am in need of your counsel. But first, introduce me to your friends?"

What followed was a surreal, slow-motion moment—two worlds bleeding into each other.

"This is Ripper," said Zoe. "And this is Val and Dallas. They're my people."

"Hello, Zoe's people," said Ripper.

She looked Dallas over approvingly, and shook his hand longer than necessary.

"How old are you, if I may inquire?" she asked him.

Dallas coughed nervously.

"Seventeen?" he said.

"Pity," said Ripper. She touched the Band-Aid on his chin with her forefinger. "I myself am nearly two hundred."

Dallas nodded.

"You look good," he said.

Ripper laughed, and proceeded to Val.

"This hair of yours," she said. "I suspect you don't care to hear anyone's opinion—but may I tell you *my* opinion?"

"Um, sure?" said Val.

"It is sublime," said Ripper. "You must not alter it until you've infuriated as many imbeciles as you can."

"Yeah, that's my plan," said Val.

Zoe felt a flood of fondness for both of them. Val was devoted to her girlfriend, Gloria, but not above being flattered by someone as gorgeous as Ripper.

"Okay, now can I ask *you* a question?" said Val. "Actually, two questions?"

"You may," said Ripper.

"What the hell is going on?" said Val. "Who even *are* you?"

"I am an associate of X's," she said. "Zoe will tell you the tale later. I promise it will not bore you."

She turned to Zoe.

"What shall we do with Mr. Mushroom?" she said.

"I don't know," said Zoe. "I hit the brake to avoid a deer, and he crashed into me—and then he just went nuts."

"Yes, well, lunatics are full of surprises," said Ripper. "I don't mean to disparage lunatics, by the way. I am a lunatic myself."

She shoved Zoe's and Ronny's vehicles apart, without any show of effort. Then she walked to the ditch.

"Mr. Mushroom," she said.

Ronny looked petrified.

"Yes, ma'am?" he said.

His shirt was twisted halfway up his torso. His gut hung over his belt.

"Are you quite finished making difficulties?" said Ripper.

"Uh-huh," said Ronny, nodding frantically. "Yes, ma'am, I am."

"Then get on your feet," said Ripper.

Ronny climbed awkwardly out of the ditch. His right eyeball was now thoroughly soaked with blood.

"If ever you mention me—or any of the inexplicable things you witnessed here—to a single person," Ripper told him, "I will find you, relieve you of your internal organs one by one, and wave them in front of your face as you die. I believe I could draw the process out for hours. Do you understand?"

"Yes, ma'am," said Ronny.

"Very good," said Ripper. She pointed at the Booty Hunter cap. "Give me your hat."

Ronny handed it to her reluctantly, and she put it on.

"Now go away," she said. "And have that eye of yours inspected by a surgeon. It is repulsive."

Ronny fled to his truck, and drove off with the ruined hood bouncing.

They all stood silently until he was out of sight.

Zoe looked at her phone—she had to be at the memorial service in five minutes. But she wasn't ready to say good-bye to Ripper.

"Come with me," Ripper said suddenly.

"To where?" said Zoe. "What do you mean?"

She heard a siren in the distance. The police.

"You recall the reason I ran from the Lowlands?" said Ripper.

"You want to see where your children are buried," said Zoe.

"Just so," said Ripper. "I have found Alfie's grave, and at last said a proper farewell, yet I cannot find Belinda. And you see the state of my dress and boots—I can hardly make inquiries. But *you* could."

"I could," Zoe said tentatively. "I'm good at inquiries."

"Zoe," said Val, "whatever this is—*no*."

"I'm with Val," said Dallas. He glanced at Ripper. "Please don't levitate me."

Ripper held Zoe's eyes, waiting.

"I have to give Bert and Betty's eulogy," said Zoe. "In five minutes."

"Afterward?" said Ripper. "I will come to you wherever you are." She paused. "I know I must seem very fierce to you, Zoe. Yet if you had seen me at the stone marker bearing Alfie's name—truly, the grass will grow taller where I sat weeping. And Belinda died in such a piteous way. Abandoned. Unloved. I myself was already in the Lowlands. Even if I could discover where they laid her body down, I could not face the place alone. So I ask you for one night." She was all but begging. "Will you come?"

Zoe gazed at Ripper. It'd be dangerous to be with her when she was on the run from the lords, and Zoe had had enough danger. She had to say no. Even though Ripper had once risked herself for Zoe's family—even though Ripper loved X as if she were his own mother—she *had* to say no.

The siren was louder. Zoe saw a squad car shoot out of the woods.

"Ripper, I—" she began.

"Before you answer," said Ripper, "let me add an inducement. Every night, the lords send bounty hunters after me. It goes without saying that I defeat them all. Last night, thinking of you, I told one of them: 'You may inform the lords that if they want me, there is only one hunter I will ever surrender to.'"

Ripper waited to see if Zoe understood, before continuing.

"I beg you to come—not just to help me find my Belinda, but so that you might be there when the lords finally send X for my head."

three

Z OE AND HER FRIENDS crept into First Presbyterian looking disheveled and dazed. The congregation was already singing "Abide with Me." Val and Dallas ducked into a pew near the back, but Zoe had to walk to the front. The hymn ended when she was halfway there, and suddenly the only sound in the church was her black flats going *squinch-squinch* on the floor. Everyone turned. Zoe gave an embarrassed wave. No one seemed to think it was funny.

Her mother had saved her a seat by the aisle, where she was sitting with Jonah and her hippy-dippy, chain saw–artist friend, Rufus. Zoe expected her mother to whisper *Where were you?* or at least give her a disappointed look. Instead, she gripped Zoe's hand warmly. She must have known she was scared to death. Zoe's heart, which had only just stopped racing from the confrontation with Ronny, now raced at the thought of giving Bert and Betty's eulogy in front of 200 people.

After Stan Manggold had killed the Wallaces, he'd dumped them in the lake by their house. Divers had recovered their bodies a few days ago. Zoe had wanted to be there when Bert and Betty were found. *Someone* who loved them should have been there. She'd actually snuck out to her car the morning of the dive, knowing her mother wouldn't approve. Unfortunately, Jonah figured out what she was up to, and hid in the backseat so he could go, too. A mile from the house, he scared the crap out of Zoe by springing up in the rearview mirror and shouting, "It's me!"

She couldn't let the little bug watch bodies get pulled out of a lake—he'd be so freaked out that he would be sleeping in her bed for a month. When he wouldn't stop saying "I loved Bert and Betty also! I loved them also!" Zoe made an illegal U-turn, and drove to Krispy Kreme, where they ate donuts and cried without talking.

Zoe's mother nudged her. The minister was leading a prayer now, and they were supposed to be standing. Zoe looked up at the altar. Her mom had chosen the flowers, which were perfect: lilies, roses, gladiolus. And Rufus had made a wooden box to hold the Wallaces' ashes. It was walnut and carved with a pair of doves in flight, like souls. Zoe liked to tease Rufus (for saying "epic" and "rad" all the time, for having the world's least secret crush on her mom), but he was an extremely good guy and more talented than Zoe had thought: the box was lovely, and there was no way he'd made it with a chain saw. Still, it was hard for Zoe to look at. She couldn't believe that everything that was left of Bert and Betty could fit inside it. Two whole lives, one little box.

The prayer ended. Zoe checked the bulletin to see when the eulogy was supposed to be. It was *right now.*

The minister was nodding at her.

Zoe realized something.

She'd left her index cards in the car.

She felt her face get hot, her throat close. The minister raised his eyebrows.

Her mother signaled for him to wait, then leaned toward Zoe and whispered the kindest thing anybody had ever said: "Do you want me to do it instead?"

Every part of Zoe wanted to say yes.

"No," she said. "I have to try. But it's gonna be messy."

"Messy is okay," her mom said. "They knew how much you loved them."

The minister looked annoyed. His eyebrows crept higher.

Zoe leaned past her mother to Jonah. He was wearing khaki pants, a red tie that he had insisted on tying himself—there was no describing the knot he'd finally come up with—and a blue blazer, the arms of which were so long that you could just barely see the tips of his fingers.

"Do you want to come up with me, bug?" she whispered.

"Yes, actually!" he said. "I think people will like my tie."

"Go, go, go," said their mom, and they climbed the steps to the altar holding hands.

The minister, seeing Jonah, said, "It seems we have a surprise guest"—which Jonah loved.

Zoe stood at the bare lectern, her pulse rushing, her mind blank as a swept room. She didn't know how to start. A dozen feelings were colliding inside her. She missed Bert and Betty almost too much to talk about them, which reminded her how much she missed X—and she just couldn't open *that* door. There was an ocean behind it.

Jonah let go of her hand, took a Sharpie out of his coat pocket, and started drawing on his palm. Maybe it was a bad idea to bring him up here. Had he taken his ADHD med this morning? Zoe looked at the congregation. They were restless. How long had she just been standing there?

Jonah tugged at her sleeve. She glanced down, annoyed.

He'd drawn a little red heart on his hand. He'd even colored it in. It was squiggly and wobbly—but it was for her.

It helped.

She leaned toward the microphone.

"I forgot the notes for my speech," she said. "I think that's god's way of telling me that my speech wasn't very good."

There was a soft ripple of laughter, even from the minister, which calmed Zoe more. She looked out at her mom and Rufus. They immediately raised their palms—they had hearts on them, too. They must have planned this out.

"I could never say everything I want to about Bert and Betty anyway," Zoe said. "They were so sweet and so funny." Bits of the eulogy she'd written started floating back to her. "You know how you'll be sitting there thinking of calling someone to see if they want to go hiking—and all of a sudden they call *you* to see if *you* want to go hiking? That was Bert and Betty. We were connected somehow." She paused. "They taught Jonah and me so much about the woods and the mountains. They also secretly gave us ice cream for years, because our mom's a vegan and won't let it in the house. Sorry, Mom—Jonah and I have actually had a ton of ice cream."

Jonah stood on his tippy-toes so he could reach the microphone, and said, "Salty caramel, please!"

Their mother made a pretend-angry face.

Zoe couldn't remember the middle of the eulogy, so she skipped to the end. She'd worked so hard on it that she'd memorized it.

"The Wallaces loved us so much that it made me feel safe—like wherever I went, they were walking in front of me with shields," she said. "The way they got killed . . . I really wish that I had been walking in front of *them*." She stopped a moment. "When something horrible and unexpected happens, like Bert and Betty dying, I try to remember all the *amazing* and unexpected things that have also happened. Getting to know the Wallaces was one of them. It's hard to breathe now that they're gone. But some people change you so much that they make any amount of pain worth it."

Zoe didn't know if she was supposed to say "thank you" or just walk back to her seat. She stood awkwardly for a second, then said, "Okay, that's all. Sorry I freaked out at the beginning."

Jonah clapped for her, then leaned up to the microphone and said, "I tied my own tie."

When they stepped down from the altar, Zoe saw that her mom and Rufus had their palm-hearts in the air.

Zoe was so relieved to be done with the speech that she felt like she was floating. The day was nowhere near over—Ripper was out there somewhere, waiting; Val and Dallas were in the back of the church, ready to barrage her with questions. But Zoe kept a box in the back of her brain for things she didn't want to think about. It was labeled Do Not Open. She pushed all her worries into it now. For the rest of the service, she laid her head on her mom's shoulder, replayed memories of the Wallaces, and stared at a spot to the left of the altar where the sun, streaming through the stained-glass windows, threw patches of blue, yellow, and green against the floor.

There was something Zoe hadn't been able to say in her eulogy because it was too weird, but it comforted her now: she knew that Stan Manggold was being punished for killing the Wallaces, because X had eventually tracked him down and taken him to the Lowlands. The fact that he was suffering was not the thing that comforted her, though. What comforted her was this: if there was a hell for Stan, there had to be a heaven for Bert and Betty.

THE PLAN WAS TO spread the Wallaces' ashes after the service. While the crowd drifted out and the organist played a few last chords, Zoe told her mom she needed a minute to say good-bye to Dallas and Val.

Zoe could almost always expect a *woot!* or a *boom!* from Dallas, but this time he said only, "You did good." Val, looking agitated and angry, gestured for Zoe to follow her, and walked out of the church without a word.

The minister stood outside amid the parishioners. Val waited on the sidewalk where they wouldn't be overheard.

"*Ripper?*" she said. "You know somebody named *Ripper?*"

"Yes," said Zoe quietly.

"You are not going *anywhere* with her," said Val.

"I am," said Zoe.

"She's psychotic," said Val.

"Only a little," said Zoe.

"This isn't funny," said Val. "Have you been lying to us this whole time—about X? About everything?"

Zoe was ashamed. She spoke even more softly.

"Not about everything," she said. "Okay, yeah, about everything."

Val turned away, too pissed off to speak.

"Why didn't you tell us the truth, dude?" said Dallas.

"I should have," said Zoe. "But the story is so crazy. And I guess—I'm just realizing this now—I guess I was afraid that once you knew who X really was, you'd tell me to stay away from him, and I knew that I couldn't."

Val turned back suddenly.

"I want to know everything about him," she said. "Right now. You know I love you, but I swear to god, one more lie and I'm done."

"X is . . . ," said Zoe. "Okay, here we go. X is a prisoner in a place called the Lowlands. They let him leave to collect souls who've been damned, but then they make him come back. Jonah and I met him during the blizzard when he came to get Stan Manggold. How was I going to explain that to you? You'd have looked at me like you're looking at me right now."

"The Lowlands? What is that?" said Val. "Are you talking about hell?"

"Yes, but—" said Zoe.

"'Yes, *but*'?" said Val. "He's from hell? How is that not a deal breaker?"

"I'm with Val, dawg," said Dallas. "You dumped *me* because I like sports."

"X was born there, okay?" said Zoe. "He doesn't know who his parents are—they're somewhere else in the Lowlands, which are gigantic, I guess. He grew up in a prison cell. I'm the first person his own age he's ever talked to, probably. I *know* I'm the first person who ever held him or kissed him . . ."

"You can skip some of this," said Dallas, reddening.

"Sorry," said Zoe. "X has been told he's a piece of shit his whole life, but somehow he's the kindest person. The most loyal person." She paused. "And he loves me so much he can barely look at me."

Val and Dallas were silent.

"I need him back," said Zoe. "I miss his hands. I miss his coat. How weird is that? I miss his coat!"

"That's the only thing you've said that actually isn't weird," said Val. "I've had sex with *all* of Gloria's coats."

Dallas was in misery. He pretended to choke himself with his tie.

Val glared at him.

"What is *wrong* with you, Hetero Norm?"

"First of all," said Dallas, "why does no one want to have sex with *my* coat—it's full of luxurious down. Also, I'm sorry but I don't want to hear about this hot-ass dude. Could you guys try to be sensitive since I'm the ex-boyfriend?"

"'Ex-boyfriend'?" said Val. "Zoe hooked up with you in the handicapped bathroom at Walmart—and now you're her 'ex-boyfriend'?"

"It was Target," said Dallas. "And that shit was hot. Back me up, Zo."

"It was," she said, mostly just to be nice. "You're sure it wasn't Walmart?"

Val yanked the conversation back on track.

"I'm sorry Bert and Betty died," she told Zoe. "I'm sorry your dad died. Obviously. Watching *you* suffer made *me* suffer. You know that. But I don't . . . I mean, I don't know what the hell is going on with you anymore."

Zoe glanced at the church. Her mother, Jonah, and Rufus had just come out. They were thanking the minister. Jonah was holding their mother's hand and swinging her arm around like it was a jump rope.

She knew that Val and Dallas were overwhelmed by everything she'd told them. She knew she shouldn't say another word. But Val had reminded Zoe of one last secret she'd been keeping.

"My father is still alive," she said. "My mom knows. Jonah doesn't. When I get back, I'll explain all that, too."

THE WALLACES HAD ASKED that their ashes be scattered on a stretch of river they loved off Tally Lake Road. Bert and Betty used to take folding chairs and read there—even in winter sometimes. It pained Zoe to remember how cute Bert and Betty looked all bundled up in their coats and scarves, how they passed a plaid thermos of coffee back and forth, how they had to keep taking off their gloves to turn the pages.

Zoe knew that Ripper, wherever she was, was waiting impatiently to find her daughter's last resting place. As she drove, she kept thinking she saw Ripper's gold dress between the trees. But Zoe didn't want to rush this. For the time being, she kept Ripper in the Do Not Open box in her brain. She smiled, imagining Ripper cursing indignantly and trying to climb out.

They had taken two cars. Zoe and Jonah were in one, their mom and Rufus in the other. Jonah had insisted that Rufus come with them, even though he hadn't known the Wallaces well. Rufus seemed to feel self-conscious about intruding on a family moment, but the Bissells had been staying with him ever since their house was destroyed, and what Jonah said, in his own strange way, was true: "You're part of our *us* now."

Jonah also insisted they bring Spock and Uhura with them to the river, because the Labs had belonged to Bert and Betty. Uhura had gotten pneumonia. Zoe was sure it was from when Stan Manggold tried to drown her in the lake during the blizzard. The dog had lost a startling amount of weight. Just picking her up was heartbreaking: it felt like holding a skeleton. The vet couldn't promise that Uhura would recover, but no one told Jonah that. He watched the dog obsessively, like he was her secret service agent.

Zoe's mother parked near the river. Zoe pulled up on the other side of a copse of trees, so her mom wouldn't see what Ronny the Unhinged Hunter had done to her car. A light rain polka-dotted the windshield.

"Do we have to get out right away?" said Jonah. "Or can we sit?"

Uhura was curled on his lap in the backseat.

"We can sit if you want to," said Zoe.

"I want to," said Jonah. "Uhura's sleeping. She still sounds rattly. Do you think she'll always sound rattly?"

"I don't know, bug," said Zoe. "But I know she loves you—and I know you love her."

"Duh," said Jonah. "I totally love her."

Zoe watched through the windshield as her mom spread a blanket by the river, and Rufus carried out flowers from the altar and the urn he'd carved with doves.

"Are you feeling sad about Bert and Betty?" said Zoe.

When Jonah didn't answer, she looked at him in the rearview mirror. He was making his scrunched-up "thinking" face.

"I'm sad-mad," he said. "I've never been here without them before. Remember their thermos? Are *you* sad-mad?"

"I am, yeah," said Zoe. "I didn't know it was called that."

"It *is* called that, I didn't make it up," said Jonah. "You know what sucks?"

"What sucks, bug?" said Zoe.

"When you go to a place and all you see is the people who aren't there," he said. "Don't tell Mom, but I'm a little glad we don't live on the mountain anymore."

"Why?" said Zoe.

"Because now it's just the place where Dad isn't," said Jonah. "Also, it's the place where Bert and Betty don't come over anymore—and the place where X doesn't play in the snow with me. You know?"

"I do," said Zoe.

She reached back and mussed his hair. Jonah grinned. He snapped his teeth at her hand, like an alligator.

"I liked your speech thing at church," he said. "You guys think I don't pay attention to stuff, but mostly I do."

"I know you do," said Zoe.

"I liked the part about X," said Jonah.

"What part about X?" said Zoe. "There wasn't a part about X."

"Yeah, there was," said Jonah. "You said, 'Some people change you so much that they make any amount of pain worth it.' See? I was listening."

"That was about Bert and Betty," said Zoe.

"No, it wasn't, duh," said Jonah. "I'm not *seven*."

"Okay, maybe it was about all of them," said Zoe. "I liked when you said, 'I tied my own tie.'"

"How else were they gonna know?" said Jonah.

Uhura finally stirred, and they left the car and walked down the slope to the river. Zoe was touched by how carefully Jonah carried Uhura, how he took only the tiniest, most cautious steps. Spock walked alongside him. He kept his worried eyes trained on Uhura, and made a wincing sound, like he was asking, *Is she okay? Is she okay?*

They all sat on the blanket, and Zoe's mom opened the wooden urn. Bert and Betty's remains were in his-and-her plastic bags. Zoe had known there would be bits of bone mixed in with the ashes, but seeing them was harder than she'd expected. She felt one of those elevator-drops in her stomach. Jonah seemed not to realize that it was bone, and Zoe was grateful for that.

Her mother asked if anyone wanted to say a few words before they scattered the ashes.

Jonah raised his hand, like he was in school.

"I want to say the words 'sad' and 'mad,'" he said.

"Me, too," said Zoe.

"Good," said their mother. "It's important to acknowledge both those things. They're both a hundred percent okay."

She looked to Rufus, who scratched his overgrown red beard thoughtfully.

"Do you want to say anything?" she said. "You can."

"No, I'm good," he said. "I like what the river is saying. I like what the *wind* is saying." When Zoe smirked—she couldn't help it—Rufus smiled unabashedly, and said, "You think I'm a goofball."

"I think you're awesome," said Zoe. "And a *gigantic* goofball."

Zoe was glad Rufus was there. Her mother refused to admit that he had a debilitating crush on her, and wouldn't tell Zoe whether

36

she had feelings for him, too. Still, Rufus was an addition to her family, which felt good and healing—they'd gotten too used to subtraction.

The rain picked up. Zoe could feel it land softly in her hair. Her mom read a Buddhist poem about how the end isn't really the end ("I don't get it," said Jonah), and put the first handful of the Wallaces' remains into the water. She had Jonah drop rose and gladiolus petals along with it, so they'd know where the ashes were as the current carried them away. The petals were a nice touch, Zoe thought. Her mom had a way with nice touches. Watching the flowers made Zoe feel peaceful for the first time since she'd woken up. They were like a fleet of red and blue ships.

Afterward, Jonah carried Uhura to the car, whispering to her as he walked. Rufus tried to distract Spock, to get him to play, but Spock wouldn't leave Uhura's side.

Zoe and her mom washed the ash off their hands in the river, which was so cold that it stung.

"I told Val and Dallas everything," said Zoe.

"Wow," said her mother. "That was maybe a decision you and I could have talked about beforehand. It has repercussions for all of us."

"I know, I'm sorry, but it kind of had to happen right then," said Zoe. "Because of . . . stuff."

"Okay, I trust you, Zo," said her mom. "How'd they take it?"

"They were shocked," said Zoe. "Obviously. Val was pissed. They're still trying to understand it. I mean, *I'm* still trying to understand it. Are you ever going to tell Rufus?"

"I'm not sure," said her mother. "It's a lot to put on the poor guy."

"Yeah, but if you don't say something, the wind or the river might tell him," said Zoe.

Her mom smiled.

"Be nice," she said. "My number one concern is that Jonah never finds out that your dad just took off on us. I hate that *you* know it."

"It's okay."

"It's not. You deserved someone better than him."

Zoe saw how tired her mother was. How depleted.

"We *got* someone better than him, Mom," Zoe said. "We got you."

Her mother surprised her by tearing up. Zoe thought of Ripper, and how badly Ripper wanted to say good-bye to Belinda, how ashamed she was for leaving her children motherless when she murdered her servant with the teakettle and was damned.

"Sorry," said Zoe's mom, wiping her eyes with her fingertips. "Emotional day. All I ever wanted to do was protect you guys from— from everything. I wanted to raise you like little lambs."

Zoe hugged her hard.

"You did good," she said. *"Baaaa."*

four

ZOE SAT BY THE river when the others had gone. Not even two minutes went by before Ripper came up quietly behind her in the Booty Hunter hat. She must have been nervous—it was such an undramatic entrance.

"You will come?" said Ripper. "You will help me?"

"Yes," said Zoe. "But I have to be back by midnight."

Ripper smiled gratefully.

"And so you shall, Cinderella," she said.

Zoe got on her feet.

"Do you think the lords will really send X for you?" she said.

"Yes," said Ripper. "I believe I have demonstrated what a nuisance I can be if they don't. Dervish, in particular, loathes the idea of us dead people running around up here. He fears we will leave evidence that the Lowlands exist. Now, you have flown with X before, have you not? You know what is involved?"

"Yes," said Zoe. "We call it 'zooming.' I throw up sometimes."

"Lovely," said Ripper. "Please bear in mind that this is my only dress."

Ripper lifted her, and they shot into the sky.

The sunlight made Zoe's eyes ache, and the air screamed past her ears. But nothing was as overwhelming as the memory of lying draped, just like this, in X's arms. She fell asleep as they flew, her senses shutting down. Her last thought was that Ripper was carrying her toward him.

ZOE WOKE HOURS LATER to the buzzing of her phone.

Ripper had laid her down beneath a tree in a meadow. She'd even folded her hands on her stomach, which was sweet, though it made Zoe feel like a corpse. Zoe sat up in the grass, so woozy she felt as if she'd been drugged. The afternoon was nearly gone. Ripper stood nearby watching for threats. Zoe couldn't see her face.

Texts from Val and Dallas had been multiplying for hours. Dallas had sent five variations on *Are you SAFE?* Val had sent eight in a row saying, *Are you INSANE?* Zoe texted them back hurriedly (*Safe! Sane!*), put the phone away, and rubbed her face.

The air was warmish and humid, and the meadow showed signs of spring—little flecks of green, like a drawing being colored in. Zoe could see a white church steeple in the distance. A stripe of blue-gray ocean. A handful of sails, tiny as commas.

"Where are we?" she said.

"Massachusetts," Ripper answered, without turning. Her voice sounded troubled. "Near the sea."

"You didn't have to let me sleep," she said.

Ripper turned her head a few degrees.

"I myself can never sleep and I like to watch others at it," she said. "I am always looking for clues as to how it is done."

Zoe walked toward her warily. The dry grass rose nearly to her knees.

"Why Massachusetts?" she said.

"Why indeed," said Ripper. "Twenty-three days after my death, my husband married a horrific American and brought my children to this . . . this *colony*."

Ripper took the Booty Hunter cap off finally, and flung it away.

"Did you love your husband?" said Zoe.

"X asked me the selfsame question once," said Ripper. "Why is it that people in love need everyone *else* to be in love—or to at least aspire to the condition?"

Zoe said nothing, afraid that she'd annoyed her.

"I most certainly did *not* love my husband," Ripper continued. "The fact that I murdered a serving girl with a teakettle speaks to my mood at the time."

Ripper stared off at the trees that separated the meadow from the town and the ocean beyond it. Zoe didn't know whether she should ask another question, whether talking more would help Ripper or hurt her.

"How do you know what happened to your children," she said carefully, "if you were already . . ."

"Deceased?" said Ripper. "I asked a bounty hunter to investigate the matter. When he returned, he assured me that I did not want to know." She paused. "Has anyone ever—in the whole history of mankind—been told they didn't want to know something and not *immediately* wanted to know it all the more?"

"You don't have to tell me what happened," said Zoe.

"My son, Alfie, died in a fire," said Ripper. "In a stable."

She explained that the boy had rushed in to save his horse, which was named Equinox. Ripper had obviously told the story many times, but it seemed as though every word was still a thorn in her throat. Alfie managed to rescue Equinox—the horse bolted free—but he himself got trapped under a beam. Belinda ran into the flames to rescue her big brother.

Zoe could see the muscles in Ripper's neck tighten.

"Belinda failed because she was very, very small," Ripper said. "I suppose X never told you any of this because you were so busy smothering each other with your bodies?"

Zoe wanted to make Ripper smile, if she could.

"There might have been some smothering, yes," she said.

"My husband's new wife apparently grew bored of hearing Belinda wail about Alfie," Ripper went on. "She shipped her off to a place with the ponderous name of The Cropsey Asylum for the Criminally Insane and Others Needful of Rest and Restraint. I know we are close, for there is an unbearable knot in my head. It is nothing supernatural, just a mother's ache, yet it tells me that . . ."

Zoe took out her phone to search for the asylum. Ripper saw what she was doing. She reached out to stop her.

"It tells me that I do not have the fortitude I imagined," she said. "You can lie in the grass a while longer, or I can spirit you home. But you need not find Belinda's grave, for I am too weak to face it."

Ripper clenched her jaw to keep from crying. Zoe went to hug her, and felt Ripper's lean frame tremble in her arms. When they stepped apart, Ripper tugged at her dress to straighten it.

"I apologize for that display," she said.

"You don't have to apologize," said Zoe. "I'm famous for my displays. My displays have fans around the world."

Someday, she was going to have to figure out if blurting weird stuff in awkward moments was a character flaw.

They stood a moment, neither knowing what came next. Ripper's eyes darted around, as if a bounty hunter might suddenly appear from any direction. Zoe remembered her saying that they always came at night. She tried not to hope for X. Despite Ripper's assurances, the chances of the lords sending him seemed impossibly small.

"Do you see something?" Zoe asked.

"No," said Ripper. "I do not."

Zoe wasn't ready to give up on finding the asylum. Ripper had been there when Zoe confronted her runaway father. She had put an arm around Zoe—whispered to her and consoled her—less than two minutes after they met. Facing her dad had been scary, humiliating, more painful than anything Zoe had ever experienced. But she was glad she had done it. It freed her somehow. It made her heart feel less like a lead weight in her chest.

She wanted Ripper to know that kind of relief.

"Look, you met my mom, right?" she said. "Did you notice her fake tattoo? Above her ankle?"

"I do not recall her ankle, no," said Ripper.

"Okay, so she's obsessed with this tattoo—she has a whole stack of them in a drawer," said Zoe. "It says, 'The Only Way Out Is Through.' I think that applies to this situation. Also to cake."

Yeah, the blurting thing probably *was* a character flaw.

"Explain," said Ripper.

"I think you can do this," said Zoe. "I think you can see this Cropsey place."

"And I assure you I cannot," said Ripper.

"Can."

"Cannot."

"X and I used to argue like this," said Zoe. "I always wore him down. I'll wear you down, too."

"Will not," said Ripper.

But she smiled.

Zoe looked again at her phone, and found the asylum within seconds.

"It's only a mile away—what's left of it," she said. "I'm going to go see Belinda. Are you going to make me go alone?"

The sun, sinking behind them, lit up Ripper's ravaged dress. Zoe would never get over how lovely, and unlikely, the woman was. Even now, even in distress, she looked gorgeous, just raw around the eyes.

"Show me the way, you obstinate thing," Ripper said finally.

Zoe beamed. She took off her black button-down sweater and handed it to Ripper.

"Put this on," she said. "It'll make you look less like a crazy dead person."

RIPPER DIDN'T WANT TO know anything about Cropsey until they got there, so Zoe read a history of the place to herself as they walked through the trees and toward the ocean. She read about why Cropsey was shut down and about the celebrations in town on the day its doors were closed. She even found—in a graduate student's thesis—an alphabetical list of every patient who'd ever walked, or been dragged, inside, including nine-year-old Belinda

Popplewell-Heath. There were a dozen words about Belinda's diagnosis, life, and death. Reading them, Zoe felt a chill spread through her. She wished she could protect Ripper from the details forever.

Zoe checked the map on her phone as they continued. The blue dot representing her and Ripper pulsed like a heartbeat.

"We're close," she said.

Ripper, trailing behind, breathed in sharply. Zoe saw her peer back through the trees.

"Do you see something now?" she said.

"I do not," said Ripper.

Zoe and Ripper exited the woods and stopped at the top of a scruffy brown hill, which tumbled down to a busy road. The sky was darkening—turning black, like ink soaking through cloth. The first handful of stars hovered over the ocean.

They crossed the road to a wide driveway that dipped toward the water. As Zoe led Ripper through a pair of brick columns, she saw the rusty hinges that used to anchor the asylum's gates, and a faded patch on the brickwork where a sign must have hung. It'd been in the shape of a family crest, as if Cropsey had been a place to be proud of.

Zoe looked to see if Ripper had noticed the remnants of the asylum. She had. In her nervousness, Ripper had begun tearing at her fingernails again—she'd bloodied the nail on her left ring-finger. Zoe gripped her arm.

"Don't," she said. "You promised Jonah you wouldn't mess with your nails if he didn't bite his."

Ripper glowered, then nodded reluctantly.

"I remember," she said.

They trudged up the drive in the dark. Hedges loomed like walls on either side, and the silence was so complete that even tiny, incidental sounds, like the *crunch* of their shoes on the gravel, seemed ominous.

"Tell me about Belinda," said Zoe. "Not how she died—how she lived."

"Oh, she was a box of fireworks, that girl," Ripper said. "Plump and mischievous. Curly-haired. Beautiful, though it annoyed her to hear it. She used to say, 'I'm only beautiful because you are, Mother—and it is *very* tedious to be complimented for something I had no part in!' She was always in motion, always up to something. She used to somersault on the carpet, then stagger around dizzily, knocking over vases."

"Jonah would have loved her," said Zoe.

"Yes," Ripper said quietly. "They'd have been a pair of bandits." She paused. "I've missed my children for nearly two centuries. If I hadn't already been dead, it would have killed me. Then—just when I thought I had subdued the pain the tiniest bit—Regent appeared at my cell, and introduced me to a ten-year-old boy."

"X," said Zoe.

"Yes," said Ripper.

Yet again, she looked back to see if they were being followed.

Zoe wanted to ask what X had been like as a child, but knew it'd be selfish. And truthfully, she could imagine X at ten perfectly: kind, watchful, sad, convinced he must be broken or wicked in some way because he'd been born in the Lowlands. Still, she wondered what he wore, if he ever laughed, if Ripper brushed his hair, even with her fingers. It was hard not to ask.

"I loved X with all that was left of my heart," said Ripper. "I still remember him releasing Regent's hand and reaching his pink palm out to me that very first time. I never told him this, but he awakened such piercing memories of Alfie and Belinda that I cannot claim to have truly slept since."

The hedges fell away, and the road arrived at an enormous lawn.

Ripper squinted into the distance.

"What, I wonder, is *that*?" she said.

A crumbling brick tower stood alone in the grass. Cracks ran down it like veins.

"That," said Zoe, "is all that's left of the Cropsey Asylum for the Whatever and Whatever."

Her words floated toward the ocean. She couldn't think of anything to say that would help Ripper now.

THE TOWER WAS LIT by a spotlight, which illuminated every fracture in the brick. Ripper motioned for Zoe to stay behind, and went forward alone. Zoe sank into the dead grass.

Ripper moved slowly. It was as if the tower were pushing back at her, trying to keep her away.

There was a plaque at the base of the monument.

Zoe knew roughly what it would say. There was no protecting Ripper from the truth.

Cropsey had been a horror—a place where patients were neglected, abused, experimented on, left in their own filth. The tower itself had had two purposes. It was used as a chute to drop the bodies of dead patients down and as a chimney for when the orderlies had collected enough corpses to burn.

Zoe watched as Ripper read the plaque. She watched as her shoulders sagged and as she fell on her knees and cried. All the tears

Ripper had been forcing back burst out at once, like windows blasting out of a building. She tore at her gold dress. The spotlight threw her shadow at the tower, five stories tall.

When Ripper finally staggered back toward Zoe, her hair had fallen loose and spilled down her face. Her eyes looked feral.

Zoe had never been scared of Ripper.

She was now.

"What did your little machine tell you about my Belinda?" Ripper asked, her voice dark and hard.

"Nothing," said Zoe.

"You are *lying*," said Ripper. The ocean hissed on the rocks a hundred yards away. A lighthouse beam swept the black water. "I must know everything."

Zoe had said the same thing to X about her father.

"I don't know very much," she told Ripper. "Belinda was committed in 1835."

"She was a child!" said Ripper. "What did they claim as her demons?"

"Grief," said Zoe. *Of course Belinda was grieving,* she thought— *she lost her mom, then her brother burned to death right in front of her.* "Grief, hysteria, and something called 'Gathering in the head.'"

She prayed Ripper wouldn't ask anything else.

"And how long was my daughter a prisoner of this place? Dammit, must I drag every detail out of you!"

Zoe just said it: "Twenty-five years. She froze to death in her bed. She was thirty-five."

Ripper stalked off in the direction of the water, then whirled back.

"And when my Belinda died," she asked, "they threw her body down this chimney—whereupon it landed atop the corpses of *other*

48

blameless sons and daughters? Is that correct? And then they consigned the mass of them to flames. Is *that* correct?"

Zoe wanted to say something comforting, but what could it possibly be?

"Yes," she said. "I think that's right."

"If our positions were reversed," said Ripper, "what would *you* do about this hateful monument lurking behind me?"

"If I had your powers?" said Zoe.

"Yes, if you had my powers," said Ripper. "*Of course* if you had my powers."

"I'd tear the thing down."

RIPPER CHARGED AT THE tower so suddenly that Zoe didn't have a chance to step back. She saw a blur of gold—Ripper's jet trail in the darkness—and heard the boom of impact. The chimney shook. The mortar between the bricks split open and sent out puffs of dust, but the tower didn't fall.

Ripper trotted back to Zoe for a second run. She was sweating and glowing with purpose now. The shoulder of her dress was torn.

"The tower and I are having a disagreement," she said. "The tower believes I am incapable of knocking it down. Yet we beg to differ, don't we?"

"*Yeah* we do," said Zoe.

She watched Ripper's second assault. Again, there was a golden blur, a concussive boom, a rush of dirt and wind. Again, the tower refused to fall.

"Bloody ignorant tower," said Ripper, readying for her third attempt. "It seems not to know who I am."

Zoe laughed.

"You remind me of Val sometimes," she said.

"I am happy to hear it," said Ripper, checking the damage to her dress. "Val has a fiery spirit and tremendous hair."

The blur. The boom. The rush.

This time, the tower hesitated—then toppled into the grass.

Ripper emerged from the rubble, coughing and waving away dust. She gave Zoe such a pleased grin that Zoe nearly cried.

Ripper adjusted her gown, and twisted her wild, raven hair back into a knot. The ritual smoothing-of-the-dress had become one of Zoe's favorite things about Ripper. The things that ball gown had survived! It was like the flag in "The Star-Spangled Banner."

"Thank you for locating that tower—and making me face it," said Ripper. She picked a brick off the ground, then said the following as if it were an afterthought: "Now, if you can survive my absence a moment, I must go dismember the bounty hunters who have been stalking us these past thirty minutes."

"Bounty hunters *plural*?" said Zoe.

"I counted three as we passed through the woods," Ripper said.

"You said you didn't see anything!" said Zoe.

"I didn't *see* them," said Ripper. "I *heard* them."

"I'm coming with you," said Zoe. "One of them might be X."

"Or all three could be deranged samurai," said Ripper. "You are not coming. You are to stay rooted here."

"I'm not good at doing what I'm told," said Zoe.

"The same's been said of me," said Ripper. "But I forbid you to follow. X would not stalk us from a distance. He would bound into your arms. He is *not* among them." Seeing Zoe's expression, Ripper softened. "I promised you X and you shall have X, even if it is only for a moment. The lords must be in a fury because of my antics, for

Dervish is not the only one obsessed with the secrecy of the Lowlands. I will disfigure these hunters. If the lords have not sent X for me by the time I'm through, I will wreak havoc all night. That lighthouse in the bay? It will not live to see the morning."

Ripper tilted her head up at the blue-black sky and shouted to the lords, "Do you *doubt* me?"

"I think the lords are down there," said Zoe, pointing to the ground.

"Ah, yes," said Ripper. She knelt and screamed at the grass this time: "DO YOU DOUBT ME?!"

"*I* don't doubt you," said Zoe.

"No one ever has and survived," said Ripper.

She shot back toward the woods.

And then: Silence. Darkness. Even the spotlight made a sudden popping noise and went out. Zoe stared at the woods a while longer, desperate for some sign or sound—for proof that Ripper was safe or that X was coming. She'd slept for hours in the meadow, but she was still *so tired*. She felt it in every part of her now. The day had unglued her. When it was over, she was going to snuggle with Jonah in a pillow fort. Her mom and Rufus could come and go around her. They could *vacuum* around her. She was going to sleep for a week.

The minutes passed slowly. Zoe imagined the heavy, iron hands of an enormous clock. She felt like she had to push them forward herself.

She turned to face the ocean. The lighthouse cast its faint circle onto the waves. Otherwise, the water was so dark it was just a vast, soft noise, an inhaling and exhaling, a presence.

The lighthouse sprouted three more beams. Zoe walked toward

it, just because it was pretty and comforting. She'd never seen one in real life before. It was like it wore a crown of light.

One of the beams began to crackle, as if it were short-circuiting. A spark drifted down toward the water.

Rather than extinguishing in the waves, the spark turned the whole ocean gold—just for a second, like a light flicked on and off.

It was a signal from X. She knew it was.

He had come.

Zoe felt the ground rushing beneath her.

She looked down and saw that she was running.

part two

Captive

five

"I LIKE IT WHEN you beseech me," she told X, as she pulled him down by his shirt. "Beseech me some more."

X grinned. Zoe was so lovely . . . He couldn't think of *anything* she wasn't lovelier than.

He'd shoved the orange rowboat away from the dock, and it was slicing through the harbor. After 200 feet, the craft finally slowed, turned in a lazy arc in the water, and came to rest in the dark. There were a few blurry clouds in the night sky. To X, it looked like someone had tried to erase the stars.

He kissed Zoe, and felt their bodies breathe into each other. She began pulling up his shirt.

"Wait," he said. "I want to *see* you."

He pressed his palms to the sides of the boat. A pale light materialized.

"You and your tricks," said Zoe.

She scanned the water to make sure no one was close.

"Only the heavens know what we do," X said.

Zoe laughed.

He was afraid he'd said something foolish, but she pulled off her shirt, and her skin shone pink in the moonlight—and she dove at him.

LATER, THEY LAY ENTANGLED at the bottom of the boat, her legs wound around him, their clothes flung everywhere.

Being with Zoe always quieted everything in X. It unclenched and unfolded him. The lords had sent him to hunt Ripper, and until he returned her to the Lowlands the fever they called the Trembling would be circulating in his blood—and worsening. But Zoe made even that easier to bear. She had her cheek against his chest. He pictured them and their boat from way up high, a bright orange triangle in a great black sea. This was all X wanted—moments like this, a lifetime's worth all strung together.

He reached into the water, and paddled them toward a beach that jutted into the harbor. They jumped out of the boat when they ran aground. Together, they dragged it away from the tide.

"I'm cold," said Zoe. "I wish we had a fire."

X pointed to a spot on the sand. A perfect flower of flame appeared, and floated just above the beach.

"Show-off," said Zoe.

They sat listening to the waves disintegrate on the sand. X liked the sound of the ocean. He'd heard it so few times in his life. Rivers, like the ones in the Lowlands, were always headed somewhere else—but oceans rushed forward to meet you. They laid themselves at your feet.

"I'm still cold," said Zoe. "Can you turn the fire up, or bring it closer or something?"

"I can do both," said X.

He summoned the flames toward them. They floated nearer, burned brighter.

"What were you like when you were a kid?" said Zoe. "When you were Jonah's age. I wanted to ask Ripper."

"How old is Jonah?" said X. "Ten?"

"He's eight but he would *love* that you think he's ten."

"When I was eight, I was . . . Well, I was thin as a needle, for one thing. I had a small pile of clothes in my cell—"

"They put you in a cell when you were *eight*?"

"Regent did, yes. But the bars were to protect me. So many of the souls were violent, and some had been damned for . . . for things they'd done to children. Do you take my meaning?"

"Yes." Zoe took X's hand and interlaced their fingers. "So you had your little pile of clothes . . ."

"That's right. Everything was either so small that I could barely pull it on, or so big that I drowned in it. The bounty hunters were made to fetch me clothes from the Overworld, and they were probably sharing a joke at my expense."

"I bet you looked adorable," said Zoe.

"I assure you I did not," said X. "I was such an anomaly in the Lowlands. Everyone else was dead, not to put too fine a point on it. Because I'd been born there, I was—I was eating. I was *growing up*. Regent was virtually the only soul who would speak to me. I used to sit at the bars of my cell and wave when he passed. Once, he stopped and begged my pardon for never waving back. He worried it would turn the other lords against me if he did, and Dervish already despised me. I remember asking Regent, 'Would it be all right, sir, if I keep waving to *you*?'"

"You called him 'sir'?" said Zoe.

"Yes, though he discouraged it," said X. "In any event, Regent smiled. Nodded. I cannot tell you how much that exhilarated me. He said I could wave to him as often as I liked, so I waved constantly—it became the chief occupation of my days. And he began bringing me tiny things he found, trinkets from the Overworld. I started a collection, which I kept wrapped in foil. I was *quite* serious about my collection."

"I love little X," said Zoe. "What happened to all that stuff?"

"*Dervish* happened to it," said X. "He was striding past my cell one day, and saw me playing. I used to pretend that I ran a store, though I wasn't entirely sure what a store *was*. Dervish demanded that I surrender my collection. Then, as I watched, he flew across the plain, and dumped everything into the river."

Zoe squeezed X's hand, as if he were still that eight-year-old boy, and in need of comfort.

"Wait," he said. "Before you pity me, there's a happy ending."

X slipped his hand into a rip in the lining of his overcoat, searching for something.

"Regent ordered ten guards into the river to recover my things," he said. "I was surprised he'd intervened so publicly—and over trinkets. It may have been because I was weeping so tragically in my cell. You know the way children cry? The way they rub their eyes with their fists? The guards dove in the cold water for an hour. Dervish was outraged. It was the first hint I ever saw of what eventually became open warfare between Regent and him. Regent wouldn't let the guards give up the search. He said they could *live* in the river until they found at least some of my collection."

"And?" said Zoe.

"Apparently, the guards did not want to live in the river," said X, smiling. "They found five of my favorite things."

He had taken a small bundle of silver foil from his coat. He opened it carefully, as if there were a living thing inside, and spread its contents on the sand: a button made of green-and-red bloodstone; an ornate silver comb; a cracked bracelet that read, *Vesuvius*; plus a shard of white porcelain and the tip of a broken drill.

"They're kind of beautiful," said Zoe.

"They are to me," said X. "Almost as beautiful as this . . ."

From a pocket, he took the letter that Zoe had written to him once. The paper had been unfolded so often that it'd begun to tear.

"Apart from my boots and the clothes I stand up in," said X, "this is everything I own."

Zoe produced something from a pocket now, too: the letter that he had written to *her*. All it said was, *X.* Yet she had stored it in a transparent bag for safekeeping. X looked at the bag covetously.

"Do you want the baggie, dude?" said Zoe. "To put my letter in?"

He said yes before she'd even finished asking.

X FELT HIS FEVER rise: Ripper had to be near. He stood, and saw that she was wending toward them down the beach. Somehow, she had changed her clothes. She had traded in the battle-torn golden dress she'd worn since 1832 for a silver ball gown decorated with crystal beading and horizontal rows of pale pink ribbons.

Zoe stood up now, too, and called to Ripper.

"You got a new dress? In the middle of the night?"

"I did, thank you for noticing," said Ripper. "I stole it."

"Ripper!"

"I know, I know. The lords can add the crime to my sentence, if they like. I can serve eternity plus a little bit extra."

"Well, it's gorgeous," said Zoe.

"And it will be easier to do combat in," said Ripper, "for it has no sleeves and a less constricting skirt."

"Cool," said Zoe. "So it's practical, too."

X found he resented Ripper's presence. He wasn't ready to leave Zoe. He had yet to tell her the most vital thing: his plan. He'd wasted his time on memories. He wished they would stop talking about the dress. Now that Ripper stood close, the Trembling made everything slip out of focus. Even the gown was just a smudge of light.

"Ripper, I need one hour more with Zoe," he said, louder than he'd meant to. "If it angers the lords, let them send another bounty hunter, and we can take turns tearing him apart."

Ripper looked at X, and seemed to see the distress he was in because of her proximity. She backed away.

"You may have your hour," she said. "But return Zoe home in the meantime, as I more or less abducted her." She snatched up the hem of her dress to protect it from the tide. "And now I shall go steal a pair of boots."

X KNEW THAT FLYING with him made Zoe nauseated sometimes, but she seemed peaceful as they shot beneath the clouds. He could see her fighting sleep. At one point, she closed her eyes and said drowsily into his ear, "Zoom zoom."

He loved carrying her because he could only truly protect her when he held her. His powers made a sort of shell around her so that she was safe from the elements—from everything. He had never told her that, but looking down at her as she burrowed into the nest made by his arms, he felt sure that she knew.

X set them down in the dark forest near the river where Zoe had left her car. Zoe looked dizzy when he released her. For a second, she staggered like a toddler learning to walk, but then turned to him and said, "Hey, I didn't throw up!"

He smiled. He had talked so long, and still hadn't told her that he had a plan, but right now he just wanted to look at her, to take her in. She had changed his life. She had *given* him a life. He thought of the rowboat, and could feel her handprints all over his body.

Zoe's car was even more battered than X remembered. She told him that a hunter had attacked it with a rifle.

"Don't worry," she added, "Ripper threw him in a ditch."

"Naturally," he said.

Zoe said she was worried about what would happen when her mother saw the car. She didn't want to tell her about the hunter because her mother had enough worries as it was.

"The lords didn't teach you how to fix cars, did they?" she said. "There wasn't, like, a shop class?"

She was joking, but nonetheless X approached the car. He ran his hand along the crumpled passenger door, heating the metal until it felt liquid beneath his palm and then smoothing it again. He'd never done anything like this before, not exactly. He liked the feeling of *undoing* violence for a change.

"That's amazing," said Zoe. "But that dent was already there, so you've got to put it back."

X laughed, and punched the door.

They circled the car together. Zoe pointed out the damage that the hunter had done, and X restored everything, even the sagging bumper and shattered headlights.

"Thank you," said Zoe when he'd completed his ministrations. "Now it's just a regular piece of crap again."

"Could you not simply acquire a new car?" said X.

"Do you know what a new one costs?" said Zoe. "We don't even have a house anymore, dude. Love *me*, love my shitty car."

"Fair enough. I love your shitty car."

THEY WENT DOWN THE slope toward the river, where Zoe and her family had spread Bert and Betty's ashes. The ground was muddy, and tried to pull off their boots.

"I've talked a storm of words this evening," said X, "yet there is something more I must tell you. I have a plan to escape the Lowlands."

He felt Zoe stop walking. They were halfway to the river.

"Why are you just telling me this now?" she said.

"Well, in the boat, my mouth was otherwise occupied—with your mouth," he said. "And truthfully, the plan is no doubt a folly, and I dreaded you telling me so."

When Zoe spoke next, X heard the nervousness beneath the humor, like a shadow following immediately behind.

"I probably wouldn't use the word 'folly,'" she said.

They sat on a tilted rock by the water. X offered to light the woods, but Zoe said she liked hearing the river in the dark—the sort of gulping sound it made.

"Tell me everything," she said. "Go, go, go."

X searched his mind for a beginning.

He told Zoe that from the moment he'd refused to take her

father's soul, he had sat in his cell in the Lowlands with barely the company of a human voice. Ripper was on the run. Another friend, Banger, had been punished for ferrying messages between Zoe and X. Here, Zoe interrupted to say that she had liked Banger—not just because he so thoroughly repented the murder he had committed when he was a bartender in Arizona, but also because she had seen him eat candy and chew gum at the same time.

"Is that not commonplace?" said X.

"Not unless you're six," said Zoe. "Also, the guy uses *really* out-of-date slang. He said I was 'the bomb diggity.'" She scowled. "I talk too much when I'm anxious. Ignore whatever I say, and keep going."

"Yes, all right," said X. "The cells on either side of me were empty for the first time I could remember. A Russian guard brought me food—he was the only one who spoke to me at all. He has been besotted with Ripper for decades, so he would linger with me awhile, moaning, 'Oh, how I *luff* my Reeper!' It was not a conversation in the usual sense."

"Does Ripper like him, too?" said Zoe.

"It would appear not," said X. "She has bitten him several times."

"*Naturally*," said Zoe, "but you're supposed to be ignoring me."

"I'm—I'm trying," said X. "Regent never visited, which wounded me. I assumed he was furious that I'd betrayed his trust, and broken the laws of the Lowlands so wantonly when I fell in love with you."

"Oh, yeah, you're from hell, but *I'm* the bad influence," said Zoe.

X pursed his lips to keep from smiling.

"I am ignoring you," he said.

X told Zoe that he'd resented Regent's absence more with every hour. He became consumed with the fact that though Regent had always watched over him, he'd gone 20 years without revealing that he had known X's mother. His whole life, X had been starved for a single fact about his parents, but only recently did Regent tell him that X's mother had once been a lord and that he had called her a friend. Even then he'd divulged virtually nothing else—just that she was punished for becoming pregnant with X, and was now imprisoned in some especially wretched corner of the Lowlands.

X stood up on the rock.

"If you don't mind, I'm weary of darkness," he said. "And I must soon return to it."

"Of course," said Zoe. "I'm sorry. I wasn't thinking."

X swept a hand through the air, and half a dozen firs across the river flushed with light.

"Today, Regent and Dervish appeared at my cell, and said they were sending me for Ripper," said X, sitting again. "I had twisted myself into a rage by now. And seeing them side by side repulsed me, for Dervish's soul is nothing but a sack of snakes. I did something that shocked them both: I refused to go."

"Wait, what?" said Zoe.

"I told them I would only bring them Ripper if they freed me forever," said X. "Remember, Ripper had already rebuffed dozens of bounty hunters. She'd stripped one man's military uniform off, and sent him back naked! The Russian had told me everything. He had even acted out some of the combat. I knew the lords needed me, so I set my price high." He paused. "Dervish cursed until there was spittle on his lips. Regent insisted that they didn't have the authority to free me, which I believed, as there is a Higher Power that presides over even them. So I said, 'Very well, then—when I return, you must bring me to my mother and father.'"

"Holy crap," said Zoe. "Look at you go."

X continued: Dervish had stormed away, telling Regent to tame the beast he'd created. Regent stepped closer to the bars of X's cell, and spoke in a low voice. He regretted that he knew nothing at all about X's father—and that, so far as he knew, there were only two people who knew exactly where X's mother was being held.

One was Dervish, who had despised her and would never help them. Regent declined to name the other person, which infuriated X. Still, Regent said that if X could capture Ripper, he would try to introduce him to this mysterious party. He swore X to secrecy, for Dervish would wreak havoc if he learned of the pact.

"Did you ask Regent why he waited twenty years to tell you he knew your mom?" said Zoe.

"Yes—and the question actually inflamed him," said X. "He said, 'I told you nothing about your mother because hope is *dangerous* here. You would have used anything I told you to torment yourself, and I had determined that your life was torment enough.' Apparently, there's a poem about hope being 'the thing with feathers'? Regent said, 'What the poet neglects to mention is that it has not just feathers but talons, too—for it is a bird of prey.' I told him I didn't care. I told him I could no longer live without hope now that you had shown me what it was. I swore I'd escape the Lowlands somehow. And my plan—my folly, if that's what it is—crystallized as Regent and I stood there with the bars between us."

X stopped again. It was time to bring Ripper home. With his index finger, as if he were striking notes on a piano, he made the firs across the river go dark one by one.

"I told Regent that I would save my mother—and then she would save me."

six

X'S FEVER DEEPENED AS they drove. He should have wrested Ripper back to the Lowlands an hour ago—but leaving Zoe would have just ravaged him in a different way. She had yet to say a word about his plan. He could tell she was ruminating over it from her silence and the way she stared at the oncoming road without seeming to see it.

When they arrived at Rufus's house, Zoe turned off the engine, and the car shuddered and bucked like it was having a coughing fit. Ten seconds passed before it quieted. X watched Zoe lean forward and push a button. A slow, sad tune replaced the silence.

"This is country music," she said.

X listened a moment. He didn't like it. Maybe it was the fever. He remembered Banger singing songs like it in his cell—badly.

"Tell me about your family," he said. "And the dogs."

"We're not doing great," said Zoe, "but compared to what *you're* dealing with . . . We lost almost everything when Dervish wrecked our house. And one of the dogs has been sick. Uhura. Since the blizzard. Pneumonia, we think."

"I remember Uhura," said X. "She is the fiercer of the two?"

"Yeah," said Zoe. "Spock's so lazy that he's basically a cat." She blew air out of her cheeks. "Uhura's lost fourteen pounds. If she doesn't make it, Jonah's heart is going to be a stain on the floor." She paused. "Every time I think we're done losing things, we lose something else."

"That does seem to be the way of the world," said X.

"Then I don't like the way of the world," said Zoe. "I'd like to speak to a manager, please."

She pushed the button again, and the song vanished in the middle of a word.

"You will not lose *me*," said X.

"You say that but, dude, your plan scares the shit out of me," she said.

"Because it could be dangerous?" said X.

"*Could* be? And what makes you think your mother will have any idea how to help you?"

"She was a lord," said X. "In any case, this is where hope comes in. And even if she tells me that escape is a fantasy, she can help me begin to understand—"

"Understand what?" said Zoe.

She never interrupted him. Only when she was frustrated.

"Who I am," he said.

That stopped her.

"Okay," she said. "Okay, I get that. I want that for you. And I'm no one to talk about, you know, healthy decision-making. *But . . .*"

All her fears came pouring out now, as if she had to exorcise

67

them. She reminded X of the last time he and Regent had plotted behind Dervish's back: Dervish terrorized her family and destroyed their house in retaliation. She reminded him that when he returned to the Lowlands, his powers would disappear. He wouldn't be a superhero anymore—"just somebody trying to do something nuts."

It became hard for X to listen as the fever sank its claws deeper. The back of his neck was sweating. His hands, which lay facedown on his lap, had begun to shake. Ripper had to be close. X turned and peered through the rear window. Yes: there she was in her new silver dress, passing under a streetlamp.

Zoe was still listing her objections. She reminded him that the reason he had to eat—the reason he was getting older—was that unlike everyone else in the Lowlands, he had been born there.

Which meant he was alive.

Which meant he could die.

Ripper tapped on Zoe's window, and made a strange gesture, as if pulling on an imaginary necklace.

"She tells us it is time," said X. "In her other life, she wore a pendant watch about her neck."

Zoe turned to him.

"Are you going to go through with it anyway?" she said. "Your plan?"

"You know that I am," said X. "All the fire I have to do this, all the certitude—it was inspired by you. Surely that is plain?"

"No, it isn't 'plain,'" said Zoe. "What do you mean?"

"Did you not search for your own father?" said X. The shaking had spread. "Did you not go into a cave so narrow that you had to crawl upon your side? Did you not confront your father about his lies, even though you were so angry and hurt you could barely stand to hear his voice? Don't pretend it didn't happen. I was right there beside you."

"I know you were," said Zoe. "I remember."

She took his face with just her fingertips, and kissed him. Her lips cooled him a little.

"Do *not* die," she said. It sounded like both an order and a prayer. "I'm not losing one more person. I won't put up with it. Not one. And definitely not you."

R UFUS'S HOUSE WAS SQUAT and green, with a sloping, red metal roof. The backyard was enclosed by a wooden fence, the gate of which banged opened and shut with the breeze, as if a line of ghosts were passing through. X stood alone, staring at the house. Zoe went to say good-bye to Ripper, who'd retreated to the road so that her presence wouldn't deepen X's pain.

A shaggy brown head appeared in the bright kitchen window.

Jonah.

He was holding Uhura. He'd pressed his face into her fur, and seemed to be murmuring to her. The sweetness of the scene struck X hard.

Behind him, Zoe was telling Ripper, "I thought you were going to get new boots!"

"Tragically, I could not find a pair that I liked," said Ripper, "at least nothing I was prepared to wear in perpetuity."

X realized as she said this that he'd given no thought at all to the fact that this would be his friend's last adventure in the Overworld. The lords would never let her return.

He turned to see Zoe hug Ripper, and tell her that she loved her and that she'd never forget looking for Belinda.

Ripper thanked Zoe for bringing her daughter, just for a moment, back to life.

X was seized with an idea.

He stumbled toward them, shrugging off his overcoat and letting it fall to the lawn.

"Is it the fever?" said Zoe.

"Doubtless," said Ripper.

He stripped off his shirt. The air felt good on his skin.

"You are aware that I carry your story in my blood?" he said to Ripper. "That the lords put it there, so I could hunt you?"

"Of course I am aware of it," said Ripper. "But you cannot possibly mean to show me my sins!"

No, she misunderstood. Zoe did, too—she almost looked frightened of him.

X turned away. He stretched out his arms. He summoned up a single image and froze it on his back.

Neither of them would look.

"It is a gift, Ripper, I swear it," said X.

His voice, even to himself, sounded like a maniac's.

But Zoe trusted him. Zoe was turning.

"She's beautiful, Ripper," she said. "She looks just like her mom."

There on X's back was Belinda. Curly-haired. Nine years old. Her mischievous eyes shining.

X prayed Ripper would turn now, too.

At last she did.

She saw her daughter and gasped. X heard nothing else. If Ripper was weeping, it was too soft for him to hear. Had he made an error? Was the sight of the girl too much?

He got his answer when he felt Ripper's palm alight on his back.

She was not touching *him*—even in his fever, he understood that. She was touching her daughter's face.

A BULB ABOVE THE front porch went on, illuminating the yard. The storm door swung open, and Jonah emerged. He wore a white shirt, a bizarrely knotted red tie, and pajama bottoms. He was carrying Uhura.

"Go back inside, Jonah," said Zoe.

"No," said Jonah. "Uhura wants to say hi."

X looked at the dog and felt himself go to pieces. Uhura was indeed nearly skeletal. Jonah carried her so carefully it was as if she were made of snow.

"Uhura's been sick since Stan Mangled tried to drown her," he said. "You can't fix her, can you? With your magic?"

"Would that I could," said X.

Blood drummed in his ears. He could barely hear his own words.

"It's okay," said Jonah. "She's gonna get better. I'm in charge. Mom said."

X petted Uhura because Jonah seemed to want him to. He could feel the stony vertebrae in her spine. Maybe Uhura *would* live, he thought. She'd survived too much not to survive this.

Jonah moved on to Ripper, and asked if she had better magic than X. It would have made X smile under different circumstances. He rubbed his forehead, trying to dislodge the spiraling pain.

He looked at Zoe, and tried to fix her image in his mind a final time. Could you memorize a person like you could a letter or a song? Could you take in every bit of them forever? Where did you start? Zoe stood on the lawn, half her face lit by the bulb over the porch. Her loveliness undid him, as always.

71

What could he say in parting? Should he tell her how moved he'd been when she told Ripper that she loved her—how moved he was right this instant as Jonah and Ripper stood comparing the state of their fingernails, which both had vowed to leave in peace?

A warmth, like a light, seemed to surround everyone.

"I will find my parents," he told Zoe, "but I have already found my family."

He knelt in the street, and slammed his fist against the asphalt. A wide fissure opened before him.

He called to Ripper. She dove into the ground first. Her dress gleamed, and she was gone.

X couldn't bring himself to look at Zoe again, but he heard her call out that she loved him as the earth pulled him down, swallowed him up—and took him back.

seven

THE LOWLANDS RIVER WAS so cold it stole his breath.

X plummeted to the bottom, and felt the rocks shifting beneath his boots before he could fight his way up. Now that he had returned, his fever was gone, but his powers were, too. Finally, he reached the surface. Ripper bobbed just ahead, the skirt of her dress spread on the water like a parachute. She turned to make sure X was all right. He was 20 years old, and still she watched over him as if his safety meant more than her own.

A rowdy crowd had assembled onshore to greet them. Guards and lords stood shoulder to shoulder, their clothes a riot of mismatched garments from across the centuries. Virtually everyone stole from the weak—Regent was the only exception that X knew of—and you could always identify the lords because they wore the grandest clothes. Of course, they had wide gold bands around their necks, too. No one claimed to have actually seen the Higher Power that ruled over even them, but it observed the lords from some remote place, and controlled them when necessary. The lords' gold bands were not just symbols of power, but hands around their throats.

X scanned the banks for Regent, as he worked to stay afloat. The lord looked stern and regal in his royal blue robes. His chin was high, his dark, muscular arms strained against his sleeves. X looked for some sign that Regent remembered the promise he'd made to introduce him to the mysterious person who knew where his mother was being held. But Dervish stood too close to Regent for any understanding to pass between them.

No matter how often X saw Dervish, the lord was always more vile than he remembered. He had splotchy gray skin, tiny yellow teeth, and white whiskers that sprouted randomly on his chin like weeds in a field.

Ripper swam for shore, and tried to clamber out of the water. X followed. He knew that Ripper would be dealt with harshly, and wanted to help her if he could. Ripper had made a spectacle of herself in the Overworld. Even the fact that she'd acquired a new dress would be considered insolence—which, in truth, it was.

A flat-nosed Cockney guard kicked Ripper back into the water. X held her above the current until she recovered. They floated in the river, gripping each other's arms, like they were dancing. Ripper looked small in the water. Her hair was in clumps, her shoulders curved against the cold.

"I fear for you," X told her.

"Try not to," she said. "There's only one thing these animals could do that would break my heart."

X waited for Ripper to name it. Instead, she gave him a

searching look, as if she were trying to memorize him the way he had tried to memorize Zoe.

Suddenly, X had an intense, bodily memory of being ten years old. He remembered Regent bringing him to Ripper's cell for his first bounty-hunting lesson. He remembered reaching out to Ripper, and waiting to see if she would take his hand. Eventually she did. She even gave his palm a squeeze. How reassuring that tiny bit of contact had been! Ripper had sunk to her knees so X wouldn't be frightened. She'd peered into his eyes just as she was peering into them now. He didn't know then that she was grieving over the loss of her children, but he remembered how kind she was. He even remembered the first words she directed to him: "I am in need of a stupendous friend. Are *you* in need of a friend—and are you stupendous?"

Dervish's jagged voice cut into X's memory.

"Take a last look at each other," he called from the riverbank. "Your conspiracies are ended."

Dervish shoved the Cockney into the water, and the guard pulled Ripper downriver. X saw no panic in her eyes, just resignation and grief. Being separated from him forever: *this* was the thing she had feared. The last thing Ripper shouted to him was, "Remember what you are worth, stupendous friend!"

Devastated and cold, and exhausted from treading water, X clutched a rock embedded in the riverbank. He looked to Regent again, but saw no sign that the lord remembered their conversation. Dervish drew even closer to Regent, not trusting either of them.

When X started climbing out of the river, Regent shook his head no. He called to the Russian guard, who stood nearby wearing a cherry-red tracksuit and sunglasses, and wielding a metal base-ball bat.

"Take him to the hill," he said. "You know the place. Take him nowhere else, no matter how he begs."

The Russian sighed, wanting no part in X's punishment. Still, he slid his sunglasses into a pocket, and dove into the water.

X was stunned.

"Have you *forgotten*, Regent?" he said. "Can it be?"

Dervish crouched, his eyes narrowing.

"Has he forgotten WHAT, exactly?" he said. "Enlighten me."

Before X could answer, Regent lowered himself as well, his blue robe falling around him.

"I have done all I can for you," he said. He met X's eyes. "I have *given* you all I can."

The Russian grabbed X by the collar of his coat, and muttered something in his native tongue. *Spokushki*, it sounded like.

He brought the bat down on X's head, and the river took them away.

JUST WHEN X COULDN'T bear the frigid water another minute, the Russian led him out of the river and into a confusing warren of tunnels. They dripped as they walked, leaving a trail of squiggles and dots. The Russian had had a limp as long as X had known him. He dragged his left foot—the edge of his sneaker had been ground down to almost nothing—but never seemed to tire. X was nauseated from the blow to his head. He struggled to keep up.

"There was no need to strike me," he said. "I did not resist."

"Was anger, if you want true fact," said the Russian. "Because of you, I lose my Reeper! You *know* how I luff my Reeper. Now my heart is leaking sack, like bag of take-out food."

"I'm sorry," said X. "Truly."

The Russian, who was two strides ahead, looked back at X to gauge whether he was sincere.

"I am accepting apology," he said. "Again we are friends."

X finally caught up to him. The tunnel was just wide enough for them to walk abreast.

"Regent spoke of 'the hill,'" he said. "I do not know it."

"Is new home for you," said the guard. "Is fairyland palace full with pillows and clouds."

"What if I asked you to release me right here and now so that I could search out my mother?" said X. "That is what Regent promised me—and you have just declared us friends."

"We are friends," said the Russian. "But we are not *best* friends."

They came to a dank cavern. Like most of the Lowlands, it was hacked crudely out of black rock. Torches sat high on the walls, their flames sputtering but never going out. At the far end of the chamber, there was an immense, medieval-looking door crisscrossed with iron.

The Russian gave X bread from a pack on his belt. It was soaked from the river, and heavy as a sponge. X ate some so as not to appear ungrateful. Eating always reminded him that he wasn't like anyone else in the Lowlands—that, as Zoe had said, he was needy and vulnerable. That he was alive.

"Are you known by any name besides 'the Russian'?" said X. "I should have inquired years ago."

"Thank you asking," said the guard. "True fact is am not Russian, okay? Am from *Oo-kra-EEN*." Seeing X's blank look, the guard added, "*Ukraine*. Yes? Okay? I try to explain this to Reeper but, of course, she is always pretending to be lunatic-type. When I tell her, she sing something about canary."

"And how did your foot come to be twisted?" said X.

"Is nothing, is defect of birth," said the Russian. "I overcome. I achieve master's degree at University of Kiev, and also lucrative life of crimes."

The guard's eyes went to the door. He listened for footsteps.

"Whom do we await?" said X.

The Russian hesitated.

"Terrible creature," he said. "I lie little bit about fairyland palace, okay? This place you go is not good. I think you don't like."

"Tell me what you know," said X. "Hold nothing back. The hill can be no worse than the hole where I've dwelt these past twenty years."

"Oh, very much it can," said the guard. "You have seen just tiny, country-club part of Lowlands in your little life, okay? We are now in kind of Wild West. Is full with most serious, prodigious criminals. Genocidal maniacs and so forth. There are no cells—just bodies everywhere like worms. There is only one lord, but she is nastiest type of person. She punishes souls however she pleases, and no one says, 'Hey, what are you doing? You must stop!' She is called 'the Countess.'"

The Russian listened again for noises, afraid of being overheard.

"When I was boy, my babushka tell me I will go to hell if I do *this*, if I do *that*," he said. "She even has painting of hell hanging over expensive stereo system. I look at painting very often as boy because it contains many naked people. This new home you have? Sorry to say, but it is like painting. I will not step foot myself. When Countess comes for you, I run very fast away."

Before X could reply, they heard footsteps beyond the door. The door groaned open, and a wedge of light widened across the floor.

Two men entered. They were almost absurdly muscled—and naked except for a just barely sufficient bit of animal hide at their waists. They had olive skin, curly hair, beards.

Greeks, thought X. *Boxers.*

They were indistinguishable. Their hands were wrapped in leather, which was spotty with blood.

The Russian acknowledged the boxers nervously. They ignored him, and stationed themselves like granite columns on either side of the door. Soon, X heard the rustling of fabric, the clicking of shoes. The Countess was coming. The boxers drew themselves up taller. They were enormous, but appeared frightened now.

The Countess swept into the chamber. She wore a burgundy velvet gown with a high white collar and a skirt that looked like an upended tulip. Her energy transformed the room. It was furious and sour, and seemed to take up physical space.

She inspected X carefully.

The Countess had an explosion of frizzy red hair, streaked here and there with gray; a small, sweaty nose; and protruding eyes that gave her a look of perpetual outrage. Her hands were raked with scratches.

She addressed the Russian, all the while scowling at X and picking at an inflamed pimple at the corner of her mouth.

"Who dost thou dangle before the Countess?"

X had never encountered a person who talked about herself as if she were someone else.

"He is good guy," said the Russian. "I can verify. Will not ruffle you."

"It shall be his undoing if he does," said the Countess. She continued scrutinizing X. "The Countess demands obeisance. Anyone who will not kneel is put to fire and sword. *Some* believe that the Countess is cruel—that her mind is disordered." She addressed the boxers: "Such things are whispered, are they not? Answer on it!"

The men shook their heads no.

"Liars," said the woman. "Cowards." She turned back to X. "These men are called Oedipus and Rex. Do not bother addressing them—they are too dumb to pile stones. The Countess found it necessary to bite one of them *here*"—she pointed to an oval wound on one boxer's side—"to tell them apart."

She jabbed the wound with the same sharp fingernail she'd used on her pimple. The boxer convulsed with pain, his torso twisting like a rope.

The Russian began to edge out of the chamber.

"Thou art too eager to depart," the Countess told him.

She hoisted the guard by his tracksuit as if he were made of straw, and heaved him at the door. Then she recommenced scratching her pimple, as if nothing had happened. She scanned the length of X's body. Her eyes felt like insects on his skin.

She noticed that his right hand was closed.

"What dost thou conceal?" she said.

X hesitated, which caused the Countess's eyes to bulge even farther from their sockets.

"Unclench thy hand," she demanded, "else the Countess shall paint a pretty picture with thy blood."

He opened his fingers, knowing everything was about to change.

On his palm lay a crust of bread.

"Wherefore would a dead man EAT?" said the Countess.

Though X had told his story many times, it still shamed him. He had to push the words out.

"I was born in the Lowlands. I am twenty years old. My name is X."

The Countess nodded, as if this was all ordinary, though she was obviously vibrating with rage. She leaned over the Russian, who was still in a heap on the floor.

"Thou shalt be our guest for eternity, too," she said. "The Countess shall not have her OWN men scurrying around the Lowlands in search of food. Thou mayest leave the hill only when this man is a hair's breadth from starvation. Tarry longer than necessary, and the Countess shall hunt thee down and—instead of bread—feed him thy liver."

The black flies of her eyes settled on X again.

"X, is it?" she said.

"Yes."

She reared back, and smashed his face with her forehead.

The last thing he heard before losing consciousness was, "Thou ART NOT special, and thou hast NO NAME."

eight

X WOKE ON A hill of prickly rock. He remembered the Countess's head rushing at him, and a wet, sickening *crack*. He touched his forehead. It was sticky with blood.

Someone must have carried him here—the Russian or maybe one of the boxers. He sat up woozily.

Bodies lay strewn all around. They coughed and gasped, slithered around the slope, stared without blinking. It was hard to move without touching one of them. Even when X sat still, someone's rubbery hand or lank, dirty hair would suddenly graze him and give him a chill. He was grateful he'd been unconscious as long as he had. Looking around his new home, he suspected that he'd never sleep again.

How could Regent have sent him here? Was he still enraged at X for breaking the Lowlands' laws? Was his promise to help him just a lie tossed out in the interest of getting Ripper back?

X stood for a better view. At the top of the hill, there was a plateau about 20 feet square, on which—unbelievably—the Countess lay on a sumptuous canopied bed, idly scratching her white stockinged feet. It was the most garish display X had ever seen. He assumed it was intended to make the souls on the hill feel even more wretched. At the end of the bed, there was a wooden box, the sides of which were cut with holes. Every so often a mewling sound escaped it. The Countess, it appeared, had a cat.

Oedipus and Rex stood immobile in front of the ridiculous bed, daring anyone to come close. There was an empty stretch of slope, about 50 feet wide, between the plateau and the mass of damned souls. It must have been forbidden ground, because the souls were careful not to cross into it. In fact, they were crammed against the invisible dividing line as if behind a wall of glass. The only other thing on the plateau was a black rectangle of rock about four feet high and eight feet long. It looked like an altar. But there was no religion in the Lowlands save the prayers that the damned whispered too low for the lords to hear. The rock had to have a less holy purpose.

High above him, X saw a rough domed ceiling. Below him, the slope was lit by torches on tall iron stands, which made the hill look like a forest on fire. Dozens of guards were on patrol, kicking prisoners aside as they went. X didn't see his friend in the red tracksuit—he must have been farther down. X would have to strategize without him. Nothing would keep him from finding his mother.

Something stirred at X's feet. He looked down to see a soul reach slowly into another soul's shirt pocket. The thief was a chalk-white figure in rags; the victim, a plump, peaceful-looking Asian man in a khaki shirt and shorts, who appeared to be meditating.

X had decided not to involve himself when he saw the thief slide a photograph out of the Asian man's pocket. It made him think of the things he himself carried: Zoe's letter and the objects in the silver foil. The photograph would mean nothing to the thief, but it might mean everything to the man he stole it from.

X knelt.

"Return the picture," he whispered, "or I will break your hands."

The thief grimaced, sized X up—and put it back.

"Wasn't gonna keep it," he said in a dry voice. "Was only gonna hold it a minute. Is it a crime now to hold something?"

The Asian man's eyes fluttered open. He patted his pocket to make sure the photograph was still there, then looked at X and the thief. He knew instantly what had gone on.

"Have you been at it again, Bone?" he said. X was surprised by how warm his voice was, how forgiving. "There's so much suffering here. Let's not compound it by turning on each other. Let's aspire to be the lotus flower that grows out of the mud. All right? All right."

"Blah blah blah," Bone said bitterly. "Easy for you to act holy. *You've* got a picture."

He crawled down the slope on his stomach, hissing at everyone in his way.

"I'm grateful to you, friend," the Asian man told X. "Not many souls would have troubled themselves to do what you did, and the photograph is dear to me." He checked to see that no guards were watching, then offered his hand to X. "I'm called Plum."

"Plum," X said, liking the sound. "I've never known the Lowlands to bestow so genial a name."

"Neither have I," said Plum. "I've become fond of it. But truth be told, I believe it refers to my belly."

He patted his stomach happily.

Plum had been sitting with his knees folded in front of him. He stretched them out now, and tried to touch his toes. Because of his size, they remained quite out of reach.

"I'm X."

"Well, that's very mysterious," said Plum. "Please don't think too badly of Bone. The Countess treats us as though we're less than human, so some of us *become* less than human. You've met her, I assume?"

"Yes," said X. "She assaulted me with—with her forehead."

"I'm not surprised," said Plum. "That woman can make a weapon out of anything."

"She seemed incensed about a blemish near her mouth," said X.

"Ah, yes, the pimple," said Plum. "It's her mortal enemy. I got here thirty years ago, and she had it even then."

X gestured toward the plateau.

"Does she lie abed all day like that?" he said.

Alarmed, Plum pushed X's hand down.

"Please don't point at her—it's like summoning a dragon," he said. "The Countess likes to be unpredictable, to answer your question. Sometimes she lets us jabber all day, sometimes she punishes us for the slightest sound. Sometimes she naps, sometimes she prowls. The only constant is that sooner or later, she will find a reason to torture somebody. She feeds on our sins. I mean that literally. It's like she's some mythological creature. The worse our crimes, the stronger she grows when she persecutes us. She has a knife. I can't tell you the things I've seen her do with it." Plum shivered. "But let's not talk about her any longer. She seems distracted at the moment. I could show you my photograph, if you'd like?"

"Please do," said X. "I carry a few tokens with me, too. Sometimes they are all that can calm me."

Plum took the picture from his pocket. It appeared to be a picture of himself when he was a younger man.

"Don't be alarmed, I'm not so vain as to carry a picture of myself around," he said. "That's my twin brother, Hai. We grew up near Lào Cai, in north Vietnam." Plum was quiet a moment. "I did a lot of horrific things when I was alive. You wouldn't know it from looking at me now. But in my day I was infamous. Hai suffered terribly as a result, not just because he was my brother but because everywhere he went, they thought he was me. I carry Hai's picture to remind myself of the wreckage I caused—and because I loved him, though I was too crippled inside to say so." Plum closed his eyes. When he opened them again, he gave X a faint, apologetic smile. "I certainly talk a lot, don't I?" he said. "You'll never make the mistake of sitting near *me* again."

X smiled back to ease his mind. Plum sat waiting for him to share his own story. There was something so peaceful about the man. X felt comfortable in his presence, even though they sat in a sea of bodies and breathed air that was foul in a dozen different ways.

"You said you carry some things yourself?" said Plum.

"Yes," said X, grateful for a way to begin his tale.

He extracted Zoe's letter from his coat. It was in the plastic bag now, safe as an ancient artifact. X set it on the tiny bit of ground between himself and Plum.

"My name is X," he said. "It is the only name I have ever had, for I was born in this place."

Plum's eyes went wide.

"And this?" he said, gesturing at the plastic bag.

"It is a letter from the girl I love," said X.

"You don't have to tell me anything else, if it's too painful," said Plum. "Your story is your own. All right? All right."

"Her name is Zoe," said X, "and I am *always* willing to talk about her."

"You met a girl here in the Lowlands?" said Plum. "It's not the most romantic place I can think of."

"I met her in the Overworld," said X. "I am a bounty hunter—or I *was*, until I broke every law they put in front of me."

"I take back what I said," said Plum. "I *must* hear your story."

THE WORDS RUSHED OUT of X like water from a burst pipe.

Plum listened, rapt. Sometimes, he got so excited that he rubbed his hands together. He frowned when X described Dervish, and laughed when he recounted Ripper's wild run from the Lowlands. He blushed when X—surprising even himself—told him about lying with Zoe in the boat, about the glow he'd made in the hull and how it lit up her body.

"I was always a disaster with girls," said Plum. "When I was twelve or thirteen, I used to write them letters. 'Dear So and So: Would you be interested in kissing me on Wednesday afternoon at 3:30 by the ironwood trees? Please circle YES or NO.' One girl—she was called Thien—taped my letter high up on a wall at school, so everybody could see it. She must have stood on a chair. I couldn't reach the thing, though I embarrassed myself by jumping up and down. Then I made the whole thing worse by walking uninvited into Thien's classroom and shouting, 'Excuse me for liking you!'" Plum sighed. "But I'm talking too much again. What else do you carry?"

X took out the silver foil packet, and unfolded it.

"May I?" said Plum.

He picked each thing up and examined it in turn, beginning with the comb and the bracelet reading *Vesuvius*, then placed them back in the foil. He was as gentle with X's things as X himself would have been.

"A lord named Regent gave me these when I was a boy," said X.

He was interrupted by a commotion farther up the slope. X and Plum turned toward the noise, and saw an elderly man wandering through the thicket of bodies. The man was stumbling, and wiping his glasses on his shirt. He had sparse, bluish-white hair that stood up in tufts like seagrass. He was perilously close to the forbidden area.

Oedipus and Rex descended, waiting to see if he'd be foolish enough to cross over. The crowd cheered the man on, though he seemed addled, disoriented. They were eager to see the boxers beat him. Even the Countess sat up in bed, ready to be entertained. The cat cried unhappily in its box.

"Oh, the poor man," said Plum.

The old soul fumbled his glasses. They fell to the ground. He bent down to search for them, a hand on his lower back which seemed to pain him, but he was too late: three ghastly looking souls were already fighting over them like children.

"Please stop this, all of you!" said the man. "My glasses are fragile and already terribly scratched!"

A woman won the struggle for the spectacles. The man held his hand out to her, but she just laughed, and threw them over his head to Oedipus.

The elderly man hung his head, his neck elongating like a turtle's, and began to cry. He pleaded with Oedipus for his glasses. His eyesight must have been terrible because he wasn't even facing the boxer as he spoke to him, not quite. It seemed to X that neither Oedipus nor Rex wanted to hurt him. But when Oedipus went to return the spectacles, the Countess bellowed from up above, "Let him fight thee for them, if they be so precious!"

The old man smoothed his few tendrils of hair. X could hear his sobs even a hundred feet away. The crowd cheered louder, and pushed him up the hill. He collapsed to his knees in the forbidden borderland, just a few steps from Oedipus.

"I can't watch this," said Plum. "I won't."

But X couldn't look away.

Oedipus pummeled the old man as if it were a regrettable chore. He left him facedown on the slope.

And then the Countess rose from her bed.

She didn't even put her shoes on—she just padded down from the plateau in her stockings.

The Countess took her knife from her belt, and sliced open the back of the elderly man's thighs, severing his hamstrings. The man reared up as if he'd been electrocuted. X knew he would never walk again. When Oedipus tried to hand him his glasses, the old man couldn't even open his hand to take them.

Mercifully, a woman in a long, black, servant's dress and a bloodied apron emerged from the crowd to help. She gave instructions to the souls nearby. Two of them lifted the man's body and pulled him back into the crowd, as if into a dark lake.

X was appalled by what he'd seen. Dizzied. The hopelessness of his own situation came flooding back to him.

He felt Plum's hand on his shoulder.

"I'm sorry you had to see that," said Plum. "But you'll see much worse before long. The Countess didn't even put him on the altar. She couldn't have been very hungry for sins."

X barely heard what Plum said.

"Can I trust you?" he said. "Tell me true, for everything depends upon it."

"You can," said Plum. "I promise you can."

"I *must* get out of this place," said X. "I vowed to myself and to Zoe that I would save my mother, and that my mother would save me. Laugh at me if you must."

"I certainly will not," said Plum.

"Regent promised to help me," said X. "I had no reason to doubt him, yet he sent me to this ungodly hill instead."

"What exactly did he say?" said Plum.

"He said he had done everything he could for me," said X. "He looked at me as if I would understand, yet how could I?"

"He didn't say anything else?" said Plum.

"He said he'd *given* me everything he could," said X.

Plum weighed this for a moment, then looked down at the objects in the silver foil, as if they held secrets.

"Is it possible that he meant all this?"

nine

PLUM WAS RIGHT—HE had to be.

X fanned his collection out in what space he had, and stared at everything with a new intensity.

A silver comb.

A red-green button made out of bloodstone.

The tip of a rusted drill.

A shard of white porcelain.

A broken bracelet.

X remembered Regent demanding that the guards recover everything from the river when Dervish dropped them in. Regent had treated these things like they were irreplaceable. X understood why now: these weren't random things from the Overworld, as Regent had claimed. They were clues somehow. They would lead him to the mysterious person who knew where his mother was being held.

Regent had sent X to the Countess's hill to fulfill his promise. Yes, X had flouted the laws of the Lowlands and shamed Regent. But through it all, and despite it all, the lord had never actually abandoned him.

X now *knew* that to be true.

He picked up the bracelet engraved with the word "Vesuvius."

He asked Plum if he knew of anyone on the hill by the name.

"The only Vesuvius I know of is the volcano," said Plum.

"I'm ashamed to say I don't know it," said X.

"No need to apologize," said Plum. "Vesuvius was the volcano that destroyed Pompeii. I don't remember if it was BC or AD, to be honest. And no, I don't know anyone here with that name. But there are thousands of souls on this hill. He could very well be here."

The idea of asking every soul on the hill if they were Vesuvius— or if they recognized the things in the silver packet—overwhelmed X. It was almost certainly impossible, especially with guards on the move and the Countess on the lookout for victims. But what else could he do?

Just holding the bracelet and button and the other items made X feel closer to his mother than he ever had. They had been in his possession many years, but he'd never known that they told a story.

X knew that his mother had been a lord. He knew that Regent had been a friend to her and that Dervish had detested her, just as he detested everyone who was not a dried husk like himself. His mother must have been bold—full of life in a place full of death.

There was one more thing X knew about her: she'd fallen in love and given birth to him. Here in the Lowlands! She had broken every law to do it. She'd lost her standing as a lord in the process, tossed it willingly away. This, more than anything else, made X feel that he knew her and that her blood coursed in him. Hadn't he done much the same as his mother when he endangered everything to be with Zoe? And wouldn't he do it again?

Plum interrupted X's thoughts.

"Guard," he said.

X closed up the foil, slipped it into the lining of his coat, and looked down the slope to see who was coming.

But it was only his friend with the baseball bat.

The guard looked miserable. He'd unzipped the top of his tracksuit because of the heat, and was dragging his foot nearly sideways behind him. His sunglasses must have made it hard to see because he kept tripping over bodies.

"Is wretched place, as in advertisements," said the guard when he reached them. "Vehement crazy. Who is large man?"

"This is Plum," said X. "He's a friend. Plum, this is the guard who conveyed me here—at great cost to himself. Don't be misled by his forbidding spectacles, he is a friend as well. I call him . . . the Ukrainian."

The guard spoke gruffly to hide how much he liked his new name.

"Everybody think sunglasses are extreme joke, yes?" he said. "But they are prescription, okay? For the *distance.*"

"Hello," said Plum. "Here's a question one doesn't ask very often: Would you please hit us with your bat—just so the Countess doesn't get suspicious?"

"Of course," said the Ukrainian. "This is tremendous point."

"I'll take the first blow myself—in the stomach, preferably," said Plum. "As you can see, I have some extra padding there."

The Ukrainian jabbed Plum in the gut. He pulled the bat back at the last second so as to inflict minimal pain. Still, Plum put on a show, tumbling backward and gasping for air, as though he had been hit by a cannonball. When he righted himself, he looked pleased with his performance and was suppressing a smile.

The guard offered X food from his pouch. X couldn't identify what it was. Something coarse and dry. It didn't matter. He was too excited about his new revelation to eat. He told the Ukrainian that the bracelet and the other objects were clues of some kind.

"Ah, the plot fattens!" said the guard. "I remember freezing my *yaytsa* off when Regent make us dive for these things. Glad to know I donate *yaytsa* to honorable cause."

Over the next few minutes, as the Ukrainian jabbed them, X declared his intention to scour the hill for the person Regent had sent him to find. He'd ask every soul he could if they knew anyone named Vesuvius or recognized the objects in his collection. In the surprised silence that followed his announcement, X acknowledged that the plan sounded ridiculous but said that unless they could conceive of a better one, he would see it through.

"I agree," said the Ukrainian at last.

"Truly?" said X.

"I agree as to sounding ridiculous," said the Ukrainian. "In fact, is loopty-loop crazy. Thousands men and women sprinkled on hill like sugar almost, and you will find *one*? Is ludicrous. Also, you will be beaten hundred times in process."

"I understand that I may fail," said X. "I understand that I may be made to suffer. But I have set a course, and I mean to follow it."

The Ukrainian shook his head wearily.

"X," he said. "You, to me, are like younger, less attractive brother. But I cannot endorse plan, and cannot assist."

"I understand," said X.

"Would be madness for me, okay?" said the guard. "Was prisoner once, before promotion. Will not be made prisoner again. Already I lose Reeper, yes? Already I lose home in country-club part of Lowlands. Am now in *leeteral* hellhole. I am sorry, but I can risk no more."

"You have nothing to apologize for," said X. "You're a good man."

The guard removed his sunglasses.

"Of course I good man," he said. "Am from *Oo-kra-EEN*. How many times am I saying this?"

X turned to Plum.

"Do you agree that I have lost my senses?" he said.

"Yes," said Plum. "Everything the Ukrainian has said is perfectly sound. But I will help you anyway—if you think a big, soft pillow like me can be of any use, I mean. Give me half of your things, and half the hill to search."

X was shocked by Plum's offer. He thanked him in a fumbling way. The Ukrainian was angry. He hit Plum with the bat.

"You have death wish or some such, Plum person?" he said. "Let me remind: you are already dead."

"Look, I know this will not end well," said Plum. "I don't see how it can. But it's a chance for me to do something good, to atone a tiny little bit—to be the lotus flower."

"Countess is psychopath," said the Ukrainian. "Do you not fear her knife?"

"I fear it more than you can imagine," said Plum.

He unbuttoned his khaki shirt slowly. There was a lurid purple scar running from his sternum to his belly button, like a zipper.

* * *

THEY AGREED TO SLEEP before starting out, but X found it impossible. His nerves were humming, and he hadn't gotten used to the noise on the hill—the awful orchestra of coughs and grunts and sobs. Plum lay close to him. X could tell from his breathing that he couldn't sleep either. Eventually, they sat up, and divided the objects in the foil between them. X had treasured these things for so long. He felt as if he were handing over pieces of his body.

Plum took responsibility for the top half of the hill because he knew souls there already. X hiked farther down. It was slow going because the hill was steep, and often clotted with bodies. They were from every country and every century, but they were all in the same torment. He thought of the painting of hell that the Ukrainian's babushka had hung on her wall. He could imagine it perfectly.

The first person X approached lay on the ground wrapped nearly head to toe in bandages like a mummy.

"I search for someone," he said, kneeling. "Someone who can help me find my mother."

He held the bracelet and the comb where the bandaged man could see them. At first, the man appeared unable to produce any words at all. X leaned close. Finally the mummy managed to whisper a few phrases, which were among the most vile things X had ever heard.

X pushed disappointment away. He thought about Zoe—about how it never occurred to her to give up on anything, ever.

The next soul he spoke to was not much older than himself. He wore a shabby uniform from the American Civil War. A woman in a bloodstained bridal gown lay next to him, either asleep or in a coma. X winced at the blood.

"Don't let her rattle yeh," said the soldier. "The Bride's not near as scary as she looks—though she did kill her husband after sixteen minutes of matrimony."

"Sixteen *minutes*?" said X.

"Marriage ain't for everybody," said the soldier. "What name yeh go by? I seen yeh. You're the feller that eats."

He spoke too loudly for X's comfort.

X told him his name.

"Please mind your voice," he added. "I cannot afford to be found out."

"Yes, sir, Captain, sir," the soldier said. He grinned as if X were worried about nothing, and did not lower his voice. "I go by Shiloh here," he said.

"I am looking for someone who answers to the name Vesuvius—or can help me in any way at all," he said. "Do you recognize these things? I beg you once more to lower your voice."

"If there's a Vesuvius in these parts, I ain't yet met him," said Shiloh, speaking so softly that he seemed to be teasing X. He indicated a few people close by. "That woman there is Dagger. And that's Stalker. That over there is a feller we call Birk, short for Birkenau. None of them ever mentioned no Vesuvius in my hearing. Whether it's worth showing them what-all yeh got there, I leave to yeh to judge."

When X stood to leave, Shiloh looked bereft.

"Aw, stay a spell why doncha?" he said. "The Bride and me don't never get company."

But X was consumed with his mission.

He questioned four more people. The first two sat side by side on a ledge of rock. One was a pink-skinned, middle-aged American, the other slightly darker and perhaps 19. They did not speak, but seemed attuned to each other's every movement. X wondered if they'd developed a code—three quick taps of the foot meant *this*, a scratch at the neck meant *that*. They stiffened when X asked their names, then argued silently about whether to answer. The American clenched his fist. The younger man, disagreeing, opened his palm.

When they finally spoke, it turned out that neither of them knew a Vesuvius, nor recognized the objects. They told X they'd met each other here because, by a quirk of fate, they'd both been given the name Bomber. They wanted to tell X their stories, but he moved on.

This part of the slope was dense with bodies. So many of them were unconscious or incoherent that it took X a long time to find another soul he could question satisfactorily. Hands, arms, feet, and legs were everywhere. They were like a net trying to entrap him. The image of his mother, the *possibility* of her, receded further and further. The image of Zoe, too. X forced himself to continue, scolding himself for his weakness. Who had told him this would be easy?

The next soul X questioned offered to trade two socks (one black, one red) for the silver comb. X ignored the offer. He asked the man if he knew of a Vesuvius. X's hands were sweating now, and the foil was turning his palms silver.

"Vesuvius? Yeah, sure, of course," said the man. He pointed to a figure a hundred feet down the hill. "That's him there."

X stumbled over bodies to get to the soul in question, only to find that he'd been lied to for sport.

He stormed back up the hill. The Liar broke into such an infuriating, self-satisfied grin that X struck him in the mouth. He had no special powers here, but he could still beat a man to the ground.

A guard heard the disturbance. X froze. The guard spit on the ground, and decided he didn't care.

Ashamed of what he'd done, X hiked back toward Plum to see if he'd had better luck.

He stopped only once more to question someone. The man he chose wore the remnants of a suit of armor, and stood at the base of one of the immense torch stands, as if he were guarding it. The knight was young, 25 perhaps, and his hair fell even farther than X's, spilling down his shoulders and over his breastplate. His helmet appeared to have been stolen, along with one of his gauntlets and both boots.

X asked the Knight his questions: Do you recognize these things? Are you Vesuvius, or do you know anyone who answers to that name?

The Knight brightened. He declared that he was indeed Vesuvius, the very same! He beat a fist against his chest, causing his armor to clank, and swore he would cut down any man who disputed it. He reached for his sword, and frowned when he remembered that it too had been taken.

X saw the desperation beneath the Knight's bravado, the loneliness. He suspected that for a few moments of company, the man would have claimed just as earnestly to be Cleopatra.

PLUM AND THE UKRAINIAN were waiting. The guard seemed even more agitated than before. He fidgeted with his sunglasses, and drummed his metal bat against his thigh. Plum was quiet. He had his arms around his knees, like he was trying to make himself small. Maybe he'd had enough of the search already, and felt too guilty to say so. He wouldn't quite look at X.

"You were kind to help me, Plum," said X. "But I release you from any obligation. I will continue on alone."

"Oh, you can't get rid of me that easily," said Plum. "We'll rest a bit, and then we'll set out again. All right? All right. Your cause is my cause."

The Ukrainian groaned.

"Is very poetical, Plum person," he said. "Now show him face."

"What does he mean?" said X. "What are you hiding?"

Plum turned to X so slowly that it was like a planet rotating. His other cheek was violent with bruises: purple, yellow, black.

"The guards beat you," X said. "Because of me."

"It's nothing," Plum said. "They have beaten me before. I pity them for what it does to their consciences."

"You think they still have consciences?" said the Ukrainian. He squatted, and whispered fiercely. "That is extremity of nonsense. As I hike on hill just now, I see other guards watching me, okay? Every move. They are suspicious, okay? They think I am not one of them. So how do I prove? I strike total innocent person with club. Then maybe one, maybe two more, why not. I hit them hard, not like I playtime with you. Always guards clap as result—they give me stupid salutes or thumbs-up, maybe. And always innocent people look up at me. *Why you strike me? What I done wrong?* Never did I do this previous, okay? Not even Dervish ask. Already, my heart hardens until there is something, I don't know what, rock or pinecone maybe, in my chest."

The guard seemed embarrassed by his tirade, but he continued.

"Plum person," he said, "you are gentle man. Good at bottom. And these guards? This Countess? They will destroy you. Little by little, or very fast, they will turn you into one of drooling people curled everywhere in balls."

"He speaks wisely, and you know it," X told Plum. "Let us agree you will not risk yourself for me again."

"No," said Plum.

"No?" said X.

"I will not agree," said Plum. "I'm not going to desert you. Let the guards be war—I will be peace." He chose his next words carefully. "Try to remember that I'm not just doing this for you. I'm doing it to redeem myself. I may seem like an innocent because I ramble about lotus flowers. But whatever goodness you see in me is just a reflection of your own, I promise you. If you knew what sort of poisonous creature I was before, up there in the world, if you knew what I did, you'd turn away in horror."

"I would not turn from you," said X.

"And I will not turn from you now," said Plum. He smiled almost beatifically. "All this fuss about my face. It was never very handsome to begin with."

The Ukrainian's anger had been percolating.

"Sorry to say, must interrupt touching TV movie," he said.

He tugged his sunglasses down over his eyes. It was like a wall coming down.

"You are idiot, X," he said. "You will not find magical person you seek. Would be impossible even for superheroes such as Rocket Red Brigade." The Ukrainian searched his pockets as he continued. "You are lucky Countess did not see your sneaking. And you, Plum, moaning about your sins—boo-hoo! We all carry guilt like bag of stones, okay? You think I am damned for stealing Pepsi from vending machine?" The Ukrainian seemed to arrive at a decision. "I hear no more plans, okay? Am out of little group. Will not watch you become drooling kind."

The guard found a piece of meat in the pack on his belt.

"What is hunger situation?" he asked X.

X looked at the dry, gray thing in the guard's hands. It was the shape of a tongue.

"I am not hungry," he said, "nor likely to be soon."

"Yes, well, take for midnight snack," the Ukrainian said, thrusting it at him. "Is last piece. I must replenish."

X slid the awful thing into a pocket.

Later, X lay on his back, his coat bunched beneath his head. Something about the conversation with the Ukrainian nagged at him. The guard knew how rarely X needed to eat—and that he'd only just fed him. Why would he ask if X was hungry?

The answer came to him.

The Ukrainian was the only one X knew on this hill with any authority at all—the only one who could roam freely and, once X learned everything he could about his mother, aid him in his escape. But now the guard needed to gather more food for him. He would have to leave the hill to do it. And X knew what his friend in the cherry-red tracksuit would do then.

It was the same thing anyone would do.

He would never come back.

ten

X DECIDED NOT TO beg the Ukrainian to stay. There was no reason the guard should be chained to him. He should flee if he could. Maybe he could find a safe haven before the Countess discovered he had gone.

X turned onto his side, so that he faced the top of the hill. Yet again he couldn't sleep.

The canopied bed sat empty. The plateau was deserted.

X sat up on his elbows, and peered down the slope. The Countess was descending—looking for victims, no doubt. Her coppery hair fell down her neck, frizzy and wild. Oedipus and Rex marched a few steps ahead, hurling bodies out of the way.

X checked to see if Plum was awake. He was. So, it seemed, was every soul on the hill. They were waiting to see who the Countess would subject to her knife.

"Close your eyes," said Plum, "and don't open them, no matter what you hear."

"Why?" said X.

"Because if you watch the violence you will never forget it," said Plum. "The Countess looks for the most depraved sinners she can find because torturing them exhilarates her the most. She hunts for them like she is looking for ripe berries."

X shut his eyes, but it only made his hearing keener.

There were noises from down below—it sounded like the boxers were descending on someone. There was kicking. Struggling. The noise grew as Oedipus and Rex shoved the soul up the hill.

New sounds, darker sounds: the soul collapsing, crying, getting dragged to his feet and thrust forward. Or was it a woman? The cries were so wild that X couldn't tell.

Plum tightened his grip on X's shoulder, imploring him not to look. But X had to watch, had to see.

He opened his eyes.

The Countess had chosen not just one victim but two: the Civil War soldier called Shiloh, and the woman in the wedding gown.

Aw, stay a spell why doncha? The Bride and me don't never get company.

Oedipus and Rex lifted them onto the giant rectangular rock at the top of the hill. So that was what the altar was for.

Sacrifices.

"The soldier," said X. "I questioned that very man."

"It's a coincidence," said Plum, his eyes still pressed closed.

But he didn't seem to believe it.

There was another flurry of sound. Guards had rounded up five more victims. X stood to see.

He knew them all.

The foul-mouthed mummy: They had to carry him up the hill.

The Bombers: They were gesturing frantically in code. The American man was already in tears.

The lonely Knight: He seemed grateful for the guards' attention. Didn't he know what was coming?

Finally, the Liar, the one X had struck: Why was *he* to be punished? He hadn't helped X at all. And it was the Ukrainian who pushed him forward. Even from a distance, X could see how disgusted his friend was to be a part of this.

"They've gathered all of them—every soul I spoke to," X told Plum. "What will the Countess do to them?"

Plum was too upset to even shrug.

"I apologize for cursing," he said, "but any goddamn thing she wants."

SHILOH AND THE BRIDE squirmed on the altar. The Countess sat on her bed, languidly putting up her hair. She was prolonging their misery. When she'd finished, she ordered Rex to tighten the laces on her shoes. She seemed to relish having a giant kneel before her. She laughed as he fumbled with the laces. For Shiloh and the Bride—and everyone watching—the delay was excruciating. The servant with the bloody apron stood at the edge of the crowd, waiting to minister to the wounded. She looked fearful. Her eyes were cast down.

At last, the Countess strode to the altar, and plunged her palm down onto Shiloh's heart.

Every torch on the hill went out. The ceiling exploded with light. It became a screen.

The Bride scrambled to get off the altar. Oedipus and Rex forced her back down. Nearby, the Ukrainian and the other guards tightened in a ring around the next victims.

Shiloh's sins began to play, loud and bright, in a movie on the ceiling. The Countess arched her back with pleasure.

"His pain feeds her," said Plum. "His sins. His humiliation. She gorges on it all. If you really have to watch, then watch how she glows as she sucks the evil into herself. I swear it makes her younger."

Every soul on the hill craned their head back to see Shiloh's sins. It was like they were gazing at stars. Light and shadow mottled their faces. Shiloh thrashed helplessly, refusing to look. The Countess spread his eyes open with her fingers.

X looked to the ceiling, too. He couldn't stop himself.

He saw Shiloh and his regiment on a plain in winter. They'd attacked a Cherokee settlement. There was snow on the ground. The trees were shaking. Shiloh forced a native father and his daughter into a wooden roundhouse. He shouted slurs at them, and prodded them with his musket. Once they were inside, he set the house alight. Flames raced onto the roof.

X should have looked away, like Plum had begged him to.

The father and daughter burst from the roundhouse to escape the fire. Shiloh laughed. He raised his musket and shot the father in the face. The girl screamed. She was maybe six or seven. Shiloh lifted his rifle again, and fired. A red stain bloomed on the girl's chest. A trail of blood ran down her dress like a tear.

Finally, the ceiling went black.

The torches whooshed back to life.

Shiloh and the Bride whimpered on the slab.

The Countess took her knife off her belt. It had a thin, curling blade about five inches long. It looked like something used to peel away an animal's hide.

All around X and Plum, souls cheered the Countess on. They were greedy to watch someone besides themselves suffer. Some got to their feet. Others shook the giant stalks that held the torches. When the Countess shined the knife on the sleeve of her dress, the cheering intensified, like a rainstorm moving in. Oedipus and Rex looked away. They seemed to have lost their taste for this.

X stood, and drew closer. Shiloh was only being punished because he had talked to *him*.

Plum heard him leaving, and urged him to come back.

X didn't listen.

The Countess raised the knife. The hill fell silent. X could hear the torches crackle. The Countess cut through the laces of Shiloh's boots, pulled them off, and flung them aside. A hunched soul in rags had been watching from the fringes of the crowd. He dashed forward and snatched up the boots. X recognized him. It was Bone, who'd tried to steal Plum's photograph.

X was close enough now to see that Shiloh wore no socks, and that his feet were horrifically swollen. The boots hadn't been off in years.

The Countess poked one of Shiloh's toes with the tip of her knife, testing the flesh. Shiloh wailed, and pleaded for her to stop. His foot shook uncontrollably.

The Countess hissed at Oedipus and Rex: "Hold him fast, else this knife shall play upon THY skin next!"

Again, the torches went out and the ceiling came to life. Again, the souls gazed upward. Everything that happened on the altar played out up there, hundreds of feet tall and wide. Shiloh's pleading was amplified so much that there was no shutting it out. The Bride writhed beside him. The men waiting to be tortured all wept, even the Knight. The servant woman with the bloody apron never lifted her eyes. Her lips moved soundlessly, apparently in prayer.

The Countess pressed the blade into the sole of Shiloh's foot, where the skin was most raw. She was about to cut him open when she paused—and looked directly at X.

She was taunting him.

She was saying, *This is your doing. This is because of you.*

The Countess pressed the blade into the ball of Shiloh's foot. She did it just hard enough to produce a single bead of blood.

And then she ripped the knife down.

Shiloh's limbs shot out in every direction, and his back flew up off the altar. He must have been in too much agony to scream. Even if he *had* screamed, he would have been drowned out by the crowd.

X did not often miss his powers—they were too tangled in his mind with the wretched business of taking souls to the Lowlands—but he craved them now. He hated his weakness. He loathed his damaged, human, near-useless body. Still, he would have to make do with it.

He stepped forward.

He shouted at the Countess.

"It is *me* you want."

The cheering stopped. Everyone turned their eyes to him. He could feel it like heat on his neck.

"Is it indeed?" the Countess said mildly.

She slipped the knife into Shiloh's wound, and peeled back the skin, revealing a bed of blood. Shiloh gave a cry that did not sound human. The Bride was sick over the side of the altar.

"You know very well that it is," X shouted.

His voice boomed all around. He looked to the ceiling, and saw that now it was he, not Shiloh, projected there.

"Regent forced me on you," he said, "without explaining who I am or even what I am—and all you could do was whimper because he is so much bolder and grander than you."

He was desperate to rile the Countess, but her heart seemed to beat slow as a crocodile's. She held a piece of Shiloh's skin in her fingers. She slid it into her mouth.

X felt his stomach rise.

"I see you are fascinated by other people's sins," he said. "I *dare* you to have a look at mine. They were too much for Regent. If you want to know why he drove me out—there is your answer."

The Countess's knife paused in the air, twitching like it longed to go back to work.

"The Countess ACCEPTS thy challenge," she said. "She shall force such cries from your throat as shall be remembered forever!"

Excitement spread over the hill. The woman in the apron helped Shiloh and the Bride down from the altar. Shiloh's face ran with tears. He looked at X, and seemed to ask: *Why would you do this for me?* He appeared stunned, ashamed.

X turned to look for Plum. He couldn't pick him out in the low light on the hill. He knew his friend would fear for him.

The Ukrainian, meanwhile, slipped away, no doubt furious at X's recklessness. The Countess would think the guard had gone for food, but X knew he would never see him again. He watched as the Ukrainian dropped his club and left it behind. It lay like a splinter on the ground.

Oedipus hoisted X onto the altar, and pushed him flat. The rock felt weirdly alive, as if it still held the heat from Shiloh's struggle. Its surface was stained every shade of red and brown. It looked exactly like what it was: a butcher's block.

"You need not hold me down," X told Oedipus. "I come willingly."

The Countess waved the boxer away. She sat on her bed with her eyes closed, as if clearing her mind. X knew that what she was really doing was giving him time to be afraid.

The truth was, he was terrified already.

X HAD DARED THE Countess to look at his sins because he believed he had none—that, unlike in everyone else she might turn her knife on, she'd find nothing to torture him for or gorge herself on. But now, as X lay on his back, a fear he had carried for years surfaced unbidden: What if the souls he had taken to the Lowlands were held against him? What if the 15 missions he'd undertaken were not just missions, but murders?

He remembered Zoe warning him once that the lords were just trying to turn him into a monster—into one of *them*.

What if they already had?

The Countess strutted toward him, her knife in one hand. With the other, she clicked open and closed the silver button on a leather sheath at her waist. For X, the clicking was somehow more menacing than anything else.

"Art thou afeard?" said the Countess.

Click, went the button. *Click. Click.*

"Of pain?" said X. "No. I have known pain before."

"Of what, then?" said the Countess.

Click. Click.

Click.

X wouldn't answer.

"So there is SOMETHING," said the Countess, digging at her pimple. "You perceive now that you are no hero. Thou hast deceived thyself at great cost."

Again, X held his tongue. One thought looped in his brain: *The ceiling will know if I am a sinner.* He couldn't wait another instant. He needed to see what was inside himself.

Click.

"Perhaps you wonder where the Countess shall guide the knife," said the Countess. "Yet the knife picks its own path."

"Why must you stoop to such depravity?" said X. "Is damnation not punishment enough for us?"

The lord seemed intrigued by the question. She stopped fiddling with the sheath.

"This 'depravity' is the only thing that brings the Countess peace," she said. "It was ever thus."

"So you're not cutting something out of us—but out of yourself?" said X.

The Countess bristled, and for just an instant spoke of herself as a more ordinary person might.

"It is a pretty theory, yours," she said. "Yet in a moment I shall slice thee apart, and we will shall see which of us screams."

She thrust her palm onto X's chest. He hadn't expected pain, not yet. But she pressed so violently that he couldn't breathe. He bucked on the altar, as Shiloh had. His vision blurred. It wasn't like when Regent put the names and stories of souls into X's body so he could hunt them down. He was not being given something. Something was being forcibly taken. The Countess was trying to pull whatever sins he had out of his heart.

This feeling, this pain—did it mean that he *did* have sins and that they were grievous? Above him, on the ceiling, something was stirring. Something was about to unfold.

X wasn't ready to look. He closed his eyes and summoned Zoe's face for comfort. He summoned Jonah. Then Ripper, Banger, the Ukrainian. Even Plum. They flitted by, one after the other. Everyone he cared about. He tried to stop the faces from flitting by so quickly, but couldn't. He tried to call Zoe to him again. Hers was the only face he wanted.

The cat cried in its box on the bed, making a desperate, strangled sound. Distracted, the Countess lifted her hand from X's chest.

"If that damnable feline erupts again, the Countess shall stop its breath," she said. "Would that the creature had been named for something mute, like a statue or the wind."

A voice X had never heard before spoke. A woman.

"Let me comfort him," she said. "He doesn't belong in a box."

It must have been the servant in the bloody apron.

"Still thy tongue, if thou means to keep it," the Countess told her.

The lord returned her focus to X, and slammed her palm back onto his chest. The pain obliterated everything else. X could feel her fingers burrowing into his ribs.

He tried to fill his lungs with air. He was frantic. His head, his body, his veins . . . Everything was poised to burst.

He screamed.

But no, he couldn't have. He didn't have enough air. The scream couldn't get out. It howled inside him.

He saw, or maybe *felt*—he couldn't tell the difference anymore— a shower of light, an exploding star.

eleven

"SLOWLY, FRIEND. COME BACK to us slowly."

It was Plum, coaxing him back to consciousness.

X felt himself slip back into his skin, like it was a suit laid out for him. His arms became his again, then his legs and feet.

Then he noticed the pain. It'd been there all along, waiting for him to wake. His body felt broken. His lungs burned when he inhaled, like a furnace lighting up.

He opened his eyes.

Plum stared down worriedly. He'd spread X's coat like a blanket beneath him. X was moved by that and by the already familiar sight of his friend's fluttering hands. Soft, kind Plum: it was good to see him.

Every soul within a hundred feet was staring at X, and murmuring. Whatever had transpired after he'd passed out on the altar had set everyone abuzz.

X didn't know if he could speak, but he had to know if his heart held sins as he feared.

He attempted a single word.

"What," he said.

"Don't try to speak," said Plum. "Not yet."

"What," X said again. *"Happened."*

"Ah, yes," said Plum. "I will tell you everything, but only if you swear you won't try to speak." He paused, adding quickly, "Swear to me with your eyes, not your voice."

X blinked.

"Very good," said Plum. "Now, I don't know how much you were aware of before you lost consciousness." Plum hurriedly put up a hand. "That was not an invitation to tell me. I will choose a starting point myself. All right? All right." He sat quietly, considering. "I was meditating. It's not that I don't let any thoughts or noises into my mind—I do—but I pretend they're soap bubbles, and I prick each one as it floats by."

"Skip," said X, *"this part."*

Plum made a wounded face, then grinned.

"If you speak again," he said, "I will talk even slower. We Buddhists have more patience than you can imagine—Buddha once sat beneath a tree for *seven days*, and I think he was just trying to decide if it was a good place to sit. Anyway, I managed to shut out Shiloh's screaming, but then I heard your voice: 'It is me you want!' I was stunned—and cross with you. I trudged up the hill with no plan at all. You were thrashing on the altar—lifting your head, then banging it back down. It struck me that unlike every other soul on this hill, myself included . . ." Plum paused, and struggled with feeling. "Forgive me. It struck me that you—my new friend and my *only* friend, if I'm being honest—could die up there. Truly die. I don't mind saying that if you died . . . Well, I'd be angry with you for a little while, but then I would miss you."

X would have smiled if he weren't in such pain. Zoe and Ripper had taught him how to let kindness in.

"I hiked closer," Plum went on. "I kept stumbling. I am not in peak condition, as we've discussed. Yes, I know I'm babbling. I'm just so excited that you're awake. Anyway, everyone on the hill was watching the ceiling and waiting. You'd gone limp. Your hands hung off the altar. It was awful."

"Sins?" X demanded—or tried to demand. The word came out like a whisper. *"Sins."*

Plum was surprised by the question.

"What do you mean, 'sins'?" he said.

"Have I," said X. *"Sins?"*

"My god, you're crying," said Plum. "Of course you have no sins! I thought you knew that—you told me yourself that you were born here! I promise you, the ceiling was so white it made us all glow. The light warmed our faces! It was like nothing anyone of us had ever seen. All right? All right."

X felt Plum's hand on his shoulder. It hurt to be touched, but again, he allowed the kindness in.

"The Countess was livid," Plum continued. "You'd promised her great sins. She expected a feast! She pressed the knife to your cheek, but before she could do anything else, she had a seizure of some sort. She tore open the collar of her dress. It turns out that she wears a gold band beneath it. She grabbed the thing like it was choking her—like she wanted to rip it from her neck. It was as if the band itself knew you were innocent, and refused to let her punish you."

X knew it was not actually the gold band, but the Higher Power that ruled the Lowlands acting through it.

Plum resumed his account.

"The Countess shoved you off the altar," he said. "You fell like a deadweight and your bones made a loud crack. Sorry—is that too vivid? I raced forward to pick you up. You don't need to thank me. I failed. You are quite heavy. Shiloh? The soldier? He was still flabbergasted by what you'd done for him, so he tried to help me lift you, but since the Countess had shredded his foot he could barely walk himself. It was actually the knight who carried you here. He's quite a fan of yours now. I think he'd follow you into battle with what little armor he has left. As for me, I did manage to at least carry your coat."

When Plum finally finished, he let X rest, though X could sense his worried friend checking on him regularly. X still felt a pain so widespread in his body that it seemed to have replaced his bones. But he felt a contradictory sense of relief now, too: taking souls as a bounty hunter had not blackened his heart. Zoe would say she wasn't surprised in the least. She'd pretend that she had never questioned that he was, as the Ukrainian had said of Plum, "good at bottom." But then . . . Then she would pull him to her and hold him so fiercely that he would know she was secretly relieved, grateful, proud. "I knew all along, you dork," she'd say. "Of course I knew. But *you* needed to know."

It was true. He did.

X stared up at the black dome of the ceiling. He couldn't remember everything that had happened on the altar. But one memory lingered. It was something the Countess had said. X struggled to call it forth, like someone trying to coax back a dream.

Finally, the memory X had been tugging at came loose.

"Take the foil packet from my coat and give it to me, if you would?" he told Plum.

"Can it wait until you've rested?" said Plum. "You've had a shock."

"It cannot," said X. "I have hold of a thought, and fear losing it."

He rolled onto his side so Plum could fish the packet out of the coat, which lay beneath him, and asked him to show him the broken bracelet that read *Vesuvius*.

"You've seen the bracelet a thousand times," said Plum. "There's nothing different about it now. This absolutely *could* have waited. You are a very irritating patient."

X only half-listened.

The Countess's words echoed in his head: *If that damnable feline erupts again, the Countess shall stop its breath. Would that the creature had been named for something mute, like a statue or the wind.*

X ran his thumb over the lettering on the bracelet.

"You said Vesuvius was a volcano," he said. "A legendary one."

"Yes," said Plum. "Can I put the bracelet back now, please?"

If that damnable feline erupts again . . . Would that the creature had been named for something mute . . .

X looked at Plum, who was staring at him with an unconvincing approximation of sternness.

"I don't believe this is a bracelet at all," said X. "I believe it is a collar."

He didn't pause for Plum to absorb this, but rather hurried on. He had to get the words out.

"And I believe Vesuvius is a cat."

twelve

THE COUNTESS WAS STILL hungry for sins. She barked for Oedipus and Rex, and set off down the hill in search of evil to feed on.

It was harder for X to watch this time, for he knew what to expect—the screams of a soul dragged up through the crowd, the light on the ceiling, the flashing knife, the sickening cheers. He also knew that if he himself had given her an infested soul to feast on, she wouldn't be searching for another.

Seeing the Countess descend, Plum sat cross-legged and began to meditate. X was jealous that his friend could escape that way, that he could disappear inside himself like a flower closing. X's own brain was in turmoil. If Vesuvius belonged to the Countess, then the items in the foil had belonged to her, too—and only she could tell X where his mother was imprisoned. His mother had been *friends* with this woman? The thought of it rattled him. The Countess was as repugnant a soul as X had ever encountered—she was Dervish in a dress.

The souls on the hill dove out of the Countess's way. To distract himself, X stared down at his silver packet, hoping to see something he had never seen before. But unlike Vesuvius's collar, the remaining items told him nothing. Every one of them was a door that wouldn't open.

Frustrated, X put the packet away. He looked up at the empty plateau: the rough-hewn altar, the absurd canopied bed, the wooden box that held Vesuvius. He remembered the mess of scratches he'd noticed on the Countess's hands. They must have been Vesuvius's work. How the animal must have hated her!

Just as X was about to look away, Vesuvius began to moan. It was a tentative cry at first, a question almost: *Is anyone there?* Not five seconds passed before the cat repeated his question more loudly: *Is anyone there? Anyone?*

It was agonizing to hear, and X saw a great number of souls turn their attention toward the cat. Vesuvius's cries grew even starker. They seemed to branch out in the air, like they were searching for something, for someone. It struck X as an incredibly lonely sound. X had been damned for no reason at all. Maybe it was foolish or sentimental, but hearing Vesuvius wail, he knew he'd found a creature even more innocent and undeserving of pain than himself. Even Plum, without opening his eyes, murmured, "Poor thing. Poor, poor thing."

There were noises from below. Someone was creeping up through the crowd. It was the woman in the servant's dress and the bloodied apron. She was approaching the forbidden borderland beneath the plateau.

X guessed that the woman was from the early 20th century. Her shiny black hair was parted, pulled back into a bun, and covered by a white kerchief. Her apron hung around her neck and flowed past her knees. Her dress was a long, severe black garment that swallowed everything but her hands and feet.

X watched as she stepped into the borderland. He remembered how the Countess had sliced open the backs of the elderly man's legs just for being *pushed* into it. He looked down the hill to see where the lord and the boxers were now. They had disappeared over a crest, but there was no telling when they would make their way back. X knew nothing about the servant woman, but now he was terrified for her.

He remembered what she had said to the Countess: *"Let me comfort him. He doesn't belong in a box."*

So *that* was it. She was coming to console the cat.

The souls on the hill watched, and whispered. But no one alerted the Countess or Oedipus or Rex. X found it touching. The servant had taken it upon herself to tend to the souls after they'd been brutalized on the altar—helped them for no reason other than that she was kind. They were grateful. They would not betray her. X thought of the Ukrainian, and wished he'd stayed long enough to see this display of solidarity.

The servant made it to the plateau, and stole toward the box on the bed. Vesuvius seemed to hear her. His cries changed: *Who's there? Do I know you?* X was consumed with a need to know the servant woman's name. He hated interrupting Plum while he meditated, but he couldn't help himself. He touched his arm.

"I apologize, but . . . ," he began.

Plum opened his eyes. He saw the servant, and the color drained out of his face.

"She has tried to get to the cat before," he said. "She's never succeeded."

He scanned the hill for the Countess.

"The lord is down below," X told him.

"But she'll be back," said Plum.

"What is the servant's name?" said X.

"I've always wondered," said Plum.

"I am sorry I disturbed you," said X. "I suppose I didn't want to be alone."

"It's perfectly all right," said Plum. "Have you heard the expression 'That's what friends are for'?"

"I have not," said X.

Plum smiled his gentle smile.

"I guess it isn't said much around here," he said.

X and Plum watched the servant creep toward the bed. Vesuvius cried louder in anticipation—*I'm in here! I'm in here!*—as if he was afraid she'd give up and turn away. The servant checked over her shoulder for the Countess. Everyone on the hill had their eyes fixed on her.

The woman removed the box's lid, and—before she even had a chance to set it down on the bed—Vesuvius sprang into her arms. The cat was puffy and gray. Even X, who had no experience with cats whatsoever, could see he was handsome. Vesuvius seemed ecstatic not just to be released from his purgatory but to see the woman. He rubbed his face against her cheek, licked her neck, put a paw on her nose. It looked to X like the servant had started crying. She was talking to Vesuvius now. He responded with a high, urgent meow as if he had *so* many things to tell her.

"She needs to put him back in the box now," said Plum nervously. "What is she thinking? She needs to *put him back*."

Fear hit X's veins and spread, like a drop of poison.

Before he could speak, the Countess came barreling up the hill.

"The Countess sees thy treachery, false jade!" she shouted at the servant.

She charged ahead so quickly that Oedipus and Rex fell behind. The servant tightened her hold on Vesuvius. It was clear to X she'd never let him go.

When the Countess reached the plateau, every torch on the hill extinguished, the ceiling lit up, and she and the servant were displayed for all to see. There was no cheering or bloodlust, which inflamed the Countess even more. No one wanted to see the woman suffer.

X found himself standing again.

For a second time, he hiked toward the Countess to stop her.

Plum begged him not to interfere. There was no time for an argument, so X just gave his friend a fond look and said, "But I have never met a cat before."

He climbed, his legs aching. He kept one eye on the ceiling. Oedipus and Rex stood just behind the Countess now, frowning. They seemed to have no stomach for this either.

"Wouldst thou risk body and breath for a creature that does naught but wail?" the Countess asked the servant.

"Apparently," said the servant.

Her tone reminded X of Zoe.

"Thou shalt regret thy impertinence," said the Countess. "For YEARS, the Countess has let thee coddle the vermin on this hill. Now we shall see if any will bestir themselves to coddle THEE."

She instructed the servant to put Vesuvius down unless she longed to see his insides. The servant set the cat on the ground, and shooed him tearfully away. The cat rubbed her leg, refusing to leave her. The woman had to stamp her foot to make him retreat under the bed.

"Vesuvius will always hate you," the servant told the Countess, "because you *stole* him from me."

The Countess yanked the woman's apron off, and wound it around her throat. The servant's neck flushed and flailed. Vesuvius howled helplessly.

Now that the servant's apron had been torn away, X could see that a long row of buttons ran down the front of her dress.

They were bloodstone.

And one of them was missing.

SO THE SERVANT HAD been his mother's friend, not the lord. X found this far easier to understand.

"Release the woman," he called out as he approached. "She will not satisfy your hunger any more than I did, for what sins could she be concealing? Nothing that would satisfy the likes of you, surely."

The Countess whirled around. She looked outraged that X had returned, but the anger turned quickly to something like curiosity.

"'Tis true, this one will make but a paltry meal," she said. "Yet *thy* interest in the matter intrigues. Dost thou care for this wretch? Perhaps the Countess has discovered a way to wound thee at last!"

She pulled the apron so tight around the servant's neck that it was like a noose. X forced himself not to react.

The Countess scowled and threw the servant down.

"So this wretch is NOTHING to thee," she said.

She stomped around the plateau, squeezing her blemish and trying to conjure a new plan for punishing X. Once again, she stopped referring to herself as if she were some exalted third party. Even the "thee"s and "thou"s fell away. X wondered if they too had been an affectation.

"You WILL kneel to me before I am through," she told X. "You WILL fear me! You say Regent is grander than I? I will disabuse you of that notion!" She gestured at the servant on the ground. "Yet if you do not truly know this trifle of a person, her suffering will not wound you—not so deep as I should like."

It struck X that he should be grateful that he'd lost so much, for now what could be used against him?

The Countess stopped circling suddenly. She grinned at X, her mouth a crack spreading fast across her face.

She called to Oedipus and Rex.

"Idiots!" she said. "Bring me Plum!"

PLUM WEPT AS HE was dragged past. X expected his friend to curse him—he had every right. Instead, Plum begged a favor of him.

"Don't watch my sins on the ceiling," he said. "*Please.* I'm so ashamed of what I was. If you care for me at all, you won't watch." One of the boxers had pinioned Plum's hands behind his back, so his tears spilled unchecked down his cheeks. "All right, friend? All right?"

Oedipus and Rex pulled him onward. X lunged at the boxers, but was batted away. He heard someone call his name from the crowd, but could not see who it was.

Plum was laid out on the altar, and the Countess pressed down on his chest. The torches went out, releasing traces of black smoke. The ceiling crackled to life. Thousands of faces turned upward, expectant as flowers.

Plum's sins began to play. X kept his promise: he didn't watch. Sounds assaulted his ears, but he dropped deep into himself and heard only an indecipherable mass of noise, like a wave crashing. Again, he heard a voice calling his name.

Eventually, the ceiling went silent. The torches reignited with a *whoosh*. Plum lay convulsing with tears.

The Countess's face was wild with ecstasy. She'd been fed by Plum's sins. Rejuvenated. The streaks of gray had disappeared from her hair, and her skin shone magnificently. Even the pimple was gone. She leaned down, tore Plum's shirt open—and saw the long, livid scar that ran the full length of his torso.

"Ah, yes, the Countess remembers thee," she said.

"Whatever you're going to do, just do it," cried Plum. "Just *do it*."

His cries were harrowing. X saw Shiloh weeping in the crowd. He saw the Knight standing forlornly in his half suit of armor, like a dragon that had lost its scales.

"Just do it!" Plum cried again. "Cut me if you're going to cut me. *Just do it!*"

Oedipus's fist shot out and struck Plum hard. X felt rage boil up in him, then realized that what Oedipus had done had been a kindness. He'd knocked Plum unconscious so he wouldn't feel the pain.

The Countess, comprehending this, too, jabbed Oedipus's shoulder with the knife.

"Thou art NEXT, traitor," she told him.

She twisted the blade before pulling it out. Oedipus dropped to one knee, howling.

Electrified, the crowd spilled into the empty borderland. X heard his name called out for a third time. This time he recognized the voice. He hadn't expected to ever hear it again.

The Ukrainian had returned.

He stood just beneath the plateau, his cherry-red tracksuit bright as a lantern.

X called to him: "Can it really be you?"

"Of *course* is me," said the guard. "What kind of question? Who else is so extremely handsome?"

X was taken aback by the bounce in the Ukrainian's voice. Did he not see that Plum was wailing on the altar?

"I did not believe that you'd actually gone for food," said X.

The guard smiled slyly.

"Did *not* go for food, if you want true fact of matter," he said. "Went for reinforcements!"

He pointed down the slope.

X turned to see Regent fly toward the altar, his robes spread like wings, and pitch the Countess down the hill.

X RAN TO PLUM. His friend was conscious but in shock. His shirt hung open, exposing his belly. X and the Ukrainian helped him down from the altar, and lay him on the Countess's bed. The servant woman handed Vesuvius to Plum to calm him. Plum hugged the cat to his chest. His breathing steadied, and he found X's eyes.

"My sins," he said. "The ceiling. Did you watch?"

"I did not," said X, trying to smile. "That's what friends . . . Forgive me, what was the expression?"

"'That's what friends are for,'" said Plum.

"Dionne Warwick!" said the Ukrainian. "Excellent soft music of 1980s! You know it?"

Before there was time to say more, a growl emanated from farther down the hill. The Countess was stalking up it again.

"FALL BACK, Regent!" she hollered. "These souls are the Countess's to govern as she pleases! Thou hast no dominion here!"

Everyone on the hill went still. The Countess's enraged face loomed above them on the ceiling. Her voice sounded loud as a god's.

Regent was unimpressed.

"You are not a countess, and you never *were* a countess—in this world or any other."

"STILL THY TONGUE OR FORFEIT IT!"

"I shall do neither," said Regent. "I sent a soul here to seek news of his mother. I knew you to be cruel and small, but I confess I did not know *how* cruel and *how* small." He looked at the souls spread all around. "Either you put an end to your savagery—or I shall put an end to you."

A cheer went up on all sides. Even the guards joined in. Even Oedipus and Rex.

The Countess flew at Regent with her knife raised.

Regent blocked the blade as it came down, but the Countess swung again, this time from below, and slashed his torso. The souls who had swarmed onto the plateau crept closer, riveted. X pushed through them so he could see. Regent knocked the knife from the Countess's hand. It skidded to a halt near Oedipus and Rex. The Countess hissed at them to bring it to her, calling them *minnows* and *maggots*.

They refused. Rex covered the blade with his boot.

While the Countess was turned, Regent locked his arms around her from behind. She screeched and threw her head back against the bridge of his nose. There was an awful *crack*, like lightning hitting a tree. Regent staggered and nearly fell. The Countess pressed her advantage. She grabbed Regent's hands, and crushed his fingers together until the pain drove him to his knees. From there, she pushed him onto his back, sat astride him, and tried to drive her thumbs into his eyes.

X knew that what he was about to do was not admirable. Still, it had to be done—and he knew Zoe would approve.

He raised his boot, and kicked the Countess in the head.

She was a thousand times stronger than he, but he had surprised her.

Regent sprang free, thanked X with a glance, and lifted the Countess from the ground.

He broke the altar with her body.

A MINUTE LATER, REGENT stood over the Countess, who writhed in the rubble. Only now did the gold band singe her neck. X could never understand why the Higher Power took so long to make its feelings known. Maybe it resented being dragged into disputes it considered mundane, or maybe the Lowlands were too vast for it to oversee properly. Either way, X felt a rare tide of peacefulness as he gazed down at the Countess now. She was gripping the gold band with both hands, grunting nonsense and profanity and trying to peel it away so the air could cool her throat.

X and the Ukrainian returned to Plum, who lay in a rippled sea of cream-colored pillows and sheets.

"Silk," he told them, still bleary with pain. "I always knew it would be silk."

"Don't get too comfortable, Plum person," said the Ukrainian. "Is my turn next."

The servant woman had never left Plum's side. She smiled now, relieved to see that he was returning to himself, and tucked a few stray hairs into the white kerchief on her head. Up close, she looked to be about 30. Her eyes were blue, or maybe gray. X couldn't quite tell, and didn't want to stare. Her face was covered with freckles, which were dense as stars on her cheeks and grew sparser as they traveled toward her chin. The woman had already demonstrated her kindness, her courage. But X sensed that she was guarded, too—as if she were judging, with every second, who she could trust and who she couldn't. It made telling her who he was, and what he needed, even harder.

"Speak to her, for goodness' sake," said Plum. He was rubbing Vesuvius under his chin with his thumbs. The cat had lifted his head to encourage him. "*Tell* her."

"I agree," said the Ukrainian. "Do not be weak at crucial intersection."

X raised a palm to silence them. The servant woman turned to him, questioningly. Still, he didn't know how to begin. Being so close to someone who might have known his mother, someone who might be able to tell him where she was held prisoner . . .

The woman saw that X was in some kind of distress, and her eyes warmed.

"They call me Maudlin here," she said. "Which I hate. Please call me Maud."

"Yes," said X. "I will. Thank you. My name is X."

"Well, that's very—short," the woman said, smiling. "What do your friends want you to tell me?"

X felt like there was a dam inside him, holding back the words.

He reached into his coat, and placed the silver packet in Maud's hands. Maud seemed not to know that she was meant to open it.

He nodded to encourage her. At last she unfolded the packet. He could see that she recognized everything inside.

"How?" she said. She couldn't even look up from the collar, the button, all of it. "I don't understand."

"I believe they belonged to you once?" said X.

Maud, dazed, shook her head no.

X worried his voice would crack with the next sentence.

"Then I believe they belonged to my mother—whom I have never known."

Maud lifted her eyes, and seemed to see him for the first time, to recognize his mother's face in his own.

"My god," she said. "You're the son."

"You know of me?" said X.

The recognition rippled through him like heat. He felt as if some part of himself had finally been colored in.

"Yes," said Maud. "I was . . . I was there when you were born."

X was stunned by this. He understood that it was his turn to say something, but couldn't.

Maud filled the silence by taking the cat from Plum and saying, "Look who it is, Vesuvius! Look! It's her son!"

"Whoa whoa whoa," said the Ukrainian, who had hung on every word. "Vesuvius is *cat*?"

No one answered.

"Do you know where my mother is being held now?" X asked Maud.

She hesitated.

"Yes," she said. "*Yes*. I think I do."

"Tell me, for I mean to save her," said X. Maud looked at him with something like pity, so he added, "You do not believe me capable of it?"

"I won't lie—I don't know if anyone is capable of it," said Maud. "But since you're her son, I'm sure no one will be able to stop you from trying."

"My mother is stubborn, is she?" said X.

Another piece of him was colored in.

Maud laughed affectionately.

"That woman could convince the ocean to part for her," she said. "Here in the Lowlands, they call her Versailles."

"Like the palace?" said Plum, sitting up in the bed.

Maud replied without taking her eyes from X, so he'd know that the answer was for him.

"Yes, like the palace," she said. "Because she's . . . Because she's magnificent."

MAUD TOLD X THAT his mother was imprisoned in a part of the Lowlands called Where the Rivers End. Regent announced that he would take not just X but Maud and the Ukrainian as well.

X glowed with happiness and hope.

But then Regent pointed over his shoulder.

"However, I cannot take *him*," he said.

X felt a hole open in his chest.

Regent was pointing at Plum.

"But he is the gentlest of us all—and brave," said X. "You cannot mean it."

"He is a stranger to me, as are the contents of his soul," said Regent. "If he was damned to this hill, he is guilty of dark doings."

"Don't worry about me, X, all right?" said Plum. "Please don't."

But as he finished speaking, he burst into sobs.

"Look at me, Regent," said X. "*I* will beg you, if he will not. I will promise you anything—just tell me what you require."

Regent sighed, approached the bed, and placed his hand over Plum's heart to see what it contained. Plum pressed his palms over his eyes as if he could physically force back the tears.

Half a minute passed—so slowly that X felt as if his body were being raked with a nail.

Regent's face clouded.

He removed his hand, and shook his head.

"I'm sorry," he told Plum.

Before X could respond, Plum stood up from the bed, and fumbled with the buttons of his khaki shirt. His pink, shining belly was exposed, with its long zipper of a scar. For the first time, he seemed ashamed of it.

"Don't trouble yourself for me, friend," he told X. "He's right, I'm afraid. I belong here."

"You do not," said X. "I won't hear it. There is so much that is worthy in you."

"It means the world that you think so," said Plum. "But as I've told you, it is a reflection of *your* goodness, not mine."

He took X's arm, and led him away from the others.

"It's time for me to tell you why I was damned," he said.

"No," said X. "I know how it shames you."

"Nevertheless, I must tell you," said Plum. "Later, when you think of me—*if* you think of me—I want you to know that there was nothing you could have done to save me. And honestly? If I can't speak my crimes aloud, then I still haven't faced them. Do you see?"

"I do," said X quietly.

"Look away from me, though, would you?" said Plum. "I don't think I can stand to see your eyes as I tell you." He sniffled and wiped his nose on his shirt. "Look at our friend the Ukrainian in his tracksuit. See how loyal he looks? Look at Maud. See how brave she is? Good. Now. I was in the military, X. A commander. Hard to believe, I know. I was an abhorrent human being. Filled with sick ideas. I decided to make an example of some prisoners. Truth be told, I wanted to be promoted—to be noticed by my superiors. I had my men line six prisoners up on their knees in a courtyard. Everyone was watching from the windows. I ordered my men to force the prisoners' mouths open. I ordered them to pour gasoline down their throats . . ."

"*Enough,*" said X.

"No," said Plum, his voice a trembling wire. "Once the gasoline had been forced down their throats, the prisoners thought I was finished with them. Their bodies sagged in relief. But I *wasn't* finished with them."

"Stop," said X. "You are not that man anymore."

"I ordered my men to light six matches," said Plum. "Do you understand where this is going? I dropped the first match into the first man's mouth myself." Plum paused. "You may think you've heard every kind of scream here in the Lowlands, X. You haven't."

Plum drew back a way, and finally looked at X. His eyes were so red it was as if fireworks had gone off inside them. X knew that his own eyes looked much the same.

"I can never repent enough for what I did, though I break my back at it most days," said Plum. "Let me stay here where I belong, my friend? Let me try to be the lotus flower?"

Regent offered Plum his hand in farewell. It was unusual for a lord to show a soul that kind of respect, and X could see that Plum was moved by the gesture.

Next, Maud hugged Plum, and lifted her cat to his face.

"Vesuvius wants to say good-bye," she said.

Plum kissed the animal awkwardly on his nose.

"Such a handsome little man," he said.

When it was time for X to say good-bye, he couldn't summon any words. He wished Zoe were there to blurt something funny and strange. The story about the prisoners, horrific as it was, had made him pity Plum even more, because he knew how his friend bent under the weight of the guilt. X had known Plum such a short time. Still, he knew he'd miss his warmth, his steadfastness, even the way he hummed sometimes when he meditated. Plum shrugged as if words were beyond him, too. He gave X a brave, almost convincing smile.

"All right?" he said. "All right."

REGENT WENT TO THE Countess, and pulled her up from the rubble by the collar of her dress, as a clutch of souls gathered around.

"Listen to every word I say, and do not utter a single one," he said. "You will never torture another soul on this hill, do you understand?"

"On whose authority dost thou speak?" said the Countess.

"My own," said Regent. "Yet I see from the way you clutch that gold band that the Higher Power concurs." He waited to see if the Countess would challenge him again. Her eyes twitched with rage but she just grunted and looked away. "If you do not entirely alter your character, I will come back," said Regent. "If you behave disagreeably toward that soul there"—he pointed toward Plum—"or those souls there"—he indicated Oedipus and Rex—"I will come back. And I will bring other lords with me, a furious flock of them. We will tear that band from your neck altogether, so that all your powers desert you, and—so help me—we will bestow it upon someone who has heard of honor."

Regent released the Countess, and she fell back to the ground like an empty dress.

X, Maud, and the Ukrainian followed Regent down the slope. The crowd parted. Some of the souls who'd been lying on the ground stood as they passed—in tribute, it seemed to X.

When their little party had descended a hundred feet, Regent paused, and they all gave the ceiling a last look.

The Countess's awful face was up there, big as the moon. She looked broken, humiliated. The pimple had returned to the corner of her mouth.

Regent asked a guard for his torch. He took it, and flung it in the air.

X watched the torch fly upward, turning end over end, shedding smoke and wisps of flame. Just as it reached the top of its arc, it grazed the ceiling—and the whole thing ignited at once.

The Countess's face was lost in a field of fire.

thirteen

AT THE BOTTOM OF the hill lay a snaking wall that kept the prisoners from escaping in the river. Regent slammed it with a fist. A jagged opening appeared. The lord helped X through the wall, telling him to avoid the edges of the hole, which pulsed in a sequence: red, orange, yellow. X emerged near the river. He watched as the others passed through. The opening glowed white, then shrank and vanished, as if it were healing itself.

The riverbank was murky, twilit. The water flowed noisily, foaming where it hit the rocks. Regent pressed a palm to the ground. A corridor of light shot along the bank, showing them the way.

"Will Dervish discover what we have done?" said X. "Will he come after us?"

"Yes—and soon," said Regent. "He has spies who are loyal to him, though I can't think why. Perhaps it is easier to believe wickedness and hate will always prevail." He turned to Maud. "The cat will slow us down. Will you part with him?"

"Never!" said Maud, holding the animal even closer, her hands lost in his abundant gray fur. "Vesuvius came to hell with me. He and I will part ways with *you* if you even ask again."

Regent seemed to have expected this response. He dropped the matter, and led the party down the riverside. They walked two by two, Maud and the Ukrainian just behind Regent and X.

"Forgive my outbursting," the guard called out before they'd gone even a hundred feet, "but as we are speaking of cat, I must ask you . . . When X is boy, you give him buttons and collars as clues. Is terrible complicated! Why not say, 'Someday you must find Maud. Thirty years old. Bloody apron like serial killer.'"

Regent looked at X.

"Tell your friend the answer," he said. "You know it, do you not?"

"I suspect he never told me about Maud for the selfsame reason he never told me about my mother," said X. "He believed that hope was dangerous—a bird of prey."

"I still do," said Regent.

"Yet you freed us," said X. "Perhaps your heart does not know how cynical you are."

Regent rubbed the top of his head, which was shaved close. It was just an offhand, human gesture, but X found it endearing.

"No, perhaps my heart does not," said Regent.

X watched the lord as they walked. Regent had been taken to the Lowlands when he was 50, yet he seemed ageless, apart from the lines worn into his forehead. Usually, Regent moved so decisively—with such long, muscular strides—that he seemed less like a person than a statue come to life. But he looked troubled now. Not so much a lord as a man.

"How is it that Maud knew where my mother is prisoner, but you did not?" said X.

"When your mother was found to be with child, there was an uproar and a trial," said Regent. "I defended her heatedly, and Dervish told the other lords that I could not be trusted. I was kept forcibly away when you were born. Yet the lords did grant two of your mother's requests. The first was that Maud be at her side when she gave birth."

Regent turned as he walked, and indicated that Maud herself should take up the story.

"I knew your mother *up there*," she said. X looked back to see her pointing at the ceiling. "I was just her lady's maid, but she was the truest friend I ever had. They separated us when we were damned because they didn't trust us together. I didn't see her for maybe eighty years. Then a guard came, and told me that I was needed—that she was in labor. 'She's having a baby?' I said. 'She's dead!' But then, I *told* you she was stubborn. Your mother was ecstatic when you were born. I feared for you. I said—my god, I should never have said it—I said I was afraid you wouldn't live. Your mother was so proud of you already. She kissed your little mouth, and said, 'Of *course* my son will live.'"

Maud stopped, overcome by memories. X said nothing, hoping she'd continue.

"They pulled you away from her almost immediately," she said at last. "Your mother's face at that moment—you may think you've seen true agony in the Lowlands, but I promise you haven't."

Maud's words were so like what Plum had said about the screams that X looked at her a second time. She stared at the ground.

The Ukrainian tapped her shoulder gently with his bat.

"Do not fret, Maud person," he said. "Everything becomes okay. Look at us now, off to rescue!"

Maud finished her story quickly, as if she wanted to be rid of it.

"Dervish and a guard dragged your mother and me away," she said. "I was left on the Countess's hill—to punish me for helping your mother, probably—and they continued on. That's when I heard Dervish tell the guard where they were going."

"You said my mother had *two* requests?" X asked Regent.

The lord slowed his pace so the others could keep up.

"Her second request was that you be placed in my care," he said. "The other lords fell about laughing. They assumed I would be horrified. Yet I was moved, for I had never raised a child, nor been *believed in* as much as your mother believed in me then."

X HAD ASSUMED THAT the way to find a place called Where the Rivers End would be to follow a river until—well, until it ended. But the light that Regent had laid before them veered from the current now, and slipped into a tunnel.

The lord stopped by the entrance to let them rest.

"This place we journey to," said X, "have you been there before?"

"No," said Regent. "The Lowlands are so vast that I shall never see them all. Yet I know that Where the Rivers End is somewhere that one rushes *away from*, rather than toward. Forgive me for lecturing again on the perils of hope, but we may not achieve what we hope to. Dervish may have foreseen the day I would look for Maud, and hence lied about where he was taking your mother." Regent looked back to the river, as if to underscore what he said next. "Even if he told the truth, he and his men will no doubt ambush us along the way."

X hadn't allowed himself to consider these possibilities, and they settled on him heavily.

"Regent, if I may outburst second time," said the Ukrainian. "You are not life of party."

The lord, who had yet to warm to the Ukrainian, ignored him and continued addressing X.

"I have risked a great deal for you because your mother was my friend—and because you are an innocent," he said. "It's as if you weren't born but rather woke up in a tomb. The injustice staggers me still. So I regret nothing I have done. If Dervish means to pull us all farther into the shadows, then I am resolved to push us all toward the light."

"Thank you," said X. "Thank you for everything you have done. If I knew grander words, I would use them."

"Yet you *must* hear what I tell you now," said Regent. "Your plan to rescue your mother—and for her to rescue you—is the plan of a dreaming child. I shall take you to Where the Rivers End, for you deserve at least to lay eyes upon the woman who gave you life if you can. In truth, I am ashamed I did not seek her out long ago. It may have been that I was afraid to see how imprisonment and degradation had altered her. Or it may have been that I needed you— your fire—to propel me."

X took this in quietly, as he leaned against the wall near the tunnel entrance. A small torch sat in a bracket above him; the torches were always bolted up high so the prisoners couldn't use them as weapons. X thought of what Regent had said about the likelihood of failure. He pictured himself trying, pathetically, to escape the Lowlands armed with nothing but a torch.

He closed his eyes, as Plum would have, and tried to quiet his thoughts. He'd heard so much about his mother, but a hundred questions still swirled inside him. After a moment, he felt a hand on his shoulder. He opened his eyes to Maud's freckled face, tilted with worry. Vesuvius lay in the crook of her elbow.

"All this must be overwhelming," she said.

"It is," said X.

"What would help?" said Maud.

"Knowing *right now* if we will succeed or fail," said X. "Knowing if I'll be able to stand in front of my mother and say, 'I am your son, and I survived, just as you said I would.' Knowing if I will make it out of the Lowlands and back to Zoe."

"It's a lot to ask for," said Maud. Then, apparently fearing she'd been too fatalistic, she nodded toward Regent and the Ukrainian, and smiled. "But you've assembled a good team."

X gazed at the lord, who, unable to stand still, was pacing sternly in his royal blue robes, and at the guard, who was trying to balance his baseball bat on one finger.

"They make a handsome picture, don't they?" said X.

"They do," said Maud. She paused. "Is Zoe a girl you love?"

"Yes," said X. "She's *up there*, as you would put it. I owe her everything, even my name."

"What does it mean? Do you mind if I ask?"

"It has something to do with mathematics, which is a jungle I have never set foot in," said X. "Zoe intended to change my name when she'd collected enough facts about my character, but then I suppose I grew into it—or it grew into me. Why are you called Maudlin?"

"Oh, it's ridiculous," said Maud. "I cried when the lords first separated your mother and me. Who wouldn't have cried? Only a monster." She stroked the cat. "Even Suvi here wailed."

141

"Why was my mother damned, Maud?" said X. "What did she do?"

Maud winced.

"The same thing I did," she said. "Nothing more."

"That's not quite an answer," said X. "You need not protect me. Tell me what you did."

Maud looked to Regent, whose pacing had brought him close. She seemed to be hoping that he'd answer for her. He regarded her gravely, and declined.

"We murdered two men," said Maud, turning back to X. "With a knife and a drill." She rushed to say more, no doubt so that the bald facts wouldn't ring as long. "You've got the tip of the drill in that silver packet of yours. Your mother kept those things to remind her of what she'd survived. There's a story behind each of them. I will tell you them all, if you'll let me, then maybe you won't judge what your mother did too harshly."

"I want to know everything," said X. "Yet tell me, if Regent was not present at my birth, how is it that you even know each other?"

Maud seemed relieved at the change in subject.

"Oh, I've known Regent since the day I died," she said.

She looked again to the lord. This time he spoke.

"Two bounty hunters were sent for Maud and your mother," said Regent. "It was a century ago, as you know—before I was even a lord."

"The first one failed to capture us because your mother was too smart for him," said Maud. "She outmaneuvered him—a mortal woman! So the lords had to send someone else."

"Dervish was the bounty hunter who failed," said Regent. "I was the one who did not."

fourteen

ONCE THEY WERE IN the tunnel, the noise of the river receded. The black walls were polished and smooth, and studded with gems, which flickered as they passed.

X turned over what Regent had told him in his mind. So Dervish had failed to bring X's mother to the Lowlands. How humiliated he must have been! No wonder he hated her—and her son. No wonder he'd ranted and stamped and railed against X at every opportunity.

And Regent . . . Regent had plucked X's mother out of the world. He had taken her life, her future, everything. No wonder he had done so much for X, even though it endangered him.

Cool air blew past them as they walked. The Ukrainian unzipped the top of his tracksuit, and gallantly handed it to Maud. He wore only a damp, sleeveless T-shirt now. X could see a field of curly black hair beneath it, as well as a silver necklace bearing a word he couldn't read, though he recognized the letters: *MAMA*.

Maud slipped on the red jacket and tucked Vesuvius inside. The cat blinked at her happily, languorously, and was snoring before they'd gone 20 paces.

"I look foolish in your coat, don't I?" said Maud. "Tell me the truth."

"Truth?" said the Ukrainian. "Truth is, you look like my tenth-grade girlfriend. Remember, however, Reeper is only true love of mine, as one day I will inform her."

The tunnel stretched indefinitely onward. For every hundred feet they walked, it seemed to grow another hundred. X was about to ask Maud to tell him his mother's story, when strange sounds flooded past. First, it was a rush of footsteps over their heads, then the roar of a wave, which seemed to barrel toward them from the other side of the wall. X stared at the rock, waiting for cracks to appear, but the noise faded fast.

Then the tunnel swerved hard, and X was met with a startling sight. On each wall, there was a long row of hands jutting through rock. And they were moving.

Regent steered everyone to the center of the passage, and told them to stare straight ahead. But X kept watching the hands. The fingers were wriggling, spasming, clutching the air. There must have been sinners on the other side of the walls. Who knew what pain they were in, or what was being done to them that he couldn't see? Two of the hands might have belonged to his mother. He felt sick as he passed.

When Regent let them rest again, X sat down next to Maud. She must have been as desperate to tell his mother's story as X was to hear it. His first question—"How old were you when you went to work for my mother?"—had barely left his lips when the answer came tumbling out.

"I WAS FIFTEEN," SAID Maud. "I was a very scared little person. About the same height I am now, but skinnier. When I looked at myself, I saw only my nose, ears, elbows, and knees. So I tried not to look at myself. I also tried to be silent one hundred percent of the time, which my parents told me was my best feature. I don't think they ever liked me very much."

Maud put her hand inside the sort of kangaroo pouch she'd made for Vesuvius, and pet him as he slept.

"When I reminded the Countess that she had stolen Vesuvius from me? When I told Regent I would never leave Suvi behind?" she said. "I could never have done those things before I met your mother. Whatever I have for a backbone, I got from her.

"I remember knocking on her door. It was the first time I ever wore this dress. This was in Montana, in 1912—"

"Montana?" said X.

He'd meant only to listen, but couldn't believe it was a coincidence that Regent had sent him to that very place as a bounty hunter. He looked to the lord, who was pacing again.

"Your mother liked the sky there," said Regent. "That struck me as odd—for isn't there sky everywhere? Yet I thought you might like it, too." The lord seemed embarrassed by the admission. He made a shooing-away gesture. "Let Maud tell her story," he said.

When X turned back to Maud, he saw that the Ukrainian, who sat across the passageway, was listening as well. X wasn't sure he liked that. He already felt protective of his mother—like he wanted to hold her story close. But when he gave the Ukrainian a questioning look, the guard said, "What? Is interesting! You want I watch TV instead?"

Maud continued.

"I remember my hand being very cold when I knocked on your mother's door. The knocker was a brass fox with a hoop through its teeth. I guess that's not important, except that your mother's husband thought of himself as very cunning and handsome, when he was actually a little knot of hate. Petty and cruel. Not that different from the Countess, in a way. He went by 'Fernley.' Your mother had been forced to marry him—something about adjoining farmland. She loathed him. He pretended he was a gentleman farmer—he had all these airs—but he was bad at everything. I remember him being confused by a *rake* one time. Your mother told me once, 'It's like he's some sort of sea creature that's been forced to live on land!' She didn't talk much, but you always knew where you stood with her because she never masked her feelings, as women were taught to—and when she did say something it was memorable. Fernley called her 'honeybun,' in a sarcastic kind of way, which she detested. So she called him Fern, which made him boil."

Maud paused. X wasn't sure why.

"I know your life's been unfair," she said. "I can't even imagine. And maybe it's not my place to say this—but it would have been unlivable if that man had been your father."

X felt as if Maud were speaking for his mother somehow, like she was a conduit.

"I believe you," he said.

"Your mother opened the door herself," Maud went on. "I can't tell you how beautiful she was. She was sort of framed in light. She looked like I *wanted* to look but knew I never would because of, like I said, the nose, ears, elbows, and knees. She used to wear her hair up while she worked. She could do absolutely anything on the farm, in the house, with the horses . . . But it was nighttime, so her hair was down. It was wavy and black, like yours. Her eyes were dark, but they never shut you out, they drew you in. She refused to use cosmetics. Fernley hated that because he didn't want people to think they couldn't afford them. Which they couldn't. Anyway, I never saw a woman who needed them less. She was twenty-six, I think— and she only had nine years left to live."

Maud frowned, and hugged her knees.

"I must have looked frightful, standing there in the doorway that first day. Terrified. Underfed. Clutching Vesuvius against my chest. I hadn't told them that I'd be bringing a cat, and I was petrified that they wouldn't let me keep him. But your mother smiled at me so warmly. She petted Suvi. She invited me in, as if I were a guest. She was showing me to my room—I'd expected a cot in the kitchen!—when Fernley accosted us in the hallway. He looked me over in the most humiliating way. I was fifteen! He was . . . Well, I forget exactly how old he was, but something like thirty-five. Finally, he looked at Vesuvius. 'Put that disgusting thing in the barn,' he said. 'If I see it again, I'll cut it open and stuff it.' Your mother saw how upset that made me. When Fernley walked away, she said, 'My husband will not harm your friend. He can barely slice a tomato.'

"But I did have to take Vesuvius to the barn, and he howled for a week. You've heard what he sounds like. The other servants warned me that Fernley wouldn't put up with it. The cook said, 'Your cat's not long for this world, girl. Best steel yourself.' I crept out to see Suvi when I could. I begged him to be quiet. But he always howled louder when I left. It was heartbreaking. One night when I went to the barn, the door swung open and gave me a start. It was your mother. She had been sneaking out to see Vesuvius, too—she'd been bringing him scraps of food! That may not sound especially brave, but believe me, it was. She might have mocked Fernley, but she dreaded his temper. We all did.

"Fernley would detonate over the tiniest thing. He was very prim and fussy, and he demanded that everything be *just so*. That silver comb you're carrying was supposedly 'electro-magnetic.' It was very expensive, and supposedly cured headaches and prevented baldness. Fernley had written away for it. One time the maid who cleaned his chamber mislaid the comb for an hour, and he beat her for it. Obviously, the comb was found, but he still deducted the cost of it from the woman's wages! That's the sort of man he was. And honestly, he was already so bald that even if god himself had forged a comb for him, it wouldn't have made a difference.

"When I saw your mother coming out of the barn, I was so moved that I cried. She hugged me, which is *not* something that employers did. It wasn't something my own mother did! We just stood there in the darkness, and when Suvi began howling again, your mother started crying, too. I knew then that I would do anything for her.

"Fernley eventually relented, and let Vesuvius live in my room. It was only because he wanted me to be grateful to him. He wanted me to lower my guard.

"One night, I was in the kitchen, up to my elbows in suds. Alone. Fernley crept up behind me, and fondled me like he owned me. I tried to elbow him but missed. He spun me around so I was facing him, and—I won't even call it a kiss—he pushed his horrible mouth at my lips. It was vile. A row of pots hung from a rack above us. I remember them banging over our heads as I struggled. I finally shoved him away, and I apologized. That's how out of mind with fear I was—I apologized to him for attacking me!

"I fled up the stairs to your mother. She glowed with rage when she heard the story. She went to Fernley's chamber, and found his beloved 'electro-magnetic' comb. He kept it—I swear to you—on a swath of red velvet, like it was the Holy Grail itself. Your mother snatched it up and, while Fernley watched in horror, combed Vesuvius with it. Fernley never touched the comb again.

"Afterward, your mother told me if I wanted to leave the household, she'd write me a sterling recommendation and give me the money she'd hidden in a boot in her closet. She showed me the boot—that's how much she trusted me. But much as I loathed Fernley, I couldn't leave *her*. So she elevated my position. She made me her lady's maid, even though she didn't need one, so I'd always be at her side and she could protect me. Fernley saw what she was up to, and seethed because she'd outsmarted him. I turned sixteen, seventeen, eighteen. Fernley leered at me constantly. Your mother was watchful—and I never went into a room unless there was at least one other person in it—and he didn't get his awful hands on me again for a very long time."

fifteen

MAUD STOPPED SPEAKING. SHE looked like someone surfacing from a dream.

"Are you unwell?" said X.

"No," said Maud, "it's just that that's more words than I've spoken in years."

Across the tunnel, the Ukrainian wore a look of disgust. He beat the bat against the ground.

"This Fernley—terrible prick," he said. "What Lowlands need are bounty hunter who can travel through time, such as Dr. Who. If I were bounty hunter of such kind, I bring sophisticated explosive device into past—and shove it up Fernley's ass, okay? Is true fact."

Maud tried not to laugh but couldn't help it.

"Fernley got what he deserved—possibly more," she said. She looked at X. "The next part of the story is terrible. I haven't let myself think about it for years. Do you mind if I rest before I tell it?"

"Of course not," said X, though he couldn't bear the wait.

Maud set Vesuvius on the ground. The cat arched his back grandly, yawned, then went back to sleep. Maud lay down and curled herself around him.

One by one they all dropped off, save Regent, who prowled the tunnels to be certain they were safe.

An hour later, X jerked up from the floor. Something had woken him. Regent was nowhere to be seen. X listened again for the noise that had jarred him. There it was again.

A scraping. A scuffling.

Boots.

It wasn't Regent. X knew the lord's tread by now.

A guard came around the corner, and stopped dead at the sight of X and the others. It was the Cockney guard who'd hauled Ripper down the river. He was one of Dervish's most sycophantic minions. For a weapon, he carried the base of a lamp.

X stood. The Cockney stepped backward.

X knew that he and his companions looked like runaways—because they *were* runaways.

"Wait," he said.

But the guard ran.

X's mind whirled. Should he wake the others?

He chased the Cockney through three twists in the tunnel. The guard had a jutting belly and a shriveled-apple of a face—Ripper used to call him Mr. Ugly—but he was quick on his feet.

When X drew close enough to reach for him, the guard spun, and jabbed him in the stomach with the lamp.

X staggered. The guard moved in on him, panting.

"Dunno wot you're up to, but it's sure to be mischief," he said.

X, still trying to find his breath, decided to gamble and tell the truth.

"I am searching for my mother," he said. "I have never known her. Never seen her." The Cockney remained stony-faced. "Was *your* mother dear to you?"

The guard eyed him.

"Let's not bring me dear mum into this," he said.

"I just want to know mine a little," said X.

The Cockney scratched the back of his neck with the broken lamp. A thatch of armpit hair poked through a hole in his shirt.

"Fing is," he said, "I don't give a monkey's arse what you want. Seems to me you fink you're royalty. You ain't. Seein' as how you made me run and lose me breath, I'm gonna beat you nearabouts to death, then haul you back to Dervish. He'll give me somethin' for my troubles, I suspect—a bit of rest, like."

"You would betray me for a little sleep?" said X.

"I'd do it for less," said the guard.

It was the last thing he said before Maud struck him from behind. She hit the Cockney once behind the legs to bring him down and once in the back of the head to knock him out.

He fell to his knees, wavered, then toppled forward.

"I didn't want to do it," Maud told X, "but he didn't seem to be listening to reason."

"You're quite right," said X. "He's one of Dervish's spies, and he was about to take me apart. I owe you a debt."

He knelt, and inspected the Cockney to make certain he was unconscious.

"Do we tell Regent?" said Maud.

"If we do, he might call off the search for my mother," said X. "He might think we've endangered ourselves."

Maud pursed her lips. X had only known her a matter of hours. He had no idea what she would say next.

"Then we won't tell him," she said.

They returned to where the Ukrainian and the cat lay sleeping. Maud had only just laid the bat near the guard's open palm when Regent approached from the other direction, and told them it was time to press on.

The Ukrainian, waking slowly, rubbed his face, and said, "Is morning, yes?"

It was an old impulse from when he was alive, from when there *were* such things as mornings. X wanted to answer, but what could he say?

Maud scooped up Vesuvius, and they headed deeper into the torch-lit tunnel. Almost immediately, the passage grew more cramped, as if it were funneling them together. Maud walked just behind X, and continued her story.

"BY THE TIME I was twenty-five, Fernley was never home, particularly in the evenings," she said. "I can't describe the relief. Your mother had always wanted a child but she refused to give one to Fernley. She used to say, 'I'd rather go to hell than make that man someone's father!' I've always remembered that, for obvious reasons. Fernley used to carouse with a surgeon friend. He'd come home at dawn, so drunk he couldn't make it up the stairs. Your mother had to have the banister rebuilt twice because he crashed through it. Fernley had stopped leering at me for the most part. He actually told me that I was too old for him now—and he had turned forty-five! But I was grateful for the peace. I got lulled by the rhythm of the days, and I made the mistake of thinking I was safe.

"It was November. Starting to get cold outside. I remember the windows were covered with bugs trying to get in. One morning, I got up especially early. Fernley was sprawled at the foot of the staircase. He was sleeping off a drunk. I couldn't get around him, so I went to step over him—and his hand shot up and clutched my leg.

"I screamed. Tried to shake free. But he pulled me to the ground, and climbed on top of me. His breath was horrid. He grabbed me, hard, between the legs. I heard a scream. It was your mother at the top of the stairs. She had the porcelain pitcher from her washstand in her hand. She flew down the steps at Fernley, and clobbered him with it. It didn't knock him out. It just infuriated him. But it made him forget about me—and go after her. I ran to my room, and pushed my bureau in front of the door."

Maud paused before going on. They walked on awhile, the story suspended in the air.

"I've always been ashamed of running away like that," said Maud. "I think it must be the worst thing I've ever done."

"Why?" said X.

"Because while I was hiding in my room—while I was holding Suvi and telling him everything would be okay—Fernley picked the pitcher off the floor, and beat your mother into a coma."

X stopped walking, and put his hands against the wall as if he might move it. The thought of Fernley hurting his mother sickened him. "Were Fernley in front of me," he said, "I would knock him down, tell him that I'm my mother's son, and put my foot upon his throat."

"I still rage at Fernley, too," said Maud. "Even in my dreams. Even after nearly a hundred years. But, if you don't mind my saying, the answer to a violent man is not always another violent man."

"I am sure you're right," said X. "Yet what is it, then?"

"In this case," said Maud, "it was two violent women."

"A STABLE HAND CARRIED your mother up to her bed for me," she said when they were walking again. "Fernley refused to do it. He sent for the surgeon he caroused with, and told him your mother had been trampled by a horse. Fernley actually winked when he said it. The surgeon pretended to believe him. 'Damned clumsy of her!' he said.

"Your mother was unconscious. Her bruises were horrific. She was sweating and swollen all over, so I packed her with ice—made a little ring around her. Days passed and the farm fell to pieces. Work came to a dead stop. Fernley was useless, and nobody would listen to him because everyone knew what he'd done. So he stood on the back steps one morning, and screeched that everyone was fired and would be jailed if they were not gone in fifteen minutes. He'd been drinking too much to afford them anyway.

"I sat beside your mother all day, every day, in a rickety chair I brought up from the kitchen. I talked to her. Cleaned her. Rubbed her limbs to keep them from atrophying. I couldn't tell if it was working. Fernley and the surgeon stumbled in every night, well and truly sloshed. They seemed *pleased* that your mother hadn't recovered yet. If I gave them so much as a cross look, Fernley would slap me across the face or pinch my arm until it was blue.

"One night, while I was pretending to sleep in my rickety chair, the surgeon announced that if your mother didn't wake before morning, he'd have to operate. He said he could relieve the pressure in her skull with some kind of drill, though it'd be dangerous and Fernley shouldn't get his hopes up. He said the procedure sometimes left patients docile and spacey—sometimes even mute! Well, Fernley's eyes lit up when he heard the words 'docile' and 'mute,' of course. He bent over your mother, and said, 'Should we give it a shot, honeybun?' Then he straightened up, and told the surgeon, 'Honeybun thinks we should give it a shot!'"

X slammed the wall with a fist as he walked.

"Don't," said Maud. "Let me finish. All this is terrible to remember, but I want you to know everything your mother knew when she did what she did."

"I understand," X said. "As far as I am concerned, you needed no more excuse to put Fernley in the ground."

X shoved his fists into his pockets, and Maud continued.

"I spent that night begging your mother to wake, and trying again to rub life into her arms and legs. She didn't open her eyes, but she wriggled a bit, which exhilarated me. Eventually I passed out next to her in the bed. I don't remember when.

"In the morning, I heard carriage wheels in the lane. The surgeon was coming. I pleaded with your mother again. I said, 'Madam, please! Can you hear me?' I said, 'Madam, if you are *ever* to wake, for heaven's sake, let it be now! The surgeon is coming, and what he intends to do to your skull . . . I cannot believe it is lawful and I *know* it is not godly!'

"I had an idea. I'm ashamed of it now. In a way, it led to everything that came after—I don't know if that makes it better or worse. Fernley had beaten your mother with the pitcher so badly that she was hard to look at, even for me who loved her. He'd shattered the pitcher doing it. I thought if I could remind him of how beautiful she was, he might change his mind about the drill. Your mother refused to keep cosmetics, as I've said. When Fernley went to greet the surgeon, I snuck downstairs and brought up a silver tray with whatever substitutes I could scare up, along with a camel-hair brush, a beet to redden her cheeks, and a broad knife to cut the beet with.

"I talked to her as I worked. I begged her not to be angry about what I was doing. I moistened her eyebrows with coconut oil, then held a dish over the candle by her bed and darkened her lashes with the soot. They were tricks my mother had taught me. I sliced the beet with the knife, and pressed it against her face. I sponged her arms with vinegar. I could hear Fernley and the surgeon conspiring downstairs. I imagined pushing Fernley into a vat of lye, and holding him under with a stick. I imagined your mother and me cutting the surgeon in half with one of those two-handed saws they use to bring down trees. I patted her arms dry, and dusted them with powder, too. It was pointless. Heartbreaking. Her arms were still a mess of bruises. They looked like the spots on a leopard. Nothing would have covered them.

"I began ranting about the surgeon and how he meant to turn her into an imbecile. I told her that I refused to lose her—that the surgeon would have to make me an idiot, too. I was just babbling. It took me a second to notice that your mother had opened her eyes.

"I fell on her chest, weeping. I saw her remember what Fernley had done to her with the white pitcher. I saw her wince when she felt the ice I'd packed around her. She began wriggling, as if she wanted to get away from it, so I swept the ice onto the floor. Fernley and the surgeon were in the parlor, cooing over the drill they'd use to open your mother's skull. Fernley sounded giddy—he asked if he could hold it!

"Your mother still hadn't spoken. She tried, but couldn't. She looked me full in the eyes for the first time. I don't know what I expected—happiness at the sight of me, maybe? relief?—but she looked inflamed. I thought she was angry about the powders and cream, so I apologized. I said I'd just wanted her to be beautiful again. But of course, she was furious at Fernley and the surgeon. She could see the state I was in. She was furious at what they'd put *me* through, too.

"I heard them mounting the stairs. There was no one to help us because Fernley had dismissed all the workers. Your mother looked around the chamber. She saw the silver tray with the candle and the brush and the beet, which was now dripping and red. She finally spoke. Just one word. *'Leave,'* she said. I refused. She shook her heard angrily, as if I hadn't understood. She tried again. *'Leave me,'* she said. Again, I resisted. I told her I'd die before I let Fernley and the surgeon have their way. She got even angrier. She was frustrated that she couldn't make herself understood. She glared at her bruises and then at my own. She wanted me to see that she saw them. Then she finally completed the sentence that'd been stuck in her throat: *'Leave me the knife.'*"

Maud paused, as if the moment were playing out again, right in front of her.

"I handed it to her," she said. "I've spent many, many years wondering if I should have refused. She took the knife, slipped it under the covers, and pretended to sleep. I sat down in my rickety chair. Fernley and the surgeon came in. Looking back, it was the only time I ever saw the surgeon sober. He looked awful. Pale. His hands were shaking, and he was so poorly shaven that I couldn't tell if he'd even tried. I'd have rather he operated on your mother drunk! He was holding this evil-looking instrument. It was like something you'd use to drill for oil or dig a well, only a miniature version. It had four little legs so you could steady it on the patient's head. There was a foot-long steel drill in the center—you carry a bit of it with you now—and a hand crank on top to make it turn. The thing wasn't even clean.

"Fernley crouched down next to your mother and said, in his phoniest voice, 'Hello, honeybun!'

"Your mother popped open her eyes.

"Fernley was astonished. Your mother said, 'Hello, *Fern!*' Then she pulled the knife out and plunged it into his stomach. She looked right at him while she did it. Then she sliced upward with the blade—like she was . . . I don't know. Like she was looking for his heart.

"The surgeon rushed forward. It was almost comic. He slipped on the ice that I'd scattered on the floor, and fell. I don't know if he could have done us any harm at that point, but I was so crazed with anger and fear that I picked up the drill, and bashed him across the mouth. Your mother begged me to stop—she didn't want me to go to jail, too—but I couldn't. I beat the surgeon until he was dead."

Maud fell quiet, like she was waiting for the memory of the murders to dissolve.

"We laid the bodies in the surgeon's own buggy, one on top of the other, and burned everything in the woods," she said finally. "Afterward, your mother said, 'It's done. It's done, and I am not sorry.' We went back to the house. She picked up a piece of the porcelain pitcher and the tip of the drill bit to save. We scrubbed the bedroom. The ice had melted and turned the blood on the floor pink.

"And then it seemed to be over. Your mother sold the house, and we moved to town. The local gossips had two theories. One was that Fernley and the surgeon had fled the state to escape creditors. The other was that they fled to get away from their wives. I doubt the sheriff even spent an hour investigating."

JUST AHEAD, THE TUNNEL divided into three. As the men clustered around, Maud repeated what X's mother had said.

It's done, and I am not sorry.

"I'm not sorry either," she said. "I hear how terrible that sounds, but I don't care." She looked at Regent. "Not being sorry," she said. "It's one of the reasons we were damned, isn't it?"

"It is," said Regent. He seemed to regret the answer. "You were unrepentant and unpunished. Each time I send a bounty hunter up to the world for a soul, I use those very words."

"Yet who could feel sorry for ridding the earth of such men?" said X. "My mother deserved a better life. As did you, Maud. *As did you.* Instead she was chained to a vile man. And when she declines to be his victim, what is her reward? She is damned! The lords send a bounty hunter to stop her breath and drag her here!" He knew he shouldn't say the words that were crowding his head now, but he couldn't hold them back. "And the one who took her life was *you*, Regent. Of all people, it was you."

Regent surprised him by nodding.

"Yes," he said. "I have grieved over my role more than you can imagine. It helps me to remember that your mother did eventually find love. She found it, and—because neither Fernley nor even the Lowlands had extinguished her sense of her own worth—she knew she had a right to it."

"Why have you never told me anything about my father?" said X. "I do not for a *moment* believe you know nothing."

"I know one thing about your father, and it is a small thing," said Regent. "I will not share it, for I cannot predict its effect on you."

"I am tired—*very* tired—of being controlled," said X. "It appears I am like my mother, and I will not apologize for it."

He stalked down the tunnel to get away from Regent. Even Maud knew not to follow.

"I know your father's name," Regent called after him. "Nothing more. And I swear to you, it is just a name, no more memorable than any other."

X turned back.

"Speak it!" he said. "Speak my father's name!"

Even Maud and the Ukrainian leaned in, waiting.

Regent closed his eyes.

"Timothy Ward," he said.

X understood in an instant why the lord had withheld the name so long. The others seemed to know as well.

"That is not a name from the Lowlands," said X.

Silence spread, like water seeking out every empty space.

"No," said Regent, "it is not."

X looked down at his battered boots to steady himself.

"My father is still alive," he said.

"Yes," said Regent.

"Is he . . . Is he an innocent, then?" said X.

"Yes," said Regent. His voice warmed. "Like his son."

The lord paused.

"I see that your thoughts are wheeling," he said. "Your father cannot help your mother, nor can he help you escape the Lowlands. Your father does not even know that the Lowlands exist."

"What if—" said X.

"No," said Regent.

"Can I not even complete a sentence?" said X.

"There's no need," said Regent. "I have known you every moment of your life. Do you imagine I'm uncertain as to what you will say next? I *cannot* send you to the Overworld to find your father. You have broken too many laws, and the retribution from Dervish and the others would be catastrophic. I am sorry. You cannot look in your father's face, nor grasp his hand."

"No, I cannot," said X. "I know that. Yet there is a girl up there who loves me—and who *can*."

part three

A Sudden Leap

sixteen

ZOE'S PHONE VIBRATED ON the windowsill, like a pair of windup teeth.

It was a text from Val.

On my way. Give me 10. Do NOT text back bc I'll be DRIVING. Texting while driving is hazardous to my beauty. I WILL NOT endanger my beauty for you.

It was April. Friday night. It'd been a little more than a week since Ripper came and went, since Zoe and X met on the dock. Val and Dallas had spent the days in shock over what they had learned about X and the Lowlands. It was as if they'd stumbled away from a plane crash in a cornfield. Then, a few days ago, Zoe's friends seemed to come back to life. They pummeled her with questions. Texts flew between them like arrows in the sky in a movie about the Middle Ages.

Zoe's friends wanted her to promise she'd never see X again. She refused. She said she'd be lying if she agreed. Already, she was letting her mother believe it was all over, though she desperately hoped it wasn't. She wouldn't lie to her best friends, too. Val was angry. Dallas seemed . . . mopey. Zoe assumed it was a drag to find out that the girl you'd made out with in the handicapped bathroom at Walmart—Zoe was positive that it had been Walmart—had graduated to a bounty hunter from the underworld. How could you *not* feel insecure?

Today, for the first time, there seemed to be a calm in the air. Dallas had texted to say that there was something he wanted to do tonight but he wouldn't tell them what it was. Val grudgingly agreed to go. Zoe was so sick of being inside her own head—so sick of wanting to help X but having absolutely no idea how—that she would have agreed to anything.

YES YES YES! she texted back. *I am DYING to do the thing you won't tell me! Can we do something I won't tell YOU after??*

Zoe was camped out on the bed in her weird bedroom at Rufus's house, and waiting for Val to pick her up. Technically, she was reading a novel for English, but she couldn't remember the main character's name or why the main character thought that her Big Plan (Zoe couldn't remember what it was) was a good idea when it obviously wasn't. (Or was it? She couldn't remember that either.) Really, Zoe was hiding until it was time to go—not from anything in particular but from everything in general, from the overwhelming evidence of life moving forward without X, which she refused to accept.

She could hear Rufus and her family beyond the door. Uhura had gotten sicker and thinner, like something was eating away at her from inside. She never moved from one particular spot on the living room rug unless they carried her. Jonah was with her every second. So was Spock, who was making his awful wincing sound, confused about why Uhura didn't want to play.

They were only going to live with Rufus a little while. Bert and Betty had left the Bissells their A-frame house by the lake in their will. Once the place had been emptied and cleaned, Zoe's family would move in. As for the Bissells' former home on the mountain, it was still rubble—a milk carton that some kid had crushed with his sneaker. The insurance money would be slow in coming, if it came at all, because the house had been wrecked by a supernatural storm for which there was no earthly explanation or evidence. State Farm ordinarily covered that kind of destruction as an "Act of God." Zoe's mom thought it best not to tell them what it had *actually* been.

Rufus had been fantastically welcoming to the Bissells. In deference to Zoe's mom, he removed every non-vegan item from the kitchen—which left tea bags, ketchup, and soy sauce. He bought them down comforters so soft that they seemed to sigh when you lay down and cotton sheets in colors he thought they'd like, based on the clothes they wore. (Zoe got purple, which would not have been her first choice, but still.) Zoe's mom slept in the main bedroom, Zoe in the small one. Jonah and the dogs resided in the living room in a complicated pillow fort that was constantly falling down. Every morning, Jonah lay on his stomach next to Uhura, eating breakfast and begging her to eat, too. Whenever Zoe passed by, she'd pet Uhura without quite looking at her. It hurt too much.

Rufus himself had moved into the sagging, moss-roofed shed in the backyard, where he made his chain-saw sculptures of bears. He still didn't know the truth about X, the lords, the Lowlands, any of it. He saw that Zoe's family was traumatized, and didn't bug them for answers. "I'm just goin' with flowin'," he said. Rufus slept in a red sleeping bag atop a folding plastic lounge chair from Home Depot. He had his electric guitar in there (it was covered with skateboard stickers from when he was a teenager) and a tiny amp. He had three space heaters arranged like a futuristic city; a stack of books about stuff like the souls of trees; and a mini fridge he called "my secret shame" because it was packed with Swiss Miss chocolate pudding and Dr Pepper.

Jonah had caught the kindness virus from Rufus. A week ago, he'd secretly given Zoe's room a makeover. He had taken everything that had been recovered from the house on the mountain, and tried to re-create her old bedroom so that she'd feel more at home at Rufus's. It was a sweet thing for the bug to have done.

But seriously, the room looked insane.

Zoe gazed around now, and saw crumpled posters, and beaten-up furniture, all of it placed carefully in the old configuration. Zoe had collected trophies from thrift stores for years because she thought it was hilarious that there were awards for so many ridiculous things. The few trophies that had survived congregated on a shelf by the door. Most were busted and chipped. (The Best Donut award that Val had once given her no longer even had a donut.) The college brochures Zoe had gotten in what seemed like another lifetime sat in a pile on her desk, untouched. If she was going to apply to college—if—it would have to wait another year. Zoe's mother couldn't even begin to afford tuition now, and what was Zoe supposed to study anyway? Every possibility felt pointless and unreal. *Hi, I'm Zoe. I'm in love with a guy named X, and I study web design.*

At the foot of the bed, Jonah had taped (with an unnecessarily big piece of gray duct tape) what used to be Zoe's favorite photo: her and her dad in their wobbly caving helmets and their mud-spattered jumpsuits. It infuriated her to look at the thing. Still, she couldn't take it down because she couldn't tell Jonah that their father disgusted her. When Zoe thought about her childhood now, it was as if everything beneath her—everything she thought was supporting her, everything she was building on—had been erased and she was suddenly standing in midair and about to fall. So the picture stayed where it was, needling Zoe with memories of a time she hoped to forget. Fittingly, it was torn down the middle.

Though Jonah had tried valiantly, Zoe's belongings didn't belong in this new space—they didn't even fit, because Zoe's room at Rufus's was smaller than her room on the mountain. The mangled remnants from her past life crowded in on her here. She sat on her bed a while longer, repeating the sentence *This is my life* in her head. No matter how many times she said it, it still sounded like a question.

It had been seven minutes since Val texted saying she'd be there in ten. Zoe decided she could handle three minutes of family time before escaping into the night. She shut the novel about the woman with some sort of plan, and dropped it to the floor.

THE LIVING ROOM WAS a museum of sadness, as she knew it would be. Jonah and Uhura lay facing each other in the pillow fort, like they were having the world's most depressing staring contest. Mist from a humidifier hung over them.

Zoe's mom wanted to put Spock outside because he wouldn't stop whining, but Jonah had forbidden it. He said that whimpering was Spock's way of being scared and that everyone was allowed to have their own way of being scared. It was so much like something their mom would say that their mom couldn't argue. Zoe waved their mother out of the room.

"I got this," she said.

"You sure?" said her mother.

"No, but you definitely *don't* got this," said Zoe.

Her mom retreated into the kitchen, and Zoe sank to the carpet. She could tell Jonah had been crying. He confirmed this by tilting his pink face toward her suspiciously and saying, "I haven't been crying."

"I know, bug," said Zoe.

She petted his hair while he stroked Uhura's fur, a little chain of love. Jonah's hair hadn't been cut in months. It curled around his ears in hooks.

"How come I'm the only one not getting any sweetness?" said Zoe, trying to coax Jonah out of his mood.

"It's not your turn," said Jonah. "Your turn is later."

"How will I know when it's my turn?" said Zoe.

"I'll tell you," said Jonah. "I keep track."

Jonah nudged Uhura's water bowl toward her nose. He'd made it for her at a pottery place back when the Wallaces were alive and the dogs belonged to them. The bowl was lumpy and yellow, as if it had melted in the sun. On the side, in blue letters, Jonah had painted, *ThrstY?*

"Come on, girl," he said. "Drink."

Uhura wouldn't drink, wouldn't raise her head. It was unclear to Zoe if she even saw the bowl. Zoe felt like she should say something wise and big-sisterly—start preparing Jonah for the worst. But she couldn't do it. Bug had already seen enough of the worst.

Jonah scooped water from the bowl with his hands, and offered it to Uhura. She drank a little. Jonah beamed.

"Boom!" he said. "Woot!"

"'Boom'?" said Zoe. "Have you been texting with Dallas? Dallas words are not normal words."

"I *like* Dallas words," said Jonah. "Ooh, her tongue feels sandy!"

Uhura drank two handfuls, then lowered her head again, exhausted. She'd barely had a quarter of a cup of water, but at least it was something—and Jonah looked relieved.

"Why are you always in your room?" he asked Zoe. "Are you being sad about X?"

Zoe wasn't expecting this. She felt an invisible finger poking at her chocolate Easter bunny heart.

"I am always in my room because I *love* my room now," she said. "You are an awesome interior decorator."

"Thank you," said Jonah. "I think so also." He paused. Zoe could never tell where his mind was going to go. "I wish I could text X, like I text Dallas," he said. "I can't, right? Because he doesn't have a phone?"

"No, bug," she said. "He doesn't have a phone."

"I could send him cool memes," said Jonah.

"I know you could," said Zoe.

"What would *you* send him?" said Jonah.

Zoe answered without thinking.

"Myself," she said.

Her phone pulsed. She knew it'd be Val, and that her text would say, *I'm here! Where are you! Let's go!* Val always texted that *before* she actually got there because she hated waiting.

Zoe checked the text to be sure. It was a minor variation: *I'm outside. Come on come on come on! WTF?*

She went and peered through the stiff, beige living room curtains.

Val was not, in fact, there.

Zoe texted her back: *Your car must be REALLY REALLY small because I can't see it.*

She let the curtains fall closed.

"Bug, you haven't talked to anyone about X, right?" she said. "I mean, about where he's from and what he can do? Not even Rufus?"

"Nobody but you and Mom," said Jonah. "Well, also Dallas."

"Dallas is okay to talk to," said Zoe. "And Val."

"Val and I don't talk, we just send each other poop emojis," said Jonah. "She's even grosser than me—and I'm in third grade." He thought for a moment. "Isn't it mean not to tell Rufus, though? Because he lets us live here? And he would tell *us*?"

It was a good point. Zoe couldn't imagine it not coming out somehow anyway. They were a family of blurters.

"Maybe Mom can think of a way to explain it to him," she said.

"Yeah," said Jonah, "she's good at explaining. It's one of her best things."

"But you and I aren't going to say anything, okay?" said Zoe. "It might freak him out. It might make him worry about us."

"Do *you* worry about us?" said Jonah.

A lock of his hair had sprung loose. Zoe hooked it back behind his ear.

"Nah," she said.

Her phone buzzed again.

OK, actually here now. Waving. Come out come out wherever you are.

Zoe kissed Jonah on the top of the head, and ruffled his hair. When she parted the curtains again, she had to laugh: Val still wasn't there.

VAL NEVER LIED MORE than twice about being there when she wasn't actually there. Zoe went to the kitchen, where Mom was teaching Rufus how to make nut milk, and Rufus, whose crush was clearly off the charts now, was doing an Oscar-caliber performance of pretending to be interested.

Her mom always brightened when she got to play vegan missionary. She looked pretty, Zoe thought. Hair up in a haphazard knot. Turquoise earrings. No makeup. She looked happy. How often had her mother looked *happy* over the last six months? Over the last six years, even? Zoe felt one of those pangs that are half gratitude, half pain.

Rufus had spent the afternoon working in his shed, covered in sawdust. But he had showered and changed into a clean work shirt and jeans. He looked shiny and new. He looked—as he always did when he spent time with Zoe's mom—like a nervous boy on a date.

When Zoe's mother looked away from the blender, Rufus tried to sneak sugar into it. She caught him, and swatted his hand.

"Hey, Mom," said Zoe. "Hey, Rufus."

"Hey, Zo, what's shaking?"

He'd never called her Zo before. He seemed not to know if he was allowed to. Zoe nodded infinitesimally to let him know it was okay.

"Mom's showing you how to make nut milk?" she said.

"Almond milk," her mother said.

"Awesome," said Zoe. "Almond milk is the best. *All* the kids love almond milk."

"Rad," said Rufus. "What's it taste like?"

"Oh, you know—paint," said Zoe.

"Ahem," said her mother. "Humans are the only—literally the *only*—species to drink the milk of another species. Think about that. It's like a sick science fiction movie."

"I could drink Red Bull instead," said Zoe. "But that's from bulls."

Her phone pulsed yet again. She could see Val's blue Jeep through Rufus's not-very-clean kitchen window. Val was parked by the giant hole that X had punched into the road.

"Before you go," said Zoe's mother, "how does Jonah seem to you?"

"He's all right," said Zoe, "but if Uhura dies—or we have to put her down—it's gonna squash him."

"It is," her mom said. "It really is. And we've all been squashed enough."

"I could talk to him, bro to bro," said Rufus. "If you want? He's always giving *me* advice about stuff. I could find a way to bring it up? I can be pretty slick."

"You can, huh?" said Zoe's mom. "Let me think about it." She turned to Zoe. "What are you and your friends doing tonight?"

"Teenager things," said Zoe.

"I used to do some *epic* teenager things, man," said Rufus wistfully. "Until I was about thirty."

"I need more information, Zoe," said her mother.

"Dallas has a plan, but he hasn't declassified it yet," said Zoe. "I'll tell you when I know. But I'm sure it's just a teenager thing."

"Okay, repeat after me," said her mom. *"I will keep my phone charged, and answer all my mother's texts promptly—with words, not emojis."*

"I will keep my phone charged, and answer all my mother's texts promptly—with words, not emojis," said Zoe.

"I will be back by 11 p.m.," her mother said. *"I will not take uncool or unnecessary risks. I will remember that I have a family that loves me and supports me and cannot function without me."*

"Yeah, I'm not repeating all that," said Zoe.

"As long as you heard me," said her mother.

Zoe hugged her mom, then shoved Rufus playfully by way of good-bye.

"No uncool or unnecessary risks!" her mom shouted.

But Zoe was already out the door.

seventeen

TRUTHFULLY, JUST LETTING VAL drive was an unnecessary risk. Val rarely used the side- or rearview mirrors—she seemed to think they were decorations—and merged into traffic not when it was safe but when she was sick of waiting. She drove in the middle of the road, with the yellow lines shooting under the car. She drove like an apocalyptic virus had broken out and she had to deliver the antidote to scientists within 12 minutes. This had become a running joke. Often, when Zoe begged, begged, *begged* her to slow down, Val would shout, "But the scientists!"

They took Highway 93 toward House of Huns, where Dallas was finishing a shift on the grill. It was seven in the evening. It had rained, and the blacktop looked silver in the headlights. Off to the right, the sun was lowering behind the mountains, like it was the end of a movie.

Dallas had quit House of Huns with a strongly worded text because King Rugila, who was actually named Sandy, had refused to let him out of work to go caving with Zoe. It turned out, however, that *many* middle-aged moms took their kids to the restaurant specifically because they thought Dallas was adorable, particularly when cooking shirtless, his pecs crisscrossed with leather straps. Eighteen mothers cosigned a complaint to King Rugila's boss, who was called Attila, though his name was Todd. Attila begged Dallas to come back—which he did, after demanding that he be promoted and called Mundzuc.

Zoe and Val were greeted at the door by the banging of a gong the size of a small pizza and a chant of *Furg! Mrgh! Furg!* from the cooks at the grill. Hailing customers as they came in was one of Dallas's "new initiatives." He'd also asked the cooks to think up backstories for their characters; to get serious about chest-hair grooming ("Some of you are already doing solid work, and that's *awesome*"); and to grow long, droopy, barbarian mustaches, or buy fake ones.

Dallas had changed into a red Grizzlies T-shirt, jeans, and a battered Carhartt jacket, but was still wearing his pointy, fur-rimmed Hun hat. He looked cute and slightly ridiculous, which Zoe had always thought was a good look for him.

"How are the 'new initiatives' going?" she asked.

Dallas sagged.

"There's been negativity," he said. "Like, somebody just poked me in the butt with a spear, and *nobody* would tell me who did it. But these guys are gonna be Huns when I'm finished with them—or, I swear to god, they can all go work at the yogurt place."

Dallas nodded *what's up?* to Val.

"I know Zoe's too cool to eat here, but you want me to cook you something before we roll?" he said.

Zoe and Val peered over Dallas's shoulder at the donut-shaped grill. It was a battlefield of unrecognizable foods, most of it frozen and sickly pink. A cook's fake mustache had fallen off, and he was trying to pick it out from a nest of sizzling soba noodles with his fingers.

"No, thank you," Val said sweetly. "I'd rather you pressed my face against the grill."

"The *hater* thing is old," said Dallas.

"I'm sticking with it," said Val. "Because I believe in it."

Zoe was relieved that the two of them were sparring again, rather than ganging up against her about X. Order had returned to their little solar system.

"When are you going to tell us where we're going tonight?" said Zoe.

"Soonish, Zo," said Dallas. "Soonish."

He removed his Hun hat, and tossed it to the cook, who was trying to reapply his fake mustache.

"*Neg khatai bugdiig, mur!*" Dallas told him.

"Mundzuc, come on, I have no idea what that means," said the cook.

"It means—" Dallas shook his head, disappointed. "It just means be careful with my hat."

DALLAS ASKED VAL IF they could make a pit stop at a gas station. He ducked inside, and came out with a half gallon of Sprite and a plastic bag full of Pop-Tarts, Funyuns, and Flamin' Hot Cheetos. He told Val to turn right onto 93.

"A clue!" said Zoe. "We're going somewhere . . . north."

They passed the rifle manufacturer, the Flathead Valley Cowboy Church, the lonely fields still waking up from winter. As always when the three of them were in a car, they couldn't play the radio without serious warfare—Zoe loved country, Val was obsessed with pop, and Dallas only listened to hip-hop—so they rode in silence. Zoe could feel Dallas grow tense in the backseat. He was not an anxious person, generally. Whatever they were going to do was making him nervous.

"You okay?" she said. "You wanna rap for us?"

"No, but thank you for recognizing my artistry," said Dallas. "I'm okay."

He clearly wasn't.

"Do you want *me* to rap?" said Zoe.

Dallas laughed.

"No, but I bet you'd crush it, dawg," he said. "You'd sling the straight shit."

"Yes," said Zoe. "Yes, I *would* sling the straight shit."

She reached back and shoved him playfully, like she'd shoved Rufus. She decided that this was going to be the new way she interacted with people she liked. Why not? It'd worked when she was 12. She felt lucky that even though she had lost so much over the winter, there were still a lot of good people she wanted to shove.

"If you don't want to tell us where we're going," she said, "what if you just told us why we need Funyuns?"

It was getting dark. They passed the car dealership, where hundreds of windshields glinted in the last light.

Dallas leaned forward from the backseat.

"Okay, listen, don't say anything until I'm finished," he said. "We're going to the mountain."

"I don't have skis," said Val. "Plus, the ski season ended yesterday, didn't it?"

"Wait until he's finished, Val," said Zoe. "Did you not hear the instructions? There was only *one*!"

"And the reason I don't have skis is that I *don't ski*, and will *never* ski," said Val. "But I'm here for the Funyuns, so keep going."

"You're so much like me," Zoe told her, "but with, like, *more* of me added."

"That's sweet," said Val. "Dallas, I'm sorry I interrupted."

"I'm gonna say this fast," said Dallas. "Yes, the ski season's over, but they're letting people ride the chairlifts while they do maintenance, and Mingyu is working the lifts—and I'm gonna ask her out."

"Wow," said Val.

"Boom!" said Zoe. "Woot!"

"I need you guys to be my . . . my wing-people or -persons, or whatever," said Dallas. "Val, I know you're gonna want to make fun of me, but please don't. Okay, dude?"

"I won't, dude-dawg," said Val. "I like Mingyu. She's weird and not that pleasant."

"Right?" said Dallas. "I love that about her."

"I mean, that band she's in is—is *horrible*," said Val. "I'm kind of obsessed with them. When everybody ran out of that dance screaming last year, me and Gloria stayed."

"Look, she could tell me no," said Dallas. He lifted the bag of junk food. "If she does, I'm eating all this myself."

"She's gonna say yes," said Zoe. "We've been calling her The Girl Who's Gonna Say Yes for months."

"Yeah, please never, ever tell her I called her that," said Dallas.

"I'm proud of you," said Zoe. "I wasn't sure you'd ever do this."

"I was positive you wouldn't," said Val.

"It's just that Val has Gloria—who I'm bummed isn't here, by the way," said Dallas.

"Thank you," said Val. "Me, too."

"And, Zoe, you've got this *hell* guy," said Dallas. "I know you don't want me waiting around. And I told myself I *wasn't* waiting around, but now I think maybe I was." He paused. "I really like Mingyu. And if she's not, like, put off by my being kind of a stud—which honestly isn't even under my control—I think she might like me."

"She will," said Zoe.

"She definitely will," said Val.

Val even reached back to high-five him, though since she was facing the wrong direction, it took her awhile to find his hand.

ZOE WAVED TO MINGYU when they spotted her at the bottom of the lift. It was a weird thing to do because they weren't really friends with her, but Zoe was excited and couldn't help herself. Confused, Mingyu frowned, and looked behind her to see who Zoe was waving at.

Dallas was jittery. He wanted to ride the lift awhile so he could figure out exactly what he was going to say to The Girl Who Was Hopefully, Probably Gonna Say Yes.

The three of them trudged up to the lift, and a volley of "hey"s pinged all around. Mingyu was dressed in black, except for a screamingly pink beanie. Her bass, which she apparently played unplugged when there was no one in line, stood propped against the control shed. She looked neither happy nor unhappy to see them, which made Zoe nervous on Dallas's behalf.

"We love your band," said Zoe.

Val gave her a look: *WTF? You don't love her band! I love her band!*

"Thanks?" said Mingyu, looking skeptical. "Chairlift or gondola? It's gonna take a minute for a gondola."

"Gondola," Dallas said, too quickly. He turned to Zoe. "Slim Reaper doesn't care if people like them—they'd actually prefer it if people didn't." He turned back to Mingyu: "Right?"

Mingyu was impressed.

"Did you look at our website or something?" she said.

"Heck yeah, I looked at your website," said Dallas. His charm seemed to be functioning again, but then his nerves overtook him and he added, "I like . . . websites."

A gondola floated like a bubble down the slope. Mingyu saw the bag of junk food hanging from Dallas's hand.

"Please don't make a mess," she said. "Because then I have to clean it up."

"We won't," they promised, nearly in unison.

"Do you want a Pop-Tart?" said Dallas.

"Okay, yeah," said Mingyu. It sounded to Zoe like she wasn't going to say anything else, but then she said: "They should make black Pop-Tarts—and call them Goth-Tarts. They could be licorice-flavored."

"That sounds disgusting," said Dallas.

Mingyu smiled for the first time.

"*So* disgusting," she said.

"Dude, I would totally eat one," said Dallas.

"I would eat a whole box," said Mingyu.

* * *

Soon Zoe, Val, and Dallas were up in a gondola, the mountainside unscrolling beneath them.

"That went pretty good, right?" said Dallas.

Zoe and Val agreed that it had.

"I think she's gonna say yes when I ask her," said Dallas.

"When exactly are you going to ask her?" said Val.

"Soonish," said Dallas.

Zoe gazed out of their big bubble as they rose up the darkening mountain. It reminded her of the end of *Charlie and the Chocolate Factory*, where Charlie and Willy float over the city in a glass elevator. Dallas was so worried about making a mess in the gondola that every time a piece of litter hit the floor, he lunged for it and stuffed it in a pocket.

Zoe felt the tiniest twinge of jealousy about Dallas and Mingyu. It wasn't because she was worried about losing Dallas as a friend—she knew she wouldn't—but because she missed X. She felt like she was part of something that had been torn in half, like one side of her body was just a long, ragged tear.

She looked at Dallas and Val, and tried to focus on the conversation. Dallas was asking how exactly he should ask Mingyu out.

"I think you should say, really loudly, 'Mingyu, I *ship* us—and I don't care who knows it!'" said Val.

"Really?" said Dallas.

"Oh my god, no—do *not* say that," said Zoe. "Val's messing with you." She made a face at Val. "Stop being evil."

"But I'm evil," said Val.

Zoe faded from the conversation. She couldn't stop wondering where X was right that second.

Some lord was probably telling him that he was *nothing* and *no one.* X had believed that once. Zoe was afraid he'd believe it again. He'd told her about one of the lords. *Dervish.* That was his name. Gray skin. Pointy face like a rat's. He was the psycho who'd wrecked their house—the one who tried to kill Jonah. Now X was back in that hole, and at Dervish's mercy, probably. Should she have begged him not to go back?

Val and Dallas were staring because she hadn't spoken in so long.

"Where are you right now?" said Val.

"Who knows," said Zoe.

The gondola slowed as it reached the platform at the top of the mountain. Zoe opened the door and got out.

"I need to walk a little," she said. "Sorry."

She pushed the door shut before they could object. The gondola swung around the turnstile. As it descended the slope, Val knocked from inside and mouthed, *Are you okay?*

Zoe gestured back: *I'm fine! I'm fine!*

She wasn't.

SHE TRAMPED AWAY FROM the lift. Her boots were too thin for this much snow. The leather had started to darken. But she wanted to be alone, to be somewhere no one could see her. She peered into the deserted lodge: The chairs were upside down on the tables. A cue ball sat on the pool table, lonely as the moon.

She tried the door. Locked, of course.

A handwritten sign said, We Ain't Open. Find Something Else to Do with Your Life!

There was a small plateau so skiers could get to the northern slopes. It was abandoned now. Zoe trudged across, and gazed out. The sun was down, but night was still forming over the valley. The darkness was bleeding into everything, eating away at light and color like a science experiment.

She started down the slope. The snow gave way. Zoe plunged down until it was up to her knees. Instead of struggling, she looked out over the valley and screamed wordlessly. It felt freeing—like she was sending the black cloud in her chest out to join the rest of the darkness.

A hundred yards down on the slope, a flashlight clicked on.

The beam swung toward her.

Shit.

Zoe couldn't see a face. No shoulders, no shape. The glare grew stronger as whoever it was came closer. She didn't like having the thing aimed at her. She scrambled back up the slope, falling through the snow, climbing some more, then falling again. She could actually feel the beam growing hot on her back. Which was impossible. Or should have been.

She heard someone behind her.

It couldn't be X—he'd know that this would piss her off.

Screw it, she thought.

She turned and looked.

A man in blue robes came toward her. He was handsome, dark-skinned, taller than X even. The light was coming from his palms. He was still a hundred feet away when he spoke, but it was as if he whispered into her ear: "I am called Regent. Is my name known to you?"

"Yes," said Zoe, relieved. "You're the nice one. What do you want? You scared the *crap* out of me."

185

"Is this the manner in which you address everyone?" said Regent.

"Generally," said Zoe.

Regent gave the tiniest hint of a smile.

"We have business, you and I," he said.

He pointed to the lodge.

"I couldn't get in," said Zoe.

"Perhaps *I* can," said Regent.

They went to the door, and he dipped his hand through the glass as if it were a pool of water. Zoe followed him into the restaurant, which was only marginally warmer than the mountain. She felt along the walls for switches, but everything had been disconnected.

"The electricity's off," she said.

All Regent had to do was touch the sconces along the walls with his fingertips, and they glowed to life, giving off not just light but heat. The two of them sat at a wooden table, which was empty except for salt and pepper shakers, a container of sweetener packets, and an ad for a drink called a Powder Hound.

Regent looked too grand for the place, like a king in a kitchen. He accidentally set the legs of his chair down on his robe. It tore a little when he pulled up to the table.

Zoe took a Sweet'N Low from the container, and spun it on the tabletop.

"This is weird," she said.

Regent seemed to agree. His eyes caught the pool table.

"You know how to play?" said Zoe.

"I do not," he said. "My father had a billiards table among his possessions in Portugal, but it had hoops and ramps. There was even a small castle, in which one had to somehow deposit the ball."

"You're thinking of miniature golf," said Zoe.

Regent gave her a confused look.

"You're Portuguese?" said Zoe. "I assumed you were from Africa."

"You are not the first," said Regent. "I corrected people for a hundred and fifty years, then realized that I didn't especially care *what* they believed."

"Sorry," said Zoe. She spun the pink packet around. "Is X okay? Why are you here?"

"He is in no pain but for the pain of missing you," said Regent. "He begged to come here in my stead. I refused him, for every time I send him to the Overworld, chaos follows."

"I know," said Zoe. "Your friend Dervish tried to kill my brother."

"Dervish is no friend to me," said Regent. "And believe this or not as you like, but I knew Jonah to be safe when we brought down your house. As did Dervish. We're forbidden from taking the life of an innocent mortal. It is a lucky thing, for Dervish would have cut a bloody swath through the world by now."

"He threatened my family so many times," said Zoe. "He was *bluffing*?"

"Even I find him convincing," said Regent.

Zoe returned to her original question.

"I want to know about X," she said. "Did he find his mother?"

"Not yet," said Regent. "But the quest continues."

"He said you knew her," said Zoe. "Is that why you're helping him?"

"It is partly that, yes, and that is no small thing," said Regent. "If you had known Versailles—"

"That was her name?" said Zoe. "It's beautiful."

"She deserved it," said Regent.

"Were you in love with her?" said Zoe.

Regent pushed himself back from the table, tearing his robe again.

"You know, it *is* possible to wonder something without immediately blurting it out," he said.

"It is?" said Zoe. She took out some more sweetener packs and built a tower. "Were you in love with her?"

"No, as it happens, I was not," said Regent. "If you must know, my heart expired many years before *I* did."

"I don't understand that," said Zoe. "What does that mean?"

Regent exhaled.

"In my nineteenth year, my father hired a woman to plant black cherry trees in his vineyard," he said. "After two months, I announced that I loved her, for I was enormously vain and assumed that she loved me, too. I remember saying to my younger brother, 'How could she not be smitten, when it is I who am the smiter?'"

"Is 'smiter' really a word?" said Zoe.

"It was once," said Regent.

He went to the pool table, and bounced the cue ball off the cushions. The ball careened around the table without stopping or even slowing down. Regent dug into the pockets, and set three more going. The balls rushed by one another without colliding.

"What happened with the girl in the vineyard?" said Zoe.

"She chose my brother," Regent said. "So I killed him."

He crossed the room to the windows. The night had turned them into mirrors.

"I strangled him," he said. "Our mother screamed for me to stop. Servants came running, but no one could pull me off. My father could have, but he was elsewhere, as he often was. Testing grapes, probably." Regent paused. "Would you believe me if I said I loved my brother very much? I did. Yet in that moment I did not see my brother. I saw only a wall standing between myself and what I wanted."

He drifted back to Zoe.

"Have I explained the death of my heart sufficiently?" he said.

Zoe nodded.

"How long have you been carrying this guilt around on your back?" she said.

"Two hundred and seventy-eight years," said Regent.

"Dude," said Zoe, "put it *down*."

"I cannot," said Regent. "The weight on my back is now a part of my body. The point is, I loved someone once, too, and well remember how it sets everything in you on fire."

"Nothing feels real right now," said Zoe. "I can't sleep. I can't concentrate. People talk, and it takes me forever to figure out that they're actually talking *to me*."

"I remember the symptoms," said Regent. "And I believe I can alleviate yours a little by offering you a task. There is someone that X is desperate to find. If you can locate the man—perhaps talk to him a little—I believe it will soothe X greatly."

Regent asked for a piece of paper and a pen. Zoe found a magic marker behind the bar, and plucked the Find Something Else to Do with Your Life sign off the door so he could write a name on the back.

Regent's handwriting looked like an invitation to a wedding.

"This," he said, "is X's father."

ZOE BURST OUT OF the lodge, desperate to google the name.

She lifted her phone up high, hoping it would help her get a signal. It didn't.

Regent swept across the snow behind her, as she descended the

189

slope beneath the chairlift, first slowly and calmly, then not so slowly and not so calmly. The paper was rolled in her hand. She couldn't bear to fold it. The paper, the name, the handwriting—it all seemed sacred.

There were stars thrown across the sky, but otherwise darkness had descended completely, like a dome. She could barely see.

She called back to Regent.

"Thank you for this," she said. "For everything."

"X's father is closer than you may imagine," said Regent. "X's mother lived in these mountains and, when she became a lord, she would sometimes return just to lay her eyes upon them."

"She lived *here*?" said Zoe.

"Her entire life," said Regent. "She met Timothy Ward twenty years ago."

"I'll find him," said Zoe. "I bet I can find him *tonight*."

She looked up at the chairlift, watching for Val and Dallas. Empty chairs and gondolas creaked overhead.

"A word of caution," said Regent. "Mr. Ward is likely unaware that he has a son—and he is certainly unaware that his son was born into a darkness beyond life. Do not let word of the Lowlands pass your lips. If the father is anything like the son, he will go on some passionate quest, enrage the other lords, and never be safe again. Even now, this gold band singes my neck to warn me that I take a grave risk in trusting you."

"I understand," said Zoe. She gestured to the band. "Why don't you just take that thing off?"

"Because my powers would disappear if I did," said Regent. "And then Dervish and others like him would run riot."

Zoe heard Val calling for her.

Regent took her small, cold hands in his own. Warmth seeped through her.

"Be well and be safe, Zoe Bissell," said Regent.

"You, too, Mr. Regent," she said.

There was something else Zoe wanted to say, but she couldn't get it out. Regent turned away. He'd be gone in an instant.

"Will I get to tell X what his father is like?" said Zoe. "Will I get to bring X to meet him?"

The next sentence was the hardest to speak aloud. The words seemed to be sewn inside her.

"Will I ever see X again?"

"He believes you will," said Regent. "I am not so certain. I see no advantage in lying to you."

"Will you tell him I love him?" said Zoe. "Will you tell him that I'm *smitten*, and he's the smiter?"

"I shall use those very words," said Regent.

A thought seemed to occur to him. He glanced around, and his eyes fell on a steep white slope where a neighboring mountain rose above them.

"I shall leave you with a gift," Regent said. "Perhaps it will give you solace."

He lifted his palm toward the cliff face, and the snow began to glow. A movie played in the wilderness.

The movie was of X.

Zoe saw him as he was that very instant. He was resting against a rock wall in a tunnel, his face in his hands. Zoe pleaded silently for him to uncover his face, so she could see his eyes.

Val crunched toward her through the snow, shouting, "Are you okay? Are you hurt? Why are you making me endanger my beauty?!"

Zoe didn't answer.

Up on the snowy screen, X finally lifted his head, and seemed to look right at her. Zoe went still—her breath, her blood, everything.

She would find X's father. And she'd see X again—she had no idea how, but she was going to. It didn't matter that even Regent doubted it.

Val trekked down to Zoe, and plopped into the snow beside her.

"What are you looking at?" she said.

Zoe gestured toward the cliff.

"X," she said.

"There's nothing up there but snow," said Val. "You're losing it. How long have you been out here?"

Zoe realized then what Regent had done.

X was only for her.

DALLAS HAD GONE TO the bottom of the mountain to finally ask Mingyu out. Zoe and Val rode a chairlift down in the dark. Just the underside of the moon was lit. It dimmed and brightened, as clouds passed in front of it. Zoe bounced her knee impatiently, as if it would make the lift go faster. She didn't tell Val about X's father. She wasn't ready. When they got off the chair, she raced for the parking lot, where she knew she could get a signal. The slush was ankle-deep, and splattered her as she ran.

Zoe could only get the call to go through if she stood on the bumper of Val's Jeep. She pulled off her gloves, and tried typing "Timothy Ward Montana." Her nerves were a mess. She misspelled the name twice. On the third try, she got 459,000,000 results, most of which weren't even close, like *Tim Montana of Ward, Florida*. Zoe had to stop herself from flinging the phone.

But wait. There was an article, from the *Flathead Beacon*, about a wilderness biologist in Glacier National Park. The headline was "A Life Apart." The photo showed a fiftyish man in his living room, a sculpture of a grizzly at his side. Zoe recognized his shy smile from X.

Holy crap. There he was.

She heard footsteps, and looked up to see Val and Dallas coming across the lot.

"What'd she say?" she shouted. "WHAT DID MINGYU SAY?"

Dallas didn't answer. It couldn't be good.

Zoe jumped down from the bumper, and walked toward them.

"Tell me," she said.

They stood in the cold lot, wisps of vapor slipping out of their mouths, like they were smoking pipes.

"She said *maybe*," Dallas told her. "I didn't even know that was an option, but it's cool. I'm cool."

"Tell her about the lists," said Val.

"She wants a list of my five favorite books, albums, and TV shows—before she makes a decision," said Dallas. "It's like, I don't know, an application process? She was pretty hard-ass about it. I said, 'Come on, I gave you a Pop-Tart!' And she goes, 'I can't be bought with a Pop-Tart!' So I said, 'What about a Goth-Tart?' And she goes, 'Okay, *maybe* with a Goth-Tart.' That's good banter, right?"

"Totally solid," said Zoe.

She told them about Regent, about the sign that said Find Something Else to Do with Your Life, about the name that Regent had written on the back of it.

Their faces fell. The whole outdoors seemed to get chillier. Zoe looked at her phone. She recognized the sculpture of the grizzly now, too. It was one of Rufus's chain-saw things. It had to be.

"I bet this guy knows Rufus," she said. "Wouldn't that be amazing? What are the chances of that?"

"They're actually pretty good," Val said coldly. "There are, like, *nine* people in Montana."

Zoe knew Val was just worried about her.

"Let's go find this guy," she said.

"Slow down, dawg," said Dallas.

Zoe thought of the tattoo on Dallas's shoulder.

"Whatever happened to *Never don't stop!*?" she said.

"Come on, I was sixteen when I got that," he said. "Now I know there are consequences to stuff. You can't just go around never-don't-stopping all the time."

"I'm with Dallas," said Val. "You need to think this through."

"I *have*," said Zoe. "Now, I just need a ride."

She was sure they'd come around. She stepped back up on the bumper and texted her mom.

Gonna be later than I thought. 1 a.m. at least. Cool? Cool.

Her mother wrote back before Zoe could even get her phone into her pocket: *Wait what no! UNCOOL. This is NOT how we do things.*

How do we do things?? I'll send you a selfie to show you I'm OK and not high on meth. (Did you smoke all our meth, btw?)

The flash on the camera lit up the parking lot.

"Val can drop me off, and you two can go," said Dallas. "But I'm not into it. I'm sorry, Zoe. Old Dallas would have gone. But old Dallas was waiting around for you."

"I get it," said Zoe. "I'm happy about you and Mingyu. It's gonna happen. I know it is."

Her phone buzzed. It was her mother again.

We do things w/ INTENTIONALITY & FORETHOUGHT, Zo. This pic only tells me u r beautiful, which I already knew. I want u back here in 20 minutes.

No, mom. Sorry

Zoe looked at Val: "Please go to Glacier with me? I'm using my sweetest voice."

Another text from her mother: *NO? SORRY? Why are u behaving like this, Zo? Are u dehydrated? NO MORE BAD DECISIONS. Is Val with u? Val knows better than this.*

Crap. Now the phone was ringing, too.

Wait, mom!! Zoe texted. *Somebody's calling me.*

It was . . . Val.

"Oh my god, I've told you not to call me when I'm standing right here," said Zoe.

"Hang on a sec," said Val. "I'm on the phone."

"I'm not gonna answer," said Zoe. "Why are you so weird?"

"Huh, they're not answering," said Val. "I'll leave a message."

Val tilted her head back and forth in a tick-tock sort of way while waiting for the beep, then left the following message: *"I'll take you to Glacier because you've emotionally manipulated me, but just to be clear: you're making a mistake, and this whole thing sucks ass."*

Zoe went to hug her. Val wouldn't allow it.

When they got to Dallas's house, he told them to wait a minute. He opened the trunk of his 4Runner, in which lay a paradise of caving gear, and pulled out two orange backpacks. He gave one to Zoe and the other to Val.

"For Glacier," he said. "Just if you need it."

When Zoe asked what was in them, he said, "Survival shit."

She turned her pack around.

"I see," she said.

On the front of the backpack, in thick block letters, Dallas had written, *SURVIVAL SH*T*. On the front of Val's, he'd written, *MORE SURVIVAL SH*T*. The asterisks made Zoe smile. Dallas always worried about offending grown-ups.

"I need them back," he said. "I made them for me and Mingyu. I got ahead of myself, I guess."

Zoe and Val thanked him, and they backed out of his driveway. Val was still irritated, and turned on the pop station that Zoe hated. Zoe just stared down at the picture of Timothy Ward on her phone. She was going to meet X's father tonight.

Her mother wouldn't stop texting. The little *bzzt*s kept coming, like she was having a cavity filled. Zoe stuffed her phone into her coat. Every so often, it lit up angrily and made her pocket glow.

The last text she bothered to read was this one:

Zo? U there? PLEASE PLEASE think about what bad decisions have done to this family.

eighteen

VAL DROVE WORSE WHEN she was annoyed: even Mad Max would have pulled over and let her pass.

The road curled and uncurled as they wound down toward the valley. Val swerved, hit the brake, swerved again. Twice, Zoe felt the tires drop off the edge of the pavement and rumble over dirt. It made her jaw chatter.

"I'm gonna go ahead and deploy the air bag now," she said. "Just so it's ready."

Val took her eyes off the road—not that they were actually *on* the road—and glared at her.

"You're being a dick tonight," she said.

"I don't think I am," said Zoe.

"'I don't think I am,'" said Val. "That's a dick-ish thing to say." She pounded her fist on the steering wheel. "When Dallas and I both think something is a bad idea? It's a bad idea."

"Why are you so pissed?" said Zoe. "This is not even in the Top Ten of the stupidest things I've ever done."

"Glacier is going to be deserted and dark as shit," said Val. "And I'm not all woodsy and intrepid like you, Zoe. I like TV. I like doing Gloria's nails. I like *napping*."

"I like napping!"

"Oh, please. You *say* you like napping, but you don't—not like I do!"

A pair of nervous deer appeared at the edge of the road, looking to cross. Val barked, "Don't even!" and shot past them.

"You've been out of control since you met X," she told Zoe.

"Wow," said Zoe.

"You're telling lies right and left," said Val. "You've got me lying to Gloria, which I've never done. The first lie I ever told her was to protect you—*and* the second *and* the third. Now I've got to lie about where I'm going tonight. That's gonna be lie number four."

"I'm sorry," said Zoe.

"Lie number four!" said Val.

"I had no idea—" said Zoe.

"I know you didn't," said Val. "Because I'm your best friend and I *want* you to have all the cute boys and all the cake and soda you want. But you're dangerous to be around. Seriously, Zo. Have you noticed that your family doesn't even have a *house* anymore?"

"Okay," said Zoe. "Okay, okay, okay."

"Okay what?"

"Okay *stop*."

Everything Val had said was true. Zoe knew she should tell her to turn around, but couldn't make herself say the words. The car felt hot now. Claustrophobic. Zoe leaned forward to turn down the heat.

"I found somebody I love, and he loves me, too," said Zoe. "You know how hard that is?"

"I'm a lesbian in Montana—with blue hair," said Val. "Yeah, I know how hard it is, thanks." She paused. "I'm gonna say something now that's gonna piss you off. But honestly, I don't care."

"Say it," said Zoe. "Go."

"I think you fell in love so fast because a ton of bad shit had just happened to you," said Val.

Zoe stared at her.

"That's your genius theory?" she said.

"Yes," said Val. "Shut up."

"Okay, yeah, it's true," said Zoe. "I was messed up because of my dad and the Wallaces. Obviously. I fell for X faster than maybe I would have because I needed it more. *However.*"

"Here it comes," said Val.

"*However,* that doesn't mean I don't actually love him," said Zoe, "or that anything you say is going to make me stop."

She stared out the window as the trees flew past.

"I don't want you to stop," said Val. Her voice was quieter now—barely audible above the radio. "I didn't say that."

"It's just . . . ," said Zoe.

"It's just what?" said Val. "What is it just?"

"I know I'm being erratic," said Zoe. "I know I'm being selfish. But I'm in love with somebody I may not be able to see—or talk to, or touch—*ever again*. I've got a dog dying in the living room. I've got a father who lied to us forever and then just took off . . ."

"Plus you suck at Spanish," said Val. "I mean, if we're gonna whine about everything. In Spain, they'd put you in kindergarten."

"Yes," said Zoe, "there's that, too. So I need a win tonight. If all that happens is I meet Timothy Ward, and he reminds me a tiny bit of X, it'll help me breathe for a while. I know it sounds dumb."

"Okay," said Val. "Okay, okay, okay."

"Okay what?"

"Okay *stop*."

Zoe let out a sigh. The right side of the car slipped off the road for the third time.

"You still love me?" Zoe said.

Val jerked the car back onto the pavement.

"Ish," she said.

THE ROAD INTO GLACIER was slick and empty under the moon. Val leaned down to fiddle with the radio when her pop station started to disintegrate, and nearly plowed into one of the ticket booths. Zoe unzipped her Survival Sh*t backpack, pulled out a white helmet, and strapped it on.

"You're funny," Val said. "Actually, I want one, too."

Zoe unzipped More Survival Sh*t, and took out a second helmet. Val leaned toward the passenger seat as she drove, and Zoe set it on her friend's head like a crown.

The deeper they went into the park, the less they talked. Val drove more slowly, which was actually a bad sign: she was nervous. A light rain started to fall, then turned to hail. The hailstones were no bigger than the head of a pin, but the noise—the insistent pecking on the roof, the way it was amplified in the dead air of the car— unnerved Zoe.

"How *is* Gloria?" she said.

"Is this the part where you ask about me because you feel guilty?" said Val.

"Yes," said Zoe, "and the next part is the one where you forgive me."

"It is?" said Val. "Really? Remind me if I forget. Gloria's a mess. What do you expect me to say?"

Gloria's anxiety and depression had burrowed in deep when, years before, she told the foster family she was living with that she was gay. Her foster father called her a vile word, then skulked out of the room like she'd contaminated it. Her foster mother grabbed the nearest object—a pair of scissors—and hurled it at her. She missed, but had thrown the scissors so hard that they stuck in the wall.

Gloria was twelve at the time.

The foster family kicked her out. The caseworker who drove her away made her sit in the backseat, which was protocol but made Gloria feel like a criminal. She'd since lived five years with a family that embraced her without qualification, but she never, ever talked about being a foster kid. Skin had never grown over the wounds.

Now, in the car, Zoe said, "Shit, I'm sorry. Is it the depression?"

"It's everything," said Val. "Part of the reason she gets depressed is that she's exhausted from being so anxious all the time. If I text her constantly, I can usually get her out of bed for school. But, I mean, I've got to be like, 'Are you brushing your teeth? Send me a picture of you brushing your teeth.' And I can never get her to hang out with us. I mean, when was the last time you saw her?"

"I can't even remember," said Zoe. "I thought it was because you guys don't like Dallas."

"Gloria actually loves Hetero Norm," said Val. "She thinks he's sweet. Do *not* tell him that, I swear to god."

They drove along the Flathead River now, the road tracing the bends in the water. There was a cliff rising only feet from the passenger side of the car. Off to the left, Zoe could just make out the black river. It reminded her of being in the boat with X, which reminded her of X's father. She stole a look down at his picture.

"So we're done talking about me?" said Val. "That's all I get?"

"No," said Zoe. "Sorry. I want to hear more. Please."

The hail slowed, then seemed to disappear. Zoe hadn't realized how much the noise had jangled her nerves. But the minute Val clicked off the windshield wipers, the storm started up again—fiercer this time. It was like someone was dropping nails from the cliff.

"The depression makes Gloria hate herself," said Val. "She thinks she's no good. You know how obsessed I am with her, right?"

"Dude," said Zoe, "you made a Tumblr about her feet."

"Right?" said Val. "And it's got, like, a thousand followers! But she doesn't believe I love her. She doesn't see how I could."

"X is like that sometimes," said Zoe. "People have been telling him his whole life that he's not worth anything. I want to hit them with a brick until they're dead."

"Aren't they already dead?" said Val.

"Then more dead," said Zoe.

"I texted Gloria twenty-two times last night," said Val. "She didn't answer once. She was too depressed."

"You must have freaked," said Zoe.

"Ya think?" said Val.

Headlights materialized in the distance, a pair of bright eyes coming toward them. Zoe winced, remembering Ronny the Unhinged Hunter. Val drove closer to the cliff to be safe.

"This morning, Gloria called and said she'd been curled in a ball on the floor all night," Val said. "Slept in her clothes. Even her sneakers and her coat. I've seen her when she's like that. I've had to pick her up off the floor. This morning, she goes, 'If you need a different girlfriend, it's okay. I wouldn't want me either.'"

The oncoming car pulled over. Val fiddled with the wipers.

"If Gloria finds out I lied about where I am tonight, shit's gonna blow up," she said. "I can't give her another reason to hate herself, or think I don't love her."

The driver got out of his car, and tried to wave them down.

"He wants us to stop," said Zoe.

"No way," said Val. "Right? I'm not stopping. Not in the middle of the night, in the middle of nowhere. Not after that freak Ronny."

"Okay," said Zoe.

"What do you mean, 'okay'?" said Val. "Should I stop or not?"

"You said you weren't stopping! I'm just saying okay!"

The man was only an outline. He'd pulled his coat over his head to shield himself from the hail. As they got closer, he waved more urgently.

"I mean, anyone who's out here right now is nuts—including us," said Val.

Zoe could see her hands tighten on the wheel.

"Okay," she said.

"Stop saying that!" said Val. "I mean, would *you* stop?"

Zoe groaned.

"Probably?" she said. "But I make bad choices!"

"You *do* make bad choices," said Val. She nodded to herself. The white helmet jiggled on her head. She floored it past the other car. "I'm not stopping. No way. Sorry, creep."

They shot past the man, feeling too guilty to even look at him.

"Are we assholes?" said Val.

"Yeah, I'm pretty sure," said Zoe.

Soon, the road forked, and the dark, rippled surface of Lake McDonald came into view. It was just past ten o'clock. The black sky was streaked with blue, like something had been scratching at it.

Zoe saw lights glinting through the trees down by the lake. Houses. Timothy Ward lived in one of them.

They were close.

As they wound around the lake, Zoe reread the article about X's father. She liked him more every time she read the story. He was a wildlife biologist who studied and cared for the bear population in the park. It sounded as if it was the only job he'd ever had, or wanted, which Zoe found touching. She was also struck by the fact that he'd lived alone on a lake for many years. Solitude almost seemed to have been passed down from father to son.

Val hit the brake, and she and Zoe jerked forward in their seats. Val let out a string of profanity.

Startled, Zoe looked out the windshield.

There was something dead in the road.

nineteen

"WHAT THE HELL *IS* that?" said Val.

She was so unnerved that Zoe had to remind her to put the Jeep into park and switch on the hazard lights.

"Dead animals," said Zoe.

"What *kind* of dead animals?"

"I don't know. I can't tell from here."

"Well, I can't get around them. And I'm not driving over them. Screw this. We're going home."

"Wait. Just *wait*."

Zoe unbuckled her seat belt, and searched Dallas's backpacks. She found two powder-blue raincoats. She tried to hand one to Val.

"You're giving me that like you think I'm gonna get out of the car and look at dead things," Val said. "In what *universe*?"

She thrust the car into reverse so hurriedly that it landed in drive instead. The car lurched forward.

"Stop!" said Zoe.

She took Val's hand off the gearshift, and hugged her to calm her down. Their helmets clacked together.

"Stay here," said Zoe. "I'll check it out."

"No, no, no," said Val, each word a rising note. "We're going home. *Look* at those things. I draw the line at really obvious omens."

Zoe pulled a pair of work gloves from the backpack. They were the creepy kind with rubberized fingertips that look like they've been dipped in blood.

"I'm not going home," she said.

"Yeah, you are," said Val. "This does not have to happen tonight. Only *you* think it does."

Zoe pushed her door open.

"Go if you want to go," she said. "I won't be mad."

"*You* won't be mad?" said Val.

Zoe walked away before her friend could say more. Behind her, Val punched at the horn, and shouted, "You *suck*, Zoe Bissell."

But she didn't abandon her.

The animals were a mountain lion and a ram. They'd died in a bend of the road. On the right, the jagged, slate cliff rose into the darkness. On the left, the mountain tumbled precipitously down to the lake. Val's high beams were still on. The light shot past Zoe. The wet road looked like a shining snake.

The mountain lion lay on its side, its tawny fur wet, its body curled. It seemed to have died peacefully, but when Zoe stood over it, she saw a ring of blood, almost like lipstick, around its mouth. She wondered if it had been hit by a car—or accidently chased the ram off the cliff.

The ram's eyes were still open. It had died afraid. The poor beast's neck was twisted backward, its teeth were shattered, and one of its big spiraling horns had broken off. The larger section lay in the road ten feet away. All that was left on the animal's head was a stub like a devil's horn. It was coated with blood.

Zoe began dragging the mountain lion to the side of the road by its legs. She could feel how stiff it was, how dead.

From behind her came a gale of noise.

Val was leaning on the Jeep's horn, as if to say, *What are you DOING?*

When Zoe got the mountain lion into the weeds, she forced herself to look at it a last time. She felt a pang, like the cat was still alive, like she was deserting it and it knew. She shook off the thought, and went back for the ram.

It was too heavy. She grabbed a foreleg and a hind leg, but got nowhere. She pulled again, harder. Still nothing. She was on the verge of crying when she heard Val get out of the car.

Val had lowered her head to protect her from the hail, and thrust her hands into her raincoat. Zoe knew how much Val hated being there, knew how much she owed her, knew that nothing she could say would be adequate.

She took in Val's helmet and blue raincoat.

"Do you have to copy *everything* I wear?" she said.

Val didn't answer. She peered at the ram out of the corner of her eye, disgusted.

"Don't look at its face," said Zoe. "It's messed up. Just look at me."

They gripped the ram's legs, and dragged it toward the shoulder of the road. Val struggled not to look down. Her face trembled with the effort. When they'd been at it for a while, Zoe checked their progress, and saw that they were barely halfway there. They jerked the ram a little farther. It streaked the road with its blood.

Zoe could see that Val was angry. They had a conversation with their eyes.

VAL: *If I can't look down, YOU can't look down!*

ZOE: *I just had to see how close we are.*

VAL: *Are we close?*

ZOE: *Do you want me to lie?*

VAL: *OF COURSE I want you to lie!*

ZOE: *We're super-super close.*

VAL: *SHIT! I'm going to throw up.*

ZOE: *No, you're not. Just keep looking at me.*

VAL: *I hate you for making me do this.*

ZOE: *No, you don't.*

VAL: *No, I don't. But would you do this for ME?*

ZOE: *I would EAT this thing for you.*

VAL: *GROSS! Now I'm DEFINITELY gonna throw up.*

ZOE: *Ha!*

VAL: *Do you think we're close NOW? Don't look. If you look, I'm gonna look. Just tell me if we're close—and remember to lie.*

ZOE: *We're super-super close.*

VAL: *SHIT!*

They left the ram in the weeds with the mountain lion. Val tore off her rubber-tipped gloves and stalked away, recoiling when she saw the swoosh of blood in the road.

Halfway to the car, Val slipped on the hail—Zoe saw the sickening moment when both her feet were in the air—then crashed onto her back.

"I am *done*," she said. "I mean it. Are you coming with me or not?"

"We got them out of the road," said Zoe, helping her stand. "You want to give up *now*?"

"I wanted to give up a long time ago," said Val. "I am all about giving up! Are you *coming*."

She said it tensely, not bothering with a question mark.

Zoe knew Val was right: X's father could wait. She couldn't keep endangering people. She looked around, surprised by how far her obsessiveness had carried them. The hail was relentless. It bounced high off the road, like something boiling in a pot.

"Yes," she said. "I'm coming."

Val returned to the car. Zoe looked back at the ram's broken horn, which lay in the road, a spiral in the moonlight. It seemed wrong to leave it there. She went back for it.

The horn was oddly heavy. Its interior was hollow and slick with blood. There was something mythological about it, something malevolent. Zoe wished she'd never touched it. She walked to the roadside a final time, grimaced at the ram's frantic face, then set the horn down beside it, like a wreath. She was twenty feet from the car when Val pounded on the car horn again: four long blasts.

She looked at Val: *What?! I'm coming! I'm five feet away!*

But Val kept honking. Zoe slid her hands under her helmet to cover her ears.

Val pointed at her frantically. Zoe couldn't figure out why.

Then she realized Val was actually pointing *behind* her.

Zoe turned in her helmet and raincoat, slow as an astronaut. Only now did the honking cease. The world rushed back in to fill the silence. Zoe heard the hail, the wind, the sound of Val rushing out of the car to help her. Why did Val think she needed help?

The ram.

It was on its feet, and charging.

ZOE WASTED A HALF second wondering if it was a different ram. No, it had only one horn. The other was just a shattered stalk. She wasted another moment wondering if maybe the ram hadn't really been dead. No, she'd looked right at it. She'd seen the blood around its mouth.

She tried to tell herself she was safe from whatever darkness this was. Regent had said not even a lord could take an innocent life.

It was no comfort now.

The ram flew at her with its head down, like it was rutting season. Zoe turned toward it, and bent her knees to brace herself. She told herself the animal would swerve at the last second, but every time its hooves hit the ground she felt a jolt, as if it were running on top of her heart.

She crouched low, like a wrestler. She'd grab its horns, or what was left of them, and twist them toward the ground. That was what you were supposed to do if this happened—except that this was never supposed to happen. Rams *never* charged at humans.

She didn't have time for another thought.

The ram slammed into her stomach, and knocked her backward. She landed hard, couldn't breathe, couldn't stand up. It was like she'd been cracked open.

The animal ran at her again. Zoe reached for its horns. She couldn't get a grip on the busted one—it was too small, too slick with blood—but she grabbed the other and tried to twist the ram away from her, which infuriated it.

Zoe kept her head down so the helmet took most of the blows.

It was like the ram thought she'd stolen its other horn. The way it was raging, driving into her, bullying her backward—it was like the ram wanted its horn back.

Zoe kicked and flailed. She heard herself scream, preposterously, "I don't have it!"

But then Val got to her. Val was there. It was going to be okay. Val was bashing the ram with a backpack.

MORE SURVIVAL SH*T.

Zoe lifted her head—a mistake. The ram sliced her cheek open with its horn. The blood felt warm on her face.

Val struck the ram again and again. She was in a rage of her own. The backpack tore open, spilling out flashlights, protein bars, bandages, rope, a whole mess of things.

The animal gave up on Zoe—and turned on Val.

It knocked her to the pavement, pushing her toward the weeds and the steep slope beyond the road. Val was on her hands and knees, trying to crawl back to the car.

Zoe searched the pile from Dallas's backpack, hands shaking. She found a can of bear spray and a knife. The knife had a six-inch serrated blade, with a notch at the tip for gutting animals. Zoe put it in her raincoat. She'd use the bear spray if she could.

She rushed to Val. The storm had let up, but the road was speckled with hail. It looked incongruously festive, like a parade had just passed.

"I'm here," Zoe told Val. "I'm here, I'm here."

She grabbed the ram's horn, and tried to spin its head toward her so she could spray it in the eyes. The ram thrashed back and forth. It was obsessed with Val now and refused to turn.

Zoe tore around to the front of the animal, her boots nearly sliding out from under her. She'd try for its eyes one more time before resorting to the knife. She'd never stabbed anything, living or dead. It occurred to her that she didn't even know which the ram *was*.

The ram slammed Val's back with its forehead. Its horn got stuck in a rip in her raincoat. It yanked her up and down, trying to shake loose. Zoe couldn't get a clear shot at its eyes.

She drew the knife from her pocket, and stuck the animal in the side. She felt the blade pierce the hide, heard it sink into the flesh. It was a nauseating sound. Zoe knew, even then, that she wouldn't forget it.

The ram reared up in shock, and glared at her. It was in no danger of dying, Zoe could see that. But it looked at her with something like outrage—and she unloaded the pepper spray into its eyes.

The ram staggered away, the knife in its side like a lance in a bull. It vanished behind the car.

ZOE BENT OVER VAL, who lay in a fetal position. She tried to uncurl her, but Val was too afraid. She clenched more tightly at Zoe's touch. She wouldn't even let her unstrap her helmet.

"It's just me," Zoe said softly. "Just me."

Val answered in a shivering voice.

"Okay . . . Thank you . . . Okay."

It crushed Zoe to see Val shaking. She leaned down and put a palm against the shaved side of her head. Val's face was cut and bruised.

"Are you okay?" said Zoe. "I'm so friggin' sorry."

"Your cheek," said Val.

"Who cares. Can you get up?"

"I think so. Crap. My *back*."

"Go slow."

"The ram . . . How was—how was that thing alive? Is this more Lowlands shit?"

Zoe wished she didn't have to answer.

"Yeah," she said. "It has to be. But we're okay. We're safe. The Lowlands can't actually hurt us."

The statement seemed to trigger something in Val. She got to her feet, refusing Zoe's help and shouting, "WTF??"—only with the real words and several extra *F*'s.

"What do you mean, they can't 'actually' hurt us?" she demanded. "We are bleeding *actual* blood. What the hell is up with you?"

Zoe was about to answer, when she heard footsteps. She took a flashlight from the supplies littering the ground—Dallas, in his optimism, had already written *MINGYU* on it—and swept the road. She saw nothing. Still, she had the prickly sensation that someone was racing just ahead of the light. Taunting her. She made a faster circle, trying to catch up with them. Nothing. No one. There was a noise near the cliff. She jerked the flashlight back. She saw—

Dervish.

She'd never seen him before, but it had to be him. He was repulsive: fussily perfect white robes, tacky diamond jewelry, sunken cheeks, skin the sickly gray of meat that had been left on the counter for days. Zoe felt only fury when she looked at him. He had persecuted X relentlessly. He'd leveled her family's house while Jonah, terrified, hid in an empty freezer in the basement.

She told Val to stay where she was. She walked toward him. Whatever part of her brain was supposed to light up when she was in danger had been overtaxed for too long. The bulb had burned out.

"I know who you are," she said. "And I know you can't hurt us."

"Regent divulged that, did he?" said Dervish. "Along with being a traitor, he takes the fun out of nearly EVERYTHING. Yet ask yourself if you are absolutely certain that I won't kill you anyway, and deal with the consequences later. Do I SEEM predictable?"

He raised a hand and somehow deflected the flashlight beam away from his face, like his palm was a mirror.

"Why are you here?" said Zoe. "What do you want?"

She'd expected him to be furious, but he seemed . . . amused. Curious. Zoe could tell he was sizing her up, trying to understand how she could have inspired so much rebellion.

"Oh, I want so many things," said Dervish. "I shall begin with the most pressing: I want you to abandon your search for X's father."

"Why?" said Zoe. "Why do you care—except that you're dead and obviously a dick?"

"How brazen you are!" said Dervish. "What on earth are they teaching girls up here these days?"

He didn't seem to expect an answer.

"Science," said Zoe. "Core strength. How to stand up to assholes."

Dervish smiled. His mouth was practically lipless. It looked like it had been sliced into his face with a knife.

"You amuse me, Zoe Bissell," he said, "so I shall tell you why I won't let you find X's father. It's because it will jeopardize the secrecy of the Lowlands—and because I am MORTALLY sick of the trouble you cause. Shall I tell you something funny? You have already SEEN X's father. He stood in the storm begging for assistance. You and your mangy friend sailed past him without a care."

Zoe flinched: the man by the car.

"No clever reply?" said Dervish. "No riposte? Good. Listen to me, little girl. The more you encourage X, the more I shall make him suffer. It's simple physics: for every action, a reaction. As Sir Isaac would say, *Actioni contrariam* ... Actually, never mind. You don't strike me as someone who speaks Latin. I have made my point."

"X is innocent," said Zoe.

"I DO NOT CARE," said Dervish. "The Lowlands aren't a country estate. If one soul breaks its laws, a thousand others will follow suit. You have given X hope, which anyone can tell you is fatal. Was it you who inspired X's mad quest to find his mother? Does he believe that if he finds her you will love him more?"

Zoe meant to say nothing.

"He's doing it for himself," she said.

"Is he?" said Dervish. "Or is he doing it to impress YOU—to prove that he is worthy, that he is WHOLE? Now I must find him, and punish him just as I punished his mother. I must dump him into a hole inside a hole inside a hole—somewhere the light cannot find. All because you 'loved' him." He waited for a reply, and when Zoe didn't speak he added, "You were not as fierce an adversary as I had hoped. Go home, Zoe Bissell. You are not needed anymore."

Val crossed the road to lead Zoe back to the car. Dervish noticed her partially shaved head, and called out, "Was it lice?"

With a bored flick of a finger, he opened a portal to the Lowlands in the cliff. Zoe watched as it turned orange, then red, then orange again.

"Didn't *you* ever love anybody?" she said.

Dervish surprised her by answering.

"You expect me to say no," he said. "Yet I did. Not in the way you think. It ended tragically, as love of every kind always does. Believe this or not, but I am doing you and X a kindness."

Val tried to steer Zoe away but Zoe wouldn't turn from Dervish. Couldn't. The image of X in some hole, lonelier even than before she met him—she couldn't shake it.

Dervish seemed to know her thoughts.

"What you have done is impressive, in a way," he said. "You have taken someone whose life was already a misery and made it a hundredfold worse. X sacrificed what little he had for you. Tell me, what did YOU ever sacrifice for him?"

Dervish lit the far side of the road with a sweep of his hand.

The dead mountain lion rose up out of the weeds.

It shook the hail from its coat—it looked as though it were shedding stars—and slunk toward Zoe and Val, the black tip of its tail sweeping the ground.

"I must leave you," said Dervish, turning to the portal. "My friend here will see to it that you pursue X's father no further."

The mountain lion came slowly at first, its back undulating up and down, like its body was made of water.

"Get on my back," said Val. "Get on my back."

Zoe looked at her, bewildered.

A half second went by.

"What's wrong with you!" said Val. "Do it!"

Zoe climbed on her friend's back, as if she were riding piggyback, and only then did she understand: the way to scare off a predator was to make yourself *big*, to make yourself *loud*.

The mountain lion picked up speed. Its eyes shone green.

"Flap your coat!" said Val.

Zoe did as she was told, but even now, she was thinking about X and watching Dervish walk to the swirling hole in the cliff.

She felt herself wave her raincoat like wings. It was like someone else was doing it.

Dervish looked back at them, grinning.

He knew where X's mother was. He was going to dump X into a hole inside a hole. What had Zoe ever sacrificed?

Val wobbled beneath her. She screamed threats as the mountain lion charged: "GET AWAY! WE'RE NOT DEER! DO WE *LOOK* LIKE DEER?!"

Zoe heard herself start screaming, too. She didn't know what words she was using, or if they even *were* words.

Dervish was almost at the portal.

Val staggered beneath her, losing her balance. She was strong, but not much bigger than Zoe. They fell to the ground just as the mountain lion leaped.

Zoe felt a rush of air. She saw the cat's claws, the white fur of its belly.

The animal shot over their heads, and disappeared down the road.

Dervish had been bluffing. Zoe knew that now. The ram and the mountain lion had confirmed what Regent had said: the Lowlands could not kill her.

She threw off the helmet and raincoat and gloves.

"I'm going to be okay," she told Val. "Don't worry about me."

"What are you talking about?" said Val.

They were both winded, panting.

"Don't tell anybody where I am," said Zoe. "Make something up."

"What are you *talking* about?" said Val. "You're scaring me."

Dervish vanished into the hole in the cliff. The portal was orange.

Zoe sprinted across the road. Val shouted something at her, she didn't know what.

Zoe rushed through the portal after Dervish.

It had just gone red.

Up close, it looked like a ring of fire.

twenty

HER CLOTHES WERE DRENCHED when she woke. She had no memory of why. A Roman in a belted tunic carried her down a tunnel.

The pain in Zoe's head was ferocious. An electrical storm. She managed to focus on the Roman: He had big, watery eyes and a cloud of curly black hair. He had to be seven feet tall. His arms were like tree limbs, and he hummed nervously, tunelessly as he walked. When he noticed that Zoe was awake, he caught her eye, then looked away fast, like *she* was the scary one.

Twenty other guards marched behind them in military formation. Dervish was up ahead, leading the way. Zoe recognized his robe, his lurching walk, his snarled gray-white hair.

The tunnel itself was rough, like animals had burrowed it. It smelled repulsive. At first, Zoe thought that it was body odor—that it was the men—then she realized it was the air itself. Her lungs didn't want it. She covered her mouth with her arm, and took shallow breaths. The Roman saw her hyperventilating and smiled cautiously. He was trying to be reassuring, but his teeth were gray green, like tiny broken tombstones. She fought down a wave of panic.

When she was in fourth grade, Zoe tried to tunnel through a snowbank in front of her house. She wanted to impress her father, the caver. She wasn't going to show him her tunnel until it was done. It was a secret. When he saw it, he was going to clap like crazy, and say it was freakin' amazing. Zoe was in the yard by herself. When she made it to the middle of the snowbank, two things happened, one right after the other. The handle of her blue plastic shovel broke off—and the tunnel came down on top of her. There was a terrifying *whump*, followed by the scariest silence she'd ever heard. She couldn't move, couldn't breathe.

That's what she felt now, that fear exactly.

Her father had been who knows where, but her mom was watching from a window. She flew out of the house without even boots on. She clawed through the snow to get to her. Zoe cried when she felt her mother's hand on her foot.

But her mother wasn't coming now.

Noises filled the tunnel as the Roman carried her. Insects, crazed animals, human screams—they all leaked through the walls. Zoe's body twitched at every sound.

What the hell had she done.

EVERY TIME ZOE FLINCHED, the giant held her tighter. Repulsed as she was, she could tell he was trying to be kind.

She remembered leaping into the portal, remembered a free fall into darkness and a violent wind shooting past. She'd braced herself to hit bottom but the bottom kept not coming. Dervish had been falling just below her. He looked up, shocked by the sight of her. He grabbed her, pulled her down, wrapped her in his robes. She fought him, even though he seemed to be trying to protect her, the way X protected her when they zoomed. When she wouldn't stop resisting, he slid a clammy hand over her eyes—his fingernails were like claws—and she passed out.

Dervish hadn't looked at her once since she woke. He just stalked down the tunnel, turning back only to bark at his men to keep up. His face was so gaunt that it looked like a skull. He was furious—and that gave Zoe the first stirrings of hope.

He didn't want her here. She'd surprised him, pushed him off balance. Good. That gave her power.

Something else occurred to her now, something so small and ordinary that it took her a minute to realize its significance: her stomach was growling. She hadn't eaten since the Cheetos and Funyuns in the gondola. She was hungry. Here in the Lowlands.

Which meant she was alive.

Zoe told herself that the Lowlands were just a massive cave—and that she understood caves. She could do this. She could survive. She'd make friends with the man who was carrying her, if she could. He couldn't possibly be loyal to Dervish.

"What's your name?" she whispered.

He was shocked that she'd spoken. He closed his eyes, as if praying Dervish hadn't heard her.

But he had.

The lord spun around and clapped his hands against the Roman's ears. The man fell forward—it was like a tree coming down—but didn't drop Zoe, though it meant smashing his elbows against the ground.

"If she can talk," said Dervish, "she can walk."

The guard put Zoe down, his ears red from the blow. Zoe tried to apologize with her eyes but he was too skittish to look at her.

Zoe knew Dervish's rage was a good sign—he was unstable, he'd make mistakes—but now she'd alienated someone who might have helped her. The Roman walked in front of her, and she saw for the first time that he had a pair of iron rods hanging from the belt on his tunic. He rested his hands on them in a way Zoe found touching: it was as if he was playing sheriff and they were his guns.

She knew she shouldn't whisper anything else.

"I'm sorry," she told the back of his head.

His shoulders tensed.

But Dervish didn't turn.

"Do you have a name?" she said.

No response.

"I'm going to call you Tree," she said.

There was a long pause—but then he nodded, as if he approved.

"Where are we going?" she said.

Tree stiffened again. No answer. She'd pushed her luck.

Tree slid the iron rods from his belt. For a second, Zoe thought he'd hit her with them. Instead, he crossed them behind his back as they walked, as if to say:

X.

ZOE FOLLOWED DERVISH AND Tree through a dozen bends in the tunnel, the other guards marching behind. Soon, she lost track of time, like she did when she went caving. An hour slipped by, maybe two. There was no point of reference here, no sun—just torches flashing past every so often like streetlights.

Zoe was exhausted. She wasn't getting enough oxygen. And though she was dying to see X, a heavy feeling had settled into her chest, like her lungs were filling with water.

He'd be furious when he saw her—when he realized that she had endangered herself for him. What could she say in her defense, except that he'd have done the same thing for her? X wouldn't accept that as an excuse. He didn't believe his life was worth as much as hers.

THERE WAS A FUZZY glow up ahead, like a dandelion puff made of light. Zoe wondered if she was imagining it. But no: the tunnel brought them to a roundish cavern lit by phosphorescent rocks, which were piled like a campfire.

"Rest if you must," Dervish told his men, then began pacing around the false fire.

The air was clearer here, and a shining curtain of water flowed down the walls. Tree and the others laid down their weapons—a wrench, a whip, a chair leg, a brick—and pressed their foreheads against the wet rock to cool themselves. They seemed to have forgotten Zoe, or at least stopped worrying about her. Where, exactly, could she run to?

She pushed her way between the men, cupped her hands, and collected some water as it ran down the rock. The first handful she dabbed on her face and neck. The second she brought to her lips. Dervish watched as he circled. When Zoe went to drink, she saw him suck in his cheeks to suppress a smile.

"No!" said Tree.

It was the first time she'd heard his voice, which sounded young and frail. Tree came over from where he'd been resting. It was amazing how long it took a person that tall to stand.

"Not safe," he said, closing a giant hand around hers. "Not for you."

Zoe let the water spill to the floor, and thanked him with a look. Dervish exploded.

"YOU!" he shouted at Tree. "How many YEARS have I endured your weakness? Hand me one of your irons."

Dervish struck Tree across the face so fast that Zoe didn't even see the blow. Tree staggered back, his hand clasped to his cheek. He sat clumsily, drew his knees to his chest, and started to cry.

Dervish turned to Zoe.

"Anyone ELSE you would like to befriend?" he said.

Tree gave Zoe a look that said, *Please don't make this any worse.* So she said nothing.

"Tell me, WHY did you follow me here?" Dervish asked her. "Did you imagine that you would rescue X—perhaps by swinging over a pit of fire on a rope?"

Zoe ignored the question. She let a moment go by.

"You said *you* loved somebody once," she said. "Who was she?"

"It was not a *she*," said Dervish. "It was my son."

Zoe tried to hide her surprise.

"What was he like?" she said.

She thought maybe she could defuse his anger a little by asking.

Dervish pushed his mousy face closer to hers. She could see tiny white hairs sprouting from the giant pores on his cheek.

"Why do you inquire?" he said. "Does the answer truly interest you? Or do you imagine that talking about my son will awaken some dormant kindness in me, and inspire me to spare your beloved?"

Apparently, she hadn't been very subtle. She considered her answer.

"Honestly?" she said. "I don't think you've got anything left to awaken."

Dervish liked this.

"Well said," he told her.

Some of the fury, the rigidity, seemed to leave his body.

"My son was older than you by perhaps twelve years," he said. "His name was Pleasant. It sounds like a name from the Lowlands, but it is in fact what we called him. I loved the boy, as I have said and shall never deny. He did not love me. Pleasant suffered from great sea-changes of emotion, which he blamed on me. I tried in every way I could to bring him peace. I raised him in the countryside. I gave him a white stallion. A violin. The whole blue firmament. Yet whenever the storms gathered in his head, everything good and hopeful was swept away, and his hatred for me revived, like a serpent rising out of the sea."

Dervish turned to his men. The nearest had been listening, which annoyed him. He sent them away with a flick of his eyes.

"One night, during some particularly grievous hours for my son, I made the mistake of leaving him alone," he went on. "We had a brown-and-white spaniel named Flossie, and I had commissioned a portrait of her for Pleasant. I went to town to receive it. I thought it might elevate his spirits. I was gone perhaps an hour."

Here, it seemed to Zoe, the weight of the story began to show on Dervish's face.

"As I trod back to our door," he went on, "I saw Pleasant standing in a window on the second floor. He was shirtless, and holding a sword that used to decorate my study. He had been waiting for me. He took the sword out of its scabbard. I knew what he meant to do. I dropped the painting. I lifted my hands, begging him to be still until I could get into the house and up the stairs. Instead, he turned the sword on himself." Dervish paused. "He opened his OWN throat, he hated me so much." He stopped again. "Later, the doctor chastised me for not reaching Pleasant in time. He said he might have lived. I told him—well, first I refused to pay him—and then I said the coldest thing I could think of, which was, 'The damned boy has ruined the rug!' After that, I did not allow a single thing on earth into my heart. I committed all manner of crimes and abominations, and have never regretted it."

Even after everything Dervish had done to X and to her family, Zoe felt an urge to say she was sorry about his son. He must have seen the pity in her eyes. In an instant, he returned to his old, inhuman self, as if his reflective mood were a coat he had tried on and not liked.

A few of the guards had fallen asleep, and lay snoring.

"Rise, IMBECILES!" said Dervish.

The men woke, grunted, grabbed their weapons. Dervish gathered them around. He told them that according to his spies, X and Regent were on the way to a place called Where the Rivers End in the hopes of finding X's mother. Dervish said that a "serving wench" named Maudlin was with them—she had a cat, which Zoe found hard to process—as well as a Russian guard. Here, Tree interrupted Dervish to say that the guard was technically from Ukraine. The lord gave him a scalding stare.

Dervish informed the squad that they would reach Where the Rivers End before X and the others—and ambush and savage them. The way Dervish beamed in anticipation of the bloodshed (just moments after telling her the story about his son, no less) convinced

Zoe, more than anything else she had witnessed, that he was a psychopath.

Dervish finished his speech by crowing that X was looking in the wrong place for his mother, though he wasn't far off. The lord looked forward to telling him how "EXCRUCIATINGLY CLOSE" he had come to finding her. Dervish seemed not to care that Zoe was listening. He appeared to relish it, in fact. He was taunting her.

As the guards lined up two by two, Dervish gave Zoe one of his revolting, lipless smiles.

"You must wonder why I have not ALREADY sent you back to your world," he said. "It is because you are my greatest weapon. When X sees you, he will be shocked. Unable to believe his eyes. Rooted to the spot. Do you follow, little girl? It shall make his capture and torture SO MUCH easier. It will not even occur to him to do the sane thing and run."

DERVISH BANISHED TREE TO the back of the squad, and pushed Zoe to the front where he could watch her. She managed to get a glimpse of Tree every so often as they made their way down the tunnel. His right hand was pressed against the violent welt on his face. The halo of his hair glowed every time they passed a torch.

Zoe tried to dream up a plan as they marched. Her father—she couldn't believe she was about to have a positive thought about him, but apparently she was—had always been an inspired improviser when he was caving or hiking. He carried the bare minimum of equipment, and made every decision half a second before he had to. He fed on the uncertainty. It scared Zoe when she was young. By the time she was Jonah's age, she and her dad had run out of gas three times in the middle of the wilderness. (Three times that she could *remember*.) Zoe would beg her dad to tell her what was going to happen next, and he'd smile wide, and say, "I have *no* idea! How freakin' *cool* is that?" As they continued to escape these situations with their lives, Zoe settled into the not-knowing. She learned to improvise, too.

Still, what could she do in the face of the Lowlands? X and the others would be taken by surprise. They'd be outnumbered five to one. Only Regent would have powers. Only the Ukrainian guard would even have a weapon, probably. What was the "wench" with the cat going to do? What was Zoe *herself* going to do? She'd defended herself before, she'd defended her friends, but she had never once hit somebody in anger. It wasn't how she was raised. Her mother had *five* playlists of Buddhist chanting on Spotify.

Zoe couldn't stop picturing X, and how shocked he'd be when he saw her. His first instinct would be to protect her—but he was powerless here, just a pale young man who grew up without enough to eat. He'd get mauled just like Dervish said he would. Zoe realized now that Dervish had made her march in front of the men partly so she'd feel ashamed: X and his friends were going to be decimated, and she herself was leading the army.

The tunnel squeezed tighter until the rock all but scraped Zoe's arms. The torches on the walls grew rarer, like a species of flowers dying off. Soon, they walked in near darkness. After what Zoe guessed was half an hour, the passageway arrived at the top of a stone staircase. It was impossible to tell how far down the steps went. Zoe put a foot on the first one, but was too tired to continue.

Dervish pushed past her and flew—literally flew—down the

staircase. The end of his robe shot out behind him, then disappeared, like the tongue of a snake.

"They are only STAIRS, Zoe Bissell," he shouted from the bottom. "Shall I explain how they work?"

Zoe breathed in heavily. The oxygen had evaporated, or done whatever it was that oxygen did, as the tunnel grew tighter.

An idea came to her.

It came to her *because* she was so exhausted, *because* she couldn't take another step. It was a small idea, but it might help X and his friends in the fight. She felt sure Dervish wouldn't have thought of it.

There was a torch in a sconce on the wall. The light fell on the first handful of stairs. Zoe nodded to herself, and descended.

One hundred and twenty-two stairs spiraled down like a corkscrew. By the time Zoe reached the bottom, her shins were prickly with the pain, but her mind was alive.

"Let's keep moving," she told Dervish. "Unless you're tired."

A DOOR CUT INTO the rock led Zoe and the others onto the ground floor of a massive stadium of cells. Level after level stretched so high above her that they blurred. The vastness of the space was shocking, especially after the narrow artery of the tunnel.

In front of Zoe, a dozen rivers cut across the rocky ground, as evenly as the lines on a clock, then spilled into a circular cavern in the center. From the cavern itself rose the most arresting sight of all: a stone statue of a face screaming in agony. The head, a man's, was bald and colossal. It was tilted back, its mouth opened hideously wide. Zoe could see the teeth, the tongue, the roof of the mouth.

Cracks in the gray stone ran down the face and neck like scars. The statue didn't look like art—it looked like a cry of pain. When Zoe stared up at the cells again, she imagined someone howling inside every one.

The cells were worse than anything X had ever described. They were essentially black-iron caskets standing in rows. There were no bars to let in light, just small oval openings at eye level. Here and there, prisoners dangled their fingers out of the eyeholes to feel the air. Or maybe they thought they could somehow pull the light in themselves.

Hundreds, probably thousands, of souls noticed Dervish and the guards' arrival. They began pounding on the inside of their doors, as if to say . . . As if to say *what*? Zoe wasn't sure. Maybe just, *We exist!* It occurred to her that the name of the place, Where the Rivers End, was an understatement. This looked like a place *everything* ended. It was her first true glimpse of the Lowlands—the scale of them, the cruelty.

"How come there's nobody but prisoners here?" she asked Dervish.

She was thinking of the model of the Lowlands that X had once made in the snow. He'd used Jonah's orc figurines to represent the guards in the hive where he himself lived, T. rexes for the lords.

"Oh, there's no need for peacekeepers here," said Dervish. "We never let these souls out of their boxes. Some have been standing for two thousand years." When Zoe blanched, he added: "You think us cruel, do you?" He gestured to the horrible Screaming Man, and smiled. "But we gave them a statue!"

A guard who hadn't been with Dervish's squad rushed through the door now. He was portly—his stomach swayed in front of him as he ran—but he had such a disproportionately small head that Zoe wondered for a second if it'd been shrunk by a witch. For a weapon, he carried a broken lamp.

He approached Dervish obsequiously.

"Guvnor, if I may?" he said. "Regardin' X and Regent and the others, if I may? They're comin', sir. They'll be enterin' frew that tunnel over there was I ta guess"—he pointed with his lamp toward a curved archway—"and I 'aven't been wrong about a single fing yet, 'ave I?"

The guard waited, obedient as a dog, for his reward. His face crumpled when Dervish turned away without thanking him.

"It is time to assemble our mousetrap!" Dervish told Zoe. "The moment has come! Oh, do not scowl, little girl, you shall have the PRINCIPAL role—you shall play the cheese!"

He ordered five guards to stand on the walkway above the arch so they could rain down on X and the others when they entered the stadium. He split the rest of the squad in half, telling the men to crouch in the nearest rivers. These guards would rush "the enemy" from either side and crush them in a kind of vise.

Adrenaline shot into Zoe's blood. She knew she should try to reason with Dervish, but also knew it was useless. All she could come up with was, "You don't have to hurt them."

"And YOU need not have come to the Lowlands to watch me do it," said Dervish.

He prodded Zoe toward the center of the arena. She understood: he wanted her to be the first thing X saw when he entered the stadium. When Zoe tripped, Dervish grabbed her up, and shoved her onward.

"I warned you that love always ends in tragedy, did I not?" he said. "That is the wisdom of a lifetime, and I bestowed it gratis! All that our hearts shall ever do is wound us when we're young—and kill us when we're old."

They neared the immense circular canyon with the Screaming Man. The rivers crashed down into it.

"Do you want to know the true—the ONLY—difference between Regent and myself?" said Dervish. "When Regent witnessed the death of all love and hope, he was devastated. When I myself did, it liberated me forever."

Zoe felt Dervish's hand on the small of her back, as he pushed her toward her place in the trap.

"I wonder," he said, "which it shall do to you."

twenty-one

HALFWAY TO THE CENTER of the stadium, Dervish stopped and turned Zoe so that she faced the archway. He slid a hand around her neck. Zoe found that she couldn't make a sound now, not even a gasp. Dervish didn't want her warning X about the ambush.

He was beaming.

She was bait.

The guards in the rivers crouched so low that Zoe could only see a row of hats and helmets, like vegetables just starting to grow. Up on the walkway above the arch, the rest of the squad killed time by trading weapons—a wrench for a whip, a hammer for a bowling pin. Tree, who was one of them, looked afraid. The others all whispered giddily, thrilled about the coming fight.

It was going to be a massacre.

The plan that had come to Zoe in the tunnel started to seem very small and insufficient. She didn't know if she'd get close enough to Regent to whisper it, or even if he would agree to it. Zoe watched the archway for X. She was scared, exhausted, overwhelmed, but she pushed past all that to access her fury—at Dervish, at the guards, at the inhuman cells spiraling up and up. Anger was what she needed now. It was energy. She could work with it.

Suddenly, there was a torch in the tunnel. And two voices.

Neither was X's. Judging from the accents, it had to be the servant and the Ukrainian guard.

Dervish signaled the men above the arch. They lifted their weapons, and jostled for position. Zoe knew they'd beat X first and worst, just to impress Dervish. Even Tree would be forced to join in.

Zoe struggled in Dervish's grip, and felt his skeletal fingers tighten around her neck.

She saw the Ukrainian and Maudlin emerge from the tunnel. The guard wore a red Adidas tracksuit. The servant held her cat against her shoulder.

"Want to know true fact?" the Ukrainian was saying. "All cats would rather be dogs. Do not dispute, you will only sound silly."

Maudlin laughed.

"Vesuvius and I are ignoring you," she said.

They stared at the ground as they walked out of the tunnel. It was agony waiting for them to look up.

And then they looked up.

They froze. If Zoe could have screamed, she would have screamed, *Run!* But Dervish wouldn't let her so much as turn her head. His men waited for his signal.

Maudlin darted back the way they'd come—to get Regent and X, Zoe guessed.

The Ukrainian stood his ground. He spread his feet and glared at Dervish, like he was trying to intimidate him.

"What a delusional little person," said Dervish.

Regent rushed up from behind and entered the stadium. He saw Zoe and stopped dead.

Dervish was clearly waiting for X to show himself. The men on the ledge leaned forward hungrily.

At last, X came out of the tunnel, with Maudlin close behind. Zoe saw him shade his eyes at the sudden light. She saw him take in the massive tower of cells. She saw him recognize Dervish.

She saw his eyes fall on her.

He stepped back in shock.

Then he moved toward Zoe—warily at first, as if he still disbelieved what he saw. Regent reached out to stop him, but X brushed him away.

"Dervish, what have you done?" said X.

"I did nothing—she followed ME!" said Dervish.

"Liar!" said X.

His voice was weaker than Zoe had ever heard it, and his face was covered with bruises she didn't remember. She had never seen X when he was . . . human. No stronger than anyone else. Ordinary.

"A liar?" said Dervish. "Me? Now you're being hurtful!"

X took off his coat, and let it fall as he came closer. Had his shirt always been so filthy and torn? Had he always winced as he walked? Zoe feared for him in a way she never had.

"Tell me it isn't you?" he called to her. "Tell me this is some mad game of Dervish's?"

Dervish gripped Zoe's throat tighter.

She tried to warn X with her eyes, but discovered that she

couldn't even move them from side to side. All she could communicate was, *It's me. I'm sorry. It's me.*

She was ashamed, but even as X came forward, she could see him forgive her. It took half a second. Maybe less. His expression just changed. Softened. She loved him for it. He was so much kinder than she was. Had he always looked so tired? Had his face always been so thin?

Regent and the others followed X protectively. Zoe was moved by their loyalty. Maudlin and the Ukrainian could have just run.

"NOW!" shouted Dervish.

His men jumped from the archway, like animals leaping out of trees. They landed loudly, grunting on impact.

X and his friends whirled around.

The rest of Dervish's men charged out of the rivers. The squad swarmed at X and the others from three sides, every man shouting some sort of war cry. A thousand prisoners pounded on their doors. The thuds made Zoe's bones vibrate.

THOUGH X HAD NO powers, Zoe could tell that he knew how to fight. She watched as he head-butted a guard and took his club. But half a dozen men were on him instantly. He was the one they were after. The prize.

Even while he was under siege, X's eyes kept returning to Zoe.

She heard him shout to Regent: "I cannot reach her."

She heard Regent shout back: "*I* can."

The lord left the melee, and moved toward Dervish and Zoe. When one of Dervish's men tried to block him, Regent stiffened his arm and swung it at his throat. The guard flew backward, spitting blood.

Zoe felt a flash of hope as Regent approached: he was going to beat the shit out of Dervish. He actually pushed up his sleeves to fight, which she'd only ever seen in a movie.

Maybe they wouldn't even need Zoe's plan.

But without Regent to worry about, Dervish's men attacked more viciously. A guard swung an ax handle at Maudlin's face. She dodged it, took the blow on her shoulder, then fell. Three others pulled X down, and took the club back. Only Tree refused to fight. Maudlin had shooed her cat to safety, and Tree stood beside the animal now, ready to defend it.

Zoe looked for the Ukrainian.

At least *he* would have a weapon.

But no: one of Dervish's men had wrenched the baseball bat away from the guard, and jammed the handle into his mouth. The Ukrainian crumpled to the ground, howling and clutching a silver necklace he wore.

X fought his way out of the knot of bodies, and ran to help him. Zoe remembered him talking about a Russian guard. This had to be the same man. She remembered X saying that he was ridiculous sometimes, but that he was a friend—that he was funny and never cruel, that he'd worn tracksuits in several different colors, that he'd had a crush on Ripper that had lasted decades.

Zoe approved of anybody who had a crush on Ripper.

Before X could get to his friend, Dervish's guard dragged the Ukrainian to the river by his necklace, and threw him in. The water rocketed him toward the canyon's edge. Dervish laughed approvingly and, with a snap of his fingers, set the river on fire.

Flames shot up like fountains.

Zoe could hear X's friend scream in his native tongue as the current pulled him away.

AT LAST, DERVISH RELEASED Zoe, and pushed her forward with a boot.

"You have served your purpose, little girl," he said.

Zoe stumbled toward Regent, and begged him to turn back and help X and Maudlin.

"Forget Dervish," she said. "Come with me."

"When did you become my commander?" said Regent.

"When I thought of a plan," said Zoe.

She brushed past him, praying he'd follow.

He did.

Outraged, Dervish shouted after Regent: "For heaven's sake, you are a LORD! At least PRETEND that you deserve that golden band! Let the insects fight each other!"

Regent didn't answer.

Three guards were pummeling X with their fists. X could barely stand. He was just taking the blows.

Zoe looked at Regent. It was time to see what he thought of her plan.

"Give X his powers," she said. "Don't think—just do it."

Regent looked shocked.

"No prisoner has ever been allowed that sort of strength here in the Lowlands," he said. "Not even a bounty hunter."

"You're *thinking*," said Zoe, "and while you're thinking they're beating the crap out of X."

The guards were now holding X up just so they could hit him.

"I will do it," said Regent.

"Thank you," said Zoe.

She looked at Maudlin, who was trying to help X, trying to crawl to him. Dervish's men struck her and kicked her, but she kept coming back. It was awful to watch.

"And also give *her* some powers," said Zoe. "I'm not kidding. Don't look at me like that."

Zoe bent over, put her hands on her knees, and drew the first real breath she'd had since Dervish released her.

"And I want some, too."

twenty-two

REGENT SPREAD HIS HAND over Zoe's face.

She felt her cheekbones ignite.

The heat shot down her neck. It made a path of her bones, her veins, her muscles, anything it could find. It was terrifying. Also awesome. Zoe felt like she was being eaten by fire.

"Is it—is it supposed to feel like this?" she said.

Regent seemed not to hear her. No, that wasn't it—she hadn't actually said it out loud.

The heat drowned her other senses. She felt her skin redden, her thoughts melt into each other. The flames crinkling in the rivers, the prisoners drumming on their doors . . . She couldn't tell if the noises were real or not, if they were happening inside of her or out.

She wriggled her fingers to prove to herself that they were still hers, that she was still present in her own body.

Yes, she was still in control.

Or maybe she hadn't really wriggled her fingers?

The heat seemed to hold her for ages, but when it vanished she discovered that not even a second had passed: Regent was still taking his hand away from her face.

As Zoe's skin cooled, the heat was replaced by a kind of euphoria. She felt golden. Invincible. Her legs, her arms, her fists—everything pulsed with power.

She gazed around the arena, her senses on overdrive. That fire in the river: she could feel the minute fluctuations in the temperature of the flames. The screaming statue: she could see into the dark pits of its pupils.

"We must test your powers to see if they have taken root," said Regent.

"Oh, they've taken root," said Zoe.

How she loved saying words, all of a sudden! She could feel her mouth and tongue shaping them. Words!

"We *must* test your powers," said Regent more forcefully.

Zoe couldn't stop smiling.

She punched him in the face.

THEY DARTED BACK TO the fight, Zoe just a few steps behind Regent. She was nearly as fast as him now. She felt as if there were stars in her blood.

X lay at the guards' feet. The Cockney was kicking him savagely in the head, as if he held a personal grudge. The other men chanted encouragement.

The Cockney heard something, and turned to see Zoe fly at him. He gave her a patronizing grin.

Mistake.

However protective she'd felt of X up in the world, Zoe felt a hundred times more protective of him now. Maybe it was because she had seen the sickening place he'd been forced to grow up in. Maybe it was just that the powers Regent had given her were amplifying her feelings like they amplified every other stimulus.

She lowered her head, and tackled the Cockney like a linebacker. She hadn't planned it. She didn't know it was going to happen until it was happening. Her muscles moved faster than her mind.

The Cockney crashed onto his back, with Zoe on top of him. He was startled but, for the benefit of the other men, he said, "Hopin' for a kiss, luv?"

Another mistake.

Zoe stood, and ripped the laces from one of his boots, her hand like a claw. She pulled the boot off his foot. Beneath it, there was a dingy, yellowed sock full of holes where the guard's toes peeked through.

Zoe beat the Cockney in the head with the boot, just as he had beaten X. The surge of feeling was so thrilling that she hit him three times before she realized what she was doing was wrong. Even then she couldn't convince her arm to stop.

From the corner of her eye, she saw Maudlin lifting a man high over her head, and throwing him down. Dervish's men were so shocked by the turn of events that they'd ceased fighting. They looked to Dervish, hoping he would give them powers, too. But he didn't trust them, didn't care what became of them. They were just plastic soldiers to him, like Jonah's figurines.

Zoe felt a hand on her shoulder. She clutched the Cockney's boot even tighter, and spun angrily.

But it was X.

He must have seen that she was shaking. He circled her with his arms. Feeling his body was like falling into bed.

"I couldn't stop myself," she said. "I couldn't stop."

"It is always that way," said X gently. "It takes you over entirely."

Zoe saw that the sole of the Cockney's boot was slick and red with blood. Disgusted with herself, she flung the thing as far as she could. It hit the door of a cell three levels up.

Dervish's men retreated toward the tunnel under the arch. Now that they were outmatched, they had lost all will to fight.

Zoe saw Maudlin grab one of the guards before he could flee.

"*You*," said Maudlin, "are not leaving here on your feet—not after what you did to my friend."

It was the guard who'd thrown the Ukrainian into the river.

"*Don't*, Maudlin," said Zoe. "It'll make you feel worse, not better."

"I killed a surgeon once—he was going to hurt X's mother," Maudlin told her. "I've never felt bad about it, and I promise you I won't feel bad about this either." She paused. "By the way, I'm very glad to meet you. Call me Maud."

Maud pushed the guard toward one of the fiery rivers. Dervish moved to stop her, but Regent flew at him to hold him back.

At the riverside, Maud stooped to pick up something that glinted on the ground. It was the silver necklace that had belonged to her friend. It must have broken off before he went in the water. Zoe's eyesight was so sharp now that she could read the necklace from a distance: It said, *MAMA*.

Zoe watched Maud knock Dervish's guard down. She watched the guard cower, trying to shield himself both from Maud and from the fire in the river.

He was sorry about the Russian, he said. *Very* sorry about the Russian.

Maud nodded, though Zoe didn't think she was listening. Everyone, even Dervish, waited for her to pitch the man into the flames. Instead, Maud just stomped on one of his hands, shattering every bone. Given the situation, it was merciful, Zoe thought.

Maud slid the baseball bat into the water, like an offering. As she walked away from the man, she called over her shoulder, "He was Ukrainian."

ZOE COULD SEE THAT Dervish had weakened. His gold band had turned his neck a deep, mottled red. He squirmed, and hissed at his men not to retreat, but Regent restrained him with what looked like very little effort. He told the squad they could return to their hives without fear of retribution.

"Forget every word of Dervish's that ever fell upon your ears," he said. "His mind is rotten with disease."

Strangely, the guards no longer wanted to leave. Zoe understood: they were enjoying the lord's humiliation.

Dervish spit some words out in disgust.

"Much as I despise you, Regent," he said, "I never thought you would actually join X's pathetic rebellion against the Lowlands—that you would jeopardize your OWN freedom for such a creature."

X surprised Zoe by answering for Regent.

"This is not a rebellion against the Lowlands, Dervish," he said. "Do you not see that at last? It is only a rebellion against *you*. The Lowlands will always stand, for there will always be vile men who deserve damnation. But I"—here, X turned to Zoe; she knew what he would say next and approved of it completely—"I am not one of them."

X moved nearer to Dervish.

"Tell me which of these cells holds my mother," he said. "Tell me *now*."

Everyone gazed up at the hateful black caskets. They were packed as densely as a honeycomb.

"I shall NEVER tell you," said Dervish. "You shall have to inspect EVERY BLESSED ONE."

X tried to lunge at Dervish, but Zoe held him back. It surprised—and thrilled—her to see that she was every bit as strong as him now.

"Your mother's not here," she said. "Listen to me: she's not here. But he said she's close."

"Please release my arm," said X.

He was still raging at Dervish. She could feel it.

"I'll let you go, but are you going to stay calm?" she said.

"No, in all likelihood, I will not," said X.

She let him go anyway. He stepped to within a foot of Dervish.

"*Where* have you put my mother?" he said. "I am going to free her, and then she is going to free me."

Dervish, even twisting with pain from the gold band, found that funny.

"I doubt it very much," he said. "For one thing, only I know where your mother is, and only I shall EVER know. For another, she has been in the dark so VERY long now that I would be surprised if she were still—how to put this tactfully?—recognizably human."

"Where *is* she?" X shouted. "She suffered enough at the hands of her husband when she was alive. I will not let her suffer another moment here."

Dervish gave another strangled laugh.

"I repeat: I shall NEVER tell," he said.

But then he said something that Zoe knew to be genuine and, for the second time since she'd come to the Lowlands, she felt a sliver of sympathy for him.

"Why should your mother have a son who loves her? I never did!"

No one spoke. The stalemate had its own particular silence.

Then a voice—shaky, but loud—called out to them.

Zoe recognized it, but couldn't place it.

The voice said: "*I* know where your mother is, X. I was the guard that Dervish took with him."

It was Tree.

twenty-three

ZOE AND X STOOD by the round canyon in the center of the stadium. The screaming head loomed in front of them. The neck, which was all muscles and veins, disappeared into the water about 150 feet down.

"This is the part where we go over a cliff together," said Zoe.

She checked to see if X smiled. He didn't.

"That was a movie reference," she said.

"From which particular movie?" said X.

"Do you *know* any movies?" said Zoe.

"No," said X.

Zoe squeezed his hand fondly. The prisoners must have been watching from their cells because they'd started banging again. Zoe wasn't sure if they were encouraging them to jump—or warning them not to.

"Do you know how to fall?" she asked X.

"Is there a trick to it?" he said. "My plan was to take one step forward."

"I can't tell if you're trying to be funny," she said. "Keep your hands at your sides, okay? You can cover your mouth, but don't hold your nose or you'll break it when you hit the water." She paused. "Were you trying to be funny?"

"A little," he said.

They stared into the canyon. The rivers flung themselves into it, as if going to their death. The white noise of the water was weirdly lulling, like the currents wanted to pull them in, too.

"This journey we undertake," said X, "is it suicidal?"

"Dallas would say yes," said Zoe. "Val would say yes. Ripper would say, 'So what?'"

"And what do you say?" said X.

"I say let's go meet your mom," said Zoe.

X breathed out slowly.

"You make meeting her sound an easy matter," said X.

"Are you nervous?" said Zoe.

"Yes," said X.

Tree had told them that X's mother was imprisoned in a hole in the canyon called the Cave of Swords. When he said it, Dervish flared, broke away from Regent, and raised his hand. The belt from Tree's tunic slithered up his body and began strangling him. It took even Regent a few moments to tear it away.

"Listen—" Zoe said now.

"You need not tell me that we don't have to do this," said X.

"I wasn't gonna say that," said Zoe. "We totally have to do this. She's in a cave. I'm a caver. I think it might be why I'm here." A thought came to her. "Are you afraid you're going to be disappointed?"

"By my mother?" said X. "No. Just wait until you hear the story Maud told me. My mother is loyal, kind, and brave. It cannot be a coincidence that I was so drawn to you."

Zoe waved away the compliment.

"Ripper is all that stuff, too," she said. "So is Banger—it's just that he's also drunk a ton of beer." She paused. "So if you're not afraid of your mother being a disappointment to you, what *are* you afraid of?"

X considered the question. A cold mist rose off the water, like a cloud coming to swallow them.

"That I will be a disappointment to *her*," he said.

"Shut up," said Zoe.

"I'm entirely serious," said X. "When I am with *you*, I feel like . . . I feel like I'm worth something. Other times, I wonder if I have ever done anything that was not violent or selfish. I dragged fifteen souls to the Lowlands—and enjoyed their suffering sometimes."

"Stop," said Zoe.

"I endangered Maud," said X. "I endangered Regent and my friend Plum. I endangered you. I endangered a cat! I watched the Ukrainian get pulled down a burning river. If I did not love you so much, I would wonder what my life was *for*. When I stand in front of my mother, what can I tell her that I am not ashamed of?" He paused. "I apologize for the soliloquy. I do not expect you to answer."

"Oh, I'm gonna answer," said Zoe. "You can tell your mother that your heart survived this place. You made Jonah really happy when we lost our dad and *nothing* could make him happy. You kissed me like I always secretly hoped to be kissed." She stopped for a second.

"Your mother is going to be so proud of you she's never going to stop crying. Trust me. I know what moms are like."

X smiled in a way that told her he believed her.

"Thank you," he said. "Your soliloquy was superior to mine."

"It was really good, I'm not gonna lie," she said.

"And I truly did kiss you like that, didn't I?" he said.

"Don't get cocky," she said.

What neither of them had said was that even if Zoe got out of the Lowlands alive, there was no reason to think he'd be coming with her. Zoe remembered what it was like to sit in her weird room at Rufus's with the torn posters and busted trophies. She remembered what it was like to miss X—and to worry about him—so much that it dug into her, hollowed her out. Standing close to him now, she tried to record every sensation. His skin smelled *so much* like his skin.

"I have to ask you," said Zoe. "When you say you're going to rescue your mother—do you mean just from the Cave of Swords? You don't think you can get her out of the Lowlands completely, do you?"

"In truth?" said X. "What I want most dearly, most fiercely, is for *you* to leave this wretched place. Then my mother. And then? If I have not used up all my wishes? I will happily go myself."

Zoe wanted X to have everything he hoped for, but feared he was asking too much.

She looked to see if he was ready to jump.

"Keep your knees bent when you fall," she said.

THEY PLUMMETED DOWN, SLICED the surface, and kept falling. The water was frigid. Zoe waited for the shock, but it never came. Her body was now immune to the cold. She was 30 feet under before she stopped shooting downward. Ordinarily, she would have fought her way back to the surface, but her lungs weren't aching. She wasn't desperate to breathe. She opened her eyes, and could see everything in high-definition. The statue's shoulders and torso lay in front of her, like a sunken ship. Its legs disappeared into the dark.

X waited for her at the surface. Because of all the rivers falling into it, the water was wildly choppy—a cauldron. But the chaos didn't frighten Zoe. It energized her. She gestured for X to follow her, and they swam the circumference of the canyon, threading in and out of the waterfalls and searching for the Cave of Swords. Tree hadn't known exactly where it was or what it looked like—when he and Dervish took X's mother, he had waited up on the canyon's edge. The water was so cold that, without powers, he'd have drowned within minutes.

Zoe assumed the name Cave of Swords had something to do with stalactites or stalagmites. Her father's voice, which always came to her when she went caving, bubbled up in her head now: "The name could also refer to ice formations, Zo. Don't forget all the cool freakin' stuff our friend ice can do!" Zoe hated that her father could still insinuate himself into her thoughts. She pictured herself pushing him out of a house, swearing at him, slamming the door on his fingers.

There were dozens of fissures in the rock along the waterline. Any of them could have led to caves. Zoe and X took turns crawling into the bigger ones and looking for something, anything, that looked like swords. Zoe didn't know the extent of her powers, but found that when she needed a particular ability it would appear, as if she had willed it into being. She'd never felt anything as weird and cool and exhilarating as the sensation of light pouring out of her palm.

For an hour, they found nothing. Then, as Zoe ducked behind one of the last waterfalls, she found an oval opening in the rock. There was a handprint beneath it. It had to be a sign.

Zoe swam back to X. She thought about how the powers that Regent gave them protected them from everything *around* them. She wished there was something that could protect X from everything inside him, too: the fear, the pain.

X treaded water, waiting.

She showed him the palm print on the rock.

Judging from the size and the elegant way that the fingers tapered, it was a woman's hand—and it was made of blood.

THE TUNNEL WAS ONLY four feet wide and had a low, jagged ceiling. X didn't want to let Zoe go in first. They argued. X pointed out that if he was behind her and got stuck, she wouldn't be able to get out. Zoe pointed out gently—okay, maybe not that gently—that she knew how to cave and he didn't and that he should suck it.

As they talked, a wind rolled out of the opening in the rock like a cold breath, followed by the unmistakable sounds of something approaching. By the time Zoe figured out what it was, there was no time for words. She pulled X under the surface with her as a torrent of water and debris shot out of the wall.

X hadn't realized it was coming.

"*Who's* going first?" said Zoe, when they surfaced again.

"Perhaps you should," said X.

It turned out that water blasted out of the tunnel every five minutes, flinging dirt and rock like buckshot. Zoe lit the passage with her hands and gazed inside. It'd be a straight belly-crawl for 500 feet. She'd never crawled more than 75. There was no way she and X were going to get in and out between the blasts of water, and they had no ropes, no drills, no bolts, no Survival Sh*t to anchor themselves. They'd have to press against the walls when the current came, and hope it didn't blow them out of the tunnel.

She didn't say any of this. It was obvious from X's face that he knew.

Zoe slipped into the tunnel on her stomach. The flood was muddy and slick, which would actually be an advantage: it'd be easy to glide. The first time she pulled herself forward, she forgot to factor in her new strength, and shot 50 feet without stopping. Behind her, X, who'd been unconsciously picking up bits of her vocabulary, shouted in a mash-up dialect: "Seriously? Is that indeed how it's gonna be?"

She smiled to herself, and slowed down.

At first, Zoe gazed straight ahead, moving quickly but carefully, listening for the telltale wind and the scary drumroll of the water. But then her father's voice returned. She'd pushed him out the door, but he had climbed in through a window: "Zoe, you're in a tunnel in the freakin' *four-billion-year-old* mantle of the earth! Are you really *not* gonna look at the walls? Are you really *not* gonna check the place out? What you're doing is epic, girl! Ponce de León only discovered Florida!"

Zoe shoved her father back out the window, and slammed it shut.

But he was right.

She lay still a second, and allowed some wonder back in. Yes, the air was sour with the smell of rotten eggs (she named the gas herself, so her father wouldn't: hydrogen sulfide). Yes, her eyes stung from the sand in the tunnel. Yes, her clothes were getting shredded. But thanks to the gifts that Regent had given her, she was sliding over busted calcite like it was nothing. She was curling around stalactites, stalagmites, and snottites as if her body were liquid. (Zoe's father had preferred, for the gooey strands of bacteria that dripped from the ceiling, the term "snoticle.") Zoe remembered how much she loved exploring. And X was with her. Every so often, he put a hand on her leg to let her know that he was there. It reminded Zoe of her mother saving her when the snowbank fell in.

For the first time, she truly looked around. The ceiling of the tunnel sparkled with gypsum crystals. The walls were embedded with the fossils of sea creatures. One looked like a tiny Christmas tree, another like a squid with human teeth, another like a mutant shrimp, another like an inch-long bear with eight legs. Zoe ran her fingers along their spines, over their legs and snouts and tentacles. She'd never seen any of them before. Probably no living person ever had.

She was mesmerized.

She didn't notice that the wind had come back.

ZOE HAD JUST ENOUGH time to thrust her palms against the walls and brace herself.

She'd never been hit by a car screaming down a highway.

Now she had.

The instant the water struck, she couldn't breathe. Couldn't see. The wave pushed her head up and back, like someone had yanked on her hair.

She didn't know the limits of her powers, didn't know what she could withstand. A very specific fear shot through her mind: the water was going to break her neck.

Zoe forced her head back down again, amazed that she had the strength, and pushed even harder against the walls.

A new fear: the water was going to tear off her arms.

And how long would it be before she needed to breathe? Why hadn't she tested her new lungs before now? Rock and sediment glanced off her. Something bigger—a stalactite, maybe?—broke off the ceiling, and flew past. Why had she wasted time on the fossils? Why had she listened to her father?

The last of the water raced past them and out of the tunnel.

Light reappeared. Air.

She felt X's hand again. He had never let go of her.

Two hundred feet ahead, the tunnel veered up steeply. Zoe wanted to get to it, and see what was up there, before the next flood. She moved faster. Occasionally, a jutting piece of rock, sharp as razor wire, would grab at her shirt and tear it—but the pain never reached her brain. Whatever happened to her body they could fix later.

A hundred and fifty feet to go before the tunnel swung upward.

She pictured X's mother urging them on.

But what if the woman had lost her faculties, like Dervish said? What if she was feral, deranged?

An old story came to Zoe. A hopeful one.

It was about six Jewish families who hid from Nazis for 18 months in an underground cave called Priest's Grotto. Zoe had done an oral report on them for school once. Half the kids in class rolled their eyes because *of course* Zoe Bissell would figure out a way to talk about caves, even in World History.

A hundred feet left to go.

The families lived in darkness, as the Germans marched over their heads. They dug toilets and showers. Foraged for food in the country-side at night. Nearly all of them survived, even when sadistic villagers blocked the entrance to the cave with dirt so they'd suffocate.

Fifty feet to go.

One of the people in Priest's Grotto was a girl whose name Zoe loved: Pepkala Blitzer. She was four. When the families finally emerged from the cave after a year and a half, Pepkala shielded her eyes, and asked her mother to please put out the bright candle.

It was the sun.

Zoe got a B+ on her oral report. The teacher said there was too much about the cave.

Just before the tunnel swerved upward, there was a giant hole on the floor of the passageway. The rock, weakened by water, must have caved in.

From behind her, X said, "I will make a bridge of my body so you can cross."

"No," said Zoe, "*I'll* make the bridge."

"Someday I will actually win an argument," he said.

She smiled, though he couldn't see her.

"Not with me," she said.

Zoe guessed they had maybe three minutes before the water returned. She pressed her palms against the walls, and leaned out over the hole.

Beneath her, there was a 50-foot drop.

She was feeling less invincible now. For a second, she thought she felt the wind coming. No, she was imagining it.

She walked her hands slowly forward. Her legs tightened as she stretched over the emptiness.

When she'd reached as far as she could, she inched her hands down from the walls and toward the far edge of the hole. She felt a rush of fear—but then her bones locked into place.

X slid over her back on his stomach. Her body held strong.

WHEN THEY CAME TO where the tunnel rose upward into a chute, Zoe saw that there was a small cove off to the right, where they could wait out the next deluge if they had to. Zoe shimmied up the chute. It was tighter than the tunnel. She had to contort her body, and grease her arms with mud to get up it. At last, she climbed into the chamber up above.

It was stunning. Snow-white crystals covered the floor in waist-high mounds. They looked like a dragon's treasure or like flowers—chrysanthemums made of ice. There were bigger crystals, too. Massive ones. They were roughly blade-shaped—hence the name Cave of Swords—but to Zoe they looked more like toppled trees. The crystals tilted in every direction. Some stretched as high as the ceiling, as if they were holding it up.

Zoe was so surprised by the beauty of the crystals that it took her a moment to see the bodies chained to them.

There were a dozen prisoners.

All their heads were covered with black hoods.

X's mother was here somewhere.

Zoe called down to X, just as he was reaching up into the narrow chute to follow her. It broke her heart to tell him that he was never going to fit. She'd have to find his mother alone.

X refused to believe it.

He started to climb, twisting his body.

Zoe felt the wind creep down from an opening in the rock over her head. She could hear the water gathering power behind it.

"Get *out* of the hole, or you'll get stuck and drown," she said.

"No," he said. "I'm coming with you."

He punched the wall to widen the chute. The rock shattered.

"Stop!" said Zoe. "You're gonna cave it in! I'll find your mother. Just tell me what she looks like."

The first drops of water fell past.

"She will appear to be thirty-five, though she's seen nearly a century," said X. "And, according to Maud, she looks . . . She looks like me."

"Okay," said Zoe. "That's all I need."

THE PRISONERS HAD BEEN left standing, their arms pulled back and chained around the crystals. Zoe moved among them as quietly as she could. Their hooded heads hung low. They made no sounds at all. If Zoe hadn't seen their chests moving, she wouldn't have known they were breathing. Only two of them were women.

She thought about how far away her own mother was. She pictured her and Jonah on the living room floor, begging Uhura to eat. The pain of missing them was so sudden and sharp that she had to force them into the Do Not Open box in her brain. They didn't want to go.

The first woman wore a pale green, medieval-looking linen dress that had been embroidered with pearls, though most had fallen off or been stolen.

"I'm a friend," Zoe whispered.

She went to remove the woman's hood so she could see her face, but her hands were shaking. She calmed herself, and tried again.

The woman's silver-white hair fell down past her shoulders. She was in her seventies.

She wasn't X's mother.

The woman had a soft, round face and gray-blue eyes, which she immediately closed against the light. There was a reason she hadn't spoken: there was a large gray stone wedged in her mouth.

Zoe wished she could have freed the woman—she wanted to free all of them—but she had no idea what the repercussions would be if she did. She touched the woman's hair on impulse. She couldn't imagine what someone like her had been sent to the Lowlands for. Without opening her eyes, the woman tilted her head and rubbed Zoe's hand, like a cat.

Zoe was close to tears when she walked away. It was partly because she missed her own mother. But it was mostly because there was only one woman left in the Cave of Swords.

Zoe had no doubt that this was the one: she could see her pale hands in the manacles and her black hair trailing down from her hood.

When Zoe got to her, she swept the crystals on the floor aside, making a clearing where she could stand.

"It's okay," she told the woman, as if she were calming a frightened horse. "I'll be gentle."

She pulled up the hood.

She saw a face so much like X's that, for a second, she couldn't breathe.

twenty-four

ZOE EASED THE STONE out of the woman's mouth. It was scratched and scored all over: tooth marks.

The woman coughed, gulped in air, winced at the light.

"Is your name Versailles?" said Zoe.

She had to speak louder than she'd wanted to because the water was falling again.

The woman looked at Zoe but her eyes didn't seem to focus. She didn't answer. Zoe wondered if she could.

Even after 20 years in a hood and chains, the woman was astoundingly beautiful—more beautiful than Ripper. More beautiful than X, even. She looked like a portrait that had been painted to flatter a queen. She had the same hair as X. She had the same dark, questioning eyebrows, the same nearly black eyes. Her clothes were simple. Functional. She wore a frayed, blue-and-white gingham dress and sturdy work boots. Zoe had expected something fancier from a lord, but maybe, like Regent, the woman refused to steal from the weak.

Her lips were cracked. Zoe took off her thin sweater, which was still drenched from the last flood. She went to wipe the woman's face. The woman jerked her back, suspicious. Zoe reminded herself that the prisoners here hadn't seen another human being in years—and that the last one had been Dervish, who barely qualified.

She had to show the woman that she wasn't a threat. She circled behind the crystal column and, without even wondering if she could do it, broke the chains. It gave her a rush to feel the iron come apart in her hands. The woman slid to the ground, rubbing her wrists and staring at her hands like she'd never seen them before. She nodded gratefully to Zoe, then looked at her feet, which were still bound.

Zoe ripped those chains apart, too.

She picked up the damp sweater again. She cooled the woman's face with it, then pressed it against her dry lips.

Zoe repeated her question: "Is your name Versailles?"

The woman's voice was raw.

"No," she said.

ZOE SLUMPED TO THE floor. A few of the other prisoners had heard voices, and were stirring. Maybe the woman was too far gone to remember her name? Or maybe Zoe had the wrong woman? She thought of X down in the tunnel, waiting. She'd promised him that she could do this.

"Are you sure?" she said.

It was a ridiculous question, but the only one she could think of.

261

The woman gestured for the wet sweater again, pressed it to her face, and sighed into it.

"Versailles," she said slowly, "is only what they call me. It's not my name. My *name* . . . is Sylvie."

Zoe shot forward and hugged her.

Sylvie was shocked, but after a second Zoe could feel her relax into the hug and return it.

"I haven't had a conversation in a long time," Sylvie said. "But I don't remember them being like this."

"Sorry," said Zoe. "We've been looking for you for a long time."

Sylvie rubbed her throat.

"Who is 'we'?" she said.

"I'm—I'm trying to think of a way to tell you," said Zoe.

"My eyes are weak from wearing the hood," said Sylvie, "but you seem very young. Just a girl."

"I'm seventeen," said Zoe.

"That's not possible," said Sylvie. "The Lowlands never take souls that age."

"I'm only visiting," said Zoe.

Sylvie shook her head in disbelief.

"My god, you do have a story to tell, don't you?" she said. She began folding the sweater. "The way you broke the chains . . . I assumed you were a lord. Now I don't know what to think."

After a lifetime of blurting, Zoe truly did not know how to begin.

Sylvie handed back the sweater.

"Thank you for this," she said. "Why have you been looking for me? Why did you break my chains?"

"Because I'm getting you out of here," said Zoe.

Sylvie looked at her warily.

"This is some joke of Dervish's," she said.

"No," said Zoe.

"Do you know why I was brought here?" said Sylvie. "Do you know what my 'crime' was?"

"You had a baby," said Zoe.

"That's right," said Sylvie. "A boy. Did you know it was a boy?"

"Yes," said Zoe.

"I gave birth almost a century after I died," said Sylvie. "Not a bad trick, if you think about it."

Her smile disappeared. Memories seemed to be crowding in.

"I named my boy before they took him away—just for myself. Just so I'd remember he was real. They couldn't stop me from doing *that*, the bastards."

"What did you name him?"

Sylvie withdrew from her memories, and looked at Zoe, as if she'd just realized she was there.

"You haven't even told me *your* name," she said.

"I'm Zoe Bissell."

"And the lords know you're freeing me?"

"Sort of? I'm not great at asking permission."

"I never was either," said Sylvie. "Be careful. *This* is where it landed me."

"I'm always careful," said Zoe. "Well, semi-careful."

"If we only 'sort of' have the lords' permission," said Sylvie, "how are we going to get out of here?"

"We're just going to walk out," said Zoe. "Actually, we're going to crawl, swim, climb—and *then* walk. Are you up to it?"

She stood, and reached down to Sylvie.

"Probably not," said Sylvie, "but fortunately, I'm stubborn—and any cell at all will be paradise compared to this." She took Zoe's hand, and stood now, too. "You have to tell me why you came for me. Please. Who *are* you to me?"

Zoe said it as simply as she could.

"I know your son," she said.

"My *son*?" said Sylvie. "My baby survived?"

"He did," said Zoe. "He's beautiful." She paused. "And I'm in love with him."

Sylvie put her face in her hands.

"This is all so much," she said. "Promise me again that this isn't a joke of Dervish's."

"I promise," said Zoe.

"How old is my baby now?" said Sylvie.

"Twenty."

"*Twenty!* I want to see him—to meet him."

"You're about to."

"Now?"

"*Right* now."

Zoe expected her to be ecstatic, but Sylvie's face darkened.

"He's here in the Lowlands?" she said. "They kept him prisoner? A little boy?"

Again, Zoe answered plainly because there was no shielding Sylvie from the truth: "They did. I'm sorry. I'm here trying to get him out."

Sylvie's jaw tightened with anger. She took Zoe's arm.

"Well, now you've got help," she said.

They walked toward the chute. The crystals crunched beneath their feet, and glowed faintly, like snow.

"My son—he loves you, too?" said Sylvie.

"Yes," said Zoe. "Can you believe it?"

"I can," said Sylvie.

When they got to the chute, the flood had only just ended. There was still a dampness in the air. They peered down and saw, just barely, the top of X's head.

Sylvie hesitated, and took a few steps back.

"My god," she said. "There he is."

"Don't be nervous," said Zoe. "He's not going to disappoint you."

"But he's expecting a lord—a force of nature, an avenger," she said. "What if I disappoint *him*?"

"That's what he said about you," said Zoe, smiling. "You're *definitely* his mom. Will you tell me what you named him?"

"Of course, but he survived with no help from me," said Sylvie. "He deserves to be called whatever he wants."

Zoe knelt by the chute, readying to help Sylvie down. She accidentally kicked a few crystals into the hole.

"You *did* help him," said Zoe. "Knowing you were out there, knowing how strong you were, knowing you loved him—it made all the difference."

Sylvie massaged some color into her cheeks.

"Thank you for saying that," she said. "You're a very kind girl. I named him Xavier."

part four

Ascension

twenty-five

X WAITED BENEATH THE chute in agony. His stomach felt like a wet rag someone was twisting.

A handful of crystals tumbled down and landed at his feet. He looked up just as Zoe's face appeared.

She was crying.

She must have failed.

He felt all hope leave his body.

"You could not find her?" he called. "It's all right. I swear it. Do not trouble yourself about it."

Zoe shook her head.

"I found her," she said.

She disappeared from view. X heard murmuring and a rustle of clothing. A woman in boots and a long blue-and-white dress descended toward him.

His mother.

After a lifetime of waiting, he didn't feel ready. He had to put his hands in the pockets of his pants because they were trembling.

Zoe guided his mother down the chute from above, pointing out where it was safe to put her feet. X heard Zoe say, "You're doing good" and "You okay?"

The first word he ever heard his mother say was *yes*.

His mother's back was to him, so he couldn't see her, which made his stomach twist tighter. As she neared the ground, she reached a hand down for support. X took it. It was warm, and felt strong. She found the floor of the tunnel. She turned her head. Her face came out of the darkness, like the moon from behind clouds.

"Is it really you?" she said.

X nodded, afraid to speak. He didn't want to cry in front of her.

He took the silver packet from his coat, and put it gently in her hands, like a gift. She looked confused. She opened it slowly as if the foil might crumble. X watched her eyes widen: Vesuvius's collar, the comb, the shard of porcelain . . . His mother's eyes got shiny with tears. She began touching everything softly, reverently. When she got to the broken drill bit, her finger hovered over it uncertainly.

"I was married to a man named Fernley," she said. "I'm afraid to tell you what I did to him."

"I have heard the whole of your story," said X. "You did only what cried out to be done."

His mother looked up at him.

"The way you speak . . . ," she said.

"Yes," said X. "I'll explain as soon as I have possession of myself again. Just now I am feeling overwhelmed."

"Me, too," said his mother. "Can I hug you? Is it too soon?"

"I'm afraid I might cry," said X.

It felt good not to pretend to be stronger than he was.

"Go ahead and cry," she said. "Your mother says it's all right."

She put her arms around him, and X—though he knew it wasn't possible—recognized the sensation somehow. He felt as if he'd hugged her before. His mother began crying first. When X felt her shaking, he broke down, too.

"You came for me," said his mother. "You *found* me."

"I wanted you to know that—that I'm okay," said X. "That I lived. That I've thought of you always."

"I'm speechless," said his mother. "I can't believe I'm looking at you."

"What should I call you?" said X.

"Anything you want," she said. "Sylvie. Mother. *You* there. Anything but Versailles. I haven't been her in a long time. And what should I call you? What does Zoe call you?"

Zoe had climbed down. She stood behind them.

"I call him X," she said.

Sylvie turned to her, stunned.

"You're serious?" she said.

"Yes," said Zoe.

"Why is that so surprising?" said X.

"When you were born," said Zoe, "she named you Xavier."

X smiled for the first time.

Up above, the water was rumbling, so the three of them ducked into the dry cove, and sat. X lit the space with a sweep of his hand. Zoe apparently felt he'd made the cove *too* bright, because she darkened it a few degrees with a sweep of her own.

"Her eyes hurt," she explained.

X couldn't stop staring at his mother. In his entire life, he'd only ever looked in a single mirror: the one in the Bissells' bathroom, which Zoe had painted purple and Jonah had decorated with stickers of bugs. Still, X recognized himself in Sylvie's face. It made him feel less alone. It made him feel *answered.* It made something inside himself—something that'd always felt slightly askew—click into place.

Sylvie stared back at him even more intensely, if it was possible. She took his hand.

"Before we say anything else," she said, "will you let me apologize?"

"For what?" said X.

"You really don't know?" said Sylvie.

"I swear it," said X.

"For giving birth to you in the Lowlands," said Sylvie. "For giving you a life that wasn't a life. For not staying with you, for not protecting you, for leaving you at the mercy of"—she gestured to the grim walls—"all this. I think I failed in every way a mother can fail."

"Don't, Sylvie," said X. "Don't." It was the first time he'd said her name. "You had no choice. As for what's happened to me, I'm not—I'm not *broken.* I found Zoe. Now I've found you. I'm not ashamed of my life—not the slightest bit—and I would not give it back."

"My god, you're kind," said Sylvie.

"No," said X. "Truly, I—"

Zoe nudged him with a foot.

"Stop deflecting," she said. "You *are* kind."

X grinned.

"You're right," he told his mother. "I am *incredibly* kind."

Sylvie laughed.

"You two are sweet together," she said.

Zoe nudged him again.

"We are *incredibly* sweet together," said X. "No one has ever been sweeter."

X wished they never had to leave the cove. He didn't know what awaited them up in the stadium, and everything he wanted or needed was here.

"When you were born, I demanded to hold you a moment—did you know that?" she said.

Sylvie had the silver foil open on her lap. She was rolling the bloodstone button on her palm.

"No," said X.

"I was surprised when Dervish agreed," said Sylvie. "He probably knew it'd make it harder to give you up. He really wanted to torture me any way he could." She paused, remembering. "I kissed your fontanel first, I think. Then your belly and toes. I may have the order wrong. I wriggled your fingers. I smoothed your little whorl of hair. Even now, I remember the weight of you in my arms—and I remember how empty my arms felt when you were gone. When Dervish shackled my wrists, I didn't resist because after losing you, I—I didn't want to hold anything else." Sylvie was crying again. "I'm sorry. I'm not a weepy person. Not usually." She pressed her fingertips against her eyes, and sighed. "Dervish and a guard brought me here—"

"I call him Tree," said Zoe.

"Oh, he must like that," said Sylvie. "He's usually called Stick."

"He told us where you were," said Zoe. "He was kind of badass about it."

"I always liked him," said Sylvie. "Such funny hair. Dervish seethed at him the whole way here, but Tree kept whispering kind things like, 'You will always be baby's mother.' And there was another one I thought about for years because it was so sweet. What was it? Oh, I remember: 'Your son is beautiful. I have five brothers—every one of them is as ugly as me.'"

Sylvie rubbed her wrists, where the manacles had stripped the skin.

"There's a lot I want to say, but I'm still feeling woolly-headed," she told X. "Will you stop me if I ramble?"

"No," said X.

His mother looked at him fondly—it was amazing how every glance of hers warmed him—and continued.

"Dervish actually hummed when he chained me up to the crystal—and sang when he stuffed the rock in my mouth," she said. "Then he put the hood over my head. The minute he was gone, I grieved over you so deeply that I didn't even care where I was. Eventually, I convinced myself that the lords had set you free. That you had a family somewhere. I pictured you out in the real world, playing in the snow in your little-boy hat and your little-boy boots. They were like bedtime stories I told myself." Sylvie stopped a moment. "It makes me sick that they kept a child prisoner. I've spent so long trying to let go of my fury at this place. My god, it comes back fast."

"I did find a family of sorts," said X. "I was trained to be a bounty hunter by a woman named Ripper. She was the rarest of people, though I don't think she believed it. I speak the way I do because of her."

"I'd love to meet her," said Sylvie. "To thank her."

"Ripper is gone," said X. "Taken. I do not know where."

"I'm sorry," said Sylvie.

X had tried not to think about how much he missed Ripper. She occupied such a particular space in his life that he couldn't imagine anyone replacing her. Who could replace Banger, for that matter, with his candy, his silly slang, his almost unbelievable loyalty? Who could replace the Ukrainian with his funny fits of outrage? Or Plum with his fluttering hands? Sitting with his mother at last, X was blindsided by how many people he'd lost on the way to finding her.

He said none of this out loud, not wanting to diminish the moment. Instead, he said: "Regent has been like a father to me."

Sylvie's eyes brightened.

"Regent," she said. "I knew he'd protect you! I should have asked—I can't believe I didn't—do you know who your father *is?*"

"His name, not much more," said X.

"I met Timothy in Montana," said Sylvie. "Once they made me a lord, I used to sneak away from the Lowlands to walk in the mountains I grew up in. There was no one to stop me."

"What about the Higher Power?" said X.

"Oh, the Higher Power isn't much of a presence, is it? You've got to do something pretty outrageous to get its attention," said Sylvie. "I came across Timothy on the trail to a place called Avalanche Lake. He picked flowers for me. No, wait, I picked flowers for him—that's what it was. He put one behind his ear and another between his teeth, and did a funny Spanish dance for me, with the clapping over the head and everything. After being married to Fernley, who was just so repellent, I didn't even know they *made* men like Timothy—men who were warm and full of life." She turned to

Zoe. "And *gorgeous*," she said. "There wasn't a plant or tree Timothy couldn't identify—or an animal he didn't respect. We ended up hiking in the woods a long time without speaking."

Sylvie smiled, and looked down at the bloodstone button on her palm.

"And then we did some *other* things without speaking," she said. "Timothy didn't know what I was. I visited him off and on for weeks. Then I realized that I was endangering him—that I was being selfish. What if another lord discovered what I was doing? So I made myself stop going. It was brutally hard."

Sylvie put the button back in the foil.

"I was shocked when I found out I was pregnant," she said. "It didn't make any biological sense. I mean, I was *deceased*. Maybe it was because I was a lord? Or because he was a mortal? I'm just guessing. When I realized that Timothy and I had *made* something together—something I could actually feel growing inside me—I wanted to tell him so badly it was crippling. I forced myself not to. I never saw him again."

As if to slough off the story's end, Sylvie turned to Zoe and said, "Montana is beautiful. Have you ever been?"

"I live there," said Zoe.

"You're serious?" said Sylvie. "What a *strange*, strange day this is." She put a hand on X's. "Now tell me about you. I've done nothing but talk. They made you a bounty hunter, you said?"

"Should I have refused?" said X. He was afraid of the answer. "I have often thought so because of the way the violence gets in your blood. Yet I was only ten when my training began, and all I knew was that something was finally happening to me."

"You were right to say yes—of course you were," said Sylvie.

"Look at me. People like you and your friend Ripper, people with consciences, are the ones who *should* be bounty hunters. They're the ones who should be lords, too, for that matter. Anyone who just craves power should be ashamed. You know why I trusted Regent from the very beginning? Because every time he had to hurt somebody it took him forever to forgive himself."

"I am no longer a bounty hunter, as it happens," said X. "I have been forbidden to leave the Lowlands. I fell in love with Zoe, and I became . . . unreliable."

"My god," said Sylvie, "your story's so much like mine. Dervish must have lost his mind!"

"I am not his favorite," said X.

"He hates us," said Zoe. *"Hates."*

"You're doing something right, then," said Sylvie. "It's important to be hated by the right people." Her brow furrowed. "Zoe, I still don't understand how *you* got here."

"I followed Dervish into a portal," said Zoe. "I just jumped. It maybe wasn't my best decision, but . . . I love your son. I was scared for him, and I thought I could help him find you. I wanted to try." She paused. "Also, him and his friends are always showing up at *my* place unannounced."

"If I didn't know better, I'd think you were out of your mind," said Sylvie. "But that's what they said about me."

Sylvie stood up in the cove. She took something from the silver foil to keep for herself—she transferred it to her pocket so quickly that X couldn't see what it was—and then returned the packet to him.

"I'm ready to face whatever it is we have to face, if you are," she said. "Who's waiting up there for us?"

"Regent, Dervish—and a mob of others with varying intents," said X. "Oh, and Maudlin, too."

"Maudlin? Really?" said Sylvie. "Her real name is Mariette, by the way. I know I'm not supposed to say that, but it's ridiculous that they call her Maudlin. She's the least maudlin person I've ever known! She beat a doctor to death with a drill, for heaven's sake." She paused. "Does she still have Vesuvius?"

"She does," said X.

"When Dervish and Regent came to take our souls, Mariette picked Suvi up to protect him, and then she couldn't bring herself to let him go," said Sylvie. "Did she tell you that?"

"She did not," said X.

"I watched her try to put him on the floor as they rushed us toward the portal," said Sylvie. "She absolutely *could not* do it. She loved him too much. So he came with us. I think he'd have wanted to, if we could have asked him. He loved her just as much."

Before they left the cove, Sylvie hugged X and Zoe in turn. X felt a strength in his mother, a resolve, that hadn't been there before.

"Thank you for saving me," said Sylvie. "Now it's my turn to save you."

X felt Zoe bump him with her hip.

"I want you to come with us," he told his mother. "To the—to the world."

"You're very sweet," said Sylvie. "But they will never let me out of the Lowlands. I did murder someone, repulsive though he was. It will be enough—so much more than enough—if I never have to go back to the Cave of Swords."

"You won't," said X. "Regent would never allow it."

"Then you have saved me from a hundred thousand—a hundred

million—days spent with a hood over my eyes and a rock in my mouth," said Sylvie. "I demand that you be as proud of yourself as I am of you."

"I shall try," said X.

"Good enough," said Sylvie. "Now let's concentrate on the two of you. Once we get up to the stadium, you may see me speak in a way, or behave in a way, that's . . . less than polite. I apologize in advance. But if Dervish thinks I will let my son—*or* the girl he loves—be imprisoned another second, he needs to be reintroduced to Versailles."

twenty-six

THE TRIP THROUGH THE tunnel was torturous. Zoe crawled in front so she could make a bridge with her body for Sylvie when they came to where the rock had fallen away. X followed so he could try to shield his mother from the floods. Sylvie didn't seem afraid, but she had no powers, no superhuman resilience. X felt as if he were transporting a pane of glass.

As he inched ahead on his stomach, he thought about what it would be like to be free. It was selfish, but he couldn't help it. Unfortunately, he couldn't stop the thought that came next either: What if the Lowlands never let him go? He imagined a guard thrusting him into the dark mouth of a cell. He imagined the bars slamming shut like teeth. Would it be enough to know that Zoe and his mother loved him—and that they loved him not because they *didn't* know what was in his heart but because they did? The answer came at him hard.

No, it wouldn't be enough.

He had to have Zoe. He had to be free.

When they reached the last stretch of the tunnel, where the fossilized sea creatures winked in the light, X got his first real glimpse of the canyon ahead. The little sea around the statue now lay utterly still. Even the waterfall that had rained down in front of the tunnel entrance had stopped—*literally* stopped, as if someone had pressed Pause. X could see the beads of water in midair.

Zoe called over her shoulder.

"Here we go."

He watched her slip out of the tunnel, then help his mother into the water. He slid forward to join them.

"This is the part where I say we've got company," said Zoe.

X lifted his eyes. There were lords up on the rim of the canyon, not just Regent and Dervish but a hundred of them, all peering down. They must have come from a dozen neighboring hives.

Word had traveled.

The three of them bobbed like corks.

"I know we don't seem like much," said Sylvie. "But we can do this."

X saw that his mother was shaking from the cold. He hoisted her out of the water, and carried her up the canyon wall. When he looked back down for Zoe, she was gone. She'd swum off in another direction.

"Wait," she called. "I think I see a friend."

X scanned the water. There was a body, clothed in red, floating on its back near the base of the statue.

The Ukrainian. His face was black with ash.

But he was moving.

X watched as Zoe lifted the guard over her shoulder and began scaling the canyon beneath him and Sylvie. Her strength was beautiful to watch.

"I thought you were dead," Zoe told the Ukrainian.

"Was *already* dead," he answered gruffly. "Please pay attention." He squinted up at Sylvie. "You are mama, of course?"

"I am," said Sylvie.

"Your boy look very hard for you," said the guard. "He was annoying about it, if I am being honest."

X CLIMBED TOWARD REGENT, ignoring the other lords. He climbed fast to show his strength. He would not be intimidated. Zoe was going home, and his mother was never going back to the Cave of Swords or any place like it.

Sylvie embraced Regent the instant they were out of the canyon. Her gingham dress was as wrinkled as a wrung-out cloth. Her boots were ordinary. But in the way she carried herself, she was more regal than any of the lords. They seemed to know it, too. They parted to give her and Regent room. They watched her with something like awe. X could hear Dervish ranting deep in the crowd, but the other lords held him back. A good sign.

"Hello, old friend," Sylvie told Regent. "Has it been dull without me?"

Regent gave her a rare, unguarded smile.

"No, it has not," said Regent. "We were joined by a mischievous young man *so* like you that it was as if you'd never left. I see that you have made his acquaintance."

"My boy has a good heart, doesn't he?" said Sylvie. "He came for me."

"He has a *very* fine heart," said Regent. "It is his mother's."

A SCREECH CUT THE air: "Enough!"

Dervish had broken away.

X and Regent moved to protect Sylvie.

Dervish moved faster.

His eyes were crazed. The gold band had eaten into his neck. He hurled himself at X's mother, and swept her over the side of the canyon.

X plunged in after them. As he fell, out of the corner of his eyes, he saw two others diving with him.

Regent. Zoe.

Dervish had his hands around Sylvie's throat, and was holding her underwater, letting her up every now and again just to see her scream.

X and Regent swam at him from one side, Zoe from the other.

"COME NEAR ME," Dervish shouted, "and I shall HOLD HER UNDER until her lungs COLLAPSE! I may not be able to kill her, yet I can turn her brain to PUDDING!"

X looked to Regent so they could coordinate an attack, but Regent was peering up at the lords. He seemed to be waiting for a signal.

"See how they STARE?" said Dervish. "You told yourself that they care, but why should they?"

He held Sylvie under again. Her legs kicked madly.

Just then, there was a scream from atop the canyon. Maud had pushed through the crowd with Vesuvius in her arms. She was watching.

X thought of the story of the drill, of how Fernley and the surgeon had tried to make his mother docile, compliant. Dervish was attempting to do the same.

Regent shouted to the lords.

"I shall end Dervish's reign with my own hands, if we are in agreement. Show me a sign!"

Of all the silences X had ever heard, the one that followed cut deepest.

It was Zoe who finally broke it.

"Regent!" she said. "It's time to *stop* asking permission!"

She cut through the water toward Dervish, but even in pain his powers were greater than hers. He swatted her away with his free hand, and she slammed against the wall of the canyon.

"How can you just *watch*?" X screamed at the lords. "Does *nothing* touch you?"

Again, they gave no answer. The silence doubled, tripled, until there seemed to be more of it in the world than air.

"How their apathy feeds me!" said Dervish. "It might as well be APPLAUSE!"

But then, one by one, the lords leaped into the water.

There were 5 of them, then 10, then 20. They swam up behind X and Regent, and—like an army, like a wave—closed in on Dervish.

Fear slid over Dervish's face. He pushed Sylvie into the water and pulled her out again. He did it faster and faster. He did it with a kind of mania. The water churned. Sylvie's body was limp as a doll's.

The fourth time he wrenched her up, she sprang to life. There was something hidden in her hand. She slashed his face with it.

It was the shard from the porcelain pitcher that Fernley had beaten her with.

A bloody seam opened on Dervish's face. Shocked, he released Sylvie, and clasped a hand against his cheek to heal it.

Sylvie swam toward Zoe, but was too spent to reach her. Zoe closed the distance in an instant. X watched as she gathered Sylvie up, and climbed with her toward safety, toward Maud.

The wound on Dervish's face disappeared beneath his touch, but the gold band burned even hotter at his throat. He fought to pull it away from his skin, just as the Countess had.

X looked at Regent, a question in his eyes.

Regent understood, nodded.

X tore to where Dervish struggled in the water.

"Let me help you," he said.

He reached for the gold band, and ripped it off Dervish's neck.

twenty-seven

X HANDED THE BROKEN band to Regent, who looped it around his arm, then dragged Dervish up the canyon like a corpse. The other lords followed. X stayed behind a moment, watching them rise up the wall en masse. With their wild colors and jewels, they looked like an ancient race of creatures finally leaving the sea.

Up on the stadium floor, the lords stood in a ring around Dervish, and debated his fate. X couldn't see Dervish himself, but he heard him wailing like an animal. No, that wasn't fair: X had never actually heard an animal cry like that. Even Vesuvius, when the Countess had stolen him from Maud and imprisoned him in a box, had protested less.

X went to Regent. He needed to know what would happen next. He'd accepted that his mother would remain imprisoned in the Lowlands forever—but what about Zoe? What about himself?

Regent turned away from the circle, annoyed at the interruption. X got a glimpse of Dervish through the other lords, though their bodies were thick as trees. Dervish had stopped screaming. He sat on the ground in shock, rocking back and forth like a terrified child.

"What is it?" said Regent. "Speak."

Abashed, X spoke only four words.

"What becomes of us?"

Regent's expression cooled.

"Zoe will be freed," he said. "As for yourself, I cannot claim to know. We have not even determined what becomes of Dervish. There are some here who believe this gold band should be returned to him."

"That would be madness," said X.

"We agree on that point, you and I," said Regent. "Now go. Do not squander your time wondering what is to come. Give Zoe and Sylvie the whole of your attention. One of them—I don't know which—you shall never see again."

Regent turned his back, and once again the circle was a wall through which no light shone.

Nearby, the Cockney and the other guards were making bets about what the lords would decide—happily flinging rings and hats and weapons in a pile on the ground.

X couldn't bear to watch.

His eyes found Zoe and the others, who sat by one of the rivers. Maud was tending to Sylvie's and the Ukrainian's injuries. Vesuvius was climbing bossily all over everyone, looking to nest. He settled at last on Sylvie's lap, remembering her even after 20 years. The two of them playfully butted heads. X saw Tree watching longingly from a distance, as if everyone's affection for one another was a fire he wished he could warm himself by.

X approached Zoe, and whispered for her to follow him.

He led her under the archway, away from the guards and the lords, away from the Screaming Man, who seemed to know everything, see everything, *feel* everything. He pressed Zoe against the tunnel wall, and kissed her. As he did, she released a breath into his mouth—a sigh—that made him shiver.

Zoe smiled, put a hand on X's chest, and thrust him at the opposite wall. X all but left the ground as he flew backward. He'd forgotten that she had powers, too. He began to speak but Zoe strode toward him, and kissed him twice—once softly and with cool, parted lips, and once so forcefully that she seemed to want to find a way inside his body.

"Which kiss did you like more?" she said.

Dazed, X said only, "Yes."

She dipped her hands just below his waistband, and took hold of his hips. He was aware of every fingertip on his skin.

"Can I tell you a secret?" she said.

"Please," he said.

"I like these powers. I kinda want to keep them."

"I do not think it will be possible."

"What if I promise to only use them for little stuff—like helping people open jars?"

X laughed.

"You are in a playful mood," he said. "I did not expect it."

She kissed him all the way down his throat. His body felt like a fuse that had been lit.

"I'm going to take you home with me," said Zoe. "I'm going to show you everything—everything good, everything the world's got."

"I pray that you can," said X.

Zoe heard the uncertainty in his voice. She pulled back.

"You don't believe you're going to get out of here?"

"I want it far too much to believe it."

VOICES CREPT IN FROM the stadium, and the moment unraveled. X and Zoe left the tunnel hand in hand. The lords had disbanded. Everyone in the stadium had moved closer to Dervish. He didn't bother standing, but seemed more in command of himself now. He glared at them all from the ground.

Regent addressed the unlikely crowd.

"It is Dervish's own doing that we are gathered in the wilds of the Lowlands, where law and morality are but ghosts," he said. "As such, it is his own fault that he shall not have the benefit of a true trial, nor have the right of redress."

"Prattle, prattle, prattle!" said Dervish. "Is my punishment being bored to death?"

Regent ignored him.

"It saddens—and sickens—me to announce that the lords are not in agreement about Dervish or the fate of this gold band," he said. "We shall hear arguments for and against him. But first I think it only right that two more of Dervish's victims be allowed to bear witness to this process. I call them to us now."

X and Zoe exchanged a confused look.

Regent lifted his arm, and pointed at two cells on the second level of the stadium. One cell door sprang open, then the other. The metallic groans drifted down. X stood frozen, waiting to see who emerged from the first cell.

It was a woman. Not many of the others recognized her because she was wearing a new gown.

Ripper descended as if she had just been announced at a ball.

X was stunned to see her again. He thought he'd lost her forever.

Banger materialized from the second cell, looking sleepy and unkempt. The purple cowboy shirt X had given him once was only half-tucked into his jeans. Amazed that he was allowed to leave his cell, Banger looked down at the crowd, and shouted, "For the reals? Coolio!"

"He's a good guy," Zoe whispered to X. "But he should be in the Lowlands just for crimes against slang."

When Ripper and Banger arrived on the stadium floor, they caught sight of Zoe, and stopped short. X waved his hands, trying to communicate that it was okay, that *she* was okay. Beside him, Zoe pounded her chest with a fist: *I'm alive.*

X pointed to where Dervish sat crumpled and diminished. Ripper and Banger saw him now, too. Another shock. Ripper streamed at Dervish, scowling. Her feet were not visible beneath her dress, so she seemed to glide through the air.

"You MAY NOT harm me, you harpy," said Dervish when he saw Ripper bearing down on him. "I am defenseless and have ALL THE RIGHTS of a citizen of the Lowlands!"

Ripper turned to Regent for clarification. Regent shrugged indifferently: *Do what you like.*

Even without powers, Ripper had no trouble pulling up Dervish's frail body. She punched him in the mouth three times in succession. When he fell, she clasped her hands, and brought them down on his head like a hammer striking an anvil.

"Did you ENJOY that?" Dervish hissed when he could speak again.

"I think you know I did," said Ripper.

Regent called the crowd back to order. He informed them that Dervish would be allowed to speak, but that first, they would hear from someone whose life he had taken upon himself to destroy.

Sylvie stepped forward. She looked strong to X. Resolute.

X caught Ripper's eye.

With a proud look, he told her: *That's my mother.*

"WHEN I WAS A lord—when I was 'Versailles'—I never understood why the Higher Power seemed to sleep through our most trying times," Sylvie began. "Why allow Dervish to wreak havoc so long? Why not put a stop to it sooner? Was it because the Higher Power was disgusted by us, and had given us up for lost?" She paused. "I had twenty years to think about those questions when my son was taken from me, and Dervish chained me up in the Cave of Swords."

Sylvie stopped again, and X feared that she wouldn't be able to go on, that the memories of losing him would be too much. He felt a flash of panic, not just because she was his mother, but because she alone now stood between Dervish and freedom.

"Do you want to hear what I realized after twenty years?" said Sylvie at last.

X exhaled in relief. Zoe looped her arm around his waist.

"I realized that when I was alive we asked the same kind of things about god," Sylvie continued. "Maybe the people in your time did, too. Why is there evil in the world? Why is there suffering? We know that there's a method to god's ways, even if we can't always divine it. So maybe there's a method to the Higher Power's ways, too. Maybe, like those poor fools up in the world, we're supposed to find the path forward ourselves—to define for ourselves what's right and what's wrong. And we have an advantage down here, don't we? We were all damned for being murderous, for being selfish and inhumane. Surely that's a sign that we should try something else?"

Zoe leaned into X, and whispered: "I had to give a eulogy for the Wallaces. It wasn't this good."

"Dervish will *never* try anything else," Sylvie went on. "He'll continue to carve his self-loathing into a weapon, and he'll continue to savage the prisoners of the Lowlands with it until the last clock in the universe stops. When it's his turn to speak, I'm sure he will tell you the same thing. Dervish must be stopped for *good*—in both senses of the word. The lords and the guards aren't supposed to beat the prisoners, or engage in any of the treacheries that Dervish is so fond of. Why? Because the true punishment here is psychic, not physical. It's making a soul who's been damned sit in the dark and contemplate his sins until his insides boil with regret. There's no pain worse than that. You all know it because you've all felt it. Probably you feel it still."

Sylvie pointed to the stone statue screaming in terror.

"That's the face of a soul being ripped apart by guilt," she said. "It's *not* the face of a soul being beaten just because some crazed lord finds it amusing. If you have any doubts about what to do with Dervish—or with Zoe and my son, for that matter—think about the fact that the Higher Power allowed Zoe to come here and challenge Dervish. Think about the fact that the Higher Power allowed my son to tear the gold band from Dervish's neck. You shouldn't need any more evidence to do what's right. Remember that the power that rules us is awake—and watching."

Sylvie nodded to indicate that she was done. There was a silence, during which X could hear the rivers whisper.

Then the applause began.

It started with Regent, Ripper, and Banger, but spread quickly. Soon, Tree and the guards were clapping, too—every one of them but the Cockney.

X looked to the lords. One or two still appeared unmoved, unsure about what to do with Dervish. How *could* they be? What would it take?

When the applause died away, Regent told Dervish he could speak if he liked, but that no one would be disappointed if he chose not to.

"I shall speak," said Dervish. "Of course I shall speak."

He stood, spreading his feet wide in an attempt to appear commanding.

"The whore we called Versailles is correct in precisely one regard: I shall not repent, nor beg for mercy," said Dervish. "Instead, I shall expound upon your idiocy a final time. You think in dispensing with me, you will save the Lowlands? The Lowlands MADE me."

He prowled toward the other lords.

"You thought you had tamed the Countess, yet, according to my spies, she has already unsheathed her knife and begun peeling the skin of a certain Plum." Dervish turned to X, and waited for the pain to show in his eyes. "And that is AS IT SHOULD BE, you worms. We are here to punish sinners, not grow goddamn DAISIES! Do what you will with me. You have become soft because of these two"—he gestured disgustedly at X and then Zoe—"and I do not fear you."

X surveyed the ranks of the lords. Surely they saw Dervish for the cancer that he was? Even the Cockney was frowning now, and fussing with his lamp, as if he'd never been devoted to him. Zoe pulled X closer. He was so tense that he'd dug his fingernails into his hand.

The lords didn't gather to debate this time. Regent only had to look them in the eyes to know their thoughts. He lingered a long time, it seemed to X, on the ones who had previously dissented.

At last Regent turned back to Dervish.

"It saddens me that you think us soft," he said. "Perhaps we can persuade you otherwise."

He nodded to one of the lords.

"Take him," he said.

The lord lifted Dervish into the air by his neck, like an osprey clutching a fish.

He flew at the statue of the screaming man, and threw Dervish into its gaping mouth. Dervish tried to scramble out, but before he could the lord made a quick motion, like the tossing of a match.

The mouth exploded in blue flame. Dervish's scream was like a twisting screw.

The lord sealed the statue's mouth with another gesture.

Dervish was swallowed whole.

ONCE HE WAS GONE, the Lowlands themselves seemed to breathe again. X felt as if a siren they'd all gotten used to had suddenly gone quiet. He watched as his friends rushed to one another, as the lords broke into a flurry of talk, as the guards settled the bets they had made by handing over weapons and rings.

X's relief at Dervish's fall was undercut only by the fear that everyone had forgotten about him and Zoe. The lords hadn't even ruled on what would become of his mother.

He found Regent in the crowd, and interrupted him a second

time. Regent didn't wait to hear X's questions. Instead, he gave him a gentle look, and said, "You will have all your answers soon. For now, rejoice. The victory over Dervish is yours more than anyone else's."

"Mine?" said X. "I did nothing."

"Why can you *never* see the good that you do?" said Regent. "Dervish couldn't bear how much you loved Zoe and your mother when no one had ever loved him. He tried to punish you for it. It became a mania. At last, the other lords—and the Higher Power, even—saw him for the horror that he was and had always been."

X thanked Regent, then turned and gazed at his friends wistfully, as if he were on a train and they were disappearing into the distance. He looked at Sylvie, Ripper, Banger, the Ukrainian, Maud. And Zoe, of course. How had he come to care about so many people? Had it all been Zoe's doing? Had she opened him up in some way—broken down a wall that had been blocking him? No, it wasn't quite that. She hadn't broken down the wall—she had coaxed him out from behind it. She had convinced him that there was nothing in his heart to be ashamed of, that it was okay to be *seen*.

X watched as Banger greeted the Ukrainian.

"Dude!" said Banger. Seeing Maud, he added, "Dude and random chick! Whoa—and a cat!"

Banger was punchy from being in the cell.

"I'm allergic, actually," he said. "Wait, are allergies still a thing when you're dead? They can't be, right? How could they? Can I pet the little guy?"

Even this exchange warmed X somehow. He turned again, and saw something that triggered an avalanche of feeling in his chest: Ripper was shyly approaching his mother.

He hurried forward to introduce them.

"Ripper, this is—"

She raised a hand to silence him.

"I know very well who she is," she said. "Madam, it is an honor. Truly. I almost feel I should kneel before you."

"And I feel like I should kneel before *you*," said Sylvie. "You raised my son as if he were your own. I can't think of a nobler act."

"I suppose we could take turns kneeling before each other?" said Ripper.

Instead, they embraced.

"That's an exquisite dress, by the way," said Sylvie.

"Thank you so much," said Ripper. "I stole it."

Zoe came to stand by X. She seemed to know what he was feeling as everyone met or reacquainted themselves, as the disparate strands of his life intertwined.

After a moment, she nudged him.

Ripper had gone to say hello to the Ukrainian.

X feared she'd say something tart or dismissive. She had never taken the guard, or his feelings for her, seriously. X wished that he'd had a chance to tell Ripper how nobly the Ukrainian had behaved. In any case, Ripper nodded politely, and even put a hand on the guard's shoulder to let him know she was glad to see him.

"Hello, Mr. Guard," she said.

"Hello, Reeper," he said.

"You have been injured," she said. She touched his face gently. "I'm very sorry to see it."

"Yes, is true," said the Ukrainian. "Had unpleasant experience while bravely defending X, okay? But in my time of agony, many things are made clearly crystal."

The Ukrainian paused to introduce Ripper to Maud, then the guard's expression turned serious, and he began what sounded like a rehearsed speech.

"I am loving you many years, Reeper," he said. "I think you are aware, yes?"

Ripper's body sagged so profoundly that the straps of her dress rose off her shoulders.

"Could we perhaps discuss this later?" she said. "Or not at all? Not at all would suit me *very* well."

"No, now is good," said the Ukrainian. "Now is important."

Maud, looking uncomfortable, tried to move away, but the guard gestured for her to stay, apparently for moral support.

"I wait long, lonely time for you, Reeper, during which you behave vehement crazy, and sing many things I think are not actual songs," he said. "I tell you now I am done waiting. My love for you is forever dead."

X could see Ripper trying to mask her relief.

"I understand," she said. "I have only myself to blame."

"Is correct," said the Ukrainian. "Now I tell you a second thing, and it may be painful in your ears: I have big new love, and it is Maud."

Startled, Maud popped her eyes. "You can't be serious."

"Is true, cat person," said the Ukrainian. "My heart is now in your hands. I promise you it is quite red and large."

JUST THEN, REGENT CALLED everyone to attention, and a hush fell over the arena.

"Our business here is not yet ended," he said.

He lifted what had been Dervish's golden band, and broke it in two. To X, it almost seemed like a religious rite. Regent slipped half the band into a pocket in his robe. The other half he held like a gift he was about to bestow.

"We are in need of a new lord to fill the void that Dervish leaves behind," he said. "I have nominated someone who has some experience in the field, and her name has been quite well received."

He looked to Sylvie.

"Come forward, if you would, old friend," he said.

Sylvie crossed the ground swiftly. X was struck by how fast she had recovered from the cave, how—even in her gingham farm dress and boots—she seemed to throw off light.

"Here I am, old friend," she said.

Regent lifted the fragment of the gold band.

"We ask you the favor of serving once more," he said. "Will you do us this honor?"

"I will," she said, "if you'll do something for me in return."

Regent smiled fondly.

"Most people regard it a great privilege to be a lord," he said.

"Then you're welcome to ask most people," said Sylvie, smiling back. "I, however, am aware that being a lord changes you—and not always for the better—so I'm not going to accept without assurances. Are you ready to hear my terms?"

"How long have I known you?" said Regent. "I'm perfectly aware of what you want—and I will do it gladly."

"I need to hear you promise," said Sylvie.

"We shall release Zoe from the Lowlands immediately," said Regent, "with the obvious admonition that she never speak of anything she witnessed here."

Relieved as he was for Zoe, X was alarmed not to have heard his own name. His heart felt like a spinning coin.

He looked to Sylvie and saw, with relief, that she was still waiting—that she wasn't yet satisfied.

Regent continued: "Yes, yes, we shall free your son, too. I believed he is called Xavier? He should never have spent a single hour in the Lowlands. I suspect the Higher Power did not know what to do with a soul so rare."

Before X could even process the words, he heard Zoe break into sobs.

Regent put the gold fragment up to Sylvie's throat. X watched, transfixed, as it grew around her like a vine and became whole.

The lords began beating their palms against their legs. It took X a moment to realize it was a kind of applause, and another to realize that it was not just for his mother but for Zoe and him.

There was still the second fragment of gold in Regent's pocket.

Regent removed it, and held it out for all to see.

"Dervish did us one courtesy in his final diatribe," he said. "He reminded us that we must remove the Countess from power as well. So it appears we require a second new lord. It must be someone inspiring enough to obliterate the memory of the Countess entirely—to stand for everything she stood *against*."

Sylvie began to interrupt.

Regent stopped her with another fond look.

"Fear not, old friend—we are in agreement on this matter as well," he said.

Regent searched the crowd with his eyes.

"Ripper, come forward, if you would."

twenty-eight

ONCE AGAIN, X STOOD staring at the green house with the red metal roof.

Rufus's house.

Zoe had gone in to talk to her mother.

It was afternoon. Already dark. The lawn was more grass than snow, but sopping wet. The portal that X had smashed into the street for himself and Ripper had been filled. X could see where it used to be because the pavement there was blacker than the road. The sight of it seemed to confirm that he would never return to the Lowlands. The way was lost—and thank god.

He'd been waiting perhaps 20 minutes. From the house, he had heard crying, shouting. But at least some of the crying had sounded loving. Conciliatory. That gave him hope. He didn't want to be the cause of even more unhappiness in Zoe's family. He'd leave if he had to, though he had no idea where he would sleep. Where did people go if they had nowhere to go?

X wore only a torn shirt, mud-streaked pants, decimated boots. He'd left his overcoat behind in the Lowlands, he couldn't remember where. But it was all right. At least he had the silver packet with everything but the piece of porcelain, which his mother asked to keep after using it to wound Dervish: the shard held two memories for her now, one layered over the other. X also had the letter that Zoe had written him once. He reached into one pocket and crinkled the foil to reassure himself, then reached into the other to feel the plastic bag that held the letter. They made him feel rooted.

In the end, it'd been his mother who freed him from the Lowlands, and Regent who freed Zoe. Sylvie had pressed her palm beneath X's eyes, as was the custom whenever a lord sent a soul to the world. Her hand was cooler than Regent's had ever been, and the pain that hummed under his skin was nothing compared to the pain of saying good-bye.

X had peered at his mother in the final seconds, desiring to say a hundred things but powerless to untangle them. After knowing her for an hour, he was losing her. What was it that Zoe said when he told her that loss seemed to be the way of the world? *Then I don't like the way of the world. I'd like to speak to a manager, please.* Someday, he'd ask her to explain the thing about the manager.

X had actually wanted to stay longer in the Lowlands—just long enough to talk to his mother, to hear more of his father's story. Sylvie had known what he was thinking. She could hear his thoughts, just as he and Zoe could hear each other's sometimes. She shook her head no. She wanted her son to live, and wouldn't risk waiting. She told X that she loved him very, very much. And then she gave the world to him—and *him* to the world. X didn't ask if she would be able to visit him sometimes, if she'd one day walk with him in the mountains. Sylvie said nothing about it either. Neither pretended to know the future.

RUFUS'S FRONT DOOR CREAKED open. Jonah rushed down the steps, and ran across the lawn. He hugged X hard around the waist.

He was crying.

"You're *staying*," he said.

"Am I?" said X, his hopes rising.

"Yes, because *I* said so."

"Ah. Thank you, Jonah. Yet we must respect your mother's decision, whatever it is. Promise me."

"Okay. I mostly promise."

"Only mostly?"

"Yes, but that's a lot. I was gonna say *sorta*."

Jonah released X from the hug, and wiped his nose on the sleeve of his navy fleece, which was covered with dog fur. A bit of fur stuck to his face. X thought with a pang of Uhura, and wondered if she had survived. He couldn't bring himself to ask.

"If my mom won't let you stay here, you and me can get our *own* house," Jonah said. "You can be in charge of cooking, and I can be in charge of answering the door. Those are the only big things."

X smiled, and tousled the boy's hair.

"Why is everybody always mussing my hair?" said Jonah. "My hair is *already* mussed."

X shook his own mane.

"Mine, too," he said. "It's even more beleaguered than yours, I fear."

"That's okay," said Jonah. "Our house isn't going to be a hair-combing house." He paused. "Zoe says you don't have magic anymore."

"That's true," said X. "I am entirely . . . I confess to not knowing the word. Magic-less? Un-magic?"

"I think it's just *regular*," said Jonah.

"Yes," said X. "I am just regular now."

"Are you sad about it?" said Jonah.

"No, I like it," said X. "I feel like my body, my blood, everything, is finally my own. I don't know if that makes sense?"

"No, it's weird."

Jonah wiped his eyes on the spot where he'd wiped his nose. Something seemed to occur to him.

"Hey, guess who did a really *big* magic trick, actually," he said. "Wait, you don't have to guess—it was me."

"Indeed?" said X. "Tell me."

Jonah flashed a giant grin.

"I'll *show* you," he said.

He dashed back up the steps, opened the door, and shouted inside: "Come here. Come on. Here we go. You can do it, girl."

Uhura came waddling out.

She was still underweight and lethargic, but clearly healthier. She recognized X and trudged heroically toward him. He met the dog halfway, and picked her up. Her fur was shining again. She felt . . . substantial. She licked his neck.

"Her tongue feels sandy, right?" said Jonah.

"It does," said X.

"I made her better," said Jonah. "Boom! And guess who's *so* happy now?"

X knew but pretended not to.

Jonah raced back to the door. Even before he'd opened it all the way, Spock bolted out, and ran circles on the lawn.

Zoe and her mother stepped outside a few minutes later. The afternoon was transitioning from blue to black. X could see the mountains in the distance, their silhouettes shaggy with trees. Zoe still had a cut on her cheek, as well as light bruises on her cheek-bones from when Regent had sent her out of the Lowlands—they were a faint copy of the ones that X had had since he was 16. Zoe walked behind her mom with her eyes cast down. Her mother looked exhausted and frazzled, and like she was trying to suppress her fury.

"Uh-oh," said Jonah.

X held Uhura tighter.

"Remember our promise," he told Jonah.

"Our *mostly* promise," said Jonah.

Zoe's mother looked X up and down. Her eyes landed on the fresh cuts in his forehead, the scars on the back of his hands. Her anger seemed to dissipate infinitesimally.

"Zoe has told me some things," she said. "I don't think she's told me everything. But I've decided to trust her. Just tell me *no one* is coming after you *ever* again. Say it so I believe it."

"I'm free," said X. "I hardly believe it myself, yet it is true."

"They don't want him anymore," said Jonah, "'cause he's just reg-ular now. Look..." He stamped on X's foot, causing X to cry out. "See!"

"Literally, what is wrong with you, Jonah?" said Zoe.

"What?" said Jonah. "I'm helping!"

"Okay, listen," said Zoe's mother. "I'm going to have to tell Rufus who you really are. I can't *imagine* how that's going to go. If he doesn't flip out—"

"He's not gonna flip out," said Zoe. "He'd do anything for you. Plus, my god, he's the emperor of mellow."

"If Rufus doesn't flip out," her mother continued, "you can stay in the shed, and he'll sleep in the living room with Jonah. For two weeks. That's it. Then Zoe and Jonah and I are moving to the Wallaces' old place, and you're gone, I don't care where."

"Thank you," said X. "I hardly know how to—"

"Stop," said Zoe's mother. "I'm not doing this because I like you. As far as you know right now, I only like you a *tiny, tiny* bit. Do you understand? I'm doing this because I love my daughter."

X nodded. Uhura licked his neck again.

"Mom's not really mad," said Jonah. "That's only her pretend-mad voice."

"No, it isn't," his mother said. "This is my *for real* mad voice."

"Nope," said Jonah.

"Yeah, it's at least twenty percent pretend," said Zoe.

Her mother rolled her eyes, then pulled Zoe and Jonah close and hugged them hard.

She spoke kindly to X for the first time.

"Zoe says you met your mom," she said.

"I did," said X.

"I'm glad," she said. "Can I ask what it was like? Uhura, *stop* licking him."

"It's all right, I've missed Uhura's company," said X. "Meeting my mother . . ." What could he say? "Meeting my mother made me feel something I have only ever felt with Zoe: a little bit whole."

Zoe's mom gave him an appraising look.

305

"Okay, I like that," she said.

She seemed to notice for the first time how filthy X's clothes were. He looked self-consciously at his feet.

"I know you're used to washing in rivers," she said. "But it's time to try a shower."

X FOLLOWED ZOE TO Rufus's small, wood-paneled bathroom, and watched as she turned on the water. There was a piece of transparent plastic hanging in the chipped pink tub. It was covered with irregular splotches of color and words that X couldn't read.

"I don't even *want* to know how long Rufus has had this shower curtain," said Zoe. She turned back to X. She must have seen how intently he was staring at it. "It's a map of the world," she said. "Have you never seen one?"

Embarrassed, X said only, "Where are *we*?"

"Here," Zoe said, pointing. "And this is Massachusetts, where we borrowed the orange boat. It's on the Atlantic Ocean. See?"

"Show me more," said X.

"This is Texas, where you captured Stan in the hair salon," she said. "This is British Columbia, where we found my father. This is Portugal, where Regent's dad made wine. This is Ukraine. What else? This is London, where Ripper lived when she—when she actually *lived*." She paused. "That's enough for now. How hot do you like the water?"

"I'm not sure," said X.

"Right," said Zoe. "Well, tell me if this is too hot or too cold?"

X reached into the shower.

"It is neither too hot nor too cold," he said. "It is just right."

"You sound like Goldilocks," said Zoe. "Goldilocks is—"

"I know who Goldilocks is," said X.

Zoe kissed him.

"Well, okay, then."

She sprayed something into the mist.

"Eucalyptus," she said. "My mom's into it."

Zoe identified the bottles that stood like soldiers along the edge of the tub, and suggested that X use her mother's soap (which was pear green and flecked with flower petals) instead of Rufus's (which was actually several small wedges of soap stuck together).

"Thank you for the tour," said X. "I believe I have all the information I need."

"Okay," said Zoe. "Just be careful in the tub—it's slippery. It'd be messed up if you survived the Lowlands just to bust your head in Rufus's bathroom."

"I will not bust my head," said X. "You have my word."

"I'm serious," said Zoe. "You're not a superhero anymore."

X closed the door behind her, but she pushed her way back in.

"Do you want music?" she said. "I can get you music, but if you dance you might fall."

"I don't think I require music," said X. "Or dancing."

"Okay," she said. "Just checking. You be you."

When he was sure Zoe had run out of questions, X sloughed off his clothes and stepped—carefully—into the tub. The water stung as it found the bruises on his chest and back, but slowly his muscles relaxed. Everything loosened, everything calmed. He soaped himself until he felt like he was covered in sea foam—he'd overdone it, probably—then watched dirt from the Lowlands run down his legs, and into the drain, away from him forever. He lifted his face to the water. He let it pound his eyelids and cheeks. He washed his hair, but he must have overdone this, too, because he found he could make clumps of it stick straight out from his head, like sunshine in a drawing of the sun. When he was clean, X found he wasn't ready to leave the comfort of the shower.

He thought about how improbably, how profoundly, how absurdly lucky he was to be free.

He turned to the shower curtain, rubbed the condensation off with his hand, and tried to memorize a little bit of the world.

X FOUND CLEAN CLOTHES of Rufus's folded in a pile outside the bathroom door, and the Bissell family around the kitchen table, waiting for him. When he asked how long he'd been in the shower, everyone laughed, but in a warm, rather than mean-spirited, way.

"An hour and a half," said Zoe.

Her mother had tended to Zoe's cuts and abrasions in the interim. She told X to take off his shirt and sit, so she could do the same for him. When he hesitated, she said, "It's okay. I went to medical school for three semesters."

X removed his shirt. He saw Zoe's mother look at the sleeves of tattoos that ran up his arms and at the damage that had been done to his body during 20 years in the Lowlands. He worried that it would be too much for her. He worried that she'd turn him out after all.

Instead, the sorry state of X's skin seemed to deepen her sympathy. She opened a metal box on the table, took out a tube of ointment, and squeezed some into her palm.

"Okay," she said, "let's fix you."

LATER, X LAY IN the plastic lounge chair in the shed in the backyard, with Zoe curled on top of him.

308

The shed was decrepit, and leaned so far left that it seemed to be in the midst of falling. Tools hung on the wall above the work-bench. Zoe had told X their names, but he'd already forgotten them all. He was thrilled to be among the living, but daunted by the ten million things he didn't know. Zoe had once said she couldn't comprehend how big the Lowlands were. X couldn't comprehend how big freedom was. He thought of the little orange boat in the vast black sea.

"I want to be of use somehow," he said.

Zoe stroked the muscle that ran along the back of his arm.

"Oh, I'm definitely gonna use you," she said.

"I am in earnest, Zoe," he said. "I want to be more than some tree stump you must drag behind you. Else one day you will wake, and wonder why on earth you saved me."

Zoe sighed.

"I shall ne'er wonder that, goodly sir," she said. "I shall ne'er ere wonder it."

"'Ere' means *before*, not *ever*," said X. "And therein lies another problem. I must alter the way I speak, the way I dress—the way I move, for all I know."

"Please don't change the way you move," said Zoe. "Look, I'll show you some YouTube videos, and you'll start picking stuff up. That's what would happen in a movie. You'd watch YouTube while I was at school, and after two days you'd be playing *Mario Kart*." She kissed him. "Please don't worry. I'll explain everything to you bit by bit, and it'll be like *I'm* seeing it for the first time, too. It's like that with Jonah, and I love it. That kid is still amazed by yogurt."

"What is yogurt?" said X.

"See!" said Zoe. "This is gonna be awesome. There are so many good yogurts."

They fell asleep without intending to, and woke when Rufus knocked on the door. The shed was dark except for the heaters, which gave off an orange light. It took X a few seconds to remember where he was.

Zoe sat up groggily in his lap.

"Come in," she said.

"Cool if I shed some light on the . . . shed?" said Rufus.

"Sure," said Zoe.

Rufus pulled a string. A bare bulb came to life, and swung back and forth. X squinted up at Rufus, who held a bottle of water, a new toothbrush, and a pair of moccasin-style slippers.

"A couple offerings," he said. "Nothing epic. I wasn't sure what you needed."

X remembered Rufus's bright eyes and his dense red beard, which seemed to be waging a military campaign to take over his face. But he was surprised by how tentative he seemed now. Rufus set the things on the workbench, and went to leave. Only then did the obvious occur to X: Rufus might not love the idea of a bounty hunter from hell sleeping in his shed. The fact that X was actually a *former* bounty hunter from hell . . . Who knew if that made it any easier?

X stood to shake his hand. He hated the idea that he'd made Rufus uncomfortable in his own home.

"Thank you for sheltering me," said X. "And thank you for these clothes I wear. I'm embarrassed by how needy I am. I have nothing but my name, and even *that* Zoe had to give me."

"It's all good, man," said Rufus, almost, but not quite, looking at him. "None of us really *own* anything anyway, you know? How long'd you wear that ratty shirt and stuff?"

"Years," said X.

"Ooof," said Zoe.

"Yes, now that I hear it aloud, it does sound unappealing," said X.

"No judgment," said Rufus. "I've still got socks from high school. Well, *one* sock."

Rufus tried again to leave, but X stopped him.

"Zoe's mother has told you my story, I think?" he said.

"Oh, yeah," said Rufus. "Yeah, yeah, yeah." He mimed his head exploding. "My whole thing is going with the flow. But I've got to admit, I'm sorta surprised by where the flow is going."

"But you do believe my story, fantastical as it is?" said X.

"Yes, I believe it," said Rufus. "I do. I mean—Zoe'll tell you—I believe some pretty weird shit anyway. I believe trees talk—to each other *and* to us. I think some Dr. Seuss books are real. I think they're actually nonfiction. Not all of them, but a couple."

"What do trees say?" said X.

Rufus laughed.

"I'm still working on that," he said. He looked straight at X finally, then took the slippers from the workbench.

"Try these on," he said. "Let's see if they fit."

The slippers were lined with fur—and so comfortable that they seemed to warm X's entire body.

"I will never take them off," he said.

"Rad," said Rufus. "They're yours."

X could see that Rufus wanted to say more. He wished he was as good at putting people at ease as Zoe was.

"Here's the deal," Rufus said finally. "I can't have Zoe or her family getting hurt. If this whole thing is *Horton Hears a Who!*—and we're protecting somebody that nobody else believes in or cares about—that's great. I am *so* down for that. But if it turns out to be *The Cat in the Hat*, and you just trash everybody's lives . . ."

"The Cat in the Hat comes back, and fixes everything," said Zoe.

"I know, I know," said Rufus. "But that part's made-up. They had to tack it on at the end because it's a kids' book."

"I'm sorry," said X. "I'm not following this conversation. The cat has a hat?"

"I just mean I care about this family," said Rufus. "Zoe, I know you think I have a thing for your mom."

"I have never, ever said that," said Zoe. "Okay, now that I think about it, I've said it a lot."

"It's cool," said Rufus. "I can see why you'd think it. But I care about you and Jonah, too. I'm like X—I don't really have a family of my own. So I can't have *any* negative stuff happen to you guys. It'd demolish me, man. I'd be roadkill."

"It's gonna be okay," said Zoe.

"It will," said X. "I know that's the hardest thing of all to believe, yet it is true. Seeing any of them hurt would break me, too."

In the silence that followed, one of the heaters went out. Rufus kicked the side of it. The coils went *thong*, and returned to life.

"I know it would," Rufus told X. "I can tell you're a solid dude. Okay, I'm all in. Let's do this, whatever this is." He shook X's hand again. "You guys need anything else?"

X could think of nothing, but Zoe said, "Actually, yeah."

She handed her phone to Rufus.

"Look at this bear sculpture, and tell me if you made it."

Rufus scratched at his beard—it was so bushy that his fingertips actually disappeared into it—and inspected the picture.

"Yeah, that's one of mine," he said. "That was a good one. I remember the guy who bought it, too. He works with bears in the park, right? Knows a shit-ton. Tim Something?"

"Timothy," said Zoe. "Ward."

"He was also a solid dude," said Rufus. "Real quiet. Little bit awkward. But I dug him for sure."

X felt something start up in his heart.

"What are you looking at?" he said, though he already knew.

Zoe held the phone out to him. It glowed on her palm.

"A picture of your dad," she said.

twenty-nine

THE NEXT DAY WAS a Saturday, blue and bright. X showered again—it only took him 45 minutes this time—then he and Zoe drove to Glacier National Park to meet Timothy Ward.

X saw Zoe resting her elbow on the open window, so he did the same. The sun warmed his skin. The wind rushed up his sleeve, making it flap like a sail.

Regent had warned them not to tell Timothy Ward that X was his son. X knew he was right. He didn't want to endanger his father by telling him about the Lowlands. He also didn't want to upend the man's life—he had upended enough lives—or make him feel beholden. And what if losing Sylvie had broken Timothy's heart once upon a time? Telling him why she'd disappeared, why she had never come back—it would only break it again.

It was Rufus who'd thought of a pretext for X to meet his father. Rufus wasn't thrilled about deceiving Timothy—he believed that lies were a kind of air pollution, like secondhand smoke—but these were what even he had to admit were "superweird" circumstances. He'd started texting immediately.

Rufus to Timothy: *Hey, man. There's a young guy who's thinking of having me make him a bear. Cool if him and his girl come check yours out? Yours is a fav of mine. I know solitude's your jam, but would you consider?*

Timothy to Rufus: *Greetings, Rufus. OK sure—my bear and I could use the company. Would tomorrow at 4 work? I'm still on Lake Lillian. You'll tell them where?*

Rufus to Timothy: *Yep. Perf. Peace.*

Now, as they passed through Columbia Falls on the way to Glacier, X's nerves began to prickle. He knew it was silly. The path to his father was not fraught like the path to his mother had been: there'd be no combat, no tunnels, no subterranean seas. Still, he'd have to sit across from the man who'd helped give him life, and pretend to be interested in a wooden bear. Ever since he'd met Zoe, holding back his feelings had come to seem stupid and futile—like trying to hold back water.

"Do you want to practice talking?" Zoe said into the silence.

"Practice talking?" said X. "Are my skills so wanting?"

"I mean talking with more of a twenty-first-century vibe," said Zoe.

"Nah, whatever, I'm cool," said X.

"Nice!" said Zoe.

"Right? I can totally hang," said X.

"Okay, maybe dial it down a little," said Zoe.

X asked Zoe if he could see Timothy Ward's picture again. She brought it up on her phone, and he stared at it as she drove. He liked the way his father looked: curly black hair, broad shoulders, shy expression. He couldn't stop looking at the picture. Zoe showed him what button to push when the screen went black.

At Glacier, a sixtyish woman in the ticket booth gave them a broad smile and said, "How you two doing today?"

X loved the uncomplicated sunniness in her voice. He loved the simplicity of the interaction. Before now, he'd been expected to kill almost everyone he met.

As Zoe fished out her pass to the park and her driver's license, X leaned forward in his seat to talk to the woman.

"We're chill," he said. "How about you?"

The woman laughed.

"I'm chill, too," she said.

"Sweet," said X.

Zoe stifled a laugh. The woman handed back her identification.

"Have a very chill day!" she said.

Zoe pulled away, and they crossed over a glittering creek. X's nervousness gave way to excitement. The immensity of the trees and mountains—the permanence of them—had never struck him so hard before, probably because he'd always been bent on some awful task for the lords. He stared at them in amazement now.

This was where his parents had met.

Zoe clicked off the radio—out of respect for what was about to happen, it seemed like. For the next few minutes, the only sound was a disembodied woman's voice from her phone.

"In two miles, turn right toward Lake Lillian."

"In one mile, turn right . . ."

"In two hundred feet . . ."

It struck X that not long ago they had been in another forest, heading toward a lake and another father.

Zoe's.

It was an awful memory—Zoe had screamed herself hoarse at her father when they found him—but it snuck into X's head before he realized what it was. It was like he'd clenched his fist around barbed wire.

"You okay?" said Zoe.

"In truth, I am thinking about your father," said X.

Zoe took a hand off the wheel, and stroked the back of his neck.

"I'm not," she said.

"ARRIVE AT DESTINATION."

X was startled by his father's house—it wasn't what he had expected, though he couldn't have said what he'd expected.

It was a tree house. It had a wraparound balcony and such giant windows that it seemed more glass than wood. It was set *among* fir trees but not exactly *in* one. X actually couldn't tell, from a distance, what was holding the house up. It seemed to hover above the ground, as if it had just taken off.

X and Zoe got out of the car, transfixed. Instead of steps or a ladder, there was a curving, wood-planked walkway that rose slowly from the forest floor to the front door. The path was bordered by carved handrails, and hung with old iron lanterns. X and Zoe were halfway up it when X's father opened the front door, waved without speaking, then retreated nervously back into the house.

The interior was a single enormous room. What little wall space wasn't dominated by windows was occupied by shelves, so that the only thing you saw—besides trees, mountains, and sunlight—was books. There were only two decorations in the entire house. One was a frame with pale fuzzy flowers pressed under glass. The other

317

was Rufus's sculpture. X had thought that Rufus only made happy, cartoonish bears that waved and held signs, but he'd carved this one as if it were sleeping. It lay near the fireplace, emanating peace.

Timothy brought out a platter overburdened with food—three kinds of crackers, three cheeses, green and red grapes, and various sliced meats, as well as dark chocolate in a gold wrapper. The minute he set it on the low wooden table he seemed to realize it was too much.

"We don't get a whole lot of guests, the bear and me, so I'm not clear on the whole portions thing," he said. "Don't feel like you have to eat it all."

X wasn't sure what to say.

Zoe said, "Oh, we're *gonna* eat it all. I'm like a seagull."

Timothy looked different than he had in the photograph, though it was only a few years old. X wondered why it hadn't occurred to him before: His father, unlike his mother, was a mortal. He was aging. Sylvie, trapped in the amber of the Lowlands, had remained 35. Timothy had edged into his 50s. His curly hair was graying at the temples, and he had a slight belly, which X found comforting. It reminded him of Plum.

X didn't think he looked like his father—his hands, maybe—but then he looked *so* much like Sylvie that he probably should have foreseen this, too. X remembered his mother saying that Timothy had been full of life when she met him, that he'd put a flower in his teeth and danced. *That* Timothy seemed to be gone. He seemed shy now, as if he wasn't sure how to proceed, as if he was more comfortable with wild animals than people. The uncertainty in him resonated with X.

X had spent his whole life wanting to say more than he knew how to.

"I've never seen a house like this before," he said, remembering to speak with "a twenty-first-century vibe."

"Seriously," said Zoe. "Are you an Elven lord?"

"I wish," said Timothy quietly. "And thank you. I put a lot of thought into this house. Maybe too much. The truth is, I—"

X and Zoe leaned forward, but Timothy decided not to finish the sentence. He looked at the platter. The silence expanded awkwardly, like a cloud that would eventually fill the room.

X needed to know what Timothy had been about to say. Zoe must have been curious, too, or she would have blurted something random to jolt the conversation forward. Fifteen seconds went by. The silence grazed the walls and ceiling. X was about to give up and ask something pointless about the sculpture, when Timothy looked up, and said suddenly, "The truth is, I built it for a woman."

X HAD NEVER CONSIDERED the possibility that Timothy had fallen in love with someone else after Sylvie disappeared—that he'd married, maybe more than once, had children, adventures, a life. He steeled himself to hear another woman's name. Then, as Timothy told his story, X felt a wave of relief, of gratitude. Maybe it was selfish, but it was what he felt. His father had never loved anyone but his mother.

"I was thirty-two," said Timothy. "Happy as hell. Already obsessed with bears, wolverines, mountain lions—all the carnivores. I just loved being outdoors. Wouldn't go indoors to save my life. Any kind of building at all felt like a—like a cell, I guess."

At the word "cell," X could feel Zoe forcing herself not to look at him.

"I'd been working for the park for two or three years," Timothy went on. "I had just come up with—you've got to be kind of a bear nerd to care about this stuff—but I'd just come up with a new way to collect DNA samples from grizzlies so we could track the population better. I got a heap of praise for it. Mail from wildlife biologists all over the place. By the way, you can skip the cheese and go right for the chocolate, if you want. There aren't a whole ton of house rules around here."

"Thank you," said X.

The idea that you ate food in a particular order made no sense to him anyway.

"The grizzly thing felt like the highlight of my life," said Timothy. "I bought myself a suit to celebrate—not a suit-suit but a kind of sleeping bag that you wear. Almost like a space suit? I always found sleeping bags constricting. Like I was a larva or something. Anyway, then I had a day off. It was September second. I remember because of what happened. I hiked up to Avalanche Lake, and met this woman, Sylvie. And all of a sudden the grizzly thing was no longer the highlight of my life. Not even close."

Timothy fell quiet.

"I just realized I don't even know your names," he said.

Zoe told him hers.

When it was X's turn, he said Xavier.

"And how old are you guys?" said Timothy. "Is that a rude question?"

"Not at all," said Zoe. "I'm seventeen."

"Twenty," said X.

The second the answer was out of his mouth, he wondered if he should have lied. Was it crazy to worry that Timothy had noticed how much he resembled Sylvie, and that simple math would lead him to the truth?

"You're not finished with your story, I hope?" X said quickly.

"Oh, I think I've probably subjected you to enough," said Timothy.

"No, no," said X. He smiled. "Please subject us to some more."

Zoe turned to him, and lifted her eyebrows, impressed by his little joke. Honestly, it was like something she herself might have said.

"People your age don't even believe in love at first sight, do they?" said Timothy.

Now Zoe came to X's aid.

She raised her hand.

"*We* do," she said.

"I DIDN'T HEAR SYLVIE come up behind me on the trail— and I'm generally pretty alert," said Timothy. "She just kind of appeared. She had a blue-and-white dress on, which I thought . . . I mean, who hikes in a dress? But she blew right past me. We were down by the gorge. You know it? I waited to see if she'd look back at me. And she did. She gave me a look like, 'Think you can keep up?' That was all I needed. I was pretty cocky in those days.

"We kept passing each other on the trail, trying to impress each other. Eventually, I realized she was just toying with me. She was ten times the hiker I was. Crazy strong. In my defense, she was so pretty that I was tripping over tree roots and stuff. I was just so taken with her. It blotted everything else out. If you had stopped me right there in the middle of the trail, and you had said, 'Do you know what day it is, Tim? Do you know where you are?,' I *might* have been able to come up with 'North America?'"

Timothy paused. X feared he would stop altogether, but the story had a momentum of its own now.

"She came back four times that month," Timothy said. "Always wearing the same dress. Just seeing her walk toward me through the trees was thrilling. When she smiled . . . I mean, it was like her body was made of light. Sounds dumb, probably."

"It doesn't," X said gently.

"Later, I figured out we spent about sixty-five hours together," said Timothy. He looked at them sheepishly. "I like counting stuff," he said. "Anyway, I bet we spent sixty-two of those hours just hiking the trails and talking. I said things that I'd never said before. To anyone. Not even to myself. Painful stuff. Joyful stuff. I feel foolish saying this because I'm a scientist—I mean, you're looking at a guy with a doctorate in biology—but the way she listened to me, the things she said, her whole kind of aura . . . I felt like she healed me in a lot of ways. Fixed some of the messed-up wiring in my head, you know? I don't know if that makes sense. She never told me a whole lot about herself, in terms of specifics, which was frustrating but also just *completely* tantalizing. For instance, ask me what her last name was."

"What was her last name?" said X.

"No idea," said Timothy.

X realized then that *he* didn't know either.

"She was from Montana, but where exactly?" said Timothy. "No idea. Later, I realized that some of what she *did* tell me about herself didn't totally compute in terms of a timeline. But being with her—I'd never felt anything like it. I didn't even know that a feeling like that was on the *menu*. She picked some plants for me at one point, and I did this goofy Spanish dance for her. You've got to understand: I was *not* the kind of guy who danced. That's how far she'd pulled me outside myself." Timothy paused. "Look, I have to stop. The rest of the story is no fun. It's upsetting even to me, and it's been a couple decades."

"She picked plants for you?" said X. "Not flowers?"

Sylvie had told them it was flowers. He needed to know which it was. He needed to know everything he possibly could.

"Yeah, bear grass," said Timothy. "Technically, it's a plant. You want to hear two interesting facts about bear grass? It's not a grass, and bears don't eat it. Not sure what the botanists were thinking. That's, uh, that's the bear grass she picked right there."

The frame with the white flowers.

Now X understood why it was one of the only decorations in the house.

"Those are the very—sorry, the *actual*—plants she gave you?" he said. "You kept them all this time?"

"I did, yeah," said Timothy. "If she had spit out a watermelon seed I would have kept it. You're thinking I'm nuts. It's fine."

"No," said X. "I'm not thinking that at all." He worried that he shouldn't say what he was about to say. "I'm thinking that what Sylvie did for you—pulled you out of yourself?—is exactly what Zoe has done for me. In truth, she's saved me many times."

Timothy seemed moved by this.

"You only get one person like that in your lifetime, I think," he said. "Keep her close."

X assumed Zoe would be uncomfortable with the praise, that she'd already be formulating a joke.

Instead, Zoe said something kind to Timothy: "I'm sure you took Sylvie out of herself, too. I'm sure you fixed *her* wiring. Actually, I'm positive that you did. It works both ways or not at all."

"I want to believe that," said Timothy. He stood, as if to underline his skepticism. "But I don't. I can't."

"Trust me?" said Zoe.

X knew how much more she wanted to tell Timothy. He longed to say it all, too.

Timothy, just to busy himself in the awkward moment, leaned down to pick up a paper napkin that had fallen to the floor.

"Then why didn't she stay?" he said. "Why have I been alone twenty years?"

WHEN X AND ZOE left, Timothy asked them—awkwardly, which made it seem all the more genuine—to come back sometime and help him finish the food. They promised they would. But the truth was that X didn't know if he could be that close to his father again without announcing, "I'm your son." Just hugging Timothy good-bye had been hard—two like objects recognizing each other right when they had to pull apart.

They'd all forgotten to talk about Rufus's sculpture.

Outside, the sun had sunk low enough to shine straight through the windows and make the house glow. X turned when he and Zoe were halfway down the curving walk. The house looked different to him now. Timothy had told them that he'd begun building it right after Sylvie disappeared, thinking that she'd come back, thinking that they'd live in it together. He had held onto the fantasy even after a year went by, two years, three. Half the books in the house, he said, were things he bought because he thought Sylvie would like them: a book about how mountains are formed; a book about a woman, known only as Agent 355, who spied for George Washington; a book about explorers on a hellish expedition to Antarctica to study penguin eggs.

Of course, Sylvie never saw the books—or the tree house.

Timothy said he thought about selling the place every few years but didn't think the house would make sense to anyone other than the woman it'd been built for. The image X took away of his father was of an enormously kind, enormously sad man. X pictured him standing on a dock and watching the whole world pull away.

X and Zoe passed the old iron lanterns, not yet lit, as they made their way down to the car. Zoe told X that it'd been brave of him to seek his father out.

"Brave?" said X. "*You* leaped into a glowing portal to hell. *I* only ate grapes."

Zoe laughed.

"I ain't scared of no portal," she said.

She drove them toward home, following the river out of the park. X watched the current—the way it crashed against the rocks, then seemed to reassemble and keep going.

"Is *wholer* a word?" he asked Zoe.

"Holer?" she said. "How would you use it?"

"'Every day, I felt a little bit wholer,'" said X.

"I'll allow it," said Zoe. She kissed her palm as she drove, then reached out to press it to X's cheek. "I really, really liked your father."

"As did I," said X. "Yet he is so much like me that perhaps I do not see him clearly."

"Like you?" said Zoe. "You think so?"

"I think he is so much like me that he could *be* me," said X.

"I mean, you've got his hands," said Zoe. "And you're both shy. But he just seems so, I don't know, decimated? Devastated?"

"That is it precisely," said X. "That is what struck me hardest as well. I think I haven't been clear. He is me—if I had lost you."

thirty

FOR ZOE, HAPPINESS WAS harder to get used to than anything else—harder to trust. When she couldn't sleep, she stared out the window at the shed X was living in. She liked seeing the glow of the space heaters under the door. It was one of the only things that soothed her. *X was in there. He was safe. They were all safe. No one was coming. No one was going away.* Sometimes, just seeing the shed wasn't enough, so Zoe would pad through Rufus's soggy backyard in unlaced sneakers. She'd pull open the door of the shed, and look at X as he slept. She had bought him one of the wearable sleeping bags that Timothy had mentioned—so he wouldn't feel constricted. It made him look like an astronaut, which cracked her up. Zoe would stand in the dark, gazing at him. It was an embarrassing thing to do. Zoe knew it, and didn't care. One night, she went out there three times.

As for X, he seemed to crave sleep. He hoarded it almost, the way a dragon hoards gold. Even the groaning of the shed door as Zoe came and went didn't wake him up. Sleep—and food and sunshine—were already healing him. His cheeks were pink. The bruises under his eyes had faded, as if his body knew he'd never hunt another soul.

When Zoe went to school, X and Rufus worked on some secret project of Rufus's. Zoe couldn't get any details out of either of them, or even out of Jonah, who helped sometimes. When Zoe and Jonah got home from school, Zoe could always hear X and Rufus laughing in the shed. Jonah would run out to join them, and he'd be in hysterics even before he knew what was funny. Hearing them all laugh: that soothed her, too.

Zoe's dream, which she didn't speak aloud, was that Rufus would let X stay after the rest of them moved to Bert and Betty's house on the lake. That X and Rufus would be roommates. Rufus would only go for it if Zoe's mom approved, and her mother hadn't adjusted to X being in their lives. More than once, as Zoe snuck back inside after checking on X, she saw her mom standing sleeplessly at her window, as if the shed were a spaceship that had just landed. To Zoe, X was an astronaut. To her mom, he was an alien.

Everybody else seemed happier with X around—*wholer*, to use his word. Zoe prayed her mother would see that. X was polite, gracious, kind. He asked what he could do to help so often that her mom and Rufus had started inventing chores, like tightening the lightbulbs and cleaning the inside of the dishwasher.

X was also more relaxed than he'd ever been. He spoke more like somebody from the twenty-first century now, and an endearing goofiness had begun to surface. X started wearing a backpack around—an old one Jonah had given him with a pixilated Minecraft sword on it—even though he didn't actually have anything to put in it. Zoe smiled whenever she saw him and his empty backpack. He was constantly offering to carry stuff for people, just so he'd have an excuse to unzip it.

The days ticked by. The Bissells began packing to move. A city of boxes grew in the living room, followed by suburbs in Zoe's and her mom's bedrooms. To Zoe, the boxes were a reminder that X could very soon have nowhere to live. She felt a pressure that increased daily, as if the boxes were being placed one by one on top of her. Rufus frowned at the sight of the stuff, too, though Zoe knew it was for a different reason: he'd just started to feel like he had a family, and soon they'd be gone.

During breakfast on Friday, Zoe's mom gave them all a sign that she was warming to X. It was a tiny thing but unmistakable. Everyone at the table stopped speaking when she did it: she put a handful of vitamins on X's napkin.

A B_{12}, a D_3, and a C.

She had to care about him at least a little.

"Holy crap," said Jonah.

X had never taken a pill before. Everybody shrieked, then laughed, when he put them all in his mouth and started chewing.

THAT NIGHT, THERE WAS an even bigger turning point.

X finally met Dallas and Val.

Zoe had postponed it all week. Val was still livid about her going to the Lowlands, and Zoe needed her to calm down enough so that she wasn't levitating off the floor with rage when she met X. In the end, Dallas suggested he cook them all dinner at House of Huns after closing. It was a nice offer, especially if Dallas still had unsimple feelings for her. Zoe said yes to the dinner immediately, even though "Hun" food creeped her out. She'd once had a nightmare about drowning in a bathtub full of brown glop.

House of Huns was empty except for Dallas, who banged the gong and chanted "Furg! Mrgh! Furg!" when Zoe and X entered. He was still wearing his work uniform and holding a rubber-tipped spear. The pointy fur hat sat just above his eyebrows. The leather straps crisscrossed his naked chest. Zoe wondered if Dallas had engineered this whole dinner just so that X could see how ripped he was. Rather than annoying her, she thought it was sweet. Dallas was never, ever going to stop being himself. She didn't want him to.

X stepped forward to shake Dallas's hand, not knowing that Dallas considered the grill a sacred place and never broke character when he was anywhere near it.

Dallas grunted. He poked X's hand lightly with the spear.

"Krot!" he said.

"Okay, now you're being weird," said Zoe.

"No, no," said X. "Dallas, you are the very embodiment of a Hun. I was acquainted with one in the Lowlands—he'd lived on the Sea of Azov—and I feel as if he stands before me now."

Hearing this, Dallas broke into an unabashed grin, and all but lunged to shake X's hand.

"Thanks, dawg!" he said. "People don't realize how much thought goes into the character. The guy I play? Mundzuc? He's complicated."

"Your work has borne fruit," said X.

"Boom!" said Dallas. "That is *so* cool to hear." He paused. "This may come out wrong, but I'm glad you're not in hell anymore. That shit was unfair."

"Thank you," said X. "I owe my freedom, and everything else, to Zoe."

"Zoe's the best, right?" said Dallas. "She crushes stuff."

"Okay, that's enough," said Zoe. "What's happening with you and Mingyu? Did she agree to go out with you?"

"She's still going over the lists I gave her," said Dallas.

"The All-Time Favorites thing?" said Zoe.

"Yeah," said Dallas. "I put stuff on there that she'd never heard of—which I'm kind of proud of, honestly. She knew all the music because she literally knows *all music*. But now she's reading the books, and watching the TV shows and stuff. She won't give me a yes or no until she's finished. She calls it 'the research phase.' She says a lot of people skip the research phase before they hook up with somebody, and then they regret it."

"You don't think all this is kind of annoying?" said Zoe.

"Are you kidding? I think it's awesome!" said Dallas. He adjusted a leather strap that had apparently been chafing a nipple. "I think it's badass. This girl is *not* playing."

"Then I'm happy for you, Mundzuc," said Zoe. "I mean it. X and I are gonna grab a table, okay?"

Dallas gripped his spear, and disappeared back into character.

"Furg zot zot!" he said. "Oh, wait, sorry—I forgot to ask what you wanted to drink."

As they drifted to a booth by the window, Zoe thanked X for being kind to Dallas about his costume.

"I can't believe you've met a Hun," she said.

"I haven't," he said quietly. "It's just that I liked Dallas immediately, and he seemed to be trying hard."

"What about the Sea of Azov?" said Zoe.

"There is no Sea of Azov, so far as I know," said X. "We'll have to check the shower curtain."

At the table, X set his backpack carefully on the chair next to him. Zoe smiled to herself. She was pretty sure it was empty. Shortly afterward, Dallas brought them their drinks (*"Furg* ice water! *Furg* Mountain Dew!"), then stomped Hun-like back to the grill.

"I was thinking about something Timothy said," said Zoe.

"Yes?" said X.

"He said he met your mother in September," said Zoe, "and that he only knew her for a month."

"I remember," said X. "But what does that signify?"

"What it *signifies*," said Zoe, "is that we're going to throw you a birthday party this summer. You were a July baby."

X seemed not to know what to say.

"A July baby," he said eventually. "I like the sound of that."

"I'm going to buy you a ton of presents," said Zoe.

"And I am going to carry them in my backpack," said X.

ZOE GOT NERVOUS WAITING for Val to show up. She was much more worried about Val meeting X than she'd been about Dallas meeting him. By the time she saw her friend's blue head approaching through the parking lot, Zoe's nerves were jangling like silverware loose in a drawer. She needed the people she loved most to love each other.

Zoe went outside to intercept Val, and gauge her mood. Val was with Gloria, which she hadn't expected.

"It's you!" Zoe shouted to Gloria, happily. "It's you! It's you! It's you!"

Zoe knew how hard it was for Gloria to be around people

because of the anxiety and depression. Now that she thought about it, maybe shouting at her hadn't been the best idea. But Zoe couldn't help herself: Val and Gloria looked so lovely arm in arm.

"It's me," said Gloria, waving back shyly. "It's me. It's me. It's me."

"Sorry we're late," said Val. "We were making out in the car."

"I assumed," said Zoe.

She hugged Gloria first.

"I love that you're here," she said. "I *love* it. Thank you."

"I wanted to meet X," said Gloria. "And I have kind of a thing for Dallas. Don't tell my girlfriend."

"Your girlfriend knows," said Val. "Your girlfriend is appalled."

Zoe hugged Val now.

"You'll be nice, right?" said Zoe.

"That kind of thing is so hard to predict," said Val.

"She'll be nice," said Gloria. "We had a long talk about manners in the car. I think she understands the basic idea now."

The three of them entered House of Huns together, and once again the gong clanged and shivered. Dallas was so surprised to see Gloria that he broke character, and let her hold his spear.

"I'm so stoked to see you guys!" he said.

X stood up from the table and came to shake their hands. He always shook hands, Zoe thought, with an adorable seriousness.

"I am stoked to see you as well," X told Val and Gloria, "though I do not know what 'stoked' means."

"It means pumped or jacked," said Dallas.

"I am pumped or jacked," said X.

There was a silence where no one knew what to say, Zoe included.

"Val, you are a legend to me," said X. "And, Gloria, I have wanted to meet you especially."

Zoe had a twinge of panic. She'd told X virtually nothing about Gloria. He had no idea how fragile she was, how guarded.

"Me?" said Gloria. She took a half a step backward. "Why?"

Everyone looked at X questioningly, and he seemed to falter.

"Because—well, because you are a foster child," he said.

Gloria dropped her head. Zoe felt her stomach lurch. She should have warned X not to bring it up.

"That is *not* a thing Gloria wants to talk about," said Val.

"Yeah," said Gloria. "I'm not . . . I don't . . . I'm not embarrassed about it. But it's hard to talk about because—honestly?—some of it sucked, and it's just kind of impossible to make anybody understand."

"I am truly sorry to have mentioned it," said X. "All I intended to say was—"

"Let it go, X," said Zoe.

"I will in a moment," he said. "All I intended to say was—"

"I mean it, X," said Zoe. "Let it go."

"It's okay," said Gloria, her head still low. "Go ahead."

"Thank you," said X. "I only wanted to say that I think I *do* understand a little." He paused. "Because I was a foster child, too."

Gloria looked up finally.

"What'd you mean?" she said.

"There was a woman named Ripper and a man named Regent," said X. "When I was little and scared and had no one at all, they took me in."

Gloria nodded, smiled, seemed to *open* again.

"Can we sit?" she asked X. "And will you tell us everything?"

* * *

WHILE X WAS SHARING his story, Zoe's phone made its little bug-zapping sound. It was a text from her mom.

About to call u. Texting first so u will pick up. It's important and involves u, X, everybody. Calling in 3 . . . 2 . . . 1 . . .

The phone trilled. Zoe slipped outside to answer. The night was clear and warm. Across the parking lot, a movie was letting out. It must have been good because everybody looked dazed, and nobody seemed to remember where they'd parked their cars.

"Hey, Mom," said Zoe. "Why are you being weird?"

"Hey, beautiful girl," said her mother. "I've got a question for you, and I want you to take all the time you need before you answer, okay? You like Rufus, right?"

"Yeah," said Zoe. "A lot."

"You didn't take all the time you needed," said her mother.

"I took twice as much as I needed," said Zoe. "It wasn't a hard question. You had to call to ask me that?"

Up in the sky, Zoe could see both Dippers, as well as a third constellation she'd forgotten the name of. She decided to call it Ripper's Dress, because of the way it glowed.

"Wait a minute," she said. "Did Rufus ask you to marry him?!"

"No, no, no," said her mother. "Stop jumping ahead."

"Did you ask *him* to marry *you*?"

"No! Stop jumping! I need you to take this seriously."

"Take *what* seriously?"

Her mother took so long to answer that Zoe wondered if she was still there.

"Rufus doesn't want us to move out," her mom said finally. "I know I've always denied this, but he *likes* me. You were right about that. He likes all of us, obviously. He's asking us to stay. He was really sweet about it. That secret project he was doing with X turned out to be a sign for the door that says, The Bissells Plus Rufus."

"He put our name first?" said Zoe. "That's kind of awesome."

"It kind of is," said her mom.

"Do you like him like he likes you?" said Zoe.

"Promise you won't tease me?" said her mother.

"You know I can't promise that," said Zoe.

"Yes, I like him a lot," said her mother.

"Then let's stay," said Zoe. "Done."

"But you hate that little room," said her mother.

"I don't care about the room, Mom," said Zoe. "I care about you. And Jonah will be bat-shit happy. Let's go for it. Let's see what happens. Let's be the Bissells Plus Rufus."

"Thank you, Zo," said her mother. "You're a good person. You always have been."

Zoe peered into the restaurant. Dallas was ferrying plates to the table. X was telling his story to Val and Gloria. He was talking excitedly, waving his hands around, which she'd never seen him do before. Even Val had bent forward.

"But what about X?" said Zoe. "What happens to him? Are you still going to make him leave?"

"Yes, but—"

"You're just gonna kick him out?"

"Yes, but—"

"He's got *nothing*, Mom. He's got nowhere to go."

Zoe looked back into House of Huns. X had stood, and was walking toward the window with a steaming plate in hand. He was asking, with his eyes, if Zoe was okay. Zoe nodded, even though she wasn't.

"Would you listen a second?" said her mother. "I had an idea. What if X lived at Bert and Betty's place instead of us? It could be cute with some work, and it's right there on the lake, and you could see him but also take some time to remember that you're still seventeen. I think Bert and Betty would have really liked X. I mean, look, he avenged their deaths, for one thing."

"Yes," said Zoe. "I love that idea. Yes, yes, yes."

X came up to the window. His plate was piled with Hun "delicacies": pork, shrimp, beef, and something that was pretending to be crab, all of it swimming in brown sauce. He smiled, and pointed his fork at the plate enthusiastically. He liked it. Zoe laughed, and shook her head at him: *You are a dork.*

She said good-bye to her mom, and hung up.

She put a palm against the window, so X would do the same, but his hands were full. He leaned toward her. From the other side of the window, he rested his forehead against her palm. She'd have sworn she could feel the heat of his face through the glass.

Zoe felt something in her chest—it was like everything that had ever hurt was being swept with feathers. It took her a moment to realize that it was happiness.

She trusted it this time.

She put her hand on her heart to hold it in.

acknowledgments

I'm grateful to everyone who had a part in this series, from the copy-shop manager who printed thousands of pages of drafts (Hannah) to the book lover in Moaning Myrtle cosplay who asked me to sign the toilet seat around her neck (Zoey).

Thank you to my sensational agent, Jodi Reamer, and my force-of-nature editor and publisher at Bloomsbury, Cindy Loh. I just reread the praise I heaped on the two of you in the acknowledgments of the first book, *The Edge of Everything*—and it all sounds like an understatement now. I couldn't do this without you and will definitely cry if you ever make me.

Thank you a thousand times over to Kami Garcia, Danielle Paige, Kerry Kletter, Kathleen Glasgow, Bridget Hodder, and Haven Kimmel. Your friendship, and your books, have meant the world to me.

Thank you, Sarah J. Maas, Jennifer Niven, and Susan Dennard, for your extraordinary generosity and support.

Thank you to Darin Strauss, Susannah Meadows, Jess Huang, and Abby West for weighing in on early drafts of *The Brink of Darkness*. A bit of trivia: Susannah begged me to never use the word *tunic* in these books (she hates that word like other people hate *moist*). I tried not to, but failed at the last second. I'm sorry, Susannah. You'll have to avert your eyes.

I'm grateful to Hans Bodenhamer for once again advising me on the fine art of caving.

I also benefited from the wisdom of three wildlife biologists: John Waller at Glacier National Park, Jim Williams (author of *The Path of the Puma*), and Douglas Chadwick (*Tracking Gobi Grizzlies*). Thank you all for your good cheer in the face of such questions as, "Well, what if the cougar was, like, *supernatural*?"

Thank you to my inspired friends at Bloomsbury, especially Cristina Gilbert and her tireless marketing and publicity team: Elizabeth Mason, Erica Barmash, Courtney Griffin, Anna Bernard, Emily Ritter, Phoebe Dyer, Beth Eller, Brittany Mitchell, Alexis Castellanos, and Alona Fryman. (Lizzy Mason: Congrats on selling your own YA novel, *The Art of Losing*. I know a *great* publicist.)

Thank you to Diane Aronson and Melissa Kavonic in managing editorial and to Katharine Weincke and Pat McHugh for being such sharp, thoughtful readers. Thank you to Bloomsbury's art director, Donna Mark; designer Jeanette Levy; and illustrator Shane Rebenschied. I love what you've done for Zoe and X.

As for the phenomenal sales team: Because of you, I've gotten to see my novels not only in amazing indie bookstores and Barnes & Noble, but also in places you can buy lawn furniture and 56 boxes of Kleenex at a time. It's all been thrilling.

Bloomsbury Publishing has been a wonderful home. I bow deeply to Emma Hopkin, the managing director of Bloomsbury Children's Books worldwide; to my UK publisher, Rebecca McNally; and to Australia's managing director, Kate Cubitt. I'm also indebted to Lucy Mackay-Sim, Emma Bradshaw, and Charlotte Armstrong in the UK, and Sonia Palmisano and Adiba Oemar in Australia.

Thank you to Hali Baumstein (Bloomsbury) and Alec Shane (Writers House) for all the things, all the time.

Thank you to Mary Pender at UTA for her vision and all-around coolness and to Cecilia de la Campa at Writers House for negotiating such beautiful foreign editions.

I'm grateful to the welcoming folks at YALLfest, Booksplosion, LitJoy Crate, and the *Quarterly Literary Box*. Thank you to Betsi Morrison and Luke Walrath at the Alpine Theater Project, and to everyone at the *Whitefish Review*. Thank you to Ursula Uriarte. Thank you to Melissa Albert, Cathy Berner at Blue Willow Books in Houston, and Cristin Stickles at McNally Jackson in New York for being early supporters.

Thank you to the friends who are always there when I'm insecure, exhausted, and hungry (usually all at the same time): Radhika Jones, Tina Jordan, Jessica Shaw, Laura Brounstein, Anthony Breznican, Erin Berger, Peternelle Van Arsdale, Robin Roe, Meeta Agrawal, Bonnie Siegler, Gita Trelease, Adriana Mather, Jeff Zentner, Missy Schwartz, Jill Bernstein, Sara Vilkomerson, Devin Gordon, Janet McNally, Susie Davis, Heidi Heilig, Marc and Francine Roston, Annie Anderson, Sabine Brigette, Diane Smith, David Pickeral, Mike Eldred, Brian and Lyndsay Schott, and Kate Ward.

Finally, thank you to my daughter, Lily, and my son, Theo: I love you more than words.

ZOE MET X ON A SUNDAY IN FEBRUARY, when there was a storm on its way from Canada and the sky was so dark it looked like someone was closing a giant coffin lid over Montana.

The blizzard wasn't supposed to hit the mountain for an hour, and her mom had gone to get groceries to tide them over. Zoe had wanted to go, too, because her mother couldn't be trusted to choose food. Not ever. Her mom was a badass in many ways. Still, the woman was a hard-core vegan and her idea of dinner was tofu or seitan, which, as Zoe had stated repeatedly, tasted like the flesh of aliens.

Her mother had insisted she and her brother, Jonah, stay home where they'd be safe. She said she was pretty sure she could get down the mountain and back up again before the storm ripped through. Zoe had driven in blizzards herself. She was pretty sure she couldn't.

Zoe wasn't thrilled to be in charge. It was partly because Jonah was a spaz, though she was not allowed to call him that, according to a sign her mother had posted above the gargantuan juicer in the kitchen: Uncool Words That I Cannot, in Good Conscience, Tolerate. More than that, though, it was because the place she'd lived her whole life suddenly seemed menacing and strange. In November, Zoe's father had died while exploring a cave called Black Teardrop. Then, in January, two of the people she loved most in the world, a couple of elderly neighbors named Bert and Betty Wallace, were dragged out of their home by an intruder and never seen again. The grief was like a cold stone on Zoe's heart. She couldn't imagine how bad it was for Jonah.

She could hear her brother outside now, chasing Spock and Uhura around like the ADHD maniac that he was. She'd let him go out because he'd begged to play with the dogs, and, honestly, she couldn't stand being with him one more second. He was eight. If she'd said no, he would have whined till her ears bled ("Just let me go out for ten minutes, Zoe! Okay, five minutes! Okay, *two* minutes! I can have two minutes? Okay, what about five minutes?"). Even if she'd managed to shut him up, she'd have been stuck with his crazy energy in a small house on an isolated mountain with a blizzard coming their way like a pissed-off army.

She went online and checked WeatherBug. With the windchill, it was 10 degrees below zero.

Zoe knew she should call Jonah inside, but kept putting it off. She couldn't deal with him yet. At least she'd wrapped every inch of him up tight: a green skater-boy hoodie, a down jacket, and black gloves decorated with skulls that glowed in the dark. She had insisted that he wear snowshoes so he wouldn't sink into a snow-drift and disappear. Then she'd spent five minutes forcing them onto his feet while he twitched and writhed like he was being elec-trocuted. He really could be ridiculous.

She checked her phone. It was five o'clock, and there were two texts waiting for her.

The first was from her friend Dallas, who she'd been seeing off and on before her dad died.

It said: *Blizzards be awesome, dawg! You doing OK??*

Dallas was a good guy. He was muscly and dimply in a baseball-player kind of way—cute, but not exactly Zoe's type. Also, he had a tattoo that used to kill the mood whenever he took his shirt off. He'd apparently gone back and forth between *Never Stop!* and *Don't Ever Stop!*, and the tattoo artist had gotten confused and the tat wound up reading, *Never Don't Stop!* Dallas, being Dallas, loved it and high-fived the guy on the spot.

Zoe texted him back in Dallas-speak: *I'm solid, dawg! Thx for checking. You rock on the reg. (Did I say that right?)*

The second text was from her best friend, Val: *This blizzard sucks ass. ASS! I'm gonna take a nap with Gloria and ignore it. I'm VERY serious about this nap. Do you need ANYTHING AT ALL before nap begins?? Once nap is in progress, I will be UNAVAILABLE to you.*

Val's girlfriend was extremely shy. Val was . . . not. She'd been crazy in love with Gloria for a year, and was always doing beautiful, slightly psycho things, like making a Tumblr devoted entirely to Gloria's feet.

Zoe texted back: *Why is everyone worried about me? I'm FINE! Go take your nap, Nap Goddess! I will be soooo quiet!!!!*

Smiling to herself, she added emojis of an alarm clock, a hammer, and a bomb.

Val wrote back one more time: *Love you too, freak!*

ZOE FOUND DUCT TAPE in a kitchen drawer and taped up the downstairs windows so they wouldn't shatter in the storm. Her mother had told her that doing this in a blizzard was dumb and possibly dangerous. Still, it made Zoe feel safer somehow, and gave her something to do. She peered outside, and saw Jonah and the black Labs jumping back and forth across the frozen river at the bottom of their yard. Their mom had prohibited this activity on another sign she had made: Uncool Behavior That I Cannot, in Good Conscience, Tolerate. Zoe pretended she hadn't noticed what her brother was doing. Then she stopped watching so she wouldn't see him do anything worse. She went upstairs and taped *X*'s on the second-story windows. She threw in a few *O*'s, too, so that when her mother finally drove up it'd look like giants were playing tic-tac-toe.

She finished taping the windows at 5:30, just as the storm finally found the mountain. She made herself a cup of coffee—black, because her mother only bought soy milk, which tasted like the *tears* of aliens—and drifted into the living room, so she could sip it at the window. Zoe stared out at the forest, which started up at the bottom of their yard and ran all the way down to the lake. Her family's land was a mostly bald patch of the mountain, but there was a stand of larch up against the house to give them shade in the summer. The wind had agitated them. Branches were stabbing and scratching the glass. It was like the trees were trying to get in.

Her mom had been gone two hours. By now, the police would have barricaded the roads and, though her mother was not usually someone who took no for an answer, the cops would never let her back up the mountain tonight. Zoe pushed the thought down into a box at the back of her brain labeled Do Not Open. She shouted out the front door for Jonah. She'd been an idiot to leave him out there so long. She pushed that thought down, too.

Jonah didn't answer. She hadn't really expected him to. She loved the little bug, but most days it seemed like his sole purpose in life was to make everything harder for her. She knew he could hear her. He just wasn't ready to stop romping around with the dogs. They weren't allowed in the house, even during storms, which Jonah thought was mean. He once protested with an actual picket sign.

Zoe shouted for her brother three more times: loud, louder, loudest.

No answer.

She checked WeatherBug again. It was 15 below.

All she could see out the window was a riot of white. Everything was shapeless and heavy with snow: her spectacularly crappy red car, the compost bin, even the big wooden bear that her mom's hippie-dippy artist friend, Rufus, had carved for the driveway. The thought of having to bundle up and trudge around in the storm just to drag Jonah's butt inside made Zoe so angry that her face started to get hot. And she wouldn't be able to complain to her mom because she shouldn't have let him outside in the first place. Jonah always found a way to win. He was nuts, but he was clever.

She yelled for Spock and Uhura. No answer. Spock was two years younger and a big-time coward. Zoe figured he was hiding under the tractor in the pole barn, quivering. But Uhura was a daredevil and scared of nothing. She should have come running.

Zoe sighed. She had to go find Jonah. She had no choice.

She threw on a scarf, gloves, boots, a puffy blue coat, and a tasseled hat that Jonah had knitted for her when their dad died (actually, Uhura had eaten the tassel and in its place there was just a hole that kept getting bigger and bigger). Zoe didn't bother with snowshoes because she was only going to be out as long as it took to march Jonah back inside. Five minutes. Maybe ten. Tops.

Zoe knew it was pointless to wish that her dad were around to help her track down Jonah. She wished it anyway. Memories of her father swept over her so suddenly it made her whole body clench.

ZOE'S DAD HAD BEEN goofy, excitable—and completely, infuriatingly unreliable. He was obsessed with everything about caves, down to bats and flatworms. He was even bizarrely into cave mud, which he insisted held the secret to a great complexion. He used to bring Ziploc bags of it home and try to dab it on Zoe's mother's face. Her mom would shriek with laughter and run away in mock horror. Then her dad would smear it all over his own cheeks, and chase Jonah and Zoe around the house, making monster noises.

So, yes: her dad was weird, as you pretty much have to be to go caving in the first place. But he was weird in a good way. In fact, he was kind of amazingly weird. He was superskinny and flexible, and if he put his arms over his head like Superman, he could crawl through incredibly narrow passageways. He used to practice by bending a wire hanger into an oval and wriggling through—or by crawling back and forth under the car. Literally, he'd be doing this stuff in plain sight when Val or Dallas came over. Dallas was a caver, too, and thought it was all deeply awesome. Val would avert her eyes from whatever bizarre thing Zoe's father was doing and say, "I'm not even noticing—this is me *not noticing*."

Zoe started caving with her dad when she turned 15. (Nobody called it "spelunking"—because why *would* they?) They caved religiously every summer and fall, until the snow blocked the entrances and ice made the tunnels treacherous. Zoe was only semi into it at first, but she needed time with her father that she knew she could count on. Unless you were going caving, you just couldn't trust the guy to show up.

Zoe had gotten used to his disappearances, just as she'd gotten used to the fact that there were things he never talked about. (His parents, his hometown in Virginia, anything at all that happened when he was young: those parts of the map were never colored in.) Her father specialized in grand gestures—he'd changed his last name to Bissell instead of asking Zoe's mom to change hers—and he could be the coolest dad in the world for weeks on end. He'd make her feel warm and watched-over, like there was a candle or a lantern by her bed. But then the air in the house would change somehow. It'd lose its charge. Her dad's SUV would disappear, and for weeks she wouldn't even get a text.

Zoe eventually stopped listening to her father's excuses. They usually had to do with some weird business he was trying to get off the ground—something about "drumming up the freakin' financing." When she was younger, Zoe blamed herself for the fact that her dad never stuck around for more than a few months at a time. Maybe she wasn't interesting enough. Maybe she wasn't *lovable* enough. Jonah was still so young that he worshipped their father unconditionally. He called him Daddy Man, and treated every glimpse of him like a celebrity sighting.

Zoe knew that she and her dad would always have their treks up to the caves, and she stopped expecting anything else. So that day in November when she'd woken to find that he'd gone caving without her felt like a betrayal.

The cops led the search for his body. Zoe had invented the Do Not Open box to hold back the memories.

* * *

ZOE CURSED JONAH UNDER her breath the minute she got outdoors and started hunting for him and the dogs. She couldn't see more than a couple of feet in front of her or walk more than a few steps without stopping to catch her breath. The wind, the snow: it was like being punched in the stomach.

The light, meanwhile, was dying fast. The coffin lid over Montana was getting ready to snap shut.

Zoe felt inside her pockets, and had a surprise bit of good luck. She found a flashlight—and it actually worked.

It took her five minutes just to zigzag down to the river where she'd seen Jonah playing. There was no sign of him or the dogs, except for a snow angel already partly filled in by the storm and two weird, blurry indentations nearby, where Jonah had apparently tried to get Spock and Uhura to make *dog* snow angels.

She screamed Jonah's name but her voice didn't travel. The wind pushed it right back to her.

For the first time, she felt dread crawl up into her throat. She imagined telling her mom that she'd lost Jonah, and she pictured her mother's heart blasting apart, like the Death Star in *Star Wars*. If something happened to that kid, her mother would never recover. Zoe tried to push that thought down, too. But the box at the back of her brain could only hold so much, and everything began seeping out.

Zoe finally found Jonah's footprints and followed them around the house. It was slow going because she had to bend down low to the ground, like a hunchback, to see the trail. Branches were breaking off trees and blowing across the yard. Every step exhausted her. Sweat was trickling down her back even though she was freezing. She knew that sweating in the frigid cold was bad news. Her body heat was evaporating. She had to pick up the pace, find

Jonah, and get inside. But if she moved any quicker, she'd sweat even more and freeze even faster.

Another thought the box didn't have room for.

Maybe Jonah was back in the house already. Yes. He definitely was. Zoe pictured him, his face and hands all puffy and pink as he spilled cocoa powder across the kitchen floor. She told herself that all this was for nothing. She followed his tracks, sure they'd lead right to their door.

But ten feet from the front steps, they veered down the hill and got swallowed up by the woods.

Zoe took a few cautious steps into the trees and shouted, but she knew it was pointless. She'd have to go in after Jonah and the Labs. Her cheeks and ears stung like they were sunburned. Her hands, even in gloves, were frozen into little sculptures of fists.

SHE USED TO WORSHIP the forest. She'd grown up running through the trees, sunlight splashing down around her feet. The trees led to the lake, where Bert and Betty Wallace had lived. They'd been like grandparents to Zoe and Jonah. They'd been there for them even when their dad was off on one of his mysterious trips, and they were a continual source of kindness when he died. But Bert and Betty had been going senile for years. This past fall, Zoe had kept Bert company as he cut photographs of animals out of the newspaper and barked random stuff like, "Gimme a break, I'm just a crazy old codger!" (When she asked him what a "codger" was, he rolled his eyes and said, "Gimme a break, same thing as a coot!") Jonah had sat crisscross-applesauce on the floor and knitted with Betty. She'd taught him how, and it turned out to be one of the few things, besides chewing his fingernails, that eased his ADHD and stopped his brain from whirring like an out-of-control blender. Toward the end, though, Betty couldn't keep her hands from shaking, and she'd forgotten everything she knew about knitting. Now Jonah had to teach *her* how.

Then, last month, the Wallaces had disappeared. Betty, the less senile of the pair, apparently got away from the intruder for a moment and rushed Bert into their truck. That was the police's theory, based on the blood on the steering wheel. The truck was found smashed into a tree a hundred yards from the house. Its engine was still running. Its doors were flung open and there was no sign of the Wallaces, except for more blood. Imagining the confused look on Bert and Betty's faces as someone scowled murderously down at them hurt Zoe's heart so much she could hardly breathe.

The Wallaces' house was left just the way it was, lonely as a museum, while their lawyers looked for the most recent version of their will. Zoe had promised herself that she'd never go near it again. It was too painful. The lake outside Bert and Betty's house was frozen over with cloudy gray ice now. Even the forest seemed scary—dense and forbidding, like somewhere your evil stepmother takes you in a fairy tale.

Yet here she was on the edge of the trees, being pulled down toward the Wallaces' place. Jonah knew better than to walk through the trees in a storm. If the dogs had gone into the forest, though, he'd have followed them. Spock and Uhura had lived with Zoe's family for a month, but they used to belong to Bert and Betty. They might have plunged into the icy trees, thinking they were going home.

THERE WAS LESS THAN a mile of woods between the Bissells' land and Bert and Betty's house. Ordinarily, it was a 15-minute walk, and it was impossible to get lost because Betty had made hatchet marks in the trees for the kids to follow. Also, the woods were divided into three sections, so you could always tell if you'd gotten spun around somehow. The first section of forest had been harvested for timber a while back—Zoe's mom preferred the term "raped and pillaged"—so the trees closest to the Bissells' house were new growth. They were mostly flaky gray lodgepole pines. They were planted so close together that they seemed to be huddling for warmth.

The second section was Zoe's favorite: giant larches and Douglas firs. They were Montana's version of skyscrapers. They were only a hundred years old, but looked dinosaur-old, like they'd come with the planet.

The trees closest to the lake had burned in an unexplained fire before Zoe was born. They'd never fallen, though, so there was a quarter-mile's worth of charred snags just standing there dead. It was a spooky place—and Jonah's favorite part of the woods, of course. It was where he played all his soldier-of-the-apocalypse games.

Walking to Bert and Betty's house meant following the path through new trees, then old trees, then dead ones. Zoe and Jonah had made the trip a thousand times. There was no such thing as getting lost—not for long. Not in decent weather or in daylight.

After Zoe had walked 20 feet or so into the young part of the forest, the world became quiet. There was just a low hum in the air, like somebody blowing across the top of a bottle. She felt sheltered and the tiniest bit warmer. She aimed the flashlight at the treetops and then at the surly sky above them, and she had a weird, dreamy impulse to plop down in the snow. She shook her head to erase the thought. The cold was already gumming up her brain. If she sat down, she'd never get up.

Zoe shone the flashlight in a wide arc along the ground, looking to pick up Jonah's tracks again. The beam was weak, either because of the batteries or the cold, but eventually she found them. Jonah probably had a ten-minute head start on her and because he was wearing snow-shoes he'd be covering ground faster. It was like a math problem: If Train A leaves the station at 4:30 p.m. traveling 90 miles an hour, and Train B leaves ten minutes later traveling 70 miles an hour ... Zoe's brain was too numb to solve it, but it seemed like she was screwed.

Jonah knew the path to the lake but he must have been following the dogs. Their paw prints were messy and wild. Maybe they were being playful. Maybe they were chasing grouse or wild turkeys, which sometimes rode out storms beneath the skirts of the trees. Maybe they were just flipping out because it was so cold.

Zoe could see Jonah's snowshoe tracks chasing the dogs every which way. She couldn't tell if he had been playing along happily or if he had been terrified and begging them to turn back. In her head, she repeated over and over: *Just go home, Jonah. This is insane. Just leave the dogs. Just walk away.* But she knew he wouldn't abandon the dogs no matter how scary things got, which made her angry—and made her love him, too.

So she just kept slogging through the woods. Which sucked. *Drag right foot out of snow, lift it up, stick it in again. Drag left foot out, repeat. And repeat and repeat and repeat.* Zoe was losing track of time. It took forever to go even a couple hundred feet—and much longer when she had to hike herself up and over a fallen tree. Her legs and knees began to ache, then her shoulders and neck. And she became obsessed with the hole at the top of her hat where the tassel used to be. She imagined it yawning wider and wider, and could feel the wind's bony fingers in her hair.

After Zoe had been in the woods for 20 minutes or so, her cheeks, which were partly exposed to the air, were scalding hot. She thought about taking her gloves off and somehow peeling the skin off her face—and then she realized that that was completely crazy. She and her brain had stopped playing on the same team. Which scared the hell out of her.

The ground started to level off and Zoe saw an enormous old fir tree up ahead. *New trees, old trees, dead trees.* She was almost a third of the way through the woods. She told herself to keep walking, not to stop for anything, until she could touch that first giant tree. That would make everything feel real again.

About ten feet from the fir, Zoe stumbled on something under the snow and belly flopped onto the ground. A bolt of pain tore through her head. She'd hit it against a rock or a stump, and could feel a bruise blooming on her forehead. She took off a glove and touched it. When she pulled her hand away, her fingers were dark with blood.

She decided it wasn't that bad.

She forced herself up onto her knees, then her feet. And, using that first fir tree as her goalpost, she walked the next few yards. When she got to the tree, she leaned against it and felt a wave of relief because, no matter how heinous things are, you gotta love a Christmas tree.

Zoe was in the second part of the woods now, with maybe half a mile to go. The trees were massive—they roared up toward the sky—and set far enough apart that what daylight was left trickled down to her. Here, Jonah and the dogs' tracks were clean and clear. They seemed to be sticking to the path now. She started off again, trying to think of nothing but the rhythm of her steps.

She imagined finding Jonah and marching him home. She imagined wrapping him in blankets till he laughed and shouted, "I! Am! Not! A! Burrito!"

Zoe had been outside for 30 or 40 minutes, and it had to be 25 below. She was shaking like she'd been hit by an electric current. By the time she'd made it halfway through the fir trees, every part of her ached and shivered like a tuning fork. And the storm seemed stronger now. The forest itself was breaking apart all around her. The wind stripped off branches and flung them in every direction. Whole trees had toppled over and lay blocking the path.

She stopped to rest against a tree. She had to. She swung the flashlight around, trying to figure out how far she was from the lake. But her hands were weak and she fumbled and dropped it in the snow.

The light went out.

She sank to her knees to search for the flashlight. It was getting dark so she had to root around in the snow. The shivering had gotten worse—at first it'd felt like she'd touched an electric fence, but now her nerves were so fully on fire that it felt like she *was* an electric fence—but she didn't care. And she didn't care about the bruise or the cut or whatever it was that was pulsing on her forehead. She didn't care that there were thorns and branches hiding under the snow and that they were tearing at the skin beneath her gloves. She could barely feel anything anyway. After a few minutes on her knees—it could have been two, it could have been ten, she had no idea anymore—her hand found something in the snow. She let out a yelp of happiness, or as much of one as she could manage, and she pulled it out. But it wasn't the flashlight.

It was one of Jonah's gloves.

The skull on the back glowed up at her, the empty eye sockets like tunnels.

She pictured Jonah stumbling through the woods, sobbing loudly. She pictured his hand frozen and raw and beating with pain. She pictured him pleading with the dogs to go home. (He *must* have started pleading by now.) His face came to her for a second. He had their father's looks, which still made her wince: the messy brown hair, the eyes you assumed would be blue but were actually a cool, weird green. The only difference was that Jonah had slightly chubby cheeks. *Thank god for baby fat*, Zoe thought. Because, tonight, it might keep Jonah alive.

She found the flashlight, and—miraculously—there was some life left in it. She got to her feet and started out again.

A few feet from the first glove, she found the second one.

Ten feet later, she found Jonah's coat.

It was a puffy black down jacket, patched with electrical tape—and he'd left it draped over the jagged stump of a tree.

Now Zoe imagined her brother dazed and wandering, his skin itchy and hot, like it was crawling all over him. She imagined him pulling off his clothes and dropping them in the snow.

Zoe was exhausted. And freaked out. And so unbelievably mad at those idiot dogs who didn't know enough to stay close to the house—who didn't realize that her beautiful brother would follow them and follow them and follow them through the snow. Until it killed him.

© BRIAN SCHOTT

JEFF GILES

is the author of *The Edge of Everything* and its sequel, *The Brink of Darkness*. He grew up in Cohasset, Massachusetts. He's been the deputy managing editor of *Entertainment Weekly* and has written for *Rolling Stone* and *The New York Times Book Review*. He also coauthored *The Terrorist's Son*, a nonfiction book that won an Alex Award from the American Library Association and has since been translated into more than twenty languages. While reporting on the Lord of the Rings movies for *Newsweek*, Jeff was invited to be an extra in *The Return of the King*. He played a Rohan soldier, and—because he didn't have a beard or mustache—they glued yak hair to his face. Jeff lives with his family in Montana.

@MrJeffGiles (Twitter)

@jeffmgiles (Instagram)